CW00968119

The Waves Between Us

Stephanie Montrose

Published by Stephanie Montrose, 2024.

This is a work of fiction. Similarities to real people, places, or events are entirely coincidental.

THE WAVES BETWEEN US

First edition. October 6, 2024.

Copyright © 2024 Stephanie Montrose.

ISBN: 979-8227595706

Written by Stephanie Montrose.

Chapter 1: An Unexpected Meeting

The sun clings to the sky like it doesn't know when to let go, stubborn and bold, casting everything in a golden haze that makes the whole world look like it's dipped in honey. I pull my sunglasses lower on my nose, pretending they're a barrier between me and reality, but nothing stops the scent of saltwater from sinking into my skin. Brighton Shores is buzzing today—families with sunscreen-streaked kids chasing seagulls, couples walking hand in hand like they invented love, and the occasional lone soul, like me, drifting through the chaos.

I don't know why I'm here. Most days I'd rather be at home with a book, curled up on the couch with a mug of tea that's gone cold twice because I was too lost in the pages to notice. But something about today pulled me outside, like a whisper I couldn't quite hear but had to follow. Maybe it was the restless ache that comes from reading too many love stories, the kind where the right person is always just around the corner, bumping into you in the most absurdly charming way. Except, in real life, the corners are always empty, and no one ever collides with you except for the occasional stray tourist who forgot to look where they were going.

The boardwalk stretches out ahead of me, a winding strip of vendors selling overpriced trinkets and food that smells better than it tastes. I weave through the crowd, letting the hum of conversation and the crashing waves blend into a backdrop of white noise. My feet are on autopilot, carrying me past the fortune teller's booth, where a woman in a turban glances up from her tarot cards with a knowing smile that makes me feel seen and unsettled at the same time.

Then, there's the crash.

It happens so fast, I barely register what I'm seeing—a blur of motion, followed by the unmistakable sound of wood hitting concrete. My head snaps to the right, just in time to see a guy go

1

down in a heap of surfboards, his limbs tangled like a marionette whose strings have been cut. I can't help the laugh that slips out, though I clamp a hand over my mouth to smother it. It's the kind of moment that would be humiliating if it weren't so ridiculously slapstick.

He's already pulling himself to his feet before I can decide whether to offer help, brushing off his jeans with an amused grin that only widens when he sees me watching. And just like that, I'm caught. The connection happens in an instant, as if something in the universe snapped into place when our eyes met. His are green, the kind of green that makes you think of moss-covered forests after a rainstorm, and there's a mischievous glint in them, like he knows a secret and is debating whether or not to share it.

"First time with a surfboard?" I call out, trying to match his easy energy despite the fact that my heart is doing a strange little tap dance in my chest.

"First time standing up, apparently," he shoots back, chuckling as he straightens the boards, one by one, like they're dominoes that need careful stacking.

I expect him to keep moving once he's got the mess under control. People like him—effortlessly good-looking and clearly comfortable with attention—usually do. But instead, he brushes his hands on his pants and walks over, closing the space between us in a few long strides. Up close, he's even more disarming. There's something about the way he moves, a casual confidence that says he's used to taking life as it comes, one fall at a time.

"Clara, right?" His voice is low, with just a hint of something unplaceable—an accent, maybe, or just the kind of voice that makes you listen carefully, afraid you might miss something important.

I blink, thrown off. "How do you—"

He laughs, a deep sound that rumbles in his chest, and points to the name tag pinned to my shirt. "I'm observant like that."

I glance down, embarrassed. Of course. The name tag. I'd forgotten I was still wearing it from the bookstore, where I'd picked up an extra shift this morning. It's a small thing, but I feel exposed, like he's read more of me than I intended to show.

"I'm Finn," he offers, extending a hand like we're at some formal event and not on a chaotic beach with a dozen people jostling past us, entirely unaware of the little moment we're having.

I hesitate for half a second before taking his hand. It's warm, his grip firm but not too tight, and the contact sends a little spark through me. I pull back quickly, folding my arms across my chest like a shield.

"Nice to meet you, Finn," I say, trying to sound casual, but my voice comes out a little breathless.

His smile widens, and for a second, I wonder if he can tell what effect he's having on me. It's annoying, really, how people like him can do that—just exist and make you feel like you're the one who's unsteady, like you're the one who might trip over your own feet next.

"You work around here?" he asks, gesturing to the bookstore behind us with a tilt of his chin. His hair catches in the breeze, tousled in a way that makes it look artfully messy, though I doubt he spent any time on it at all.

"Yeah, part-time," I reply, feeling a sudden need to downplay it. "It's not glamorous, but it pays the bills."

He shrugs, like he understands that better than I'd expect. "There are worse ways to spend your time."

His gaze flickers over the shelves visible through the shop window, rows of spines in every color, and I can't help but wonder what kind of books he'd pick if he came in. Something adventurous, I imagine, or maybe philosophical, like the kind of guy who reads Nietzsche and debates the meaning of existence over black coffee. Not that I'm overthinking it.

"I'm actually looking for a good book," he says, as if reading my mind. His grin softens into something a little more genuine. "Any recommendations?"

It's a simple question, but the way he asks it feels like an invitation, as if there's more weight to his words than just idle conversation. I hesitate, torn between answering with something safe or throwing caution to the wind and letting him see a little more of me than I usually do.

"Do you read fiction or non-fiction?" The question slips from my lips, surprising even me with its boldness. It's not that I'm typically shy; I just usually reserve my enthusiasm for the dusty pages of my favorite novels, not for spontaneous conversations with strangers. Finn's eyes spark with amusement, a flicker of something unspoken swirling between us, and it makes me wonder if this is what they mean by chemistry.

"Fiction, definitely," he replies, leaning back slightly as if weighing my reaction. "I like stories that sweep me away. Reality has a tendency to be a bit... dull, don't you think?"

"Dull?" I echo, my eyebrows raised in disbelief. "You just crashed into a pile of surfboards, and you're calling reality dull?"

He shrugs, unabashed. "What can I say? I thrive on chaos." There's a lightness in his voice that feels infectious, and for the first time in a long while, I find myself smiling genuinely. The world around us fades into a backdrop, each passing surfer and beachgoer blurring into insignificance as we stand there, wrapped in our own conversation.

"I can't say I've ever been swept away by chaos," I admit, feigning a dramatic sigh. "More like... gently nudged. With a side of awkwardness."

His laughter is rich and deep, echoing off the nearby shops and mingling with the distant sound of crashing waves. "I bet you've had your fair share of adventures, Clara. You strike me as someone who has a good story or two up her sleeve."

The compliment warms me, filling a space in my chest that had been gathering dust for far too long. "Most of my adventures take place between the pages of a book," I confess. "It's safer that way. I can explore foreign lands, fall in love with impossible heroes, and conquer mythical beasts without ever leaving my couch."

Finn leans in, as if sharing a secret. "But what if the real adventure is out here?" He gestures around, encompassing the sun-soaked boardwalk, the smell of caramel corn and fried dough wafting from the stands, and the laughter of children splashing in the waves. "What if there's a whole world waiting for you to dive into?"

For a moment, I'm tempted to tell him that the only thing waiting for me is the latest bestseller I've been itching to read. I'm quite content to live vicariously through the characters on the page, where the stakes are high but the dangers are safely contained in fiction. But his earnest gaze urges me to reconsider, to step outside the confines of my own narrative.

"What do you do for fun, Finn?" I ask, shifting the focus away from me as my curiosity blooms.

"I surf, obviously." He chuckles, motioning to the boards still strewn across the ground like oversized dominoes. "But I also play guitar. Sometimes I write songs, though they're mostly terrible. I'm a work in progress."

The image of him playing guitar, perhaps serenading the sunset or strumming quietly by a bonfire, ignites a spark of imagination in my mind. "That sounds lovely," I reply, picturing it vividly. "Do you ever play at the beach?"

"Only when I'm feeling brave," he admits with a wink. "The waves are a fickle audience."

"Perhaps you need a better approach," I suggest playfully. "A little charisma never hurt anyone. And if all else fails, just throw in a tragic backstory."

"Ah, yes, the old 'my dog died' routine," he laughs, a genuine, carefree sound that resonates with the joy of a summer afternoon. "You're a natural at this, you know?"

"Maybe it's just that you're fun to talk to," I say, feeling a light blush creep up my neck. My words hang between us like the last note of a song, both thrilling and terrifying.

"Is that so?" Finn grins, and there's a teasing glimmer in his eyes. "Then let's make this an adventure to remember." He steps back slightly, scanning the bustling boardwalk with an exaggerated flourish. "What's your first suggestion for fun?"

Before I can think of a suitable response, he steps closer to the surfboards, expertly righting one that had toppled over. "You could try surfing," he suggests with mock seriousness. "I promise the water is refreshing. You'll only swallow half a gallon of it."

I can't help but laugh at the image of me, an awkward beach-goer with little more than an affinity for reading and daydreaming, trying to balance on a surfboard. "And what happens if I wipe out? I'm not sure I'm ready to be the town's latest viral sensation."

"The way I see it," he says, leaning in closer, "every good story has a hero who stumbles before they learn to soar. Plus, it'd make a great chapter in your memoir."

I shoot him a playful glare. "You're an awful influence, you know that?"

"I'm just here to help you embrace the chaos," he replies, feigning innocence. "Besides, you can't live life on the sidelines forever."

A hesitant excitement dances in my chest. I glance back at the surfboards, then at him, imagining the thrill of the waves crashing around me, the exhilaration of being out of my comfort zone. Maybe he's right. Maybe stepping into the chaos might be just what I need.

"What if," I say, "I agreed to try surfing, but only under one condition?"

Finn raises an eyebrow, clearly intrigued. "I'm listening."

"If I wipe out—and let's be honest, I probably will—you have to promise to help me up without laughing. No matter how ridiculous I look."

He bursts into laughter, and the sound feels like sunlight breaking through clouds. "Deal! But only if you promise to take my guitar lessons seriously afterward. I have a feeling you'll need them."

"I have no musical talent," I counter, already envisioning my attempts to strum a guitar while standing on a board. "This is a fair trade. I'll get wet, and you'll get a laugh. Sounds like a win-win."

"Absolutely. But just so you know, I'll probably laugh anyway," he grins, his eyes sparkling with mischief.

With an unexpected surge of courage, I nod, determined. "Alright, then. Let's go surfing."

"Perfect!" he says, clapping his hands together, his excitement infectious. "But first, we need to get you a wetsuit. Can't have you freezing out there." He gestures toward a small shop nearby, and I follow him, my heart pounding with a mix of anticipation and disbelief.

As we make our way to the surf shop, the world around me transforms. The salty breeze carries the echoes of laughter and distant music, wrapping around us like a warm hug. It feels as if the universe is conspiring in our favor, turning an ordinary day into something extraordinary.

In that moment, standing next to Finn, I realize that life, with all its unexpected twists and turns, might just be the adventure I've been searching for all along.

Finn leads the way into the surf shop, a small haven adorned with vibrant surfboards lining the walls like colorful soldiers ready for battle. The scent of coconut and sunscreen fills the air, mingling with the faint whiff of the ocean just outside. My heart races in a delightful flutter as I step inside, half-expecting someone to ring a bell and announce that I'm about to embark on a new adventure. The walls are plastered with posters of surfers defying gravity, hair whipping in the wind, faces alight with the thrill of the waves. It feels alive in here, a pulse of energy that vibrates in the air.

Finn, with his easy demeanor, strolls to the counter, where a grizzled man with a beard that looks like it belongs on a pirate leans casually against a stack of boards. "Hey, Sam! Got any wetsuits that might fit this one?" He gestures to me, the gleam in his eyes both teasing and inviting.

The man squints at me through thick glasses, then smirks. "Sure do, but I can't guarantee it'll do anything for her looks." His voice is gruff yet friendly, the kind of tone that suggests he knows more than he lets on about the mysteries of the ocean and the people who dare to ride it.

"Very helpful, Sam," I retort, shooting Finn a look that's half amused, half mortified.

He chuckles, enjoying the banter. "Don't worry; you'll look fantastic in whatever you choose."

As Sam rummages through the rack, I find myself scanning the shop, my fingers grazing over the soft fabric of beach towels emblazoned with whimsical designs of sea turtles and sunsets. It's all so vibrant and inviting, a stark contrast to the solitary confines of my apartment. Here, people come and go, sharing laughter and stories in a sun-soaked tapestry of community.

"Here we go!" Sam exclaims, pulling out a black wetsuit that looks more intimidating than I expected. "This one should fit you just fine."

I take the suit from him, feeling the sleek material beneath my fingers, and I can't help but imagine how ridiculous I'll look trying to squeeze into it. "Um, I might need a moment," I say, clutching it awkwardly as I retreat to the changing area.

Once I'm alone, the small space feels oddly confining. The suit smells faintly of the ocean, and as I pull it on, I can't help but think of the countless stories woven into its fabric—stories of adventure, of triumph, of people who dared to take a leap. It's a small moment, but it feels significant, as if this one act of stepping outside my comfort zone is the first page of a new chapter.

When I finally step out, Finn's expression is one of mock seriousness, his eyebrows raised high. "You look... ready for battle."

I can't help but laugh at myself, the slick suit hugging every curve in a way that feels both empowering and entirely foreign. "I look ridiculous, don't I?" I spin playfully, eliciting another chuckle from him.

"Not at all! You look like you're about to conquer the waves," he assures me, his enthusiasm contagious. "Now, let's get you a board."

As we move to the back of the shop, I spot an array of surfboards, each one painted with unique designs, vivid colors swirling together in artful chaos. There's something enchanting about them, like they each hold their own story, a testament to adventures waiting to unfold. Finn picks one up, a beautiful turquoise board with a sunburst design. "This is my favorite," he says, admiration lacing his voice. "It's called 'Ocean Dreams.' Perfect for someone who's about to experience their first ride."

"Not sure if I'll be dreaming or drowning," I quip, but the excitement in his eyes ignites a spark within me, fanning the flames of anticipation.

He hands me the board, and its weight is both foreign and familiar, sending a thrill through my veins. "You've got this, Clara. Just remember to breathe."

As we step outside, the sun has dipped slightly, casting a golden glow over the sand and water, and the sound of crashing waves fills the air like a soothing symphony. I take a deep breath, filling my lungs with salty air, feeling the weight of the moment settle on my shoulders. This isn't just about surfing; it's about breaking free from the routine that has kept me tethered to the same four walls, about embracing the unknown and letting it sweep me away.

We walk toward the shoreline, the sand warm beneath my feet, each step a reminder of how far I've come just by being here. "What's the worst that could happen?" Finn asks, glancing at me with a grin that could easily light up the darkest corners of my imagination.

I shoot him a sideways glance, a teasing smile playing on my lips. "You mean besides face-planting into the ocean and being dragged under by an angry jellyfish?"

"Okay, that's a fair point," he concedes, his laughter mingling with the distant cries of seagulls overhead. "But you know what they say—no great story ever started with someone sitting on the couch."

I roll my eyes playfully, letting his words sink in as I grip the board tightly, feeling its pulse against my own heartbeat. "Alright, wise guy. Let's see if I can manage to not embarrass myself too badly."

The water glistens in the fading sunlight, and as I approach the waves, the thrill of the unknown quickens my pulse. Finn walks beside me, giving me encouragement that feels genuine, warming me from the inside out. "We'll start with the basics—just paddling out and catching small waves. You ready?"

"Ready as I'll ever be," I reply, though my voice is shaky. He flashes me an encouraging smile, and I can't help but feel as if I've known him forever, as if we're not two strangers in a vast ocean but rather partners in an adventure that's just beginning.

With a deep breath, I step into the water, the coolness a shock against my skin. I wade in slowly, the waves curling playfully at my feet, teasing me to venture deeper. Finn stays close, guiding me as we paddle out, the rhythm of our movements synchronized like a well-rehearsed dance.

"Just keep your eyes on the horizon," he advises, his voice steady. "Don't focus on the water or the shore. Feel the wave instead."

I nod, concentrating on the horizon, the colors shifting and blending in the twilight. The world narrows to just me, the board, and the vast expanse of the ocean. It's exhilarating, the freedom washing over me, drowning out my self-doubt.

When the first wave approaches, I feel my heart race, the adrenaline surging through me. "Now!" Finn calls, and I push off, riding the wave, my body instinctively adjusting to the swell. I can hardly believe it—I'm actually surfing!

For a brief moment, everything aligns. I feel the rush of the water beneath me, the wind whipping my hair back like I'm a character in one of my beloved novels. But then, inevitably, the wave crashes, and I'm thrown into the water, the salty ocean enveloping me like a chilly embrace.

Emerging from the surf, sputtering and laughing, I look up to see Finn grinning from ear to ear, his laughter echoing in the air. "Welcome to the club! It's a rite of passage!"

"Did I at least look cool for a second?" I ask, shaking my hair out and trying to regain my composure.

He flashes a thumbs-up, eyes sparkling with mischief. "For a fleeting moment! But you're definitely going to need a lot more practice."

I wipe the water from my face, feeling a sense of exhilaration unlike anything I've experienced before. The thrill of the unexpected, the laughter, and the connection we're building—I can feel it deep within me, like the beginning of something magnificent.

As the sun dips below the horizon, casting a warm glow across the sky, I realize that this is more than just a day at the beach. It's an awakening, a reminder that life is meant to be lived fully, unpredictably. Finn's presence at my side ignites a flame within me, pushing me to embrace all that life has to offer, to step outside the pages of my novels and into a narrative all my own.

And as we dive back into the waves, laughter spilling between us like sunlight on water, I can't help but think that this is just the start. The ocean stretches wide and endless, full of potential, waiting for me to explore its depths and weave my own story into the fabric of life.

Chapter 2: Love in the Unlikeliest of Places

The salty air mingled with the scent of sunscreen and distant barbecues, wrapping around me like a warm embrace as I settled into my beach chair, my toes sinking into the soft, sun-warmed sand. The sound of the Pacific crashing against the shore was both exhilarating and calming, a rhythmic heartbeat echoing through the vibrant Southern California coastline. This was my sanctuary, a place where the worries of everyday life seemed to dissolve into the ocean mist, leaving behind only the sound of laughter from sunbathers and the occasional shriek of delight from children chasing the retreating waves.

I leaned back, letting the sun envelop me, feeling its warmth seep into my skin. I had come to this beach to escape the frenetic pace of my daily routine, where deadlines loomed like ominous clouds threatening to burst. Each summer, I would grab my favorite book and find a spot along the shoreline, hoping to dive into stories far removed from my own. However, this year was different. This year, my gaze drifted away from the pages and toward the horizon, where the ocean met the sky in a brilliant blend of azure and gold. It was there I spotted him for the first time.

Aiden Callahan. His name danced on my tongue, as elusive as the spray from the surf. He emerged from the waves like a sun-kissed god, water cascading down his toned body, glistening in the fading light. His hair was tousled, bleached by the sun, and his laughter rang out like a melody, inviting and infectious. I felt an inexplicable pull toward him, an undeniable connection that transcended the mundane and sent my heart racing.

He walked with a swagger that spoke of confidence and a carefree spirit, leaving a trail of laughter and admiration in his wake.

As he caught my eye, a playful smile crept across his face, and I suddenly felt like a character in one of those romantic novels I often escaped into. I was merely a spectator in a world of adventure and charm, yet something deep within me urged me to step forward, to break the spell of my quiet existence.

Our first encounter was unceremonious—a brief exchange as he brushed sand off his board and offered me a casual "Hey" with a grin that lit up his whole face. I couldn't muster a witty retort or a flirtatious quip; I simply blinked, my tongue stumbling over words that had never felt more foreign. Instead, I offered him a wave, which he returned with a mischievous nod. The moment lingered like the fading colors of sunset, igniting a spark within me that I couldn't quite understand.

Days passed, and the chance meetings became more frequent, each encounter punctuated by shared laughter and playful banter. We found ourselves gravitating toward one another, often seated on the warm sand, watching the sun dip below the horizon as it painted the sky in brilliant hues of pink and orange. Aiden's stories unfolded like the tide—wild and unpredictable. He spoke of his love for surfing, how the ocean was not just a playground but a sanctuary where he found freedom. Each wave he rode became a metaphor for life's challenges, and I couldn't help but admire his unwavering passion.

As the sun sank lower, I'd find myself leaning closer, captivated by the way his eyes sparkled with excitement when he shared tales of conquering the toughest breaks or the thrill of catching the perfect wave. It was as if he poured pieces of his soul into those stories, revealing layers of himself that the world rarely got to see.

He challenged me in ways I hadn't anticipated. One evening, as the salty breeze tugged playfully at my hair, he suggested we try surfing together. The idea sent a rush of panic through me, intertwining fear and thrill. I had always been more comfortable in the shallows, content to watch from the sidelines, but Aiden's infectious enthusiasm ignited a fire within me. What if I could break free from my carefully constructed comfort zone? What if I could learn to ride the waves, just as he did?

"Come on, it'll be fun! I'll teach you," he urged, his voice smooth like the ocean's gentle lull. The way he looked at me, filled with encouragement and mischief, made me feel invincible, as if I could tackle anything the world threw at me—even the fierce waves of the Pacific.

With a deep breath, I agreed, my heart pounding with equal parts dread and excitement. The next morning, we met before dawn, the sky still draped in darkness. I could barely suppress my nerves as Aiden led me to the water, the moonlight shimmering on the waves like a silver path. With each step into the surf, I felt more alive, the cool water washing over me, invigorating my spirit.

"Just relax and go with it," he instructed, his voice a comforting presence amid my swirling apprehensions. As he demonstrated the art of balancing on the board, I watched him glide effortlessly across the water, his movements graceful and fluid, a dance with the ocean.

My first attempt was, as expected, a spectacular failure. I stumbled and fell, splashing into the surf with a yelp, the cold water crashing around me. Laughter erupted from Aiden, not in mockery but in genuine joy. His laughter was infectious, and soon I found myself laughing too, the tension of the moment dissolving into a delightful blend of exhilaration and embarrassment.

"See? You're already getting the hang of it," he teased, helping me up. "You've got to embrace the wipeouts." With each fall, I felt a strange sense of freedom, a release of the fears that had anchored me for so long. Aiden's encouragement became my lifeline, pulling me closer to a sense of self I hadn't realized I was missing.

As the sun rose, casting a golden hue across the water, I began to find my balance. Each wave that threatened to toss me aside became a challenge to conquer, and Aiden was always by my side, cheering me on. The connection we forged deepened, entwined in the laughter and shared moments of vulnerability that washed over us like the tide.

Every sunset we shared brought us closer, revealing the threads of our dreams and fears, intertwining our stories in ways I never thought possible. The world beyond the beach faded into a distant echo, the hustle and bustle of life replaced by the soothing sound of the waves. I could feel my heart opening, its rhythm syncing with the pulse of the ocean, as Aiden helped me embrace the unpredictable nature of love and life.

I started to wonder if perhaps he was my wave, an unexpected force that could sweep me off my feet, pulling me into the depths of something beautiful and terrifying. In his presence, the walls I had so carefully constructed began to crumble, leaving me exposed yet exhilarated. The summer sun illuminated our journey, and I realized that in the unlikeliest of places, I was discovering not just the thrill of riding waves, but also the deeper tides of my heart, where love was patiently waiting to emerge.

The summer stretched on, and with each passing day, my laughter mingled with the sound of the ocean, wrapping me in a cocoon of newfound joy. Aiden became the sun around which I orbited, pulling me from the shadows of my safe little world into the brilliance of his vibrant one. Mornings were filled with salty air and crashing waves, afternoons surrendered to the thrill of surfing, and evenings transformed into long talks beneath a sky scattered with stars. Each moment felt like a treasure I had stumbled upon, a discovery I never knew I needed.

Our connection deepened, the playful teasing of our early encounters giving way to something more profound. Aiden had this way of drawing out my thoughts, coaxing me to share the dreams that had been tucked away in the corners of my mind. I revealed my aspirations of becoming a writer, my words flowing like the tides, sometimes crashing and messy, other times gentle and poetic. I told him about the stories I'd penned in the quiet solitude of my room, stories that had never seen the light of day.

"Why haven't you shared them?" he asked one evening as we sat on the beach, the golden glow of the setting sun illuminating his features, making him look like some kind of hero from a novel. His gaze was unwavering, a challenge wrapped in sincerity.

"I guess I'm afraid," I admitted, picking at the sand beneath my fingers. "What if no one likes them? What if I fail?"

Aiden shrugged, a carefree smile playing on his lips. "You won't know unless you try. And besides, what's failure, really? It's just another wave to ride." His eyes sparkled with mischief, but there was an underlying sincerity that sent my heart racing. It was true; his perspective was fresh, unclouded by the fears that had long shackled me.

I started to see the world through Aiden's lens, one that allowed for flaws and failures, where mistakes were simply opportunities to learn and grow. The more I opened up, the more I felt like I was shedding layers of insecurity. I began to see writing not just as an escape but as a form of self-expression—an extension of the joy I found in sharing moments with him.

Our shared evenings melted into laughter as the stars twinkled overhead. Aiden would often lean back on his elbows, looking up at the vast expanse of the night sky, and recount tales of constellations and the myths that surrounded them. He made everything seem magical, painting stories with his words, igniting my imagination in ways I had never experienced before. Each night, under the starlit canvas, we found ourselves wrapped in an intimacy that felt both exhilarating and terrifying.

One particular evening, as the moon hung low and bright, casting a silvery glow on the waves, Aiden suggested we take a midnight swim. "C'mon, it'll be amazing! Just you, me, and the ocean," he coaxed, his eyes dancing with a daring gleam.

I hesitated, the idea of plunging into the cool waters under the moonlight swirling through my mind. "What if it's cold?" I countered, a feeble attempt to cling to the safety of my reservations.

"Exactly! What if it's cold? What if it's the best thing you ever do?" His grin was infectious, a daring spark that ignited something deep within me. I found myself smiling back, the thought of stepping into the unknown becoming less frightening with his encouragement.

With a deep breath and a racing heart, I nodded, a silent agreement to embrace the thrill of spontaneity. Together, we dashed toward the water, laughter spilling from our lips as the waves lapped eagerly at our ankles, inviting us into their depths. The shock of the cool water was exhilarating, sending shivers down my spine and washing away the remnants of my hesitance.

Once submerged, the world above faded into a distant echo, and all that mattered was the exhilaration coursing through me, the sensation of freedom that enveloped us. We splashed and played, diving beneath the waves, the moonlight shimmering like scattered diamonds on the water's surface.

In those moments, I felt truly alive, the worries of life dissipating with every wave that rolled over us. Aiden's laughter mingled with the sounds of the ocean, creating a symphony of joy that resonated within me. As we floated on our backs, gazing up at the vast expanse of stars, he turned to me, his expression softening. "See? Sometimes you just have to leap."

With Aiden beside me, I felt invincible. It was as if he held the key to a world where fear could transform into exhilaration, where each wave was a possibility rather than a threat.

Our friendship blossomed, evolving from lighthearted teasing into a deep-rooted bond that felt almost tangible, like the cool breeze wrapping around us. We started exploring the local haunts together—quaint coffee shops tucked away in vibrant alleys, surf shops brimming with eclectic gear, and food trucks serving mouthwatering tacos that filled our stomachs as we shared our dreams over spicy salsa and laughter. Each outing felt like a mini-adventure, a stepping stone in the journey we were unknowingly navigating together.

But it wasn't just the thrill of our adventures that captivated me; it was the little moments too. The way his fingers brushed against mine as we passed a bowl of guacamole, the warmth in his eyes when he spoke of his family, and the sincerity in his voice when he shared his fears. It was all those simple gestures that began to weave a tapestry of intimacy between us, one that felt like it was meant to be.

As the days turned into weeks, the summer began to shift, the golden light of August slowly giving way to the softer hues of early fall. I felt the gentle tug of change in the air, a reminder that nothing lasts forever. With that thought, a pang of uncertainty settled in my chest. Was this fleeting moment meant to be just that—a summer fling, destined to dissolve with the warmth of the sun?

One evening, sitting on the beach as the sun dipped below the horizon, I found myself lost in thought. Aiden leaned back, his head resting on his arms, his eyes scanning the endless waves. I admired him in that moment—the way the dying light danced in his hair, how the breeze played around him as if it, too, wanted to be near him.

"Penny for your thoughts?" he asked, turning to me with a smile that made my heart skip.

I hesitated, caught in the web of my own feelings, unsure of how to voice the turmoil within. "Just... wondering what happens next," I finally said, my voice barely above a whisper.

Aiden's expression shifted, the carefree sparkle dimming for a moment as he regarded me with an intensity that made my heart race. "What do you mean?"

"I mean, this summer—us—it's been incredible, but..." My voice trailed off, the weight of my words hanging in the air between us. "What happens when school starts again? When life goes back to normal?"

He took a moment, his gaze fixed on the horizon, as if searching for answers in the ever-rolling waves. "Normal can be overrated," he finally replied, his voice steady. "But I get it. Change is scary. But what if we embraced it instead? What if we let it be an adventure?"

His words hung in the air, and I felt a flicker of hope ignite within me. Maybe he was right; perhaps I could learn to ride this wave of uncertainty, to trust that whatever lay ahead would unfold in its own time.

As the stars began to dot the sky, I realized that my heart had already decided. No matter what came next, I was ready to dive into the depths of whatever this was, even if it meant facing the fear of the unknown head-on.

As the days rolled on and the warmth of summer slowly faded into the gentle chill of autumn, the beach transformed into a canvas of shifting colors and emotions. Mornings turned misty, with the sun struggling to break through the horizon, casting a golden glow that shimmered on the water's surface like a thousand tiny mirrors. The shifting tides reflected the complexities of my heart, each wave echoing the unspoken feelings that bubbled beneath the surface, caught between exhilaration and trepidation.

Aiden and I fell into a rhythm, our days filled with spontaneous adventures that made the ordinary feel extraordinary. Each morning, the beach became our playground, where we surfed until our muscles screamed for respite, then retreated to our favorite café—a tucked-away spot where the barista recognized us and always knew to prepare two iced coffees and a plate of banana pancakes. Aiden insisted on extra syrup, and I found myself indulging in his whims, giggling as he smothered the pancakes in a glossy layer of sweetness.

With every laugh, with every shared glance, a deeper connection anchored itself within me. Aiden had this uncanny ability to see right through me, to sift through my layers of self-doubt and insecurity. He would tease me about my tendency to overthink, a habit honed through years of trying to be perfect. "Just let it go, Penny! Life's too short to be so serious," he would say, shaking his head in mock dismay.

And he was right. In his presence, I learned to embrace the messiness of life—the imperfections that made each moment worth living. On one particularly sun-drenched afternoon, after our surfing session, we sprawled on the sand, our bodies exhausted yet buzzing with a kind of energy only summer could provide. The warmth of the sun wrapped around us like a familiar blanket, and the distant sounds of laughter from beachgoers created a soothing backdrop.

"Have you ever thought about what you want to do after this summer?" he asked, propping himself up on one elbow, his gaze serious yet soft.

My heart raced at the question. I had been avoiding the reality of my imminent return to school, where responsibilities awaited like uninvited guests at a party. "I've thought about it, but it's a little overwhelming," I admitted, tracing patterns in the sand. "The thought of fitting back into my old life makes me anxious."

Aiden's expression shifted to one of understanding, the kind that made me feel like he was truly listening. "You're not defined by what you've always done. You're free to change your narrative." His voice was calm, almost hypnotic, as if he were imparting a secret that could unlock my future.

"Easy for you to say," I teased, half-heartedly, "you're a surfer. You don't have deadlines or assignments."

"True, but I still have dreams, and sometimes, chasing them means taking risks." He grinned, his eyes twinkling with mischief. "What's your dream? What's the one thing you'd do if you knew you wouldn't fail?"

I paused, the question swirling around my mind. What would I dare to do if failure wasn't a possibility? The answer bubbled up slowly, a tender whisper. "I want to write a book."

Aiden's grin widened. "Then write it. Why not? The world deserves to hear your voice, your story."

His unwavering belief in me ignited a spark, one that flickered with the possibility of change. That evening, as we sat beneath a tapestry of stars, I found myself crafting ideas, plotting characters, and dreaming of story arcs that would bring my thoughts to life. The excitement surged within me, an electric current that danced through my veins.

As the summer waned, I felt a bittersweet ache settling in my heart. I dreaded the end of our endless days together, but Aiden was determined to make the most of every moment. He suggested we embark on a road trip to the nearby beach town of Laguna, known for its stunning sunsets and artistic vibes. "We can catch some gnarly waves and explore," he urged, eyes sparkling with enthusiasm.

I agreed, excitement bubbling in my chest. We packed up his trusty surfboard, a cooler filled with snacks, and an eclectic playlist that ranged from classic rock to the latest indie hits. The drive was filled with laughter and sing-alongs, the wind whipping through the open windows as we belted out our favorite tunes. The coastline unfurled before us like a cinematic masterpiece, each twist and turn revealing breathtaking views that felt straight out of a postcard.

When we arrived, the vibrant artsy atmosphere enveloped us. Colorful murals adorned the walls of quaint shops, and the aroma of fresh churros mingled with the salty sea air. Aiden and I explored hand-in-hand, our fingers brushing together as we wandered through galleries showcasing local artists. The energy of the place sparked something within me—a renewed sense of inspiration.

Later, as the sun dipped below the horizon, we made our way to a secluded beach, where the sand felt cool beneath our feet. The sky transformed into a breathtaking palette of purples, oranges, and pinks, the sunset casting a magical glow over everything. Aiden and I sat in comfortable silence, the waves lapping at the shore, as the beauty of the moment enveloped us.

"Isn't it incredible?" I murmured, my voice barely above a whisper.

Aiden nodded, his gaze fixed on the horizon. "Moments like this remind me of what really matters. It's not about the past or the future; it's about right now."

I turned to him, catching the intensity of his gaze. "What do you see when you look out there?"

He contemplated for a moment, the soft breeze tousling his hair. "Possibility. Every wave is a new opportunity, a chance to ride or wipe out. It's exhilarating and terrifying all at once."

"Just like life," I added, the realization settling over me like the warm glow of the sunset.

With the sun kissing the horizon, Aiden shifted closer, his arm brushing against mine. I felt the heat radiate from him, an electric connection that sent shivers down my spine. "You know, I think you're going to do great things," he said quietly, sincerity etched across his features.

"Thank you," I replied, my heart swelling. His words felt like a lifeline, a promise that I could break free from the chains of self-doubt that had held me back for far too long.

As the stars emerged, twinkling like tiny beacons of hope, I felt a sense of clarity wash over me. The uncertainty that had once felt overwhelming now transformed into something beautiful. A wave of acceptance surged through me, and I leaned into the warmth of Aiden's presence, grateful for the connection we had forged.

But as our time together began to draw to a close, the looming reality of my return to school tugged at my heart. I had spent the summer growing and changing, feeling more alive than ever, yet I was terrified of the void that Aiden's absence would leave in my life. Each day felt like a countdown, a reminder that the summer days were slipping away like grains of sand through my fingers.

On our final evening together, we returned to the beach, the air thick with unsaid words and emotions. The sun dipped low, casting a fiery glow over the water, and I felt a mixture of sorrow and gratitude swell within me. Aiden seemed to sense my turmoil as he turned to me, his expression softening.

"Penny," he began, his voice low and sincere, "whatever happens next, remember this summer. Remember that you're capable of so much more than you think."

His words resonated deep within me, a guiding light against the impending darkness. I felt my heart race, the weight of what I wanted to say pressing against my chest. "Aiden, I—"

Before I could finish, he leaned in, his lips brushing against mine in a soft, tentative kiss. Time seemed to freeze, the world around us fading into nothingness as I melted into the moment. It was sweet and gentle, a promise wrapped in the heat of summer, and as he pulled away, my breath caught in my throat.

"I'm going to miss you," he said, his voice barely above a whisper, but his eyes held an unwavering intensity.

"I'll miss you too," I replied, the truth of my words crashing over me like a tidal wave. "You've changed everything for me."

In that moment, the sunset transformed into a tapestry of colors, our unspoken feelings swirling around us like the very waves that had brought us together. I knew that this summer had not just been a fleeting escape; it had been a turning point, a time when I learned to embrace the uncertainty of love and life. And as I looked into Aiden's eyes, I realized that I was ready to ride whatever waves came my way, armed with the belief that I could carve out my own path, no matter how unpredictable it might be.

With one last glance at the horizon, I felt a sense of peace wash over me. This was not the end, merely a new beginning, and I was ready to face it, heart open and eyes wide, knowing that Aiden would forever be a part of my story, no matter the distance that lay ahead.

Chapter 3: Secrets Beneath the Surface

Salt clung to my skin, a reminder of the afternoon spent laughing under the relentless sun. The beach stretched endlessly, a canvas painted in hues of azure and gold, where laughter and the distant cries of seagulls melded into a soundtrack of summer. Aiden stood beside me, a sun-kissed figure framed by the shimmering waves, his laughter bright and effervescent like the fizz of soda on a hot day. Each flick of his wrist sent droplets of water arcing through the air, catching the light like tiny diamonds before crashing back into the surf. I watched, entranced, as he challenged the waves with the same bravado he applied to life—a confidence that felt both exhilarating and disconcerting.

We had spent countless afternoons like this, tracing the shoreline and letting our feet sink into the warm, yielding sand. Each step left a fleeting imprint, quickly erased by the relentless tide, much like the ephemeral nature of our burgeoning relationship. Aiden had this way of drawing me in, his charm as intoxicating as the salty sea breeze, but there were moments when his laughter would falter, shadows flickering across his features before he expertly masked them with a smile.

The sun dipped low, casting a golden glow that ignited the horizon, and Aiden suggested we head back to his family's beach house. It loomed in the distance, a weathered structure of bleached wood and bright blue shutters, its charm enhanced by the tangled vines that snaked up the sides. It was a home filled with memories, each creak of the floorboards whispering tales of summers gone by. But I sensed there were more secrets buried beneath its sunlit exterior—an undercurrent of sorrow that clung to the air, just as the scent of brine lingered in the breeze.

Once inside, the familiar scent of grilled fish wafted through the open kitchen, mingling with the lingering notes of coconut sunscreen. Aiden's mother had prepared one of her famous feasts, the kind that brought the whole family together, and my stomach grumbled in anticipation. The dining table, adorned with vibrant, mismatched plates and flickering candles, welcomed us like an embrace. Laughter echoed from the living room, where Aiden's siblings gathered, their banter a tapestry of teasing and warmth that wrapped around me like a cozy blanket.

But even as I settled into the rhythm of the evening, I couldn't shake the feeling that Aiden was holding back—a silent storm lurking just beneath his sun-drenched exterior. After dinner, we retreated to the deck, the evening air thick with the scent of ocean spray and woodsmoke from the nearby fire pit. The sky transformed into a tapestry of stars, twinkling like scattered diamonds, each one holding a story, a secret, much like Aiden.

He leaned against the railing, his silhouette etched against the night sky, and I couldn't help but admire the way the moonlight danced across his skin, highlighting the contours of his jaw and the playful curl of his hair. We talked about everything—the mundane and the profound, the future and fleeting dreams. Yet, there was a tension in the air, a weight that pressed down on our lighthearted conversation, urging me to delve deeper.

As the night wore on, I excused myself, the need for a breath of fresh air guiding my steps toward the dimly lit hallway. A curious pull led me to a small room at the end of the corridor, a door slightly ajar, beckoning me to peek inside. I hesitated, the quiet hum of laughter and music fading into the background, replaced by a sense of trespassing. Yet the urge to explore, to uncover the layers that made Aiden who he was, compelled me forward.

Inside, the room was a sanctuary of memories—surfboards lined the walls, trophies glimmered in the soft glow of a lamp, and scattered photographs lay strewn across the desk, their corners curling as if desperate to escape the confines of time. As I sifted through the pictures, a chill ran down my spine, each image a snapshot of joy overshadowed by a lurking sadness. There, amid the sun-kissed faces, was Aiden—his smile radiant, but there was something else; a heaviness in his eyes that spoke of loss, a grief carefully tucked away beneath layers of bravado.

My fingers traced the edges of a photograph showing Aiden standing beside a young girl with golden hair, their smiles bright against the backdrop of a summer carnival. But in the next image, the laughter seemed to dissipate, replaced by a grim silence as Aiden stood alone, staring at the sea with a haunting emptiness that made my heart ache. I could feel the weight of his sorrow, a palpable thing that wrapped around me, urging me to understand the depth of his struggle.

With each image, my heart clenched tighter, realization dawning like the slow creep of dawn. Aiden was not merely a boy with an infectious smile; he carried the weight of tragedy, a loss that haunted him like the very waves that kissed the shore. My thoughts spiraled—should I confront him about this shadow looming in the corners of his life, or should I give him the space he so desperately needed?

As I closed the door, the echo of laughter resumed in the distance, the warmth of the evening contrasting sharply with the chill of my discovery. I stepped back into the glow of the shared memories, heart racing as I grappled with the newfound knowledge. Aiden deserved to share his burdens, but the question lingered like the salty air—was I ready to peel back the layers of his heart and reveal the secrets that lay beneath the surface?

The laughter from the living room danced around me like a gentle caress, pulling me back into the present, yet the weight of what I had discovered lingered like a persistent shadow. I could hear Aiden's voice rising above the others, full of warmth and light, a stark contrast to the quiet turmoil brewing inside me. With a deep breath,

I forced a smile, hoping to cloak my concern in the layers of joy surrounding us.

Gathering my thoughts, I slipped back into the living room, where the atmosphere was vibrant with the flickering light of candles and the soft hum of conversation. Aiden was animatedly recounting a tale from last summer, his hands gesturing wildly as his siblings leaned in, captivated. It was a beautiful scene, one of those moments where laughter becomes a language all its own, and I felt the sharp edges of my worries soften, if only for a heartbeat.

As the evening unfolded, I joined in the storytelling, weaving my own memories into the tapestry of shared laughter. Each anecdote was punctuated by bursts of humor, Aiden's laughter contagious, and soon I found myself relaxing into the rhythm of the night. But beneath my smile, a question lingered: How could I breach the chasm between his past and present without tearing apart the fabric of our connection?

After dessert, a chaotic yet delightful affair of ice cream and homemade pies, Aiden suggested we head outside to the bonfire. The fire pit awaited us, a cozy glow beckoning in the twilight, where the embers would flicker like stars fallen to earth. I followed him, the warm sand sinking beneath my feet, its heat still radiating from the sun's embrace earlier that day.

We settled into the weathered adirondack chairs, a perfect circle surrounding the crackling fire. The flames danced playfully, illuminating our faces in an orange glow, and Aiden tossed a log into the flames, sending sparks spiraling into the night sky. I nestled deeper into my chair, glancing sideways at him, the glow reflecting in his eyes like a warm invitation, yet those shadows still lingered behind his smile.

As the night progressed, the conversation ebbed and flowed like the tide. Stories about school, travels, and dreams intertwined with playful banter, and for a moment, I allowed myself to forget the darkness lurking behind Aiden's laughter. His brothers engaged in friendly rivalries, each boasting about their latest exploits, while his sister joined in, her laughter bright and melodic, filling the air with a sense of belonging that wrapped around me like a soft blanket.

But then, as if drawn by an invisible thread, my gaze found Aiden's once more. He sat slightly apart from the group, a contemplative look in his eyes as he stared into the flames. The laughter faded into the background, replaced by the sound of crackling wood, and I sensed the change in the atmosphere, a subtle shift that hinted at the weight he carried within.

I hesitated, the weight of the moment pressing down, urging me to reach out, to bridge the gap that had silently grown between us. My heart raced as I leaned forward, the warmth of the fire contrasting the cool air wrapping around us. "Aiden," I began softly, feeling the words hang between us, "what do you think about when you look at the fire?"

His gaze shifted from the flames to me, an intensity in his eyes that both thrilled and unnerved me. "It's like a mirror," he replied, his voice low, barely above a whisper. "You see the beauty, but if you stare too long, it can burn you." There it was—the first crack in his carefully constructed facade, the glimpse into a world beyond the laughter.

I nodded, not wanting to break the moment. "I've always thought fire has its own stories. Each spark is a memory waiting to be told." My heart pounded, the vulnerability of my words hanging in the air like the smoke that curled above us. "Sometimes, those stories are beautiful, but sometimes... they're painful."

He hesitated, the silence stretching between us, heavy with unspoken thoughts. I could see the gears turning in his mind, the internal battle raging as he grappled with whether to let me in. It was a delicate dance, and I didn't want to push too hard, yet the desire to know him, to understand the heartache behind his smile, urged me forward.

The silence was filled with the symphony of the night—the distant crashing of waves, the rustle of palm leaves swaying in the gentle breeze, and the crackling of the fire, each sound an echo of life that surrounded us. Finally, he spoke, his voice barely audible over the whisper of the wind. "There are things in my past I haven't wanted to talk about, not because I'm afraid of sharing, but because I don't know how to explain them. It's like they're a part of me I can't quite grasp, and if I try to hold on too tightly, I might shatter."

My heart ached at his admission, the raw honesty piercing through the layers of his bravado. "You don't have to explain it all at once," I reassured him gently, my fingers brushing against the warmth of my knee as I leaned closer. "I'm here, and I'm not going anywhere. You can take your time."

He met my gaze, and for a moment, the flickering light of the fire illuminated the depth of his sorrow, the vulnerability in his eyes a soft plea for understanding. I could see the turmoil swirling beneath the surface, a tempest battling against the tranquility he projected.

"I lost someone very important to me," he finally confessed, the words tumbling out like stones dropped into the stillness of the night. "It was sudden, unexpected. And ever since, it feels like I'm carrying their memory like a weight, a constant reminder of what was lost."

The confession hung heavy in the air, each syllable laden with the weight of grief. I felt a pang of empathy, a visceral connection to his pain, and my heart swelled with a fierce desire to help him carry that burden, even if just a little. "I can't imagine what that must feel like," I murmured, my voice steady. "But I'm here, Aiden. You don't have to face it alone."

As he gazed into the fire, a flicker of hope ignited in his expression, and the shadows that had clouded his features seemed to lighten just a fraction. In that moment, the distance between us began to close, the warmth of the fire reflecting the warmth in our hearts. We sat in comfortable silence, the bond between us growing deeper, a fragile yet resilient thread connecting our souls as we both began to share the parts of ourselves hidden beneath the surface.

The fire crackled softly, a comforting rhythm against the backdrop of the ocean's lullaby. As the flames danced, they flickered shadows across Aiden's face, illuminating the deep lines of emotion etched there, a map of grief he carried quietly. It was an invitation, an opening I desperately hoped he would take, a chance to share that heavy load with someone who could bear witness to his pain.

"Sometimes it feels easier to pretend," he continued, his gaze fixed on the flames as if they might hold the answers to his questions. "Like if I keep smiling, keep laughing, then the hurt will stay hidden. But the truth is, it never really goes away, does it?" His voice was steady, yet I could feel the tremor of vulnerability beneath the surface, like the distant rumble of thunder before a storm.

I shook my head gently, my heart aching for him. "No, it doesn't. But pretending can be exhausting. You're not alone in this, Aiden. You don't have to carry it by yourself. It's okay to feel lost sometimes."

He turned to look at me then, his eyes reflecting a flicker of gratitude mixed with disbelief, as if he had never expected anyone to truly understand. "You don't know me well enough to say that," he replied, but his words held a softness that betrayed his skepticism.

"Maybe not, but I know loss. I've felt its grip too." I took a breath, the cool night air filling my lungs, and allowed myself to share a piece of my own heart. "When I was younger, I lost my grandmother. She was my anchor, my confidant. Without her, it felt like I was adrift on an ocean without a compass, struggling against waves that pulled me under."

The admission hung in the air, fragile yet powerful, and I could see Aiden processing it, the gears of understanding turning slowly in his mind. "You never really get over it, do you?" he asked, his voice quiet.

I shook my head. "No, you learn to navigate around it, to carry it with you. It becomes part of who you are."

We fell into a contemplative silence, the kind that wrapped around us like a cozy blanket. It felt like a shift had occurred, a small fracture in the walls we both had built, revealing the fragile humanity beneath. The laughter from the living room faded to a gentle murmur, replaced by the rhythmic sound of waves crashing against the shore, a comforting reminder of the world beyond our shared sorrow.

As the fire crackled, Aiden finally spoke, his voice a low rumble, like distant thunder. "Her name was Lily." The name floated between us, delicate yet heavy, like a feather caught in a storm. "She was my little sister. She loved the ocean—every summer, we'd build sandcastles, race waves, and collect shells until our pockets were overflowing. But one day, everything changed."

His gaze drifted back to the fire, the flames illuminating the sorrow etched in his features. "We were at the beach, just like this, and she... she never came back from the water. It was like the ocean swallowed her whole."

My heart ached at his words, the imagery powerful and visceral. I reached for his hand, our fingers brushing gently, a silent promise that he was not alone in this memory. "I'm so sorry, Aiden," I whispered, feeling the weight of his grief settle around us like a heavy fog.

"I spent months trying to blame myself," he continued, his voice thick with emotion. "If I had been watching her, if I hadn't let her swim alone... I thought if I could just turn back time, I could save her. But no matter how hard I tried, the ocean kept its secrets, and she was gone."

Tears pricked at the corners of my eyes, and I squeezed his hand tighter, my heart breaking for him. "You were just a kid. You did everything you could. It wasn't your fault."

He turned to look at me, his gaze searching mine, and in that moment, I saw a flicker of hope igniting within him. "But that loss... it still follows me, like a shadow. I put on a brave face for everyone, but when I'm alone, it all comes rushing back. It's suffocating."

The fire crackled again, and for a moment, I was struck by the beauty of his honesty, the rawness of his emotion that spilled forth like an overflowing tide. "You don't have to be brave all the time, Aiden," I said softly, the words spilling from my heart. "It's okay to feel. It's okay to grieve. You don't have to hide from it."

He took a deep breath, and for the first time since I'd met him, I saw a hint of vulnerability mixed with something else—relief. The weight of unspoken words had begun to lift, and I could see the possibility of healing glimmering in the distance, like the first light of dawn breaking through the darkness.

"Thank you for listening," he said finally, his voice thick with emotion. "It feels... freeing, I guess. Like I've been holding my breath for too long, and now I can finally exhale."

The honesty between us felt like a fragile thread, weaving our stories together. "You're not alone in this, Aiden. I'm here for you. And when you're ready, we can navigate this together."

He smiled, a slow, genuine smile that lit up his face and reached his eyes, banishing the shadows that had lingered there. "I'd like that."

The fire continued to crackle, its warmth wrapping around us as we sat together, hand in hand, our shared moments of vulnerability creating a safe space that felt almost sacred. The stars twinkled overhead, a canopy of light watching over our conversation, and for the first time in a long time, the ocean felt like a friend rather than an adversary—a reminder of the ebb and flow of life, of loss and healing.

As the night deepened, we began to share lighter stories, tales of childhood mischief and embarrassing moments that made us laugh until our sides hurt. Aiden recounted a time he had tried to impress a girl by surfing but ended up tumbling into the water, the image so vivid it made me giggle. "I swear, I looked like a flailing octopus!" he said, mimicking the scene with exaggerated gestures that sent me into fits of laughter.

With each story, the air between us grew lighter, and as the fire dwindled to glowing embers, I realized how far we had come in just a few hours. The night had transformed from one filled with heartache to one brimming with connection, laughter, and shared understanding.

Eventually, the chatter from inside the house began to fade as Aiden's siblings wound down for the night. I could hear their laughter in the distance, a soothing reminder of the love that surrounded him, of the support he had yet to fully embrace.

"Maybe it's time we get some sleep, huh?" Aiden said, glancing at the embers. "We can always continue this conversation tomorrow."

"Sounds good to me," I replied, standing and brushing the sand from my legs. He reached for my hand, and as we walked back toward the house, I felt a sense of hope blooming within me—a promise that the path ahead, while uncertain, was one we would navigate together.

As we stepped inside, the warmth of the house enveloped us, the flicker of the firelight dancing behind us like a beacon of light. In that moment, I understood that our connection was no longer just a fleeting summer romance but the beginning of something deeper—a shared journey of healing, laughter, and love that would continue to unfold beneath the vast tapestry of the stars.

Chapter 4: A Career Breakthrough

The golden hues of the late afternoon sun spilled through the half-open blinds, casting intricate patterns on the worn wooden floor. It was the kind of light that filled a room with warmth, yet I sat in the corner of my tiny living space, the air heavy with the mingled scents of brewed coffee and old books. My fingers hovered over the keys of my laptop, betraying my unease. There it was—a blinking cursor, as insistent as my own restless thoughts.

Aiden had been the catalyst for this moment, the one who nudged me beyond my doubts, like a push from a friend on a swing that finally made me soar. His words had lingered in my mind, a gentle insistence wrapped in warmth. "Just submit it," he'd said, his deep voice laced with encouragement. "You've poured your soul into it. Let the world see." But now, as I prepared to take that step, my heart raced with equal parts excitement and dread.

I glanced around my small apartment, its walls lined with shelves overflowing with dog-eared novels and scattered pages filled with my own musings. Each item held a story, a fragment of my journey—a journey that had, until now, felt a bit too quiet. It was as if the universe had conspired to keep my voice hidden, but here I was, finally ready to share it. Yet, the moment I clicked "send," a sharp pang of anxiety coiled in my stomach, as if I had just thrown my heart into an abyss without knowing if it would ever return.

Days passed with the weight of that submission pressing down on me, transforming the ordinary into a tapestry of the extraordinary. Aiden and I spent evenings wrapped in the familiar comfort of his presence, our laughter mingling with the distant sounds of traffic outside his apartment. He had a way of making the mundane feel like an adventure—turning grocery shopping into a scavenger hunt for the best avocados, or our late-night talks on the balcony into philosophical debates about everything from the meaning of life to the best way to brew coffee. Each moment felt precious, yet I sensed an undercurrent of tension growing between us, like an unspoken promise that was slowly unraveling.

Then came the email—the one that shattered my quiet world with the force of a meteorite. "We are thrilled to accept your piece." I read those words over and over, the screen blurring with disbelief. My heart pounded wildly in my chest, drowning out the world around me. I clutched the phone, my breath hitching in my throat. I was elated, yet a sense of impending doom loomed over me like storm clouds gathering on the horizon. What did this mean? Would my newfound success pull Aiden and me apart, like two ships sailing in opposite directions?

I rushed to Aiden's place, the city alive around me. The chatter of pedestrians, the aroma of street food wafting through the air, and the distant sound of a saxophonist playing a soulful tune created a symphony of urban life. I arrived at his door, breathless, my mind racing with a mixture of anticipation and fear. When he opened the door, the warmth of his smile momentarily calmed my fraying nerves.

"What's wrong?" he asked, his brow furrowing as he stepped aside, inviting me in. "You look like you've seen a ghost."

I swallowed hard, a lump forming in my throat. "I got accepted... by the magazine." The words tumbled out, and for a moment, all I could do was watch as his face lit up with pride, his eyes sparkling like sunlit seas.

"Are you serious?" He grabbed me, pulling me into a tight embrace that felt like a shield against the world. My heart raced, a wild thing trapped in my chest, but soon it fluttered into a dance of joy.

"I am! I can't believe it," I managed to say, pulling back to see the genuine happiness etched across his face. Yet, beneath that happiness lay an unspeakable tension that pulled at my heartstrings.

"See? I told you!" he exclaimed, his enthusiasm infectious. "This is just the beginning for you."

But as the hours unfolded, our conversations began to shift. Where once we had bantered about life's little absurdities, now there lingered an air of seriousness, as if my success had carved a new divide between us. I could sense Aiden's internal struggle, the way his gaze sometimes drifted when we spoke, as if he were searching for something that lay just beyond reach.

I spent my days wrapped in a whirlwind of preparation for interviews and social media engagements, each one a step deeper into a world that was both thrilling and terrifying. But every achievement, every accolade, felt heavy with the burden of expectation. Would my life now belong to the world? I feared that Aiden, with his quiet dreams and aspirations, might feel overshadowed by my sudden spotlight.

We began to dance around each other, a subtle shift that played out like a well-rehearsed performance. I longed to share my triumphs, yet feared that each shared victory would only serve as a reminder of what he had not yet accomplished. The conversations, once rich with shared laughter, became laden with the weight of unsaid words. I couldn't help but wonder if this new chapter of my life would turn out to be the end of our own story.

Sitting alone in my apartment, I scrolled through social media, catching glimpses of my name alongside the likes of established authors. It felt surreal, a dream cloaked in doubt. With every notification that buzzed, I found myself seeking reassurance that I was still anchored in reality. The validation was sweet, but it was also a bittersweet reminder of the uncertainty that loomed over me—over us.

As night fell and the city lights flickered to life, I stared out at the sprawling skyline, a glittering tableau that seemed to mock my uncertainty. The vastness of it all felt both exhilarating and terrifying. It was a world teeming with possibilities, but with each passing moment, I could feel Aiden slipping further away, our laughter echoing in the distance like a fading melody.

Evenings turned into a familiar blur of deadlines and edits, my mind racing like the subway trains that rumbled beneath the streets of New York. Each day felt like a balancing act, a precarious dance where I teetered between the thrill of success and the gnawing worry that my burgeoning career was slowly but surely pulling me away from Aiden. The irony wasn't lost on me—what I had always longed for, a platform to share my voice, was now the very thing that could silence my most cherished connection.

Aiden continued to be my sounding board, but I began to notice a subtle shift in the rhythm of our conversations. The once-easy banter now felt like it had taken on a weight of its own. Our talks had a tendency to linger on the edge of silence, each pause laden with a question neither of us dared to voice. "How does it feel?" he would ask, genuine curiosity sparkling in his eyes, yet I could sense a shadow of something deeper lurking beneath.

"It's overwhelming," I confessed one night, our knees brushing together on his worn-out couch as we watched the cityscape twinkle through his balcony door. "Like I'm floating on a cloud, but the ground keeps slipping away." I laughed, but the sound felt brittle, almost hollow.

Aiden turned to me, his brow furrowed in concern. "You're still you, right? Just with more readers?" His attempt at levity fell flat, and the room grew quiet, the air thick with tension. I wanted to reassure him, to remind him that success wouldn't erase the girl who once wrote stories tucked away in the corners of coffee shops. But the more I tried to explain, the more I realized that words felt inadequate, like trying to catch smoke with my bare hands.

Weeks turned into a montage of interviews and social media engagements that made my head spin. I reveled in the excitement, yet felt as if I was wearing a costume that didn't quite fit. I smiled for the camera, rehearsed my answers, and celebrated each milestone, but as the praise and attention poured in, the hollowness within me deepened. My heart tugged at me, calling me back to Aiden, but I was afraid—afraid that my achievements would dim his light, overshadow his aspirations, and make me something I never wanted to be: a distant star in a sky filled with other celestial bodies.

One late afternoon, I found myself alone at a café I often frequented, the comforting clatter of cups and the rich aroma of freshly brewed coffee wrapping around me like a familiar embrace. I should have been basking in my success, yet I felt adrift. Aiden had texted earlier, his message a simple inquiry about dinner plans. But what once felt like a lighthearted exchange now felt heavy, as if we were trying to stitch together a quilt of connection, but each patch was a reminder of the distance that had crept in.

As I sat, staring at my reflection in the café window, I was struck by a realization: I was afraid of the person I was becoming. Would I be the author who moved on, leaving behind the threads of my life, or the woman who found a way to weave Aiden into the fabric of my new reality? It felt as though I stood at a crossroads, each path glimmering with its own promise and peril.

That evening, I decided to surprise Aiden. I wanted to reignite the spark of our connection, the one that had flickered in the midst of my whirlwind life. I arrived at his apartment with a small bouquet of wildflowers, each bloom a vibrant testament to the world outside our bubble. The door swung open, and there he stood, a picture of warmth, his features softening as he took in the sight of me.

"Wow, look at you!" he exclaimed, his voice filled with genuine surprise. "What's the occasion?"

I stepped inside, a wave of nostalgia washing over me. The familiar scent of his cologne mixed with the faint aroma of cooking.

"I thought we could celebrate," I said, my heart racing as I handed him the flowers. "Celebrate us."

His smile faltered for a brief moment before he recovered, his hands gently cradling the blooms. "You know how to brighten a day," he said, setting the flowers on the kitchen counter. But the moment felt heavy, as if we were standing on a tightrope, balancing between celebration and uncertainty.

As we settled into a comfortable routine of chopping vegetables and stirring sauces, I realized how much I missed the simplicity of our time together. We shared stories, laughter, and playful jabs over who was the better cook—his insistence that his pasta was unbeatable versus my unwavering belief in my chili's supremacy. The kitchen hummed with life, yet in the background, I could feel the shadow of unspoken words lurking, casting a pall over our lighthearted banter.

"Are you happy?" Aiden asked suddenly, his voice cutting through the simmering pots, his gaze piercing into me with an intensity that made my heart race.

"Of course I am," I replied, but the words felt inadequate. I searched his expression, trying to decipher the layers of concern etched in his features. "Why do you ask?"

He hesitated, the kitchen filled with an uneasy silence. "I just... I don't want you to feel like you have to hide how you're really feeling, you know? Things are changing."

I took a deep breath, the tension between us palpable. "I don't want to lose what we have. But I'm scared, Aiden. Scared of losing you to all of this," I gestured vaguely, the air around us thick with the enormity of my unfiltered thoughts.

Aiden stepped closer, the warmth radiating from him wrapping around me like a blanket. "You won't lose me. I'm here for the journey, remember? I want to be part of it, all of it." His sincerity shone through, illuminating the room in a way that made the shadows recede, if only for a moment.

But that moment was fleeting, and as we shared a meal, I felt the familiar ache of unaddressed emotions between us. The plates clinked, our forks scraped against the porcelain, but each bite tasted bittersweet as I pondered the uncertainty that lay ahead. I yearned for connection, yet feared the implications of my newfound fame.

The evening drifted into night, our conversation dipping into comfortable silences interspersed with laughter. Aiden's presence felt like a balm to my restless spirit, reminding me of the warmth we shared. But in the back of my mind, the worry lingered. Would this moment slip away like grains of sand through my fingers, leaving me grasping for something I could never quite hold?

As I gazed out at the city skyline through Aiden's window, the lights shimmering like stars scattered across a vast ocean, I realized that the road ahead would be anything but straightforward. The choices I made would shape not just my career, but the very fabric of my life and the relationships I held dear. My heart ached with a longing for clarity, for a way to navigate the uncharted waters of my aspirations and the fragile thread of connection that bound Aiden and me together.

Even as the vibrant colors of dusk unfurled beyond Aiden's balcony, casting a warm glow across the room, a subtle heaviness nestled in my chest. Each flickering city light seemed to pulse with the energy of possibility, yet the brilliance felt dimmed by the shadows lurking in the corners of my heart. I craved to dive into the exhilarating whirlwind of my newfound success, yet the threads of anxiety wove tighter around me, binding me to the fear of what I might lose in the process.

Aiden and I stood shoulder to shoulder in the kitchen, where the aroma of sautéed garlic and herbs filled the air, a comforting reminder of simpler times. We chopped vegetables and stirred sauces, the act familiar yet tinged with an unspoken tension that hung between us like an unfinished sentence. I felt as if we were two stars on the brink of colliding—drawn to each other yet battling the gravitational pull of our individual aspirations.

As I diced a ripe tomato, the knife glided through the flesh with ease, yet I couldn't shake the feeling that every slice was a potential fracture in our bond. Aiden, with his easy charm and deep laughter, remained a constant in the chaos of my life. He'd always been there, offering me support and encouragement, yet now, with my piece published and doors flung open, I sensed a subtle shift, like the movement of tectonic plates beneath our feet.

"Do you ever think about what happens next?" I asked, my voice barely above a whisper, the question hanging in the air like the steam rising from the pot. Aiden looked up, his brow furrowing as he set down his knife.

"What do you mean?" His eyes searched mine, trying to unravel the complexities I had wrapped around my heart.

"The future," I replied, a hint of vulnerability creeping into my tone. "I mean, I've dreamed of this for so long, but now that it's happening, it feels... uncertain. What if this new world pulls me away from what we have?"

Aiden stepped closer, his presence warm and grounding. "You're the same person, no matter how many articles you write or awards you get," he said, his voice steady like the heartbeat of the city outside. "I'll always be here. I want to share in your journey, not watch you disappear into it."

His words ignited something deep within me—a flicker of hope amid the turmoil. Yet, I couldn't help but wonder if the world I was stepping into might swallow us both whole. The glow of ambition shone bright, but beneath it simmered the fear of what might be sacrificed on the altar of success.

That evening, as we dined on pasta adorned with basil and a drizzle of olive oil, the conversation flowed like the wine in our glasses. We spoke of dreams, of aspirations that stretched beyond the confines of our respective worlds. I shared my vision for the next piece I wanted to write, a narrative that danced between the lines of personal experience and broader truths. Aiden listened intently, his eyes alight with passion, and for a moment, the tension dissipated like steam from a kettle.

"Why don't we do a little writing retreat?" he suggested suddenly, a playful grin spreading across his face. "We could escape the city for a weekend—find a cozy cabin in the woods, somewhere we can write and unwind. You know, just breathe."

I considered the idea, envisioning a rustic cabin nestled among towering pines, a crackling fire, and the serene sounds of nature wrapping around us like a familiar blanket. "That sounds perfect," I replied, my heart lifting at the thought. "It would be nice to step away from everything, just for a little while."

As we planned our getaway, a renewed energy coursed through me. I wanted to reclaim the magic of our connection, to remind myself that beneath the excitement and pressure of my career, I was still just me. The girl who scribbled dreams in the margins of notebooks, who adored the soft warmth of Aiden's laughter, and who found solace in shared moments of silence.

The days leading up to our retreat passed in a whirlwind, each hour punctuated by new messages from readers and a flurry of social media interactions. I reveled in the attention but felt my heart tugging back towards the simplicity I craved. I found myself waking up in the middle of the night, my mind racing with thoughts of articles and interviews, only to drift back into dreams of quiet woods and starlit skies.

Finally, the weekend arrived. Aiden and I loaded his old Jeep with bags filled with cozy sweaters, notebooks, and an endless supply of snacks. The road ahead unfolded like a ribbon, weaving through the heart of the countryside, lush greens stretching as far as the eye could see. The trees whispered secrets to one another as we drove, their leaves shimmering in the sunlight like emeralds.

Upon arriving at the cabin, the air was crisp, infused with the earthy scent of pine and damp earth. The wooden structure, rustic yet inviting, stood like a sentinel guarding the peaceful oasis around it. We stepped inside, greeted by a cozy interior that exuded warmth, the fireplace beckoning us to gather around it later.

Aiden and I settled in, laughter bubbling forth as we unpacked our belongings and arranged our makeshift writing sanctuary. I claimed a small desk by the window, where sunlight streamed in, illuminating the pages of my journal waiting to be filled. Aiden set up a cozy nook with cushions and blankets, promising to indulge in a few chapters of the novel he'd been reading.

"Promise me we won't get distracted by Netflix," I teased, my voice playful as I settled into my chair, pen poised and ready.

He chuckled, his eyes twinkling with mischief. "No promises. But let's make a pact: write for an hour, then we'll take a break. Sound fair?"

I nodded, exhilaration bubbling within me. The soft hum of nature outside replaced the clamor of the city, and I could feel inspiration coiling within me like a spring waiting to release. We dove into our writing, each lost in our worlds, the only sound being the scratching of pens on paper and the occasional rustle of leaves outside.

As the sun began to set, painting the sky in hues of pink and gold, I leaned back in my chair, glancing over at Aiden. He was deeply engrossed in his book, a content smile playing on his lips. The sight warmed my heart, anchoring me to the moment. I realized then that this was what I had longed for—the convergence of my personal and professional lives, each enriching the other rather than pulling them apart.

"Hey," I called softly, breaking the silence. "What do you think about the piece I'm working on?"

He set his book aside, curiosity lighting up his features. "I'd love to hear it."

As I read aloud, weaving together the threads of my thoughts, I could see Aiden's expressions shift—from amusement to contemplation, then back to joy. His reactions grounded me, reminding me of why I wrote in the first place. It wasn't for accolades or validation; it was to connect, to share my heart and experiences with others.

When I finished, Aiden's applause filled the room, rich and genuine. "That was incredible! You have a way of making the words come alive."

I felt a flush of warmth at his praise, my heart swelling with affection. "Thanks! But it's easier when I know you're right there, rooting for me."

Aiden's gaze softened, and for a heartbeat, time stood still. It was a moment of clarity, a gentle reminder that while my journey was mine alone, it could coexist beautifully with our shared path. The world I was stepping into didn't have to overshadow our connection; instead, it could illuminate the way forward, blending our dreams into a vibrant tapestry.

Later that night, we huddled by the fireplace, the flames crackling and casting flickering shadows across the walls. I felt the weight of the day's worries slip away, replaced by a lightness I hadn't felt in weeks. As we talked about everything and nothing, laughter danced between us, an echo of the bond we'd cultivated over time.

Underneath the star-studded sky, I allowed myself to imagine a future where both our dreams could coexist. In that moment, I grasped the essence of what it meant to truly share a life with someone. It wasn't about sacrificing one passion for another; it was about supporting each other, navigating the complexities together, and celebrating the triumphs along the way.

In the quiet of the cabin, with the scent of pine and warmth enveloping us, I realized that the journey ahead wouldn't be about choosing between love and ambition. It would be about weaving them together, forging a path that embraced both my aspirations and the cherished connection I had with Aiden. Together, we could write our own story—one filled with adventure, love, and the beauty of shared dreams.

Chapter 5: The Rift

The gentle hum of the air conditioner blended with the soft patter of rain against the window, creating an almost lullaby-like atmosphere in my little writing nook. Sunlight was a rare guest these days, often overshadowed by the gloomy clouds that rolled over the Seattle skyline. I used to thrive on the chaos of the weather—how the clouds would darken before bursting with rain, mirroring the tumultuous thoughts I translated into words. Now, though, I felt like the sun that had lost its way, trying desperately to shine through the thick, oppressive layers of my life.

As I stared at the blank page on my laptop, the cursor blinked at me, a taunting reminder of my struggle. I took a deep breath, inhaling the rich scent of freshly brewed coffee that wafted from the kitchen. It wrapped around me like a comforting embrace. Each sip of that dark, bitter brew became my lifeline, fueling the words that needed to spill onto the page. I let my fingers dance across the keys, feeling each letter form into words, each word weave itself into a sentence. The rhythm of my thoughts mirrored the rain outside, pouring out in an unrestrained torrent.

Yet, amidst the clatter of my creative process, Aiden's silence echoed louder than the storm. Once, our apartment buzzed with laughter and banter, a sanctuary of warmth. Now, it felt like a hollow shell, haunted by his absence. Aiden, with his tousled dark hair and deep-set eyes that held stories of his own, had been my muse and my grounding force. But lately, I noticed how he seemed to fade into the shadows of our life together. His once-vibrant spirit now lurked behind a veil of unspoken emotions, a weight I couldn't shoulder alone.

I glanced at the clock on the wall—two hours had slipped by unnoticed, but in that stillness, a small part of me held on to hope. Maybe he would emerge from his brooding and join me. Perhaps he would sit beside me on the couch, flipping through my latest manuscript, sharing the excitement and trepidation of watching my dreams take flight. But the only sound was the steady rhythm of the rain, relentless as my swirling thoughts.

A night like any other turned into a scene I could never have scripted, a tempestuous clash of words and feelings that erupted like the storm outside. We were huddled in the kitchen, a battleground strewn with dirty dishes and half-finished takeout containers. The flickering overhead light cast erratic shadows on our faces, and I could feel the tension thrumming between us like a taut string ready to snap.

"Why can't you just be happy for me?" My voice, although steady, quivered with an undercurrent of desperation. "You act like my success is a personal affront."

Aiden leaned against the counter, arms crossed, his face a mixture of frustration and hurt. "It's not that, and you know it. I'm just... trying to find my place in all this. I thought we were in this together."

"What do you mean by that?" I stepped closer, my heart racing, feeling the air thickening with unspoken fears. "You're the one who's distanced himself! I can't chase you down every time I want to share something important."

He scoffed, the sound cutting through me like ice. "Important? You mean your book tour? Your interviews? That's what matters now, isn't it? You're too busy chasing fame to notice the cracks forming around us."

The words hung in the air, heavy and stinging. I could feel the heat of my cheeks flushing as anger bubbled to the surface. "You don't get to dismiss my hard work! You've always been my biggest supporter until now. What changed?"

His eyes darkened, a storm of their own brewing. "Maybe I'm just tired of being in the background while you bask in the limelight."

With that, the dam broke. My voice rose, echoing off the kitchen walls, our argument spiraling into a frenzy of hurt feelings and unfiltered truths. Each word was like a thunderclap, shaking the very foundation of what we had built. I could see the walls closing in around us, an invisible rift splitting our hearts.

Finally, in a fit of anger, Aiden slammed his hand against the counter, the sound reverberating like a gunshot in the confined space. "I need air," he spat, turning on his heel and marching toward the door.

"Where are you going?" I shouted, panic slicing through my anger. I wanted to reach out, to stop him, to fix what was unraveling before my eyes. But he didn't turn back.

The door slammed shut behind him, echoing like the finality of a closing chapter. I stood there, a storm of emotions swirling inside me—betrayal, confusion, heartbreak. My world had been reduced to the sound of the rain, each drop tapping against the window like a reminder of everything that had slipped through my fingers.

Alone, I sank onto the couch, my heart racing as the reality of the moment hit me. I was left with the remnants of our argument, and my fingers trembled as I opened my laptop once more, the screen illuminating my face in a soft glow. Yet, as I tried to type, my thoughts fell into a disarray, a chaotic jumble of uncertainty and longing. The words that had once flowed so freely now felt heavy, trapped within the confines of my heart.

What had once been a partnership felt fragile, and I couldn't shake the feeling that our dreams, once intertwined like ivy on a trellis, were now spiraling apart, leaving me to grapple with a haunting question: Was it my success that drove him away, or was it his own ghosts that he couldn't confront? The rain continued to pour outside, a mirror to my turbulent thoughts, as I surrendered to the solitude of that evening, feeling the distance between us grow like an insurmountable chasm.

The rain had finally relented, leaving behind a glistening tableau on the streets of Seattle, each puddle reflecting the muted glow of streetlights as the sun dipped below the horizon. It was one of those evenings where the world felt both expansive and impossibly small, a paradox that echoed in my heart. I sat on the edge of our bed, the crisp white sheets tangled around my legs like a cocoon I couldn't escape. I had always found solace in the familiar, but now every corner of our apartment seemed to carry the weight of Aiden's absence, like the ghost of laughter trapped in the walls.

I wrapped my arms around my knees, staring into the void where Aiden should have been. The silence was deafening, punctuated only by the soft ticking of the clock, each second a reminder of how much time had passed since he left. My heart raced as I replayed our argument, the hurtful words exchanged like daggers. How had we reached this point? The promise of a shared life, once vibrant and full of color, now felt like a faded photograph, edges frayed and colors dulled.

The glow of my laptop caught my eye, a beacon calling me back to the one thing that had always grounded me—writing. I opened it, hoping to find comfort in the familiar rhythm of my words. But the blinking cursor felt like a taunt, a reminder that inspiration didn't blossom in the midst of chaos. I wanted to write something profound, something that would pull me from this abyss, but every thought I tried to harness felt tangled and frayed, much like my heart.

With a sigh, I closed the laptop and wandered to the kitchen, seeking distraction. The faint aroma of garlic still lingered from dinner, a hasty affair I'd prepared for us before the storm of emotions had blown through. I poured myself a glass of wine, its deep crimson hue reflecting the remnants of my mood. The first sip was both bitter and sweet, a taste that reminded me of late nights spent sharing dreams and fears. I leaned against the counter, staring out the window at the glistening street below, each droplet catching the glow of the streetlamps, sparkling like stars fallen from the sky.

Memories crashed over me like waves—lazy Sunday mornings spent curled up in bed, Aiden's laughter ringing in the air as he flipped pancakes, the way his fingers would graze my arm when he thought I wasn't looking. Each moment felt precious yet tinged with sadness. I reached for my phone, the familiar comfort of scrolling through our shared photos tugging at my heart. I lingered on one particular shot, us grinning against the backdrop of the Space Needle, sunshine dancing in our eyes. We looked so happy, so oblivious to the turbulence brewing beneath the surface.

Suddenly, my phone buzzed, jolting me from my reverie. A message flashed across the screen, the name familiar but the sentiment unknown. It was from Mia, my closest friend, and a beacon of sanity amidst the chaos. "Thinking of you. Want to meet at The Pike?" My heart fluttered at the idea of escape, of pouring my heart out to someone who understood the intricate dance of love and ambition.

I quickly typed a response, my fingers moving with urgency. "Yes! I need to get out. Be there in 20." The prospect of a night out filled me with a rush of hope, the anticipation of laughter mingling with the promise of catharsis.

Dressed in my favorite teal dress that clung in all the right places, I stood before the mirror, studying my reflection. I wanted to be someone who radiated confidence, someone who could let go of the burdens weighing on her heart. A light breeze greeted me as I stepped outside, the cool air refreshing against my skin. The streets were alive with energy; people buzzed around me like fireflies, each with their own stories, their own struggles. I inhaled deeply, allowing the scents of street food and damp pavement to wash over me, a reminder that life was still happening, even if my world felt paused.

The Pike Place Market was a kaleidoscope of sounds and colors, laughter mingling with the distant call of vendors peddling their wares. Mia was already waiting for me at our favorite little café, a cozy nook tucked away from the bustling crowd. She waved as I approached, her smile brightening the dimness that had settled in my heart.

"You look amazing!" she exclaimed, wrapping me in a warm embrace. "I've missed this! You and me, girl time."

As we settled into our seats, the weight of the day began to lift, replaced by the familiarity of our shared moments. Mia, with her wild curls and infectious energy, had a way of lighting up any room. She ordered us drinks—a peach bellini for her, a glass of red for me. As we clinked our glasses together, I felt a small spark of joy ignite within me, a reminder that there was still life to be lived, even amidst the turmoil.

"I can't believe how much you've been juggling," Mia said, sipping her drink as she leaned forward. "Your book launch, interviews, and everything else. How are you handling it all?"

I took a moment to gather my thoughts, swirling the wine in my glass. "It's exhilarating and terrifying. I've worked so hard for this, but sometimes I feel like I'm losing myself in the process. And Aiden... he's not exactly making it easier."

Mia's brow furrowed slightly, her playful demeanor fading as concern etched her features. "What's going on with him? I know he's been quieter, but I thought maybe he was just adjusting."

I sighed, the frustration bubbling up again. "It's more than that. I can see him slipping away, consumed by his own doubts. It's like he's drowning in the shadows of his past while I'm trying to reach for the stars. I just wish he could see that I want him there beside me, cheering me on, instead of retreating into his shell."

Mia reached across the table, her hand clasping mine tightly. "You both need to talk. It's the only way to bridge that gap. You can't carry this alone."

Her words resonated deeply, and for the first time that evening, I felt a flicker of resolve igniting within me. "You're right. I need to confront this. We need to figure it out before it's too late."

As the evening wore on, laughter bubbled up between us, washing away the heaviness of the past days. I felt lighter, almost giddy, sharing stories and plans for the future. But even in my joy, a shadow lurked, a reminder of the rift that had formed in my life. I knew I had to face it head-on, to pull Aiden back from the brink before it was too late.

Leaving the café, I walked through the bustling market, the vibrant energy of Seattle surrounding me. The sounds of life resonated in my heart, a reminder that while storms may come, so too could the sun. I was determined to reclaim that light—not just for myself, but for Aiden and the future we had envisioned together.

The soft glow of the city lights cast an ethereal hue over the streets as I made my way back home, the night air brisk against my cheeks. Each step echoed with purpose, a heartbeat against the stillness that had settled in our apartment. I replayed Mia's words in my mind like a mantra, the echo of her encouragement wrapping around me like a warm shawl. I couldn't shy away from confronting the storm brewing between Aiden and me any longer. It was time to break the silence that had hung over us like a thick fog, obscuring everything we had shared.

As I reached our building, the familiar sight of the brick façade and potted plants lining the entrance felt both comforting and suffocating. Inside, the hallway smelled faintly of lavender, a fragrance I had always found soothing but now only served to heighten my anxiety. My heart raced as I approached our door, the wooden surface smooth under my fingertips. Taking a deep breath, I turned the knob, the creak of the hinges a herald of the tension that awaited me inside.

The living room was dimly lit, the shadows stretching along the walls as if they too were afraid of the confrontation looming ahead. Aiden was sitting on the couch, his back to me, an unkempt mess of hair and a rumpled T-shirt that had seen better days. He was lost in thought, a half-empty glass of whiskey resting on the coffee table before him. The sight of him made my heart ache, a heavy weight settling deep in my chest.

"Aiden," I said softly, stepping further into the room, feeling the air grow thick with unspoken words. He didn't turn around at first, the silence stretching like an elastic band between us, taut and ready to snap.

"Can we talk?" I ventured, my voice barely more than a whisper, as if the mere act of asking could somehow shatter the fragile barrier that had formed.

Finally, he turned, the shadows casting a deep line under his eyes, a storm brewing beneath the calm surface. "Sure," he replied, his voice low and rough like gravel, tinged with a hint of vulnerability.

I perched on the edge of the armchair, the fabric rough against my skin, grounding me in the moment. "I've been thinking about our conversation the other night. I don't want this distance between us. I want to understand what's going on with you."

His eyes flickered with a mixture of emotions—surprise, frustration, and a glimmer of hope that made my heart flutter. "I don't know, Jess," he said, running a hand through his hair. "It's just... everything has changed so fast. You're out there, achieving your dreams, and I feel like I'm still stuck in the past."

"It's not just your past that matters," I insisted, leaning forward, desperate to bridge the gap. "It's our future. I want you to be part of it. I need you to be part of it."

His gaze dropped to the floor, and I could see the internal struggle playing out behind his eyes. "What if I can't be what you need? What if I'm just... not enough?"

I could feel my heart crack at his admission, each word an echo of insecurities that had long haunted him. "Aiden, you are more than enough for me. Your support has always been my anchor. But I can't carry this alone. We're a team, remember? We've always been stronger together."

He remained silent, and the stillness of the room became almost unbearable, a heavy blanket smothering any warmth between us. I reached for his hand, my fingers brushing against his. It was a small gesture, yet it felt monumental in the moment, a lifeline thrown into turbulent waters. "Please, let me in. Talk to me about what you're feeling. We can face it together."

Slowly, he intertwined his fingers with mine, and the contact ignited a flicker of warmth. "It's just hard to see you shine so brightly while I feel like I'm fading into the background," he admitted, his voice barely above a whisper.

"It's not about outshining each other," I replied, squeezing his hand gently. "Your dreams matter too, Aiden. I want us both to succeed. But we can't if we don't face this together."

He nodded, a hint of tears glistening in his eyes, and my heart ached for him, for both of us. "I guess I just got scared. Scared that you would leave me behind for something bigger and better. I've seen it happen before."

"I'm not going anywhere," I promised, my voice steady and unwavering. "We're in this together, through the highs and the lows."

The weight of the moment hung between us, a delicate balance of hope and uncertainty. I could see the flicker of resolve in his eyes, the beginning of understanding that perhaps we could bridge the rift that had threatened to swallow us whole.

After a few moments of silence, he exhaled slowly, the tension in his shoulders easing ever so slightly. "Okay. I want to try. I want to make this work. But I need you to know that it's going to take time."

"Time is what we have," I assured him, a smile breaking through the clouds of worry hovering above us. "We've built something beautiful. Let's not throw it away over misunderstandings."

The conversation flowed more easily after that, a steady current of shared feelings and dreams. We spoke of our hopes for the future, the plans we had once laid out but had been shrouded in doubt. It felt like pulling back the curtain on a darkened room, allowing light to seep in and illuminate the shadows.

As the night wore on, I found myself laughing, the sound ringing through the air like a melody that had long been silenced. Aiden's laughter joined mine, and for a moment, the world outside faded away. The fears and insecurities that had threatened to drown us seemed to dissipate, leaving behind the promise of new beginnings.

Eventually, we settled into a comfortable silence, our fingers still intertwined, a silent agreement of unity. I leaned against the couch, resting my head on his shoulder. The warmth of his body enveloped me, and I could feel the steady rhythm of his heartbeat beneath my ear, a soothing balm to my restless spirit.

"We can do this, you know," I murmured, my voice a soft whisper in the stillness. "We just have to keep talking, keep being honest with each other."

"Yeah," he replied, his voice low but steady. "I think we can."

As I closed my eyes, the city outside hummed with life, and I felt a glimmer of hope take root within me. We had faced the storm together, and while the path ahead was still uncertain, we were no longer standing on opposite sides of a rift. We were side by side, ready to navigate whatever challenges lay ahead, hand in hand, heart to heart.

Chapter 6: Reflections in the Waves

The salty breeze whipped through my hair, each gust a gentle reminder of the chaos swirling within me. Standing at the edge of the Atlantic, I could hear the familiar roar of the waves crashing against the jagged rocks, their rhythmic cadence echoing my heartbeat. The sun hung low in the sky, casting a golden hue over the surf, where the water shimmered like liquid glass, and I found solace in the chaos of nature, hoping to untangle the knots in my heart.

I sank onto a weathered log, its surface worn smooth by countless tides and the weight of years, my fingers clutching a frayed journal, the pages imbued with my thoughts and dreams, my struggles and fears. The scent of the ocean mingled with the faint trace of jasmine from the nearby dunes, creating an intoxicating blend that made me feel both alive and achingly nostalgic. I opened the journal, the crisp pages inviting me to pour out my soul onto their blank canvas, and I began to write.

The ink flowed like the tide, each word crashing onto the page with the same fervor as the waves lapping at the shore. I wrote of laughter, those fleeting moments when we'd danced on the beach under a sky bursting with stars, our laughter mingling with the whisper of the ocean breeze. I wrote of the way his eyes sparkled with mischief, how he could turn a mundane Tuesday into an adventure with just a hint of spontaneity. But now, those memories felt like shards of glass, beautiful yet sharp, each slice a reminder of the argument that had ripped through our lives like a storm.

I pressed the pen harder against the paper, pouring my heart into each line, hoping to make sense of what had happened. It was easy to forget the softness of his touch, the warmth of his embrace when all I could see was the hurt. The ocean's roar seemed to echo my frustration, a cacophony of emotions I couldn't quite articulate. Love had never promised to be simple, but the complexity of it felt heavier now, as if the weight of the world rested on my shoulders.

With each wave that crashed, I recalled the words we'd hurled at each other, sharp as the shells scattered across the sand. "You never listen!" I had shouted, my voice carried away by the wind. "You're always so wrapped up in your own world!" He had countered, frustration etching lines across his brow. It felt like a betrayal, the way our love could so quickly spiral into anger, and as I relived those moments, I felt the sting of tears threaten to spill. I blinked them away, focusing instead on the horizon, where the sky met the water in a blur of blue and gold, a reminder of the beauty that still existed.

I flipped through the pages of my journal, pausing to revisit old entries that chronicled our journey. There was a time when everything felt effortless, as if the universe conspired to keep us together. I wrote of the day we found that hidden cove, the way the sunlight danced on the water as we splashed in the surf like children. "This is our secret," he had declared, his laughter ringing out like music, echoing in the vast emptiness around us.

But now, the weight of unresolved emotions settled heavily in my chest. Love was not just those beautiful moments; it was the commitment to weather the storms together. I realized that confronting our fears was part of the package, even when the darkness threatened to swallow us whole. Perhaps love meant leaning into the discomfort, reaching out even when it felt easier to retreat. I pondered this notion as I watched the waves crash and recede, the ebb and flow a testament to resilience.

As the sun began its descent, painting the sky with strokes of orange and lavender, I felt a flicker of hope ignite within me. I closed my journal, the words now etched in my heart as well as on the page. Maybe this was the first step in mending what had been broken, a promise to myself to communicate openly, to face the fears that lay buried beneath the surface. My breath steadied as I watched the tide shift, the waves whispering secrets only the ocean knew.

With renewed determination, I stood up, brushing sand from my jeans and squaring my shoulders. The horizon beckoned, and I turned away from the tumult of emotions that had momentarily consumed me. I had the power to change the narrative, to seek out understanding rather than dwell in resentment. My heart felt lighter as I walked back along the shore, the waves retreating at my feet, leaving behind glistening foam that sparkled like diamonds.

The world around me seemed to vibrate with possibility. I realized love was never about perfection; it was about the messy, beautiful journey we navigated together. I took a deep breath, letting the salty air fill my lungs, feeling a sense of clarity wash over me. Perhaps it was time to share my thoughts with him, to open the door to conversation rather than letting the silence fester between us.

As I neared the path leading back to the beach house, the last rays of sunlight dipped below the horizon, casting a warm glow on the sand. I could see our home nestled among the dunes, a beacon of light in the encroaching twilight. Each step brought me closer to the man who made my heart race, the one with whom I'd shared not just laughter but also pain. In that moment, I understood that while storms could rage and tempests could shake us, it was the quiet moments of reflection and resolve that would ultimately define us.

As I stepped onto the wooden porch, I felt a mixture of trepidation and anticipation. Love, I decided, was worth fighting for.

The wooden steps creaked beneath my feet as I made my way toward the house, the soft glow of the lanterns casting playful shadows on the porch. The scent of the ocean lingered on my skin, mingling with the faint aroma of the rosemary plants that lined the walkway. I paused for a moment, my heart racing at the thought of what lay beyond the door. Inside was more than just a house; it was a sanctuary of shared memories and whispered promises.

Taking a deep breath, I pushed open the screen door, the familiar sound of it swinging on its hinges a comfort against the growing tension in my chest. The cozy living room was illuminated by the soft, flickering light of a candle, and I could see him sprawled on the couch, his brow furrowed as he focused on the book in his hands. The sight of him made my heart twist with a mixture of longing and fear. How could I bridge the chasm that had opened between us so suddenly, so violently?

"Hey," I said, my voice softer than I intended. He looked up, surprise flashing across his face before quickly being replaced by a guarded expression. The tension was palpable, thick enough to cut with a knife, and I felt as if I were wading through an invisible fog.

"Hey," he replied, his tone flat, the warmth I had come to rely on feeling distant. I could sense the walls he'd built around himself after our fight, a fortress I feared would be difficult to breach. I took a step closer, my pulse quickening as I searched his eyes for a glimmer of the love we'd shared.

"I went to the beach," I said, trying to break through the silence that draped over us. "I wrote some things." My fingers toyed with the edges of my journal, the ink still wet with my unfiltered thoughts. It was a vulnerable moment, revealing my inner turmoil to the very person who had been the cause of it. Yet, it felt necessary—like opening a window to let in fresh air after a long, stagnant winter.

He shifted, his eyes drifting to the floor, the conflict within him palpable. "You didn't have to do that," he muttered, his voice barely above a whisper. "I mean, you didn't have to go by yourself."

"I needed to," I said, feeling the urge to push back against his retreating demeanor. "I needed to think." I stepped forward, the small distance between us feeling like an entire ocean. "We need to talk, don't you think?"

He nodded slowly, his fingers curling tightly around the book as if it were a lifeline. "Yeah, I guess we do." There was a tremor in his voice that didn't go unnoticed. I could see the shadows of doubt flitting across his face, a storm brewing just below the surface.

Sinking onto the edge of the couch, I placed my journal on my lap, my heart pounding like the waves outside. The sound filled the silence between us, a reminder of the connection we had forged through laughter and shared dreams. "I wrote about us," I began, my voice steadier than I felt. "About what we've been through and how things got so... messy."

He finally looked up, curiosity igniting a flicker of light in his eyes. "And?"

"And I realized that love isn't just the fun times. It's also the hard conversations—the ones we've been avoiding." I opened the journal, my fingers grazing over the words I had penned earlier, feeling each sentence resonate within me. "I wrote about our fight, how it felt to see you pull away. It hurt more than I expected."

He shifted, the air thick with unspoken words and emotions. "It's just... sometimes it feels like you don't see me," he admitted, his vulnerability piercing through the tension. "Like you're in your own world, and I'm just here, trying to keep up."

The honesty in his voice struck a chord deep within me, and I felt the weight of his words settle like stones in my heart. "I never meant to make you feel that way. I've been lost in my thoughts, trying to figure everything out, but I see you. I really do." I met his gaze, letting the sincerity of my words wash over him.

"You have this way of making everything seem effortless, and I guess I got scared. Scared of not measuring up, of losing you," he confessed, his shoulders slumping slightly as the words spilled out like a dam breaking. I could see the vulnerability in his eyes, the cracks in his armor, and I wanted to reach out, to bridge the distance between us with the warmth of understanding.

"I'm not going anywhere," I reassured him, my voice softening. "I want to face this together. But we have to talk about what's bothering us, the fears we're hiding."

He exhaled, the tension in his body easing just a bit. "It's just... when we argue, I feel like I'm losing you, and it scares the hell out of me." The raw honesty of his confession hung in the air like the scent of salt and earth, and I could see the fear that flickered in his eyes, mirrored in my own.

"We're in this together," I reiterated, reaching for his hand, intertwining my fingers with his, feeling the warmth radiate between us. "Let's promise to be honest, to share our fears rather than letting them fester."

His grip tightened, and for the first time since our argument, a hint of a smile tugged at the corners of his mouth. "That sounds... good. I want to make this work."

In that moment, the shadows that had loomed over us began to recede, replaced by the faint glimmer of hope. The air felt lighter, charged with possibility, and I knew that together, we could weather any storm. The journey ahead wouldn't be easy, but facing it side by side made all the difference.

As the night deepened and the stars blanketed the sky, we sat together, sharing our fears and hopes, laughter spilling into the spaces where silence had once reigned. It was a start—an imperfect but beautiful beginning toward healing. With each word, we stitched the fabric of our love tighter, determined to face the world outside our door, hand in hand.

The conversation flowed like the tide, our words ebbing and flowing, crashing against the shores of our insecurities and washing away the remnants of misunderstanding. I could feel a sense of ease settling in the room, a sanctuary of vulnerability, and as the candle flickered softly, I leaned into the warmth of our connection. The shadows danced around us, weaving through the air as if celebrating the tentative bridge we were building.

"Do you remember that time we got lost on the way to the lighthouse?" he asked, a smile creeping onto his face, its warmth radiating like the sun spilling across the horizon. His eyes glimmered with mischief, the corners crinkling as he recalled the memory. "You insisted we take that 'shortcut' through the woods, and we ended up knee-deep in mud."

I laughed, the sound echoing like music in the quiet room. "I was convinced it would save us time! I swear the map looked different back then. Besides, I think the mud was the best part." I could see the shared moment glinting between us, that familiar spark of joy igniting the air once more. "We made up the silliest songs about being stranded. I thought we'd be stuck there forever."

"Those songs were terrible," he teased, leaning closer, his fingers brushing against mine, sending a delicious shiver up my spine. "But at least we made each other laugh, right?" The sincerity of his gaze made my heart flutter, each beat resonating with the realization that even amidst the chaos, there was a bond that could not be severed.

"Yes," I said, my voice dipping to a whisper, as if speaking too loudly would break the fragile magic of the moment. "It's those memories that remind me why we fight for this, for us." I felt a flood of warmth surge through me, igniting hope and determination. It was the moments woven from laughter and shared dreams that formed the tapestry of our love, binding us through both the sunny days and the storms that threatened to pull us apart.

"I don't want to lose that," he confessed, his voice thick with emotion. "But sometimes I feel like we're drifting apart, like we're on different currents." The vulnerability in his admission tugged at my heart, and I could see the worry etched in his brow, the depth of his feelings laid bare before me.

I shifted closer, the space between us shrinking until I could feel the warmth radiating from his body. "Then let's be the anchors for each other," I suggested, my voice steady with conviction. "Let's hold on tight when the currents get strong, and promise to navigate through it together. We've always found our way back before." The metaphor felt like an incantation, summoning the strength of our shared experiences, each one a testament to our resilience.

"Together," he echoed, and a soft smile spread across his face, lighting up the room like the dawn breaking after a long night. "Together sounds good."

As we settled back into our conversation, the worries that had once threatened to drown us began to recede like the tide. We reminisced about the little things—the way he'd sneak extra fries off my plate, how I'd steal the blankets at night. With each shared laugh and tender moment, I could feel the weight of our earlier fight lift, replaced by a renewed sense of connection.

The glow of the lanterns illuminated the room, casting a golden hue around us. Outside, the ocean continued its ceaseless dance, waves crashing against the shore, a reminder of the world that lay beyond our sanctuary. I found comfort in knowing that just as the tides ebbed and flowed, so too could our emotions, as long as we navigated them together.

Eventually, the conversation shifted to dreams—the future we both yearned for but often felt too fragile to grasp. "What do you want?" I asked, my curiosity piqued. "What do you see for us?"

He paused, his gaze drifting toward the window, where the moonlight painted silvery patterns on the floor. "I see a house," he began, his voice filled with hope. "Not just any house, but a place filled with laughter and chaos. Maybe a little garden where we can grow things, even if they only survive on our attempts at nurturing them."

I imagined it vividly—the vibrant colors of flowers bursting to life in the sunlight, the laughter of children echoing through the halls, our shared dreams taking root in every corner. "And what about adventures?" I added, leaning in. "I can't picture us settling without exploring the world."

"Of course! We'll have to travel," he said, a grin breaking across his face. "Road trips to nowhere, spontaneous flights to somewhere. And you know I'll always let you pick the music, even if it means enduring your terrible playlists."

"Hey!" I protested playfully, feigning outrage. "Those playlists have character! Besides, they're part of the experience."

We shared a laugh, the sound mingling with the rhythmic crashing of waves outside, a perfect harmony that underscored our dreams. With every laugh, every shared secret, it felt as if we were weaving the fabric of our future together, stitching together a life filled with color and light.

As the night wore on, we spoke of challenges, the storms we would inevitably face, but it felt different now, as if naming them somehow diluted their power. "I think we can handle anything," I said firmly, feeling the strength of our bond. "Even if it means navigating through the rough seas together, I believe in us."

He nodded, the sincerity in his eyes reflecting my own resolve. "I believe in us too. And I'm ready to face whatever comes, as long as we're together."

In that moment, the weight of our earlier fight dissipated, replaced by a sense of shared purpose. We were two imperfect people, willing to embrace our flaws and forge ahead together. Outside, the moon illuminated the waves, casting a silver sheen over the water, an ethereal reminder of the beauty that still existed in the world.

As we turned toward each other, our hands entwined, the connection felt stronger than ever. It was as if the universe had conspired to bring us to this very moment, where the past was just a stepping stone to a more profound understanding. Together, we would navigate the depths and the shallows, guided by the light of our love, refusing to let the storms define us.

With a renewed sense of purpose and hope, we leaned in, sealing our commitment with a kiss that spoke volumes—a promise to weather any storm, to cherish the laughter, and to embrace the beautiful chaos that was life. In that moment, I knew we were not just two souls adrift; we were a force intertwined, ready to conquer the waves together.

Chapter 7: The Turning Tide

The sun hung low over the horizon, painting the sky in hues of burnt orange and lavender, as the gentle roar of waves lapped rhythmically against the shore. I stood at the water's edge, feeling the cool foam curl around my ankles, a stark contrast to the warmth of the fading day. Each wave brought with it a whisper of the ocean's secrets, promising adventure and a sense of freedom that felt like a long-forgotten embrace. The beach was alive with the laughter of children, their gleeful shouts rising and falling like the tide, mingling with the sound of seagulls circling overhead.

I breathed deeply, letting the salt air fill my lungs, savoring its briny tang. It was a typical summer evening in Cape May, a place steeped in nostalgia, where Victorian houses stood sentinel against the pastel sky, their ornate gables silhouetted in the dying light. This was my refuge, my escape from the cacophony of life that often felt too heavy to bear. Here, I could shed the weight of my worries, even if just for a moment.

Then I saw him. Aiden. He stood a little way down the beach, the wind tousling his dark hair as he crouched low, seemingly focused on something in the distance. My heart did an involuntary flip. It had been months since we'd last spoken, since our world had splintered like driftwood under the relentless tide. I thought I had buried my feelings, but seeing him now, the ghosts of our shared past clawed their way to the surface. A sudden shout broke my reverie, and I turned just in time to see a small figure, a child, struggling against the surging waves.

Time froze as I watched, my breath catching in my throat. The child flailed, the joyous laughter of earlier now replaced by desperate cries for help. Panic surged through me, but Aiden was already in motion. He shot into the water, his form cutting through the surf with an ease that belied the danger. I could see the determination etched on his face, the way his muscles flexed with each stroke, as if the ocean itself had become a part of him.

The moment felt surreal, like I was watching a scene unfold in a film—one that I desperately wanted to turn away from but couldn't. Every part of me screamed to intervene, but I was paralyzed, captivated by the sheer force of his instinct. With swift precision, he reached the child, wrapping an arm around her waist as the waves crashed around them like angry giants. I held my breath, willing him to bring her back safely, my heart racing with each passing second.

Aiden's silhouette emerged from the water, triumph and relief mingling in the air as he carried the child back to the shore. She coughed and sputtered, but the moment her feet hit the sand, her laughter returned, a sweet, melodic sound that cut through my anxiety. He knelt beside her, checking for injuries, his voice soothing, gentle—a stark contrast to the chaos of the ocean moments before. I felt an overwhelming surge of pride wash over me; this was the man I had fallen for, the protector I remembered so fondly.

As the crowd began to gather, the little girl's parents rushed over, their faces painted with gratitude and relief. I stayed back, hesitant to intrude on their reunion, but my eyes remained glued to Aiden, who radiated warmth and confidence. It was in that moment, as he brushed the sand from her cheeks, that our eyes met. An electric current passed between us, a silent acknowledgment of everything we'd lost and everything that still lingered in the depths of our hearts.

The beach slowly emptied as the sun dipped below the horizon, leaving behind a canvas of twilight hues. I could feel the coolness creeping in, wrapping around me like a familiar shawl. Aiden walked toward me, shaking droplets from his hair, a sheepish grin plastered across his face. "Hey," he said, his voice deep and warm, igniting the embers of hope flickering inside me.

"Hey," I replied, my words catching somewhere in my throat. It was as if the world around us had fallen away, leaving just the two of us suspended in time.

He shifted on his feet, the weight of our shared past hanging heavily in the air between us. "I didn't expect to see you here," he said, glancing back toward the waves as if seeking reassurance from the very ocean that had nearly claimed that child.

"Neither did I," I admitted, the memories of our last encounter flooding back—the bitterness, the heartbreak, the unsaid words that had echoed between us like a haunting melody. But now, there was a spark, a chance for something new to take root in the soil of our shared experiences.

We found a quiet spot on the sand, the night sky stretching above us, painted with a thousand stars shimmering like diamonds. The gentle sound of the waves created a soothing backdrop, a lullaby that coaxed secrets from our lips. As the night deepened, Aiden began to open up, his voice low and raw, revealing the shadows of his past—the loss that had haunted him, the fear that had held him captive. It was a confession soaked in vulnerability, each word a stepping stone toward healing.

I listened intently, my heart aching for him, but also swelling with a fierce determination to help him carry that burden. With each revelation, I felt the distance between us shrinking, the barriers we had erected slowly crumbling like sandcastles under the relentless tide. In that moment, beneath the expansive sky and the watchful eyes of the stars, we began to weave a new tapestry of understanding, one thread at a time. The night stretched on, heavy with promise, and for the first time in a long while, I felt a glimmer of hope—a flickering flame that might just guide us back to each other.

The stars twinkled above us like scattered confetti, each one a little whisper of hope in the expansive darkness. As we sat on the cool sand, I felt the comforting weight of Aiden's presence beside me, a warm contrast to the evening breeze that teased the edges of my hair. We both gazed at the water, now a velvety expanse reflecting the night sky, the waves gently kissing the shore in a rhythmic embrace. The energy between us had shifted, crackling with unspoken words and a shared understanding that transcended the past.

"What was it like?" I asked, my curiosity slipping into the air like a fragile balloon. "The moment you jumped in after her?" My voice was steady, but inside, I felt a tumult of emotions swirling. I wanted to understand the depths of his instincts, the rush of adrenaline that had propelled him into danger, and how it felt to be the hero in that moment.

Aiden's eyes narrowed slightly, the flicker of a smile dancing on his lips, almost teasingly. "It was terrifying," he admitted, his tone thoughtful, as if he were carefully unpacking layers of experience. "You see the water, and it's beautiful, but there's this power beneath it, waiting to swallow you whole." He paused, lost in his memories for a moment. "But then you see a child in trouble, and all that fear gets eclipsed by something deeper—a need to protect, to act."

I nodded, feeling the weight of his words settle around us. "It's like everything else fades away," I mused. "Your fears, your doubts... they just don't matter anymore."

"Exactly," he said, his voice barely above a whisper, as if sharing a secret. "In that moment, you become part of something larger than yourself. It's as if the world narrows to just that instant, and nothing else can touch you."

I could see the flicker of light in his eyes, the very fire that had drawn me to him in the first place. It sparked memories of lazy summer afternoons spent on the same shore, sunbathing and laughing until our sides ached, the sound of his voice mixing seamlessly with the ocean's lullaby. We had shared dreams, fears, and ambitions, but life had steered us apart, leaving fragments of what once was.

"You've always been like that," I continued, my voice now barely above a murmur. "The protector, the one who runs toward danger instead of away from it." I turned to face him fully, wanting him to see the sincerity in my gaze. "That's why I was so scared when we... when we drifted apart. I felt like I lost my anchor."

His expression softened, and for a moment, I caught a glimpse of the man I had loved so fiercely, the one who still held pieces of my heart. "I didn't want to hurt you," he said, his voice heavy with regret. "I thought pulling away would shield you from my chaos."

The honesty in his tone stirred something within me, a deep yearning to bridge the gap that had grown between us. "But the chaos is a part of you," I insisted, my heart racing. "You don't need to hide it from me. I want to share that burden, Aiden. I want to be here."

A silence enveloped us, thick with unexpressed emotions and the weight of unhealed wounds. The waves continued their timeless dance, but the world around us had shrunk to just the two of us, suspended in a moment that felt both fragile and infinitely strong.

After a while, Aiden turned to me, his expression serious, almost vulnerable. "I lost someone once," he began, his voice steady but heavy. "Someone I should have saved." The words hung in the air, palpable and raw. "It was my brother. He drowned during a storm a few years back. I had tried to reach him, but the currents were too strong, and by the time I got to him... it was too late."

A chill ran through me at the intensity of his confession. "Oh, Aiden," I breathed, my heart aching for him. "I'm so sorry."

He continued, his eyes distant, reflecting the turmoil of that day. "Ever since then, I've been haunted by that moment. It's like a ghost that follows me everywhere I go. I thought if I could just distance myself from everyone, I wouldn't have to live through that pain again. I didn't want to lose anyone else."

His admission cut deeper than I expected. The guilt and sorrow clung to him like a second skin, and I yearned to reach out, to offer him the solace he so desperately needed. "You don't have to bear that alone," I said softly, my voice steady. "I'm here for you, Aiden. I can help you carry that weight."

He turned to me, his expression a mix of disbelief and longing, as if he were allowing himself to hope for the first time in years. "You really mean that?"

"More than anything," I replied, leaning closer. "Let's stop hiding from the hurt. We can face it together. You've already started by saving that little girl. That's a step in the right direction."

A smile broke through the darkness of his sorrow, and it lit up his face like the dawn breaking over the horizon. "You always did know how to pull me out of the shadows," he said, a note of warmth returning to his voice.

The connection between us felt renewed, the distance we had allowed to grow slowly eroding under the tide of understanding and shared pain. I could sense that we were on the cusp of something beautiful, something worth fighting for.

As the night deepened, our conversation flowed easily, weaving through stories of our childhood, dreams we had shelved, and hopes we still dared to harbor. Laughter bubbled up like champagne, effervescent and heady, and I found solace in the rhythm of his voice, each word a thread stitching our hearts back together.

The salty breeze carried the scent of the ocean, mingling with the warmth of the night, and as we sat side by side, I felt an exhilarating sense of possibility unfurling within me. Maybe, just maybe, the tide was turning, bringing us back to shore where we could rebuild the love we once had, one wave at a time.

With the stars as our witnesses and the waves as our lullaby, I knew this was just the beginning of our journey back to each other. The road ahead would be fraught with challenges and echoes of the past, but for the first time, I felt ready to face it all, hand in hand with the man who had once stolen my heart.

The night wore on, and the cool breeze turned crisp, a harbinger of autumn creeping into the heart of summer. Stars twinkled above us, each a silent witness to our conversation, our laughter drifting upward like a prayer. Aiden's demeanor shifted as we shared stories; the weight of his earlier sorrow seemed to lighten, like the tide slowly receding. The shadows that clung to him faded under the glow of our renewed connection, each shared word stitching together a tapestry of hope and possibility.

We lingered on the beach long after the sun had surrendered its reign to the moon, the golden light of day giving way to a silvery luminescence that transformed the world around us. Aiden tossed small pebbles into the water, watching them skip across the surface, his face illuminated by an uncharacteristic softness. "You remember those summers when we were kids?" he asked, a nostalgic smile playing at the corners of his mouth.

"How could I forget?" I chuckled, my heart warming at the thought. "You would always drag me to the lighthouse, convinced you could find buried treasure."

A playful glimmer danced in his eyes. "And we did find treasure, didn't we? It just wasn't gold."

A tender silence enveloped us, and I felt the familiar warmth of connection unfurling, rekindling the flames of a bond I thought had been extinguished. "We found our own little world," I replied, my voice barely above a whisper. "A sanctuary away from everything."

He nodded, his gaze drifting back to the horizon where the moon kissed the water. "I miss that simplicity," he confessed, his tone laden with longing. "Before everything became so complicated."

The memory of carefree days, spent searching for seashells and chasing waves, filled the space between us. I thought about the last summer we had spent here together, laughing until our sides ached, dreams woven into the fabric of our friendship. But life had a way of fraying those threads, leaving us in a tangle of unspoken truths and missteps.

The sounds of the beach had softened, the laughter of distant revelers fading into the night. As the moonlight danced upon the water, casting shimmering reflections that flickered like fireflies, Aiden turned to me, his expression serious yet gentle. "Can we try to be friends again? I know I've made mistakes, and I don't want to keep running from them."

A rush of warmth flooded through me at his words, igniting the flickering hope that had been buried beneath layers of hurt and resentment. "I'd like that," I said, my heart racing. "I've missed you."

The honesty in his gaze held me captive as he reached for my hand, our fingers intertwining effortlessly, as if they had always belonged together. It felt like a promise, a quiet vow to navigate the uncertainties ahead, to face whatever demons still lingered between us.

As the tide began to pull back, revealing glistening strands of seaweed and small shells, we rose to our feet, the sand still warm beneath us. The beach was ours again, a canvas waiting to be painted anew. "Let's explore the lighthouse tomorrow," I suggested, a playful spark in my voice. "You can show me all the secret spots again."

Aiden grinned, the boyish charm I had always adored flashing in his eyes. "You mean my expert treasure-hunting skills? I've still got some tricks up my sleeve."

The lighthearted banter felt like a balm, soothing the wounds that had festered for too long. Together, we walked along the shoreline, our footsteps tracing a path through the sand as the waves lapped gently at our ankles. The night felt alive with possibility, and as we talked and laughed, I began to believe that perhaps we could carve out a new chapter, one filled with laughter and healing.

As the first hints of dawn began to color the sky, the horizon transformed into a palette of pastel hues. I marveled at the beauty of it all, the sun peeking shyly above the waves, casting golden rays that danced upon the water. "Look at that," Aiden said, pulling me closer, his warmth wrapping around me like a cherished blanket. "It's breathtaking."

"It really is," I replied, my heart swelling. "Just like this moment."

The world around us faded away, the worries and fears of yesterday swept out to sea. In the light of a new day, I felt a sense of clarity wash over me. We were standing on the precipice of change, and this time, I was ready to dive into the depths with him, to face the currents that threatened to pull us apart.

The lighthouse stood tall in the distance, a beacon guiding lost souls back to shore. As we made our way back to the boardwalk, the salty air filled with the sounds of seagulls and the distant hum of the town awakening, I couldn't shake the feeling that something significant had shifted between us. The laughter and lightness that had once defined our friendship were creeping back in, and with them, the hope of a future that felt attainable.

Over the next few days, we explored the coast, rediscovering the hidden nooks and crannies that had once been our playground. We climbed the rickety stairs of the lighthouse, the view from the top breathtaking as we surveyed the expanse of the ocean, its vastness echoing the newness of our relationship. Aiden pointed out landmarks from our childhood, recounting stories that made me laugh until tears streamed down my face.

Yet, amidst the joy and laughter, the weight of Aiden's past lingered like a ghost, always hovering just out of sight. I saw it in the way he would sometimes stare off into the distance, his smile faltering for a fraction of a second as if caught in a memory he couldn't quite shake. I wanted to reach out, to help him navigate those turbulent waters, but I understood that healing takes time, just as the tide ebbs and flows.

One evening, as we sat on the porch of a quaint café overlooking the beach, the sunset painting the sky in brilliant oranges and purples, I sensed the heaviness creeping back into the air. "What's on your mind?" I asked, my voice gentle but probing.

He sighed, running a hand through his hair, the sunlight catching the strands and casting a warm glow around him. "I don't want to drag you into my darkness," he admitted, his eyes clouded with uncertainty. "You deserve to be happy, and I... I'm still trying to figure out how to move forward."

I reached across the table, taking his hand in mine. "We all have shadows, Aiden. You don't have to face yours alone."

His gaze met mine, a mixture of vulnerability and gratitude swirling in his eyes. "It feels so easy to fall back into the past," he confessed. "But with you, I want to keep looking forward."

"Then let's look forward together," I urged, my heart racing. "No more running. We'll take it one step at a time."

As we watched the sun dip below the horizon, casting shimmering reflections on the water, I realized that our journey had just begun. The complexities of our past would always linger in the background, but they no longer felt insurmountable. With each shared smile and whispered secret, we were forging a new path, one that honored our history while bravely stepping into the future.

And just like the tide, I knew we would rise and fall, ebb and flow, but together, we could weather any storm that came our way. The beach had always been our sanctuary, and now, as the waves lapped at the shore, I felt a renewed sense of purpose and belonging. We were more than just fragments of a broken past; we were two souls navigating the waters of life, ready to embrace whatever came next, hand in hand, heart to heart.

Chapter 8: Tides of Change

The air hung heavy with the scent of freshly brewed coffee and the unmistakable sweetness of pastries, creating an intoxicating blend that wrapped around me as I pushed open the door to the quaint café. The bell chimed overhead, a cheery greeting that echoed my excitement as I stepped inside. My eyes quickly adjusted to the warm glow of the amber lights, illuminating the rustic wooden beams that crisscrossed the ceiling. Each table was adorned with little vases of wildflowers, their petals delicate and unassuming, yet bursting with life.

Nestled in the corner, Aiden sat with his back to the wall, his head slightly tilted as he scanned the room. He had a way of looking at the world that made it seem like every detail mattered. As I approached, his face broke into that easy smile, the kind that made the corners of my heart tug with familiarity and something deeper. It was a smile that made me believe in good days and the promise of shared moments, no matter how mundane.

"Hey, there you are!" he exclaimed, his voice rising above the soft chatter of customers. "I ordered you a caramel macchiato. Figured you'd need the extra energy." He gestured to the steaming cup waiting on the table, frothy swirls of milk floating atop dark coffee like a painter's canvas awaiting its first stroke.

"Perfect choice," I replied, sliding into the seat across from him. The warmth of the cup seeped through my fingers as I lifted it, inhaling the sweet aroma. This moment felt significant, a thread weaving us closer in a tapestry that had once seemed frayed and tangled.

The café was alive with the gentle hum of conversations blending into the background, punctuated by the clinking of cups and the hiss of the espresso machine. Outside, the street was a rush of autumn colors—trees adorned in vibrant yellows and reds, their leaves dancing down in a graceful flurry. Each leaf seemed to whisper stories of change and renewal, mirroring my own journey with Aiden.

We spoke of everything and nothing, our laughter punctuating the air, as easy as the way the sun filtered through the windows, casting golden rays upon us. I watched him, his eyes crinkling at the edges as he shared a story from his childhood, a time filled with mischievous escapades that made his past seem almost mythical. It was refreshing to see him peel back the layers, revealing bits of himself that he had once kept guarded. In that moment, I realized how much I wanted to be part of his narrative, how much I craved that connection—a longing that had sprouted quietly, unfurling its petals with every shared glance and fleeting touch.

"Do you ever think about how far we've come?" I asked, my voice soft yet tinged with a hopeful reverie. "I mean, a year ago, I was just a girl chasing a dream, and you..." I paused, trying to capture the essence of his presence in my life. "You were just trying to find your place in the world."

He looked at me then, a contemplative expression taking over his features. "Yeah, I think about it a lot," he admitted. "I didn't expect to find someone who could see me for who I am, not just the façade I put on." There was a vulnerability in his admission that made my heart flutter, each beat echoing the depth of our shared understanding.

We spent hours there, lost in our bubble of conversation and laughter, occasionally drawing glances from nearby tables. I reveled in the way his gaze would linger on me, as if he were trying to memorize every detail of my smile. The world outside continued to bustle, people hurrying by, but inside this little sanctuary, time seemed to pause, allowing us a moment of respite from our pasts.

As the sun began to dip below the horizon, casting a warm glow across the café, I felt an urge to embrace the future that lay ahead of us. Aiden was more than just a chapter in my life; he was a collaborator in my story, one that would intertwine with mine in beautiful, unexpected ways.

"Can you come to my book signing next week?" I asked suddenly, the question tumbling out of my mouth before I could fully process the implications. The thought of him standing beside me, cheering me on as I showcased my work to the world, sent a rush of excitement coursing through me.

His eyes lit up, a spark igniting the air between us. "Absolutely. I wouldn't miss it for anything." There was a sincerity in his voice that made my heart swell. In that moment, I knew that whatever challenges lay ahead, we would face them together.

Leaving the café felt surreal, as if we were stepping out of a dream and back into reality, hand in hand. The cool evening air wrapped around us like a soft embrace, sending shivers down my spine as we walked side by side. Aiden's warmth radiated beside me, a comforting presence that felt as familiar as the well-loved pages of my favorite novel.

We navigated the streets with a sense of purpose, our footsteps echoing against the pavement, blending with the sounds of laughter and distant music wafting from open windows. As we strolled, the vibrant city came alive around us—street performers showcasing their talents, couples laughing as they shared secrets, and the sweet scent of food vendors lingering in the air. It was the perfect backdrop for the promise of a new chapter in our lives.

I glanced at Aiden, his face illuminated by the streetlights, and for a brief moment, everything felt right in the world. With him, I was no longer just a girl lost in her dreams; I was a writer with a story to tell, and he was the muse who inspired every word.

The book signing loomed ahead like a thrilling but nerve-wracking wave on the horizon, and I could feel the anticipation thrumming in my veins. The quaint little bookstore where I had spent countless hours lost in worlds not my own transformed into a canvas where my dreams would be unveiled. It was an enchanting space, the air thick with the smell of old pages and fresh ink, and the soft glow of fairy lights strung across the wooden shelves cast a gentle, welcoming ambiance. As I stood at the entrance, taking in the familiar surroundings, I felt a flutter of excitement mixed with trepidation—this was it, my moment.

Aiden arrived just as I was about to sink into my own thoughts, his presence commanding and comforting. He looked effortlessly handsome in a fitted navy shirt that accentuated the strong lines of his arms. His hair was tousled, as if he'd just run his fingers through it in a moment of distraction—an endearing quirk that made me smile. As he approached, the corners of his mouth turned up in that smile that made my heart skip like a pebble across water.

"You ready for this?" he asked, tilting his head slightly, his eyes searching mine for any trace of doubt.

"More than ready," I said, my voice steadier than I felt. The truth was, with him by my side, I felt invincible.

As we made our way inside, the gentle buzz of conversation enveloped us. Friends, family, and supportive strangers were already milling about, flipping through the pages of my book that sat stacked on the small wooden table adorned with a simple bouquet of sunflowers. Their cheerful faces and animated discussions about literature filled the space with warmth. I felt the nerves twist in my stomach, a whirlwind of excitement and anxiety that threatened to spill over.

"Hey, let's take a quick walk around," Aiden suggested, sensing my unease. We wandered through the aisles, surrounded by towering shelves that held the stories of countless authors. The light chatter faded into the background as I focused on the comforting presence beside me, a sanctuary amid the swirling sea of anticipation.

"Look at all these books," I said, my fingers trailing along the spines, feeling the rough texture beneath my fingertips. "Every one of them has its own story, just waiting to be discovered." I paused, glancing at Aiden. "And here I am, about to add mine to the mix. It's surreal."

"It's more than that," he replied, turning to face me, his expression earnest. "You're not just adding to the mix; you're creating something unique. Something that's a part of you." His words wrapped around me like a warm blanket, infusing me with courage.

We returned to the signing area, where a small line had formed, eager faces glancing at me expectantly. I took a deep breath, channeling the energy around me. The first person stepped forward, a beaming girl with a stack of books cradled in her arms. Her eyes sparkled with excitement as I signed her copy, my hand moving instinctively across the page, my signature flowing like a dance.

"Thank you so much!" she gushed, her enthusiasm infectious. "I've been waiting for this day! Your book means so much to me."

The words melted my apprehensions, and with each signature, I began to feel the rhythm of the moment settle into a joyful cadence. Aiden stood close by, his presence a steady anchor as I greeted readers, sharing snippets of inspiration behind my writing. With each conversation, the atmosphere buzzed with shared excitement, and the connection between us all felt palpable.

As I signed the last book for a shy young woman who barely met my eyes, I glanced up to find Aiden watching me with a proud smile. It was a moment of pure elation, and I could hardly contain the warmth spreading through my chest. "You're amazing," he said softly, and those two words felt like a gentle caress.

"Thanks to you," I replied, allowing myself a moment to bask in the glow of his encouragement.

The signing concluded, and the crowd began to dissipate, leaving behind echoes of laughter and the sweet, lingering scent of coffee.

I turned to Aiden, feeling an overwhelming rush of gratitude. "I couldn't have done this without you. You believed in me when I was still trying to believe in myself."

His gaze softened, and for a moment, the world around us faded. "I believe in the you that's yet to come, too," he said, his sincerity washing over me like a tide.

We stepped outside, the cool evening air refreshing after the warmth of the bookstore. The sunset painted the sky in hues of pink and orange, a breathtaking backdrop that matched the exuberance bubbling inside me. We walked side by side, our fingers brushing against each other, a small connection that felt electric and tender.

"Let's celebrate," he suggested, a glimmer of mischief dancing in his eyes. "I know the perfect place."

Before I knew it, we found ourselves at a nearby rooftop bar, the city sprawling beneath us like a twinkling sea of stars. The ambiance was alive with laughter and the clinking of glasses, and I could hardly believe the day had turned into such an adventure. As we settled at a small table, the glow of string lights overhead created an intimate atmosphere, setting the stage for a celebration of dreams realized.

Aiden ordered us a round of drinks, his ease with the waitress drawing me in further. When he returned, a cool cocktail in hand, he raised his glass. "To you," he declared, his voice full of genuine admiration. "To every page you've written and every story you have yet to tell."

I clinked my glass against his, warmth flooding my chest as I met his gaze. "And to us," I added, the realization washing over me that this was just the beginning. We were two people entwined in each other's journeys, navigating our aspirations together, discovering strength in vulnerability.

The night deepened, and as laughter spilled between us, I marveled at how effortlessly we connected. Aiden shared stories of his own dreams, hopes flickering in his eyes like candle flames. Each revelation brought us closer, stitching together the fabric of our lives with threads of shared ambition and tenderness.

With the city sparkling below us and the stars winking overhead, I found myself surrendering to the moment. I felt anchored by Aiden, buoyed by the possibilities ahead. In that embrace of the night, everything felt possible, as if the universe conspired in our favor, whispering secrets of hope and the promise of love.

The night unfolded like a beautifully scripted play, each scene illuminated by the flickering lights of the bar and the ambient hum of laughter surrounding us. Aiden's presence was both invigorating and calming, a rare combination that made me feel as though I could conquer any challenge, be it a blank page or the remnants of self-doubt that threatened to surface. The taste of victory was still fresh on my tongue, and as we shared a round of drinks—his choice being an artful concoction of gin and tonic with hints of rosemary—every sip tasted like a celebration of newfound possibilities.

As the evening deepened, I found myself leaning closer to him, caught in the magnetic pull of his charisma. We exchanged stories, weaving tales from our pasts like colorful threads in a tapestry. I listened intently as Aiden recounted his childhood in a sleepy little town, painting vivid images of summer days spent on bicycles and endless adventures in the woods. His laughter resonated, bright and unguarded, and I could see the boy he had been still flickering beneath the surface of the man he had become.

"Sometimes I think those simpler times were the best," he mused, glancing out over the cityscape. "Everything was more straightforward. You rode your bike until dark, and your biggest worry was making it home before dinner."

I nodded, recalling my own memories of carefree afternoons spent in treehouses, armed with a notebook and a pen, crafting entire worlds within the pages. "And then you grow up and realize that adulting comes with a whole new set of complications," I replied, a playful sigh escaping my lips. "Like taxes and making decisions that actually matter."

His chuckle rippled through the air, and for a moment, the world around us faded, leaving only the connection we shared. "Yeah, I think we should all be given a 'do-over' button," he said, his eyes sparkling with mischief. "Imagine if we could press it every time life threw us a curveball."

"Or when we accidentally sent a text to the wrong person," I added, laughter bubbling up between us like a fizzy drink, lightening the mood. It was in these moments of banter that I felt our bond solidify—a dance of wits, of shared laughter that drew us closer.

But the conversation turned serious when I noticed a shadow pass over his face, a fleeting glimpse of the weight he carried. "What about you?" he asked, his voice softer now. "What's your biggest worry these days?"

I took a moment to consider my answer, glancing at the twinkling lights of the city below us, each one a tiny beacon of hope. "Honestly, it's this," I admitted, gesturing between us. "I've never really allowed anyone into my world like this before. What if I mess it up?"

Aiden reached across the table, his fingers brushing against mine, sending a thrill up my arm. "You're not going to mess it up," he assured me, his gaze steady. "We're both in this, and I promise to navigate the storms with you."

His words settled in my chest like a warm embrace, wrapping me in reassurance. It was a simple promise, yet it felt monumental in its implications. We were two imperfect souls, forging a path through the complexities of life, and with every shared moment, I felt a deeper sense of belonging blooming within me.

As the evening wore on, we moved to the edge of the rooftop, where the cool breeze tousled our hair, and the city stretched out like a vast, glittering ocean. The skyline loomed tall, buildings reflecting the soft glow of the moonlight, while the distant sound of music drifted up from street performers below.

"Let's make a pact," Aiden suggested, leaning closer, his voice barely above a whisper. "No matter what happens, we'll always be honest with each other."

My heart raced at the sincerity in his eyes. "Deal," I replied, my voice steady. The gravity of our unspoken agreement hung in the air, a binding thread connecting our fates.

The following days unfolded like the chapters of a book, filled with vibrant scenes of exploration. Aiden and I dove headfirst into the rhythm of our lives intertwined, navigating our individual pursuits while making room for each other. We frequented art galleries and hidden cafés, our laughter echoing against the walls like a melody that belonged to us. He introduced me to his favorite hiking trails, where the scent of pine trees and the sound of rustling leaves became the backdrop to our adventures.

One particular Saturday, we found ourselves at the local farmer's market, the sun shining brightly as we wove through stalls brimming with colorful produce and homemade delights. The air was rich with the scent of fresh bread and blooming flowers, creating a vibrant atmosphere that invigorated the senses. Aiden picked up a plump heirloom tomato, examining it with the seriousness of a connoisseur.

"Here's a secret," he said, leaning closer with a conspiratorial grin. "The riper the tomato, the better the caprese salad."

"Is that so?" I replied, raising an eyebrow, playful skepticism dancing in my voice. "And what makes you such an expert on tomatoes?"

"I had a summer job at a local deli," he explained, his expression turning reminiscent. "We made the best sandwiches with fresh ingredients. You wouldn't believe how much love goes into a good caprese salad."

I laughed, charmed by his earnestness. "Alright, then. Show me how it's done."

With a playful determination, he led me to a vendor who boasted the freshest mozzarella. We gathered ingredients, our arms brushing against each other as we moved through the market, and each touch sent a spark of warmth through me.

Later that evening, in Aiden's small but cozy kitchen, we transformed our haul into a culinary masterpiece, laughter and conversation flowing as freely as the olive oil drizzled over our creation. The simplicity of the moment felt profound—a snapshot of our lives converging, weaving together a shared experience.

We sat at the table, surrounded by the aroma of fresh basil and the clinking of glasses as we toasted to the simple joys we had found together. "To good food and even better company," Aiden declared, and as we sipped our wine, the warmth of the moment enveloped us, a cocoon of burgeoning intimacy.

But beneath the surface, there was a current of unease tugging at me. I could sense the layers of Aiden's past still lingering in his gaze, shadows that danced just beyond reach. While he was present, I often wondered how much he still carried with him—the scars from battles fought and lost.

One night, as we lounged on his couch, surrounded by the remnants of takeout and the glow of a movie playing softly in the background, I decided it was time to delve deeper. "You know," I began cautiously, "I feel like there's so much you haven't shared with me. It's like you're still holding on to pieces of your past."

He turned to me, his expression shifting, uncertainty flickering in his eyes. "I'm still figuring it all out," he admitted, his voice low. "There are things I don't know how to talk about."

"I get that," I said softly, reaching for his hand, intertwining our fingers. "But I'm here for you, Aiden. You don't have to carry it alone."

The tension hung in the air like a storm cloud, but I could see a flicker of hope in his gaze, a willingness to open up. It was a pivotal moment—one that could either draw us closer or set us adrift.

With a deep breath, he began to share, each word carefully chosen but infused with emotion. As he recounted fragments of his life, from the challenges he had faced to the dreams he still clung to, I felt the weight of his burdens slowly lifting, a shared vulnerability weaving us together even tighter.

As the night deepened, I realized that we were not just navigating our dreams individually but also learning to confront our fears together. Each revelation added depth to our relationship, building a foundation that felt sturdy and resilient. And as I nestled against him on the couch, the warmth of his body against mine, I knew we were embarking on something extraordinary—a journey of love and healing, side by side, ready to face whatever came next.

Chapter 9: Whispers of Hope

The sun dipped low behind the hills of Jackson, casting long shadows that tangled with the tall grass in my backyard. Each blade swayed with a whisper, as if sharing secrets of the summer days gone by. I leaned against the weathered porch railing, my fingers tracing the rough wood, taking in the scent of freshly cut grass mingling with the rich, earthy aroma of the nearby woods. This was my sanctuary, a modest house surrounded by the kind of wildness that had become my solace, where the air crackled with the anticipation of an approaching storm.

Aiden was inside, his presence a comforting hum against the backdrop of nature's symphony. I could hear the rhythmic tapping of his fingers against the keyboard, a familiar sound that felt like home. He was lost in his world, a creative space where words flowed like water from a mountain spring. I envied that flow—his ability to harness emotions and craft them into something tangible. My own thoughts often felt muddied, tangled in a web of uncertainty, but Aiden had a way of turning the murkiest feelings into poetry.

The sun finally sank below the horizon, painting the sky in hues of orange and deep indigo. Fireflies began to flicker to life, their tiny lights illuminating the encroaching darkness, reminding me of the fleeting moments we often took for granted. But it was the silence that followed the day's end that felt heavier than expected, laden with the weight of unsaid words and unaddressed feelings. I could sense it—the stillness had shifted.

The door creaked open, and Aiden stepped out, the glow from inside spilling over him like a warm embrace. He wore that familiar expression, the one that held a mix of joy and vulnerability, a look that made my heart swell and ache all at once. "What are you thinking about?" he asked, his voice soft yet charged with curiosity.

"Just how beautiful it is out here," I replied, forcing a smile that didn't quite reach my eyes. He didn't need to know about the knots tightening in my stomach, the worries unspooling in the back of my mind like a long-forgotten thread.

"Yeah, it is," he said, leaning against the railing beside me. The warmth of his shoulder against mine felt electric, grounding me in the moment. "I was just working on that piece. I think I finally found the words for it."

"Really? That's great!" I feigned enthusiasm, though a part of me felt heavy with the anticipation of what was to come. Aiden had a way of pulling me into his world, but I could feel the shift brewing in the air—a storm of emotions that threatened to overshadow our quiet evening.

He turned to face me, the last rays of sunlight catching the edges of his tousled hair, illuminating the intensity of his gaze. "I feel like something is about to happen," he murmured, as if he could sense the tension in the air, the change brewing just out of sight.

Before I could respond, the doorbell rang, its chime slicing through the evening stillness. I felt my heart leap into my throat, a harbinger of something unwelcome. Aiden's expression changed, confusion etching lines across his forehead as he glanced back toward the house. "I wasn't expecting anyone," he said, the words trailing off into a heavy silence.

"Do you want me to get it?" I offered, instinctively sensing that whatever lay beyond that door was not going to be the casual visit we both hoped for.

Aiden hesitated, and I could see the flicker of apprehension in his eyes. "No, I'll get it. Just... wait here."

He stepped inside, leaving me alone in the fading light, the weight of uncertainty thick in the air. I could hear the muffled voices, the rustle of papers, and the unmistakable shift of tension. My mind raced, envisioning a million scenarios that could unfold with each passing moment.

When Aiden returned, his face was pale, the warmth of the evening air suddenly feeling cold. Clutched in his hand was a letter, its envelope stark white against the darkening sky. "It's from my past," he said, the words a fragile whisper that carried the weight of years.

The world around us seemed to fade, the chirping of crickets silenced by the gravity of the moment. A storm had arrived, uninvited and forceful. I felt the knots in my stomach tighten further as Aiden's fingers trembled slightly as he opened the envelope, each tear of paper echoing in the growing silence.

"What does it say?" I asked, my voice barely above a whisper, as if raising it would somehow conjure more shadows.

"It's... complicated," he admitted, his brow furrowing deeper as he scanned the contents. "It's about things I thought I had moved on from, things I didn't even know were still affecting me."

His gaze lifted to mine, and I could see the turmoil swirling behind his eyes, the battle between wanting to protect me from his past and the need to confront it. "I need to deal with this," he said, and my heart sank. "But I'm afraid. I don't know if I can face it alone."

The weight of his words wrapped around me like a shroud, pulling me into the depths of his struggle. I wanted to reach out, to tell him he didn't have to face it alone, but a part of me recoiled at the thought of being dragged into the shadows of his history. What if those shadows consumed him? What if they consumed us?

In the hush that enveloped us, the moon emerged, casting a silvery glow across the yard, illuminating the uncertainty that loomed over us. I took a deep breath, filling my lungs with the cool night air, trying to clear my mind of the swirling fears. "Aiden," I began, my voice steadying as I focused on his eyes, "whatever it is, we can face it together. But you have to be honest with me."

His eyes searched mine, and in that moment, I knew we stood on the precipice of something significant. A whisper of hope flickered between us, a fragile light amid the growing shadows.

He nodded slowly, the tension easing just slightly. "I want to, but it's going to take time. There are things I need to sort out."

"Then we'll take it one step at a time," I promised, though doubt lingered like the distant rumble of thunder. "I believe in you, Aiden. I believe in us."

As the night deepened, we stood together in the embrace of uncertainty, the weight of the past pressing down but softened by the light of a shared future. The fireflies danced around us, their delicate glow a testament to the beauty that could flourish even in the dark. In that moment, with the moon overhead and the world hushed, we realized that love, in all its messy, complicated glory, was worth fighting for, even when the tides threatened to pull us under.

The night unfurled around us like a blanket, soft and dark, allowing only the luminous glow of the moon to penetrate the canopy of shadows. As Aiden and I stood on the porch, a palpable tension lingered in the air, thick enough to almost touch. I could see the gears of his mind turning, each thought a clashing wave against the shore of his resolve. The letter lay crumpled in his hand, a paper weight tethering him to the past.

"Do you want me to read it?" I asked gently, hoping to guide him through this uncertain territory. There was a flicker of hesitation in his eyes, the kind that spoke of ghosts long buried, and I wondered if he could even bear to let me see the specters of his past.

"No," he replied, his voice steady but strained. "This is something I need to do on my own." The strength in his words was admirable, but I felt a tug of disappointment, as though he was building a wall between us, brick by brick.

The air was charged, and I was acutely aware of every sound—the rustle of leaves, the distant bark of a dog, the rhythmic chorus of cicadas. Each noise felt amplified, a reminder that life continued to hum around us, while we stood on the precipice of something immense. I wanted to reach out, to tell him that confronting the past didn't have to mean facing it alone. But I hesitated, unsure if my words would bridge the gap or deepen the chasm.

"Okay," I said finally, leaning against the porch railing, a move that seemed to ground me in this moment. "Just know that I'm here when you're ready."

He nodded, a ghost of a smile flickering across his lips, and for a moment, I saw a glimpse of the Aiden I loved—the one who laughed easily, who brought light into my life like the dawn breaking over a sleepy town. But then that smile faded, replaced by shadows that loomed large in his expression.

"Thanks," he murmured, his gaze drifting to the horizon where the last remnants of sunlight melted into the night. The darkness felt thicker than ever, wrapping us in a cocoon of uncertainty. "It's just... there are things I thought I had put to rest, things I buried deep. I don't know if I'm ready to dig them up."

I could almost feel the weight of his memories pressing down on him, a mountain he had climbed and now had to confront once more. It was disconcerting, the way the past clung to him like a heavy mist, refusing to dissipate despite his best efforts. "Sometimes the past doesn't let go, no matter how hard we try," I replied softly. "But facing it might be the only way to truly move forward."

His eyes searched mine, and I could see the flickering candle of hope struggling to stay alight amid the gusts of uncertainty. "You really think so?" he asked, a hint of desperation creeping into his voice.

"I do. It might hurt, but sometimes the hardest paths lead us to the most beautiful destinations."

Aiden's lips curved into a hesitant smile, and the tension in his shoulders eased, if only for a moment. I felt a warmth surge within me, a spark igniting in the dark. Perhaps this was a step, however small, toward confronting those old demons. "Maybe you're right," he said, sounding more resolved. "It's just that—"

"Whatever it is, I'll stand by you," I interrupted, feeling an urgency to assure him that he wasn't alone in this fight. "I'm not going anywhere."

With that reassurance lingering between us, we descended into a silence that felt more comfortable, as if the moon above us were shining a path through the fog of uncertainty. The fireflies flickered around us, their tiny bodies mirroring the hope I clung to.

Then, as if the universe had decided to intervene, Aiden's phone buzzed from inside the house, shattering the stillness. He glanced back at the door, torn between the weight of the moment and the modern-day interruptions that always seemed to find a way to intrude. "Let me check that," he said, reluctantly stepping away from our cocoon of intimacy.

As he turned to grab his phone, I caught a glimpse of his struggle—a beautiful soul grappling with the remnants of a past that refused to stay buried. The night air felt electric as I watched him, my heart swelling with a mixture of admiration and concern. I wanted to pull him back into the safety of our shared silence, to cocoon him in warmth and love.

When he returned, the flicker of his phone screen illuminated his face. "It's from my sister," he said, his brow furrowing as he read the message. "She wants to know if I'll be coming to the family dinner this weekend."

"Are you?" I asked, curious about how the invitation sat with him. Family dinners were always a mixed bag for Aiden, a delightful yet daunting maze of laughter and unresolved tensions.

"I don't know," he replied, rubbing the back of his neck as if trying to ease the tension that had returned. "It's complicated."

"Complicated seems to be the theme of the night," I said, trying to lighten the mood with a teasing smile, but it didn't quite land.

"I should probably go," he said, his voice dropping to a whisper, as though the thought itself was a betrayal. "I can't keep avoiding them, especially with everything that's happened."

The flicker of fear coursed through me. I didn't want to be the anchor that held him back, but the thought of him walking into a situation fraught with old family dynamics, especially now, felt like a risk I wasn't ready to take. "What if it's too soon?" I asked gently, searching his eyes for reassurance.

Aiden met my gaze, and I could see the conflict raging inside him, a battle between wanting to face his past and the desire to protect our present. "I can't keep running," he replied finally, resolve creeping back into his voice. "I need to confront it, to let them know I'm still here, still trying."

"Then we'll go together," I blurted out before I could think twice, a spontaneous offer borne from love and a desire to shield him from the weight of that family history.

His eyes widened in surprise, a mixture of gratitude and disbelief etched across his features. "You'd do that?"

"Of course. We'll face this together," I said, the conviction in my voice surprising even me. I knew family dinners were a minefield, a tightrope walk between nostalgia and regret, but I wouldn't let him do it alone.

"Okay," he said, a small smile breaking through his earlier hesitation. "Let's do it."

And just like that, in the shadow of uncertainty, a plan began to form. We would confront not just the past but the fears that had kept us both tethered to old wounds. The night stretched on, but with every passing moment, I felt that whisper of hope gain strength, the promise that love could light the way through even the darkest corners of our lives. Together, we would find our way, hand in hand, stepping boldly into the unknown.

As dawn began to crack the horizon, spilling a wash of soft gold over the world, Aiden and I sat in the kitchen, the air thick with the smell of fresh coffee and the bittersweet scent of uncertainty. I had thrown together a simple breakfast—scrambled eggs, toast, and slices of ripe tomato, their vibrant red a stark contrast to the heaviness lingering in the room. Aiden picked at his food, his fork moving absently across the plate, while I watched him, trying to decipher the thoughts swirling behind his stormy eyes.

"Are you going to eat that?" I asked lightly, gesturing to the half-eaten toast, but he simply shrugged, lost in his own labyrinth of worries. I couldn't help but feel the weight of the unspoken words hovering in the air like a thick fog. Each passing moment felt like a countdown, as if we were both acutely aware that something monumental was on the horizon.

"Just thinking about today," he said finally, his voice low, barely above a whisper. "I haven't seen my family since... well, since everything fell apart."

I could see the shadows dancing on his face, each flicker a reminder of the turmoil that had brought him to this moment. The thought of him stepping back into that world filled with familiar faces—but not the same ones—sent a shiver down my spine. "You know they miss you," I said, trying to infuse some lightness into the conversation, but the words felt weighty, almost burdensome. "Even if it's complicated."

"Complicated is an understatement," he replied with a wry smile that didn't quite reach his eyes. "It's like trying to navigate a minefield in a blindfold."

I reached across the table, taking his hand in mine. His fingers felt warm and solid against my own, grounding me in this moment of uncertainty. "You don't have to go in blind. You have me. I'll be there with you."

He looked up, his expression softening. "Thank you. It means more than I can say."

As the last sips of coffee disappeared from our mugs, a sense of determination settled over us. We would face whatever was waiting for us at that dinner, and though I felt trepidation bubble in my chest, I also felt an unyielding sense of purpose. We weren't just confronting his past; we were claiming our future, one hesitant step at a time.

The drive to his family's house was filled with an uneasy silence, punctuated only by the soft hum of the tires on the asphalt. The road wound through a landscape that felt both familiar and distant—rolling hills speckled with wildflowers and the occasional lazy cow chewing its cud. I tried to distract myself with the scenery, but my mind kept drifting back to Aiden and the shadows that loomed ahead.

As we pulled into the driveway, the familiar sight of his childhood home washed over him. The house stood proud, a two-story frame nestled among the trees, its pale blue paint faded from years of sun and rain. I could almost see the echoes of his childhood in the way the porch sagged slightly, the swing that hung loosely from the frame swaying ever so slightly in the breeze. This was a place steeped in memories, some joyful and others tinged with pain.

"Are you ready?" I asked, squeezing his hand gently as we sat parked in front of the house. He took a deep breath, his chest rising and falling as he contemplated the threshold that lay before him.

"As ready as I'll ever be," he murmured, a mix of resolve and apprehension in his voice.

Together, we stepped out of the car, the gravel crunching beneath our feet, a cacophony of sound that felt painfully loud in the quiet morning. Aiden's family was inside, a world of warmth and chaos waiting just beyond the door, a sharp contrast to the stillness that enveloped us outside.

The moment Aiden opened the door, a wave of sound rushed over us—laughter, the clinking of silverware, and the unmistakable smell of home-cooked food wafting through the air. It was a sensory overload, pulling me in while simultaneously pushing me away, as I felt the weight of expectation settle on my shoulders.

"Look who finally decided to show up!" His mother's voice rang out, warm and welcoming yet edged with concern, a subtle undertone that hinted at the years of distance between them. The room fell quiet as Aiden stepped inside, and I felt the eyes of his family turn toward us, an unspoken judgment that both thrilled and terrified me.

"Hey, Mom," he replied, his voice steady despite the emotions flitting across his face. I could see the way he braced himself for the waves of questions, the probing inquiries that would come.

"Come in, come in!" she exclaimed, enveloping him in a tight hug, her warmth wrapping around him like a safety net. I stood back, watching the scene unfold, the bond between them both comforting and unsettling.

As I crossed the threshold into the house, I was greeted by the familiar sights of family photos lining the walls, each frame a testament to the life Aiden had lived before the shadows crept in. There was a photo of him at a high school graduation, his goofy smile stretching from ear to ear, a memory frozen in time. Next to it, a snapshot of a family vacation, sun-kissed faces grinning against the backdrop of a shimmering ocean.

"Who's this?" Aiden's younger sister, Emma, chimed in, breaking the momentary silence as she eyed me with a mix of curiosity and caution.

"This is my... friend," Aiden said, the word lingering on his lips as if testing its weight. "This is [Your Name]."

"Nice to meet you," I said, offering a smile that felt a bit shaky but genuine. Emma's eyes widened, and I sensed the gears turning in her mind, the family's collective curiosity piqued.

"Friend?" she repeated, a teasing lilt in her voice, a hint of the mischief that had often danced between siblings.

"Yes, friend," Aiden said, a blush creeping up his cheeks. "For now."

The laughter that erupted in the room eased some of the tension, the familial bond weaving its way through the air, reminding us both that love often existed in the complicated spaces. I settled into the conversation, weaving in and out of various discussions, learning the intricate dynamics of Aiden's family.

As the dinner progressed, I watched Aiden navigate the conversation like a seasoned sailor charting a course through turbulent waters. His laughter came more easily, and I could see glimpses of the boy he once was, tucked away beneath the layers of past hurt. But each time a question arose about his absence, I could feel him stiffen, a shadow flickering across his features.

"Why did you stay away so long?" his father asked, the words hanging in the air like a lead weight.

"I just needed time," Aiden replied, his voice steady but laced with vulnerability. "Things got complicated."

The table fell quiet, the clinking of forks halting momentarily as his family absorbed the weight of his words. I felt a rush of sympathy for him, knowing how difficult it was to confront those painful realities. Yet, at that moment, I also sensed an unspoken understanding in the room. They had missed him, and perhaps, like Aiden, they were ready to navigate the complexities together.

After dinner, as the sun dipped lower in the sky, casting long shadows across the backyard, Aiden and I found ourselves outside, the air thick with the scent of freshly mowed grass. The evening was cool, a refreshing breeze sweeping over us, and the weight of the dinner began to lift.

"Thank you for coming with me," Aiden said, his voice low, almost drowned out by the distant sounds of laughter from inside.

"I wouldn't have it any other way," I replied, stepping closer to him, the warmth radiating off his body a comforting presence. "You don't have to carry all of this alone."

He took a deep breath, a hint of relief flickering across his face. "I know that now," he admitted, his voice barely above a whisper. "And I'm glad you're here."

In that moment, we stood together beneath the sprawling branches of an ancient oak, the stars beginning to twinkle above us, reminding me of the fragility and beauty of life. There was still a long way to go, but for the first time in a long time, hope felt tangible. The whispers of our pasts might echo in the corners of our lives, but we were ready to fight against the tide, hand in hand, crafting a future defined not by what we had lost, but by the love we had found.

Chapter 10: The Calm Before the Storm

Brighton Shores thrums with the energy of summer, its shores kissed by the rhythmic embrace of the ocean waves. The sun hangs like a molten coin in the sky, spilling gold across the beach where families picnic, their laughter and shouts mingling with the scent of salt and sunscreen. Vibrant umbrellas bloom in every color imaginable, dotting the sand like wildflowers in a meadow, and beneath each, stories unfold—tales of sunburns, spilled ice cream, and the tender bonds of friendship. I find myself wandering this sun-soaked paradise with Aiden, our laughter a counterpoint to the crashing waves, a symphony of joy punctuated by the occasional soft whispers of shared secrets.

Aiden and I have become an inseparable duo, weaving through the town's winding streets and discovering hidden nooks that are as much a part of Brighton Shores as the ocean itself. We often stumble upon the quaint coffee shop, The Drifting Bean, its rustic charm drawing us in with the aroma of freshly brewed coffee and the tantalizing promise of pastries that crumble delightfully at the touch. The barista, a silver-haired woman with a warm smile, knows our orders by heart—an iced caramel latte for me, dark roast with just a splash of cream for Aiden. We settle into a window seat, the gentle breeze fluttering through the open door, making the pastel curtains dance like seaweed in the current.

In those moments, I study Aiden—the way the sun highlights the tousled strands of his dark hair, the way his green eyes crinkle at the corners when he laughs. I catch myself stealing glances, marveling at how effortlessly he navigates our conversations, his humor both sharp and endearing. There's an ease between us, a comfort that feels as if we've known each other a lifetime rather than just a few fleeting weeks. But even as we share these simple joys, a thread of tension pulls at the fabric of our happiness.

Aiden's laughter, though frequent, sometimes gives way to silences that stretch like the horizon, filled with unspoken thoughts and shadows. I can see it in the way he gazes out at the ocean, his expression turning contemplative as he watches the boats bobbing gently on the water, their sails unfurled against the cerulean sky. It's in these moments of distance that I feel a chill, an undercurrent of something unresolved stirring beneath the surface. I want to reach out, to tether him back to me, but there's a fear that lingers—a fear of pushing too hard, of unearthing something he isn't ready to face.

One evening, we find ourselves wandering along the beach as the sun dips low, painting the sky in hues of orange and pink, the clouds appearing like strokes of a painter's brush. The warmth of the sand seeps into my bare feet, grounding me as I lean against Aiden, the salty breeze tousling our hair. We walk in companionable silence, our shoulders brushing, the intimacy palpable, yet I can't shake the feeling that the tide is turning, that something is about to change.

"Have you ever thought about what lies beneath the waves?" Aiden muses, his voice low and thoughtful, breaking the silence. I glance at him, surprised by the depth of his question, by the way his gaze remains fixed on the ocean, as if seeking answers from the depths.

"Like secrets?" I reply, my curiosity piqued. "Or maybe a treasure chest just waiting to be discovered?"

He chuckles softly, the sound warm and inviting. "More like the parts of ourselves that we bury. What if we're all just like the ocean—calm on the surface, but turbulent below?"

His words hang between us, heavy with meaning, and I realize that we're standing on the edge of something profound. I want to dive deeper, to plunge into the depths of his thoughts, but the weight of unspoken fears pulls me back. Instead, I simply nod, the uncertainty in my heart mirrored by the distant rumble of thunder, a warning of the storm that's brewing both in the skies and in our lives.

As the sun sinks lower, casting long shadows across the sand, I feel an electric charge in the air, a whisper of the change that's coming. We decide to build a fire, the flames flickering to life as the first stars appear overhead, bright against the encroaching darkness. Aiden pokes at the embers while I unwrap the s'mores supplies, our fingers brushing occasionally, sending tiny shocks of warmth through me.

The fire crackles, casting a golden glow around us as we roast marshmallows, the sweetness of the chocolate and graham crackers melting together in blissful harmony. "You know," I say, savoring the treat, "there's something magical about fire. It draws people together, almost like a lighthouse in the night."

"Or a beacon for trouble," Aiden replies, a shadow crossing his face. "Sometimes, the brightest flames burn the hottest, and they can consume everything in their path."

His words strike a chord, and I want to ask him what he means, to peel back the layers of his guarded heart, but the moment passes. Instead, we sit in a comfortable silence, the sounds of the night wrapping around us—the distant laughter of beachgoers, the soft lapping of waves, the occasional call of a gull. But beneath this serene exterior, a tempest brews, and I feel the weight of the storm that looms ahead.

As the fire dwindles and the stars begin to fill the sky, I lean against Aiden, my heart racing with a mix of anticipation and dread. The world around us may be vibrant and alive, but inside me stirs a tempest of emotions—love, fear, and the longing for the connection I sense teetering on the edge of revelation. The night holds its breath, and so do we, caught in a moment that feels both fragile and infinitely powerful.

The air thickens with a strange, electric tension, the kind that clings to your skin before a storm breaks loose. As summer swells into its full bloom, the vibrant hues of Brighton Shores grow richer—the cerulean sky deepens to a sapphire blue, and the lush greenery around the town flourishes, breathing life into every corner. Even the salty scent of the sea seems more pronounced, mingling with the sugary allure of ice cream wafting from the local parlor, a siren song beckoning beachgoers to indulge in a sweet escape. I find myself irresistibly drawn to this paradise, yet my heart is tethered by the unseen threads of uncertainty that bind Aiden and me together.

Days melt into a comfortable routine, each moment with him a cherished treasure. We venture to hidden coves, discovering secret beaches where the waves curl and crash with a seductive whisper. Aiden is fearless in the water, diving into the depths as if seeking something he cannot find on land, while I linger on the shore, wrapped in a sun-soaked towel, my heart racing at the sight of him breaking through the surface like a sunlit dolphin. Every splash sends ripples through me, but the joy of his laughter always fades into the background when I sense the shadows that follow him.

One afternoon, we stumble upon a quaint antique shop tucked away between two bustling cafés, its windows fogged with time and secrets. The doorbell jingles as we enter, a whimsical sound that seems to awaken the dusty relics housed within. The shopkeeper, an elderly man with spectacles perched precariously on his nose, looks up from behind a cluttered counter, his eyes twinkling with mischief.

"Welcome to the Treasure Trove," he announces, gesturing with a flourish at the eclectic collection around us—faded photographs, tarnished silverware, and shelves lined with books whose spines are cracked like the dry earth. I run my fingers along the spines, imagining the stories they hold, while Aiden meanders deeper into the shop, drawn to a brass telescope that gleams with promise.

"Think it works?" he asks, lifting it to his eye, gazing out the window with an expression of childlike wonder. "I can almost see the future through this thing."

I can't help but chuckle, the sound lightening the weight in my chest, if only for a moment. "Or perhaps it just shows us what we already know," I reply, my voice softening. "That we're standing at the edge of something amazing, but we can't quite grasp it."

His gaze remains fixed on the distant horizon, where the ocean meets the sky in a seamless blend of blues. There's a moment, fragile and ephemeral, when I think he might open up, but instead, he lowers the telescope, a flicker of something indecipherable flitting across his features.

We purchase a small ceramic turtle, an odd trinket that seems to beckon us with its simplicity. "A reminder to slow down," I say with a grin, and Aiden nods, a smile ghosting his lips, but it doesn't quite reach his eyes. The turtle becomes our talisman, a symbol of the moments we share and the uncharted waters we have yet to explore together.

As twilight descends, draping a silken cloak over the town, we find ourselves on the familiar beach, the waves whispering secrets that only we can hear. A bonfire flickers nearby, its orange glow casting playful shadows on our faces as we settle into the warm sand, the soft crackle of wood echoing around us. Laughter from the other beachgoers mingles with the gentle rush of the tide, creating a symphony that feels both familiar and alien.

"Do you ever wonder what's out there?" Aiden asks suddenly, his voice barely rising above the sound of the waves, his gaze fixed on the darkening sea. "What's beyond the horizon?"

"Of course," I reply, the question igniting a spark of curiosity within me. "But I think the real adventure is right here. It's in these moments, in the people we choose to spend them with."

He turns to me then, his eyes piercing, searching for something beyond the playful banter we've woven. "But what if those moments come with their own storms?" he presses, vulnerability threading through his tone. "What if they unravel everything we think we know?"

I feel the weight of his words, the heaviness settling into my bones as I meet his gaze. "Maybe we have to embrace the storms," I counter gently, my heart pounding. "Because the calm can be just as misleading."

Silence stretches between us, thick with unspoken truths and hidden fears. I want to reach for him, to bridge the gap that threatens to widen, but I hesitate, unsure if I'm ready to dive into the turbulent waters of his soul. The distant rumble of thunder in the background seems to echo our unspoken turmoil, a reminder of the chaos that lies just beyond our blissful façade.

The wind picks up, tousling my hair, and I take a deep breath, filling my lungs with the briny scent of the sea. I wish for courage to unravel the tension, to dig deeper into his thoughts, but Aiden seems lost in his own contemplation, the shadows once again flickering in his eyes.

In an attempt to lighten the mood, I throw a handful of sand at him, laughing as it rains down like glitter. He grins, the warmth returning to his expression, but I can still sense the battle raging within him. We spend the rest of the evening trading lighthearted banter, our voices competing with the crackling fire, yet I remain acutely aware of the distance that stretches between us.

As the last embers die down and the stars blanket the sky, a shiver runs through me, not from the coolness of the night but from the realization that we are teetering on a precipice. The air is thick with unexpressed emotions, and I can feel the storm brewing not just outside, but within Aiden's heart. There's a longing to grasp the truths hidden beneath the surface, to navigate the depths of his troubled thoughts, yet I hold back, fearing what might surface if I pry too deeply.

With the world hushed around us, I lean against him, our shoulders brushing, my heart racing at the intimacy of the moment. The flickering light dances on his face, illuminating the resolve that often feels just out of reach. I want to believe that we can weather whatever storm looms on the horizon, that our laughter can drown out the thunder rumbling in the distance. But as the stars shimmer above, I realize that every beautiful summer day is but a prelude to the storms that must follow. And in that realization lies both fear and hope—the hope that we will find a way through the tempest together.

The tide ebbs and flows with a languid grace, a perfect metaphor for the rhythm of my life as I navigate these sun-drenched days alongside Aiden. Each sunrise ignites the sky in a breathtaking explosion of color, casting a glow over the sandy shores and reflecting off the gentle waves that lap eagerly at our feet. Yet, amid this picturesque paradise, an invisible weight tugs at my heart—a silent plea for understanding, an urgent longing for clarity that seems to elude both of us.

It's on one such sun-kissed afternoon that we find ourselves drawn to a hidden alcove just beyond the bustling main beach, a secluded haven where the rocks jut out like ancient guardians. The air is thick with the intoxicating scent of wildflowers, their colors vibrant against the backdrop of craggy stone. We sit on a large boulder, our legs dangling over the edge, the ocean below shimmering like a thousand scattered diamonds. Aiden's expression is pensive as he tosses pebbles into the water, each splash echoing the unvoiced thoughts swirling in his mind.

"Do you believe in fate?" he asks suddenly, his voice low and contemplative, as if he's trying to decipher a riddle hidden in the depths of the sea. I catch the glint of sunlight dancing in his eyes, a fleeting glimpse of vulnerability that both captivates and terrifies me.

"I think we create our own fate," I reply, drawing a breath to steady my racing heart. "Every choice we make weaves our story, one thread at a time."

He nods, but a shadow flits across his features, a reflection of the storms brewing within him. "But what if some things are meant to happen? What if they're out of our control?" The weight of his words sinks deep, stirring a tempest within me, igniting a desire to unearth the truth hidden beneath his guarded exterior.

"It's all part of the journey, right?" I counter gently, trying to weave a bridge between us. "Those unpredictable moments, the ones we never see coming—they can lead to the most beautiful destinations." My gaze drifts toward the horizon, the undulating waves a constant reminder of the unpredictable nature of life.

Aiden's silence stretches, filling the air with an uncomfortable tension. I can see the internal battle waging behind his expressive eyes, a tempest of thoughts battling for dominance. He turns his gaze to the sea, and I sense his reluctance to share the weight he carries. I long to pry open the depths of his mind, to coax out the fears that hold him captive, but my own heart hesitates, unsure of how to breach the divide that grows ever wider.

As the afternoon sun begins its descent, casting elongated shadows across the rocky shore, Aiden reaches for my hand. His touch is warm, electric, grounding me in the moment as if to reassure me that we're still connected despite the turbulence swirling around us. "I wish I could just... let it all go," he admits, his voice barely above a whisper, the vulnerability in his tone almost palpable. "But sometimes, the past has a way of holding onto you."

I squeeze his hand, my heart aching for the burdens he bears. "You don't have to carry it alone, you know. I'm right here." The sincerity in my voice feels like a lighthouse in the fog, but I can't ignore the flutter of fear within me—what if he can't see the shore, even with my guiding light?

The silence that follows is filled with a tension so thick I can almost taste it, the impending storm of unspoken words looming just over the horizon. Just as I think he might unearth his secrets, a distant rumble of thunder rolls across the sky, startling us both. The sun, which had basked us in its warm glow, suddenly retreats behind a blanket of clouds, casting the alcove into shadow.

"Maybe it's a sign," Aiden quips, a nervous laugh escaping his lips, but there's an edge to his humor that suggests he's not entirely convinced. The clouds swirl overhead, dark and menacing, and I can feel the cool breeze picking up, sending a shiver down my spine. It's as if nature itself is echoing the turbulence between us, a silent testament to the chaos that threatens to unravel our fragile connection.

We decide to head back to town, our fingers still entwined, the storm overhead mirroring the uncertainty brewing within our hearts. The familiar path feels different now, each step resonating with the weight of the revelations that linger just beyond reach. As we navigate the rocky terrain, I steal glances at Aiden, searching for answers in the lines of his profile, but he remains an enigma, a riddle that eludes my grasp.

When we reach the beachfront, the winds have begun to howl, whipping up the sand and sending it swirling around us like tiny tornadoes. The beach that once buzzed with laughter and chatter is eerily quiet, the gathering storm prompting most visitors to seek refuge. Yet, something compels me to stay, to stand firm against the storm both outside and within.

"I love storms," I declare suddenly, surprising even myself with the admission. Aiden raises an eyebrow, his expression a mixture of skepticism and curiosity. "There's something exhilarating about them. The raw power, the unpredictability—it's like a reminder that we're alive, that we can feel so deeply."

He watches me, his gaze piercing, and for a moment, I think he might finally share what weighs on him. Instead, he merely nods, a flicker of understanding passing between us, but the barrier remains unbroken. The first droplets of rain begin to fall, and I can feel the tension coiling tighter, an unspoken truth waiting to burst forth.

"Let's get out of here," he says abruptly, breaking the spell. We dash for the nearest café, laughing as we dodge the raindrops, our footsteps echoing against the cobblestones slick with rain. We burst inside, the warmth wrapping around us like a comforting embrace, and I can't help but feel a pang of disappointment that the moment didn't unravel the way I'd hoped.

We take refuge in a cozy corner, the scent of roasted coffee wafting through the air, mingling with the sweet notes of pastries cooling behind the counter. I watch as Aiden removes his damp jacket, revealing a fitted T-shirt that clings to his frame, accentuating the muscles beneath. A flush creeps into my cheeks as I try to focus on the moment, on the mundane act of choosing a pastry, but the electric energy between us hums in the air, undeniable and alive.

As we sip our drinks, the café fills with the sound of rain drumming against the windows, creating a soothing melody that contrasts sharply with the turmoil churning inside me. I'm determined to push through, to find a way to connect the dots that seem so distant yet so intertwined. "So, what's your favorite storm story?" I ask, hoping to shift the conversation toward lighter territory, to coax him into revealing a piece of himself.

Aiden chuckles, his smile transforming the atmosphere around us. "I remember once, when I was a kid, I got caught in a thunderstorm while camping. I thought I was going to be struck by lightning or something." His eyes twinkle as he reminisces, and I can't help but smile, grateful for this glimpse into his past.

"What happened?" I lean in, captivated.

"We huddled in our tent, terrified, while my dad told ghost stories to distract us. He said if we were too scared, the storm would hear us and get angrier." He chuckles again, the sound echoing like music, but I notice a slight shadow in his gaze, a hint that his past is far from simple.

"Sounds terrifying," I tease lightly, but the laughter fades as we lock eyes, the weight of our unvoiced fears settling between us once more. The rain continues to fall in sheets outside, the world beyond obscured, and for a fleeting moment, I wonder if it will wash away our worries or simply heighten them.

As the storm rages outside, I realize we are at a crossroads, teetering on the edge of revelation. With each heartbeat, I feel the walls around his heart shift slightly, and I know we're inching closer to the truth, to understanding what binds us and what threatens to pull us apart. Aiden leans back in his chair, a thoughtful expression replacing his earlier mirth. "You know," he says softly, "sometimes it feels like the storms are the only things that make sense."

His words hang in the air, heavy with the weight of unspoken truths, and in that moment, I can see the yearning for release flickering behind his eyes. Perhaps this storm, this chaotic moment, is just what we need to confront the truths we've both been avoiding. My heart races, the air thick with anticipation as I brace myself for the journey ahead. The winds may howl, the rain may fall, but maybe—just maybe—this storm can lead us to a place of clarity, where the past can be faced and the future can begin anew.

Chapter 11: Confronting Shadows

The wind whipped through my hair, tangling it in playful knots as we navigated the rugged trail winding along the coastal cliffs. Each step was a dance with nature, my boots crunching against the scattered pebbles, the earthy scent of salt and damp earth filling my lungs. I glanced sideways at Aiden, his silhouette framed against the expansive canvas of the ocean, a canvas painted in shades of azure and emerald that shimmered under the sun. He walked with his usual quiet intensity, but today there was a tension in his posture, a stiffness in his shoulders that suggested the weight of his thoughts was almost too much to bear.

I had spent the last few weeks wrestling with my own emotions, but this trip was about him. The cliffs had been a refuge for Aiden, a sanctuary he had described with a nostalgic twinkle in his eye—a place where the world's chaos fell away like the shells cast aside by the waves. If I could just coax him into that peace again, perhaps I could help him confront the shadows that lingered in his mind, the ones that seemed to cloud his every thought.

As we reached a particularly steep ledge, the vista before us unfolded like a breathtaking painting. The cliffs jutted out into the ocean, their rugged surfaces kissed by the frothy waves that crashed and retreated, as if engaged in a timeless conversation. I felt my heart swell with the beauty of it, the wildness of the landscape mirroring the tempest within me. I motioned for Aiden to join me at the edge, my fingers grazing the weathered rock as I settled down on a flat stone. The sun bathed everything in golden light, creating a halo effect around us, a fleeting moment of warmth amidst the chill of the sea breeze.

"Aiden," I said, my voice almost lost in the symphony of the waves below. I turned to him, trying to gauge his expression. The way the sunlight caught the angles of his jaw made him look ethereal, but

I could still see the shadows flickering in his dark eyes, those eyes that held galaxies of unspoken words. "You need to let go of whatever is holding you back. I know it's not easy, but I promise you're not alone."

He shifted uncomfortably, his gaze fixed on the horizon as if the answer lay hidden somewhere among the wisps of clouds. I could feel my heart race, each beat echoing the urgency I felt to break through the wall he had built around himself. The air between us crackled with an unspoken tension, a mixture of apprehension and the undeniable chemistry that had drawn us together.

Aiden finally settled beside me, his knee brushing against mine—a brief connection that sent an electric thrill through my body. I looked at him, urging him to meet my gaze. "Please, talk to me. I can't help you if you don't let me in."

He exhaled, a long, slow breath that seemed to release some of the tension that had been wound tightly within him. "It's just... hard," he said finally, his voice barely above a whisper. "There are things I've done, things I haven't faced. Sometimes it feels easier to just pretend they don't exist."

The confession hung in the air like a heavy fog, suffocating yet strangely liberating. I could feel the weight of his pain, the layers of guilt and regret that clung to him like shadows in the fading light. "I know you think you can carry it all alone, but it's okay to share that burden. I want to help you, Aiden."

The waves crashed below us, and for a moment, the sound filled the silence that stretched between us. I sensed a flicker of hesitance in his eyes, a struggle between the desire to confide in me and the instinct to retreat. He swallowed hard, his throat working as if the words were lodged there, fighting to be released.

"I lost someone," he began, the tremor in his voice hinting at the depth of his pain. "A friend. It was my fault. I could have done something, but I didn't." He paused, eyes darkening with the weight of his memories. "We were out on a hike like this one, and... it happened so fast. One moment he was there, and the next—" His voice cracked, and he took a shuddering breath, as if the very act of remembering threatened to drown him.

My heart ached for him, each word he spoke piercing through the barriers I had been trying to dismantle. "Aiden, it was an accident. You can't keep punishing yourself for something that was out of your control."

He shook his head, anguish etched across his features. "You don't understand. I should have seen the signs. I should have known he was struggling. Instead, I was too wrapped up in my own life to notice he was in trouble." His fists clenched in his lap, the knuckles whitening as he wrestled with the remorse that threatened to engulf him.

The sun dipped lower in the sky, casting long shadows that danced across the rocky surface around us. I reached out, placing my hand over his, feeling the warmth of his skin against my palm—a reminder that he was still here, still alive, despite the burden he carried. "You can't change what happened, but you can choose how to move forward. Holding onto this pain will only keep you trapped."

He turned his head, finally meeting my gaze, and for a fleeting moment, I saw a glimmer of hope battling against the darkness within him. "I don't want to feel like this anymore," he admitted, vulnerability lacing his words. "But letting go feels impossible."

"Then let me help you," I urged, my voice steady and reassuring. "Together, we can face the past, no matter how terrifying it seems. You don't have to do this alone."

As we sat on the edge of that cliff, the world around us fading into a blur of colors and sound, I felt a shift between us—a connection forged in the crucible of shared pain and the hope of healing. The wind whispered promises of new beginnings, and for the first time, I dared to believe that the shadows could recede, if only we had the courage to confront them.

The sun sank lower, painting the sky with a riot of oranges and purples that bled into each other like an artist's palette gone wild. I watched as Aiden's features softened in the fading light, shadows casting fleeting patterns across his face, illuminating the struggle I knew was still etched within him. As the ocean roared below, a powerful reminder of nature's force, I felt the urgency of the moment pressing in, urging him to release the burdens he had kept locked away. The crashing waves provided a rhythm, a pulse that seemed to synchronize with the rapid beating of my heart.

"Aiden," I said, my voice threading through the air, laced with determination. "You've carried this for too long. You're not defined by this tragedy. You have the power to write your own story from here."

He looked away, his gaze drifting to the horizon where the last rays of sunlight kissed the water goodbye. There was a moment of silence, heavy and profound, where I felt the weight of the world hovering just between us, teetering on the edge of revelation. Then, finally, he nodded slightly, as if acknowledging the truth buried deep inside him, one that had been too painful to confront until now.

"I always thought if I didn't talk about it, if I just kept it buried, it would fade away," he admitted, his voice thick with emotion. "But it hasn't. It's like this ghost, always lurking. I can feel it whispering to me in the quiet moments, reminding me of what happened, of what I could have done."

As he spoke, I could sense the bitterness of regret coating his words, the way they tumbled out like stones dropping into the ocean, creating ripples that expanded outward but never truly dissipated. I squeezed his hand, willing him to look at me, to see that he wasn't alone in this fight. "What if, instead of hiding, you faced it? What if you let it out?"

He turned to me then, his eyes reflecting the tumult of emotions swirling within. "And what if it's too much? What if talking about it only makes it worse?"

The fear in his voice struck a chord within me. It echoed my own anxieties, those nagging worries that had plagued me throughout my life. The fear of confronting the past, of unearthing memories that could prove painful. Yet, as I looked at him, I realized that the real horror lay not in the pain itself but in the act of avoidance, in letting the shadows stretch and grow until they enveloped us whole.

"I'd rather face it head-on with you than let it fester in silence," I said softly, meeting his gaze with unyielding resolve. "Together, we can find a way to navigate through it. You're stronger than you think, Aiden. You've shown me that time and again."

He took a deep breath, the kind that filled his lungs with air yet still felt heavy with apprehension. "Okay," he whispered, as if speaking the words aloud had pulled a heavy weight off his chest. "But it's not pretty. It's messy and complicated."

The sound of the ocean seemed to hush for a moment, as if holding its breath in anticipation of his next words. I leaned closer, willing him to share, to peel back the layers of his heart and reveal the raw truth hidden beneath.

"It was a few years back," he began, his voice trembling slightly as he recalled the memory. "We were camping, just a group of us from school. It was supposed to be a fun weekend—a chance to escape, to enjoy the outdoors. We were laughing, telling stories around the fire, feeling invincible." He paused, the light fading from his eyes as he ventured deeper into the shadows. "But we got careless. We went hiking without checking the weather. It turned into a stormy night, and we didn't make it back in time. Jake... he slipped."

The confession hung in the air, heavy with unspoken grief. I felt my breath hitch in my throat as I imagined the scene he described—young and reckless, laughter echoing in the woods, only to be shattered by the sudden chaos of a storm. "What happened?" I asked gently, my heart aching for the pain he carried.

Aiden's brow furrowed, the memories flashing across his face like scenes from a haunting film. "He fell off a ledge. I was right there, and I— I didn't reach for him. I thought he could hold on. I thought..." His voice cracked, and the tears that brimmed in his eyes reflected the anguish of a heart grappling with its own limitations.

The world around us faded, and for a moment, it felt as though we were suspended in time, the cliff and the ocean both becoming mere bystanders to the rawness of his admission. "I thought he could make it, but he didn't. I could have saved him, and I didn't."

I wanted to reach out, to comfort him, to wipe away the torment etched in his features. "Aiden," I whispered, my heart breaking for him. "You were just a kid. You couldn't have known what would happen."

"But I was supposed to be the one looking out for him," he insisted, his voice rising, the anger and regret spilling over like the waves crashing against the rocks below. "I let him down. He was my best friend, and I failed him."

The sorrow in his voice clawed at my insides, twisting and turning until it felt like I could hardly breathe. "You're not a failure. You're human. We all make mistakes; we all have moments we wish we could change."

"But this isn't just a mistake," he countered, his voice hardening, laced with disbelief. "This was a life. I took his life away because I didn't act."

The finality of his words hung heavy between us, and I could feel the ache in my chest widen. "Aiden, you need to forgive yourself. You can't carry this weight forever."

He looked at me, and in that moment, I saw the storm swirling within his soul—the turbulence of guilt, the ferocity of sorrow, and the fragile hope flickering like a candle fighting against the wind. "I don't know how," he admitted, the vulnerability raw and unguarded.

I felt a flicker of determination ignite within me, an unwavering belief that healing was possible, even in the face of the darkest shadows. "Let's start small," I suggested, squeezing his hand tighter. "Let's share the weight. You don't have to face it alone anymore."

As the sun dipped below the horizon, casting a blanket of stars across the sky, I knew we were standing on the precipice of something transformative. It wouldn't be easy, and the journey would likely be fraught with tears and pain, but in that moment, with the ocean crashing below and the promise of a new dawn on the horizon, I felt an unbreakable bond forming between us—one that could withstand the storm. Together, we would confront the shadows, one step at a time.

As the stars blinked awake one by one, the deep indigo sky transformed into a canopy of sparkling diamonds, twinkling with a vibrancy that felt both intimate and vast. The air carried a cool breeze, fragrant with the salty tang of the ocean mingling with the earthy scent of the cliffs beneath us. Sitting side by side, the gentle caress of the wind seemed to wrap around us like an embrace, whispering promises of solace and understanding. I could feel the weight of Aiden's pain pressing down on him, but amid the tension, there was also a flicker of hope—the realization that he was beginning to share the burden that had haunted him for too long.

"Aiden," I ventured softly, breaking the comforting silence that had settled around us, "what do you think Jake would want for you now?"

He remained silent for a moment, his gaze fixed on the horizon where the water met the sky, as if searching for answers among the stars. "I don't know," he finally admitted, his voice barely above a whisper. "He was always the one who pushed me to go after what I wanted, to take risks and live life fully. I wish I could just channel that part of him, but it feels impossible without him here."

"Maybe that's exactly it," I said, feeling the warmth of his presence beside me, illuminating the darkness that had shrouded his heart. "You have to live for both of you now. Carry his spirit with you, honor his memory by allowing yourself to be happy."

A flicker of understanding crossed his face, though it was still clouded by the shadows of grief. "How do I even start?" His voice was tinged with despair, the weight of his memories threatening to pull him under once more.

"By taking it one day at a time," I replied, determined to guide him toward the light I sensed flickering within him. "Begin with small steps. Embrace the things you love, the things that make you feel alive."

I turned my gaze to the sea, mesmerized by the waves dancing in the moonlight. "Look at how the ocean flows, always moving forward, never looking back. Even in its most tumultuous moments, it finds a way to keep going. You can do that, too."

He shifted slightly, absorbing my words as the wind tousled his hair, creating a wild halo around him. "You make it sound so easy," he chuckled, a hint of irony lacing his voice. "But life isn't exactly a stroll on the beach."

"No, it's not," I acknowledged, my heart pounding at the sincerity of the moment. "But it can be a beautiful mess, just like this view." I gestured toward the ocean, its tumult reflecting the complexities of life. "Let's embrace the chaos together."

As I spoke, I felt an overwhelming desire to push him further, to urge him into the unknown. "You should allow yourself to feel joy again, Aiden. There's so much beauty in this world, and you deserve to experience it."

He looked at me, and for a moment, his guarded expression softened. "You really believe that?"

"Absolutely." I met his gaze, willing him to see the truth in my words. "And I want to help you see it, too. You don't have to carry this alone."

The moon climbed higher, casting a silvery glow over the cliffs, transforming the rugged landscape into something ethereal. In that moment, I felt a shift, as if the very air around us had begun to vibrate with a new energy—one filled with potential and possibility.

"Okay," he said finally, the corners of his mouth twitching upward in a faint smile that felt like the first crack in a dam. "I'll try."

"Good," I said, my own smile breaking free, a mirror of his reluctant acceptance. "Let's make a pact, then. This weekend, let's celebrate life. We can hike during the day, find a cozy spot to watch the sunrise, and explore all the little joys this beautiful place has to offer."

"Okay, deal," he replied, his voice firmer now. "But if I start brooding again, you're not allowed to let me slip back into the shadows."

"I wouldn't dream of it." I leaned closer, feeling the warmth radiating from him, the distance between us collapsing as we began to redefine our connection. "We're in this together, remember?"

The stars twinkled above us as the first light of dawn began to creep over the horizon. Together, we sat on that cliff, the dawn illuminating our uncharted path, a shared journey filled with laughter, tears, and perhaps even the beginnings of healing.

The next morning arrived with a gentle nudge from the sun, breaking through the horizon with a soft, rosy glow that spilled over the cliffs, warming the cool air and coaxing the world to wake. I stirred awake to find Aiden already up, sitting at the edge of the cliff, his silhouette framed against the vibrant colors of the morning sky. I watched him for a moment, the light casting an ethereal glow around him, illuminating the contours of his face and the dark strands of hair tousled by the breeze.

"Morning," I called out, my voice thick with sleep.

"Morning," he replied, turning to me with a sleepy smile that sent a flutter through my chest. "You ready to conquer the day?"

"Absolutely." I climbed to my feet, stretching my arms toward the sky, embracing the crisp morning air. "What's the plan?"

"I thought we could hike a bit further along the coast, find a secluded beach," he suggested, a hint of excitement breaking through the heaviness of his earlier confessions. "Somewhere we can just... breathe."

"Lead the way, adventurer," I grinned, the spirit of camaraderie invigorating me as we set off. The trail wound ahead, flanked by wildflowers swaying gently in the morning light, their colors bright against the backdrop of green. Each step felt like a step away from his past and a leap toward a more hopeful future.

As we hiked, the conversation flowed easily between us, laughter punctuating the silence, each chuckle peeling back another layer of the weight Aiden had been carrying. I shared stories about my childhood, the countless adventures I had embarked on, each one tinged with the vibrant hues of youth and the magic of exploration. He listened intently, his eyes sparkling with curiosity, and for a moment, the shadows of regret seemed to flicker and fade.

We reached a small, hidden cove, the beach cradled by tall cliffs that sheltered it from the world. The sand was a soft, golden hue, and the waves lapped gently against the shore, a soothing rhythm that felt like a heartbeat.

"This is perfect," I breathed, glancing around at the untouched beauty surrounding us. "How did you know about this place?"

"It was a spot Jake found," he explained, a bittersweet smile crossing his lips. "We used to come here to escape everything. It felt like our own little sanctuary."

There was a softness in his voice, a reverence for the past that reminded me of the memories we often hold dear, even when intertwined with sorrow. "It's beautiful," I said, feeling the weight of his words. "And now it can be our sanctuary, too."

We settled on the sand, the warmth soaking into our bodies, and I pulled out the small picnic I had packed—a simple assortment of sandwiches, fresh fruit, and drinks. As we shared our meal, I could feel the tension ebbing away, the air around us filled with laughter and lightness. Aiden's smiles became less tentative, more genuine, as he recounted stories of mischief and adventure, his laughter ringing like music in the salty air.

"Okay, your turn," he said, nudging me playfully with his shoulder. "Tell me about your most embarrassing moment."

I laughed, the sound bubbling up like effervescence, and as I recounted a particularly awkward tale from high school involving a failed talent show performance and an unfortunate wardrobe malfunction, I felt the bonds between us strengthen. Aiden's eyes sparkled with mirth, and I could see the shadows receding, bit by bit.

As the sun arched higher in the sky, the warmth enveloping us became more than just the heat of the day; it became a reminder that life, despite its complications and heartaches, held moments of unparalleled beauty. Together, we embraced the simplicity of being, of laughing freely and letting the tide wash away our worries, if only for a little while.

"I think Jake would be proud of you," I said softly, my gaze shifting to Aiden's contemplative expression as the waves crashed against the shore. "He would want you to enjoy life, to find joy in the small moments. You're honoring him by living fully."

He nodded, the reflection of the ocean sparkling in his eyes. "I hope so. I just want to make him proud, to feel like I'm living for both of us."

"You are," I assured him, the sincerity in my voice wrapping around us like a protective cocoon. "You've taken the first steps, and that's what matters most. We'll keep moving forward, one adventure at a time."

With that promise hanging between us, we rose from our spot, the laughter and lightness carrying us back toward the trail. I felt a sense of anticipation swelling within me, the kind that comes from knowing we were embarking on something profound—a journey woven together by shared pain, blossoming trust, and the indomitable spirit of friendship.

As we set off along the beach, the horizon stretched endlessly before us, a world brimming with possibilities waiting to be explored. The shadows that had once loomed over

Chapter 12: The Crashing Waves

The moment I step into the San Francisco air, it feels as if I'm breathing in not just oxygen, but the very essence of possibility. The salty tang of the ocean mingles with the scent of fresh bread wafting from the nearby bakery, creating an intoxicating blend that both excites and unnerves me. I glance up at the iconic Golden Gate Bridge, its rusty orange beams cutting through the fog like a giant, welcoming embrace. The city sprawls beneath me, a kaleidoscope of vibrant neighborhoods and eclectic souls. I can feel the pulse of creativity thrumming through the streets, a rhythm that beckons me to lose myself in its symphony.

My suitcase, a faithful companion clad in a mosaic of stickers from my previous adventures, rolls unevenly behind me. I find myself smiling at its imperfections; it mirrors my own chaotic life, worn yet resilient. As I make my way towards the retreat, nestled in a quaint Victorian house perched on the edge of the cliff, I can't shake the nagging sense of Aiden's absence, an uninvited specter trailing me like a shadow. The excitement of this moment collides with an aching loneliness that feels almost like a physical weight on my chest. What would he think of my decision? Would he see me as someone who runs from challenges, or as someone brave enough to chase their dreams?

The house is a breathtaking testament to the past, painted a soft blue that echoes the color of the sky just before sunset. Ivy climbs its walls, weaving an enchanting tapestry that whispers stories of old, stories that feel both foreign and familiar. As I step inside, the warm glow of the interior lights envelops me like a hug, casting playful shadows that dance along the walls. The inviting aroma of coffee mingles with the sweet scent of pastries, grounding me in the moment as I remind myself why I'm here.

The retreat is buzzing with fellow writers, their laughter spilling into the hall like champagne bubbles. I catch snippets of conversations about characters who have clawed their way to life and plots that twist like the streets of the city outside. My heart swells with anticipation; I belong here, among these passionate souls who understand the joy and pain of creation. As I introduce myself to a group gathered around the kitchen island, I feel a sense of warmth wrap around me. They are all eager to share their stories, their aspirations spilling forth like the overflowing mugs of coffee cradled in their hands.

But beneath my cheerful exterior, the internal storm rages on. Aiden's last words echo in my mind, each syllable a haunting reminder of the love I left behind. "You know I support you, but it feels like you're running away." His voice was laced with that familiar blend of understanding and hurt, the kind that gnaws at your insides long after the conversation has ended. I can't help but wonder if he's right. Am I simply trading one emotional struggle for another, escaping the heavy weight of our relationship only to find myself adrift in a sea of strangers?

As the retreat progresses, I delve into the world of my writing, each word unfurling like a delicate petal. I discover a solace in crafting characters who battle their own demons, mirroring my own turmoil. The writing sessions are punctuated with laughter and the sharing of vulnerabilities, a testament to the bonds forged through ink and paper. I meet Claire, a fiery poet with wild curls that frame her face like a tempest. She speaks with a fervor that ignites something within me, a spark that makes me feel alive. We trade stories late into the night, the sound of the waves crashing against the cliffs a constant reminder of the world outside, a world I can't help but long to return to.

Yet, the evenings grow heavier with the weight of my decisions. The shadows deepen, and I find myself retreating to the small balcony off my room, the chilly breeze wrapping around me like a familiar shroud. The ocean sprawls below, the moonlight dancing on its surface like thousands of tiny diamonds scattered across velvet. It's beautiful and haunting, a reflection of my own heart. With each wave that crashes against the rocks, I feel a pang of nostalgia for Aiden. I can almost hear his laughter, the way it resonates with the very core of my being. The intimacy we shared felt woven into the fabric of my identity, and without him, I'm unsure of who I am.

Days blur into one another, filled with workshops and late-night brainstorming sessions that stretch into the early hours. My heart races as I write with newfound vigor, my fingers dancing across the keys, pouring my soul into the pages. I draft scenes that echo the longing I feel for Aiden, the complexity of love interwoven with the fear of abandonment. The words flow effortlessly, as if the characters are whispering their truths to me, begging to be heard.

But with every triumph comes the weight of my absence. I reach for my phone countless times, the urge to message Aiden clawing at my insides. Each time I hesitate, a mixture of pride and fear holding me back. I want to share my successes with him, to let him know that I'm not running away but rather discovering the parts of myself that were lost amidst the chaos of our lives together. But what if he interprets my silence as a retreat? What if he thinks I'm better off without him, reveling in this new chapter while he grapples with our unfinished story?

The retreat culminates in a showcase of our work, a moment where we pour our hearts out to one another, our vulnerabilities laid bare like open wounds. As I prepare to read my piece, a lump forms in my throat. I realize then that the words I'm about to share carry the weight of everything I've been grappling with—my dreams, my fears, and most importantly, my love for Aiden. The audience hangs on my every word, and in that moment, I am both terrified and liberated, straddling the line between two worlds that seem ever so far apart. The crashing waves below echo my heartbeat, reminding me that even amidst uncertainty, there exists a beauty in letting go and embracing the unknown.

The moment I step onto that makeshift stage, the air thick with anticipation and the scent of fresh coffee mingling with the salty breeze, a wave of vulnerability washes over me. The wooden floor creaks beneath my feet, a reminder that this space holds countless dreams and fears of writers just like me, who have dared to bare their souls to the world. My heart thrums in my chest, a wild, uncontainable thing that feels as if it might leap from my ribcage at any moment. I clutch the pages of my piece, their edges slightly crumpled from the countless times I've revisited them, hoping they would somehow transform into something that captures the whirlwind of emotions inside me.

The audience, a sea of eager faces—some familiar, some strangers—leans in, their eyes shimmering with curiosity. Claire sits near the front, her wild curls bouncing as she gestures for me to begin. The soft glow of the overhead lights bathes the room in warmth, and for a moment, I feel cocooned in this little world of words and dreams. My throat tightens as I clear it, the familiar sensation of impending exposure sending shivers down my spine. I remind myself of the purpose behind my writing: to connect, to share, and to heal. With a deep breath, I start to read, letting my words spill into the air like petals caught in a gentle breeze.

As I weave the story, I conjure images of love intertwined with uncertainty, of a woman standing at the precipice of her dreams, staring into an abyss of what-ifs. The characters take shape, their voices a symphony of hopes and fears that reflect my own tumultuous journey. I can feel the tension in the room as I describe the moments of longing and the bittersweet taste of love tinged with distance. Each line draws me closer to Aiden, his laughter and warmth flickering like candlelight in the corners of my mind, reminding me of everything I left behind. The waves crash against the rocks outside, a constant reminder of the world I yearn to share with him, yet feel so far removed from.

As I reach the climax of my piece, the emotions rise to a crescendo, and I can no longer suppress the swell of tears that threatens to spill over. It is a catharsis, a release of everything I've been holding inside—the fears of inadequacy, the guilt of leaving, and the fervent hope that my journey will lead me back to him. When I finish, the silence lingers for a heartbeat longer than it should, and then the applause erupts like fireworks on a summer night. I blink away tears, overwhelmed by the kindness and understanding etched into the faces before me. In that moment, I know that I've touched something within them, a shared struggle that binds us all together, a reminder that we are not alone in our battles.

The days that follow blur into a whirlwind of creativity and camaraderie. I feel like a moth drawn to a flame, basking in the brilliance of the other writers who share their tales, each one more poignant than the last. We form bonds over late-night snacks and the inevitable caffeine highs, our conversations weaving between laughter and profound vulnerability. Claire becomes my confidante, her spirit infectious, her laughter a balm to my frayed edges. We explore the city together, wandering through streets lined with pastel-colored Victorian houses that stand proudly against the backdrop of rolling hills.

In the evenings, we often find ourselves at a local bar, the dim lighting creating an intimate atmosphere where dreams feel tangible. We sip on cocktails that taste like summer, their vibrant hues reflecting the excitement of our shared ambitions. Each clink of glasses rings with the promise of the future, a future that I am desperate to envision with Aiden. But as I sit there, surrounded by newfound friends, a pang of guilt slices through the warmth. I can't shake the feeling that I'm living two lives—one vibrant and electrifying in this city of dreams, while the other languishes in uncertainty, waiting for my return.

The retreat culminates in a final night of sharing, an open mic where writers spill their hearts one last time. As I listen to my fellow attendees, I notice how their words resonate with me, echoing the doubts and fears that haunt my own journey. It's an unspoken agreement among us—a commitment to vulnerability and honesty that transcends our individual stories. Yet, as the hours slip away, I can feel Aiden's absence pressing against me, a reminder of what I've left unfinished.

That night, I retreat to the balcony once more, the moonlight spilling over the ocean like liquid silver. I pull out my phone, heart racing, fingers hovering over the screen. What do I even say? Should I tell him how much I miss him, or would that only amplify the pain of our distance? I wish I could bridge the gap between this moment of joy and the sorrow I left behind, to let him know that my heart is still tethered to him, even as I explore new horizons.

After an internal debate that feels like a battle between my heart and my head, I finally start typing, my breath hitching with every word. I pour out my feelings, letting them spill across the screen like an open wound. I tell him about the retreat, the beauty I've discovered in the written word, and the unexpected joy of meeting people who understand my struggles. I admit my fears, my guilt about leaving, and the ache of missing him that gnaws at my insides. The thought of sharing my experiences with him fills me with both excitement and trepidation, as if I'm unraveling a tapestry that could either bind us closer or tear us apart.

As I hit send, the weight of my confession settles over me like a heavy blanket. I don't know what will come of it, whether my words will soothe the storm brewing in his heart or deepen the rift between us. But in that moment, I know I've chosen to be honest, to embrace the complexity of love and distance. The crashing waves below echo my heartbeat, a reminder that every ending holds the promise of a new beginning. I step back from the railing, my heart racing, and take a deep breath, preparing to face whatever comes next, tethered to hope like a lifeline amidst the tumultuous sea of uncertainty.

The response to my message arrived sooner than I expected, a beacon of hope flickering in the darkness that had begun to creep into my heart. The familiar sound of my phone buzzing cut through the quiet, and I felt my stomach tighten in a mixture of anticipation and dread. I read his words, each one a lifeline tossed into a turbulent sea. "I miss you," Aiden wrote. "But I want you to embrace this opportunity. You deserve it. Just remember that I'm here, waiting for you." The relief that washed over me was intoxicating, yet tinged with an ache that resonated deep within.

This was the connection I had been craving, the thread that anchored me to him while I navigated this wild new adventure. The retreat unfolded like the pages of a novel, each day more vibrant than the last. With every workshop, I found new layers to my writing, my characters evolving into something more profound. The quiet corners of the Victorian house became my sanctuary. I would often escape to the sunlit parlor, where a cozy nook filled with plush cushions offered a perfect view of the bay. The gentle lapping of the waves against the cliffs outside became a soothing soundtrack, guiding my thoughts as I poured myself into my work.

One afternoon, as I penned a particularly gripping scene, Claire burst through the door, a whirlwind of energy and inspiration. Her eyes sparkled with excitement as she launched into a story about a chance encounter with a local artist who had painted a mural on the side of a building. "You must come with me! His work is incredible, and he has this vibe about him that just screams creativity," she insisted, pulling me from my reverie. I hesitated at first, feeling the familiar tug of guilt for stepping away from my writing. But Claire's infectious enthusiasm was hard to resist.

Stepping into the streets of San Francisco felt like entering a living canvas, colors splashed across every surface, each alleyway telling its own story. We wandered through the Mission District, where murals adorned nearly every wall, vibrant depictions of culture, love, and resilience. The sun hung low in the sky, casting a golden hue over the city, illuminating the artistry in a way that felt almost magical. I could feel inspiration bubbling up inside me, a surge of creativity that made my heart race. We reached the mural Claire had raved about, and I gasped at the sight. It depicted a phoenix rising from the ashes, its feathers ablaze with fiery oranges and reds, a symbol of rebirth that resonated deeply with my own journey.

The artist, a rugged man with inked arms and a gentle smile, caught my gaze. His presence was magnetic, and as he spoke about his work, his passion flowed effortlessly, a river of creativity spilling over. I found myself drawn to his words, but even more so to the way he seemed to embody everything I aspired to be—a person unafraid to dive into the depths of their own imagination, to create without hesitation. I could feel the weight of Aiden's absence beside me, but there was a comfort in this moment, a reminder that beauty could be found even in the midst of uncertainty.

As the sun dipped below the horizon, painting the sky in shades of lavender and gold, Claire and I shared our own stories with the artist, our laughter weaving through the air like the colors of the mural. I felt lighter, as if the burdens I had carried were slowly dissipating with each passing moment. We exchanged contact information, and the artist promised to send us updates about his upcoming projects, an invitation to stay connected to this newfound world of creativity.

Returning to the retreat that evening, the weight of inspiration danced on my shoulders. I sat on the balcony, allowing the cool breeze to wash over me, the sound of the ocean whispering secrets to my soul. I opened my phone and found Aiden's message waiting for me: "Tell me about your day. I want to be part of this journey with you."

My heart swelled as I crafted my reply, sharing the vibrancy of the city, the artist, and the murals that had breathed new life into my imagination. I wrote of the phoenix and how it mirrored my own struggles, the need for rebirth resonating with every word I typed. I wanted him to know that while I was far from home, my heart still beat for him, each pulse a reminder of the love that tethered us together despite the miles.

As the days flowed into one another, I found a rhythm—a delicate balance between my passion for writing and my desire to remain connected to Aiden. I would wake early, fingers flying across the keyboard as dawn broke over the city, casting soft pinks and oranges across the sky. The afternoons were filled with exploration and camaraderie, while the evenings returned me to my sanctuary of words.

Yet, with each passing day, the emotional tide began to shift. The thrill of discovery was tempered by a growing restlessness within me, a sense that I was dancing on the edge of something significant. The bond I had forged with Claire deepened, her laughter echoing like music in my heart, but the void Aiden left behind loomed larger. I began to question the distance between us—was it really just a geographical separation, or was it something more profound?

One evening, after another exhilarating day filled with inspiration, I sat at my desk, staring out at the shimmering water below. The moonlight kissed the surface, creating a path of silver that seemed to beckon me closer. I pulled out my notebook, letting the words flow freely, pouring out my thoughts and fears onto the page. My pen danced across the paper, drawing connections between my writing and my heart, the two intertwined like vines climbing toward the sun.

It was in this moment of vulnerability that I recognized the truth: I was afraid. Afraid that the distance would change us, that my pursuit of dreams might pull us apart rather than draw us closer together. I was torn between the exhilaration of chasing my ambitions and the gnawing fear of losing the one person who truly understood me.

Just as I was lost in thought, a knock at the door startled me from my reverie. It was Claire, her eyes alight with excitement as she held up two tickets. "We have to go to a spoken word event tonight! It's going to be amazing, and I promise you'll find inspiration!"

The enthusiasm in her voice was infectious, and while I initially hesitated, I could feel the urgency of her spirit urging me forward. "Alright," I said, a smile breaking across my face, "let's go."

The event turned out to be a melting pot of voices, each one powerful and unique. Poets took the stage, sharing their truths in a way that resonated deeply within me. Their words wrapped around my heart like a warm embrace, igniting a fire that I hadn't realized had dimmed. As I listened to the stories of love, loss, and resilience, I felt a renewed sense of purpose ignite within me. This was why I had come here—to find my voice, to understand my place in the world, and to weave my story into the fabric of humanity.

Amidst the crowd, I spotted a familiar face—the artist from the mural. He was seated at the back, nodding along to the rhythm of the words, his presence a comforting reminder of the beauty I had encountered on this journey. Our eyes met for a fleeting moment, and a spark ignited, reminding me that connections are fragile yet powerful, often waiting in the wings to take center stage.

The evening unfolded like a vivid tapestry, and I could feel my heart swelling with every performance, every echo of emotion reverberating through the room. Yet, as the night wore on, a sense of longing for Aiden crept back in, weaving its way through my exhilaration. I wished he could be here, sharing this experience with me, the two of us lost in the magic of creativity together.

When the final performance came to an end, the crowd erupted in applause, the sound ringing through the air like a declaration of triumph. I found myself caught in a whirlwind of emotions, each wave crashing against the shore of my heart, pulling me in different directions. I turned to Claire, her expression mirroring my own, and we both knew that we had just witnessed something monumental.

The ride back to the retreat was filled with a buzz of excitement, our minds racing with thoughts and ideas. But amidst the thrill, I felt a stillness settle in my heart. I realized that I had to confront my fears head-on, to embrace the vulnerability that came with love and ambition. The moonlight illuminated the path ahead, and as we neared the house, I made a silent promise to myself: I would reach out to Aiden once more, allowing the distance to become a bridge rather than a barrier.

Once inside, I pulled out my phone, my heart racing as I crafted my message. This time, I would share everything—the beauty, the inspiration, the doubts that had shadowed me. I would let him in on my journey, inviting him to be a part of this chapter of my life, not as a distant memory but as an integral piece of my ever-evolving narrative.

As I pressed send, I felt an exhilarating sense of release wash over me. I was no longer just a writer searching for her voice; I was a woman ready to embrace love and dreams in equal measure, fully aware that both could coexist. The waves crashed against the rocks below, their rhythm a reassuring reminder that change is both a constant and a gift, and with each ebb and flow, I was learning to navigate the depths of my own heart.

Chapter 13: A Heart Divided

The clamor of San Francisco surged around me like an ever-flowing tide, each wave crashing against the shores of my mind. The city was a collage of colors and sounds; the orange and gold hues of the setting sun draped themselves over the iconic Golden Gate Bridge, making it appear as if it were aflame. I stood on the balcony of the retreat, the scent of saltwater mingling with the earthy aroma of the city below, creating a bittersweet perfume that pulled at my heartstrings. The chatter of accomplished writers filled the air, each voice rising and falling like the lapping waves beneath me, but their words were mere echoes, reverberating in the vast expanse of my discontent.

As I raised my glass, the rich red wine glimmered under the fading light, mirroring the complexities of my feelings. Each sip was like an infusion of memories—Aiden's laughter, the way his eyes sparkled when he was deep in thought, and the warmth of his hand brushing against mine. I closed my eyes, letting the taste transport me to moments long past, where we wove our dreams together under starlit skies. I could almost hear the gentle strum of his guitar, a melody that lingered in the air, mixing with the heady scent of summer evenings spent beneath a canopy of twinkling stars. But now, the world felt jagged and incomplete without him, and the words I penned felt like mere shadows of what my heart truly wanted to express.

The writers around me were brimming with ideas, each one eager to share their latest breakthroughs, their struggles, and their triumphs. I watched them, a flicker of admiration igniting in my chest, yet the warmth quickly faded as I felt like an outsider in this sanctuary of creativity. My fingers danced over the page, crafting sentences filled with yearning and nostalgia, but the pulse of my pen seemed stifled by the absence of Aiden. Every stroke of ink was a testament to the connection we shared, yet it also served as a reminder of the distance that now stretched between us like an unyielding chasm.

As dusk fell, the city transformed into a glittering jewel, lights twinkling like stars against the deepening blue of the sky. I found solace in the beauty that enveloped me, but my heart ached for the familiar cadence of Aiden's voice, the gentle teasing that had always been the foundation of our bond. I recalled the day we met at that small café tucked away in the Mission District, a place filled with murals that whispered stories of love and loss. He'd sat across from me, his easy smile disarming and his laughter infectious. It was in those moments that I felt a spark igniting, a flicker of possibility that sent shivers racing down my spine.

I had been an aspiring writer then, fumbling through my own insecurities, but Aiden saw something in me that I often failed to recognize. He challenged me, pushing me to explore the depths of my creativity while simultaneously unveiling the layers of my heart. Together, we painted a vivid tapestry of shared dreams and whispered hopes, each thread binding us tighter, entwined in a connection that felt like a warm embrace. But now, that embrace was absent, leaving me floundering in a sea of uncertainty, each wave threatening to pull me under.

As I turned back to my notebook, the pages were filled with reflections of my discontent, words spilling onto the paper like an uncontrollable tide. I wrote about the beauty of the bridge, its graceful lines mirroring the curves of my own longing. I penned poems laced with the essence of our love, each line echoing the sweetness of shared laughter and the tenderness of whispered secrets. But no matter how I tried, the ache of separation loomed over me, a heavy blanket smothering the spark of inspiration I so desperately craved.

A faint chill swept through the air, wrapping around me like an unwelcome reminder of the solitude I found myself in. I shivered, pulling my shawl tighter around my shoulders, the fabric worn and soft, much like the memories that draped over my heart. The retreat was meant to be a sanctuary, a place to hone my craft among like-minded souls, yet all I felt was the growing distance from the one person who understood my spirit in a way no one else could. My love for Aiden had become both my muse and my prison; he was the ink in my pen, yet the specter of his absence taunted me with every word I struggled to write.

Night fell, draping the city in a velvet darkness punctuated by streetlights casting golden pools of light on the pavement. I leaned over the railing, gazing out at the flickering lights, and for a moment, I imagined Aiden standing beside me, his laughter mingling with the night air, his warmth enveloping me. The thought sparked a fire in my chest, igniting a flicker of hope that perhaps this distance was merely a test—a trial meant to strengthen the bonds we'd forged.

But as I sat there, the wine cooling in my glass, the reality of my situation pressed heavily on me. What if the distance was more than a test? What if it was a fracture that could never be repaired? The fear clawed at me, an unwelcome intruder in my heart. With each passing day, the fear grew more tangible, threatening to strangle the dreams we had built together. The battle within me raged on—how could I embrace my aspirations when the one who inspired them was miles away, pursuing his own path, perhaps forgetting the very dreams we had nurtured together?

The weight of uncertainty hung thick in the air, and I took a deep breath, attempting to dispel the clouds of doubt. I picked up my pen once more, the familiar feel grounding me, the ink flowing freely as I let my thoughts spill onto the page. Each word became an act of defiance against the loneliness that threatened to consume me. I was here, in this vibrant city, surrounded by writers who breathed life into their stories. I would honor our love, even from afar, letting it guide my pen through the darkness. The connection we shared deserved to be etched into existence, and I was determined to immortalize it, even if it meant navigating the stormy seas of my own heart.

The clinking of glasses and the murmur of laughter from the retreat's communal area filtered through the open door, a symphony of voices that blended together in a cacophony of joy. I could hear snippets of conversation drifting up the stairwell, tales of literary triumphs and the weighty presence of unfulfilled aspirations. Each laugh, each spirited debate over the merits of a freshly penned story, was a reminder of what I felt I was missing, the lighthearted camaraderie that infused the air. And yet, here I was, tethered to my own bittersweet reverie, like a moth drawn to the flame of what had once been—a relationship that was both a beacon and a burden.

The soft glow of the lanterns outside flickered, casting shadows that danced along the balcony railing, and I marveled at how a mere change in light could create such different emotions. Where the day had been suffused with warmth, night now cloaked the world in mystery. I set my glass down, its rim still wet from the wine that had slipped through my fingers during my moment of reflection. I wanted to reach for my pen and share every thought that fluttered through my mind, every moment that felt too heavy to keep bottled up. Aiden's absence was more than just a physical separation; it was an echo of laughter unshared, a heartbeat that had fallen out of sync with my own.

With each stroke of my pen, I crafted letters that would never be sent, each word laden with longing and the weight of what we had built together. I described our afternoons wandering through the colorful streets of San Francisco, where murals told stories that mirrored our own—tales of love, loss, and everything in between. I captured the taste of our favorite coffee shop, where the rich aroma of freshly ground beans mingled with the sweet scent of pastries. The intimacy of our shared spaces filled my pages, bringing to life our late-night conversations that flowed like wine, intoxicating and revelatory.

Yet, even as I filled the notebook with ink, a shadow lingered in the back of my mind, whispering doubts I struggled to silence. Would these words mean anything without him? Every heartfelt sentiment felt like a drop in an endless ocean of silence. The distance that had crept between us wasn't merely geographical; it felt as if we were two planets, orbiting in separate galaxies, tethered only by the fragile strands of memory and hope.

The cool breeze danced through my hair, sending a shiver down my spine as it mingled with the warmth of the wine in my belly. I closed my eyes and inhaled deeply, allowing the salty air to fill my lungs. I could almost conjure Aiden's voice in my mind, his teasing tone asking what I was working on this time. The memory struck me like a jolt, igniting the kind of fierce longing that kept me up at night. We had made promises—dreams wrapped in laughter, plans that stretched across timelines like a string of lights waiting to be plugged in. But with every passing day, the idea of "us" began to feel more like a fairy tale, beautiful yet unattainable.

The heart wants what it wants, they say, but my heart felt like a puzzle with missing pieces, leaving behind a void that gnawed at my spirit. My fingers trembled as I wrote, the ink flowing with the same chaotic energy that thrummed beneath my skin. I wondered if Aiden felt it too—the pull, the push, the ache that resonated through our shared dreams. I longed for him to sit beside me, his presence like a warm blanket on a chilly evening, his laughter punctuating the silence in a way that made everything feel possible.

I looked out at the city sprawled beneath me, each light a flicker of life. San Francisco had always been a city of stories, and yet, standing there, it felt empty without my favorite character at my side.

A surge of resolve washed over me, and I took a deep breath, trying to find the balance between embracing my own journey and yearning for the one we had embarked on together. The retreat was meant to nurture my craft, to immerse me in a world of creativity, and I refused to let my own insecurities dim that light.

As the night deepened, I decided to venture inside. The common area was alive with laughter and spirited debates about the craft of writing, and for a moment, I hesitated at the threshold. I felt like an intruder in their happiness, yet I knew I had to step forward, to immerse myself in the very thing I loved. I pushed the door open and let the warmth wash over me, the voices blending together like a melodious song that filled the room with camaraderie.

I spotted a small group gathered around a coffee table, their faces animated as they shared stories about their writing processes. With a gentle smile, I joined them, introducing myself and offering my own experiences, weaving my thoughts into the tapestry of their conversations. I could feel the familiar pulse of connection beginning to form, the laughter breaking the ice of my solitude. I spoke about my love for storytelling, how it wrapped around me like a warm embrace, and I noticed how their eyes lit up, mirroring my own passion.

Hours slipped away as we shared anecdotes and discussed the struggles inherent in creating something meaningful. The heaviness in my heart began to lift, replaced by the electric energy of collaboration and inspiration. Yet, even amidst the laughter and creative fervor, Aiden lingered in my thoughts, a ghost I couldn't shake.

As the night wore on and conversations flowed like the wine that filled our glasses, I found myself caught in a moment of clarity. Maybe it was the realization that distance doesn't always mean disconnection. Perhaps the very act of sharing my journey—my vulnerabilities, my dreams—could bridge the gap between us. I could write about the distance, encapsulating our love in words that might reach him, drawing him back to me, if only through the pages of my heart.

That thought ignited a spark within me, a flicker of hope that I clutched tightly. I didn't have to choose between my passion and my love; I could weave them together, creating a story that encompassed the entirety of my experience. As I spoke, the pieces of my heart began to align, blending the excitement of this new chapter with the lingering echoes of the past. I was a writer, after all, and my story was still being written, one beautiful, messy word at a time.

The laughter in the common area crescendoed, a musical interlude that harmonized with the clinking of glasses, igniting a warmth within me that I hadn't anticipated. I found myself drawn into conversations that flowed effortlessly, like the wine spilling over the edges of our cups, each participant weaving their unique tales into a communal fabric of creativity. The camaraderie felt invigorating, but the ghost of Aiden lingered at the edges of my thoughts, a bittersweet reminder of what was absent yet ever present in my heart.

Seated among these literary souls, I began to feel the tendrils of connection tightening around me, a welcoming embrace that gently drew me away from the isolation I had initially felt. One woman, her hair a cascade of chestnut curls, spoke passionately about her upcoming novel, a historical romance set against the backdrop of the roaring twenties. Her words painted pictures in my mind, flapper dresses swaying to the rhythm of jazz, the intoxicating scent of smoke and perfume wafting through dimly lit speakeasies. It was a world alive with color, a stark contrast to the grayscale shadows that clung to my own thoughts about Aiden.

Yet, for every laugh that erupted, a pang of longing threaded through my heart. I shared my own project—stories of love lost and found, an exploration of connection that danced around the theme of distance. As I recounted my adventures with Aiden, the room quieted, each pair of eyes drawn to the raw emotion that infused my words. I described the tender moments—the way he would brush the hair from my face, his fingers grazing my skin as if he were sketching me into existence. The air thickened with empathy, the understanding that came from shared experiences of love, desire, and heartache.

As I spoke, the clock on the wall ticked away the hours, time slipping through my fingers like grains of sand. The conversation flowed seamlessly into deeper discussions about the complexities of relationships, the ways in which love could uplift or unravel us. Each anecdote shared felt like a key turning in a lock, opening doors to revelations about our shared humanity. There was a sense of freedom in this communal vulnerability; it emboldened me to confront the insecurities that threatened to drown my spirit.

The night stretched on, and as the crowd began to thin, I lingered near the coffee table, my heart still racing from the connections I had forged. I caught the eye of a fellow writer, a tall man with a wild mop of curls and a spark of mischief in his gaze. He approached me, his enthusiasm palpable. "You have a way with words," he said, his voice warm like the sun breaking through clouds. "You should consider sharing those stories beyond these walls."

His encouragement sparked a flicker of determination within me, a light that cut through the haze of doubt. I realized that perhaps this retreat wasn't merely about honing my craft; it was about rediscovering the courage to bare my soul, to allow my experiences with Aiden to find their place on the page. My longing didn't have to be a burden; it could be the very thing that propelled me forward, transforming heartache into art.

The thought lingered as I finally made my way to bed, the weight of the day resting heavily on my eyelids. I lay there, the cool sheets cradling my body, my thoughts a whirlwind of inspiration and longing. Each moment with Aiden replayed like a film reel, from our first hesitant encounters to the sweet familiarity of our quiet moments together. The ache of missing him pressed down, a constant reminder of the life we had shared.

But as I drifted off to sleep, I felt a flicker of resolve spark within me. I could write him a letter, an open heart spilled onto paper. It wouldn't simply be a message; it would be a manifesto of my love, a testament to the bond that transcended distance. My heart might be divided, but it was also fiercely resilient, capable of holding onto love even when miles apart.

Morning arrived with the sun spilling golden light through my window, casting playful patterns across the floor. I rose with a newfound energy, the remnants of my dreams igniting a sense of purpose within me. After a quick breakfast, I grabbed my notebook and made my way to the balcony once more. The view of the Golden Gate Bridge, now shrouded in a soft morning mist, felt like a metaphor for my journey—beautiful yet obscured by uncertainty.

Settling into my familiar spot, I opened my notebook and began to write, letting the words flow freely as I poured my heart out onto the page. I described Aiden's laughter, the way it filled every room with light, how it danced around the edges of my soul, pulling me into a warmth I could never have anticipated. I wrote about our dreams, the plans we had made, and the love that felt like a tether binding us even across the expanse of the ocean.

With each sentence, the weight in my chest began to lift, and I found solace in the act of creation. Writing about our connection transformed my longing into something tangible. I could feel Aiden's spirit lingering in the lines, guiding my hand as I poured out my affection and fears. I wrote about the distance between us, yes, but I also wrote about the moments we had shared—the stolen kisses, the quiet nights, and the way our hearts had always seemed to speak the same language, even when words failed us.

Hours melted away as I crafted this letter, every stroke of my pen a heartbeat echoing through the silence. I envisioned Aiden reading it, his face lighting up with recognition as he felt the love embedded within my words. The thought propelled me, each line a bridge spanning the gulf of our separation.

Eventually, I paused, glancing up from my notebook to take in the beauty around me. The sun now shone brightly, illuminating the bay in a brilliant display of blues and greens. I felt invigorated, my heart lighter than it had been in days. This retreat, this beautiful city, and my burgeoning friendships were all helping me rediscover my voice. I realized that I had been holding onto the past, but it was time to embrace the future—time to let my heart be both a vessel of love and a beacon of hope.

As I sealed the letter, my heart raced with the thrill of sharing my truth with Aiden. I understood now that love wasn't merely an emotion; it was a force that demanded to be acknowledged, cherished, and shared. The distance that had once felt insurmountable began to shrink in the light of this realization. My heart, divided yet whole, could carry both the sweetness of what we had and the promise of what could still be.

The rest of the retreat passed in a blur of inspiration, each day a new canvas filled with stories and laughter. I delved deeper into my writing, crafting characters that reflected my experiences and channeling the raw energy of my connection with Aiden into every word. The retreat had become a sanctuary of sorts, a place where I could explore the intricacies of love and loss, where my heart could expand to embrace the complexities of life.

And as the final night arrived, I stood on the balcony once more, the city alive beneath me, a tapestry woven from countless stories. I felt a sense of belonging and possibility, a warmth enveloping me like a familiar embrace. I knew I would carry the lessons learned here into the world beyond the retreat, into the arms of a love that was waiting for me. With Aiden in my heart and my words as my compass, I was ready to navigate the journey ahead—one that promised to be filled with new beginnings, boundless creativity, and the ever-present spark of love.

Chapter 14: An Unexpected Connection

The air in the retreat center was thick with the scent of pine and the underlying hum of creativity, a delightful blend of expectation and quiet desperation. Nestled within the sprawling woods of the Pacific Northwest, the rustic cabin had seen generations of aspiring writers pass through its doors, each seeking solace, inspiration, and perhaps a little magic. My fingertips danced over the worn wooden railing of the porch, a chorus of crickets chirping their evening serenade, a soundtrack that felt like an invocation to the muses. Each thrum of their song made me acutely aware of the swirling thoughts in my mind, a blend of longing for the gentle sea breezes of Brighton Shores and the fiery desire to carve my name into the literary world.

Jenna appeared as if summoned from the shadows, her dark hair cascading around her shoulders in wild waves, as untamed as her spirit. She held a steaming mug, the steam curling into the cool evening air like a whisper of secrets waiting to be shared. "Mind if I join you?" Her voice had the soothing quality of a distant lullaby, yet there was an edge of urgency beneath it, a tantalizing invitation to dive deeper into conversation. I gestured to the seat beside me, my heart racing as she settled in, her presence magnetic.

As the sun dipped below the horizon, casting the sky in hues of orange and violet, we found ourselves enveloped in an intimate cocoon of shared dreams. Jenna spoke with a fiery passion about her journey, her struggles echoing in my own heart. "You know, writing feels like standing on the edge of a cliff," she mused, her eyes sparkling with fervor. "You're terrified of the fall, but the view is so breathtaking that you can't help but leap." I admired the way she wielded words like paintbrushes, each stroke vibrant and evocative.

Listening to her, I couldn't help but feel a kinship, a shared yearning that bound us together in that moment. We exchanged stories late into the night, our laughter mingling with the rustling leaves, the solitude of the forest cradling our vulnerabilities. I shared my own aspirations, the flickering flame of ambition that had dimmed under the weight of love and self-doubt. Jenna leaned forward, her intensity drawing me in. "You can't dim your light for anyone else. Love should amplify your dreams, not silence them."

Her words reverberated through me, igniting something deep within. I realized I had been treading water, caught in the delicate balance of love and ambition, afraid to embrace one without sacrificing the other. Aiden, with his easy charm and unwavering support, had become my anchor. Yet in that moment, I understood that I didn't have to choose between my heart and my passion. I could weave them together, creating a tapestry of dreams that included him.

As the retreat unfolded, Jenna and I became inseparable, our late-night conversations evolving into a sanctuary where we could bare our souls without fear of judgment. She introduced me to her favorite writing exercises, each designed to strip away the layers of self-doubt that clung to me like a second skin. We ventured into the woods, notebooks in hand, our surroundings becoming a living, breathing muse. The smell of damp earth, the crisp bite of the mountain air, and the chorus of nature surrounding us formed the backdrop of our creative revival.

"Let the forest speak to you," she urged one afternoon as we settled beneath the sprawling branches of an ancient cedar. The sunlight filtered through the leaves, creating a kaleidoscope of shadows on the ground. I closed my eyes, allowing the sounds of the forest to wash over me—the whisper of the wind, the distant rush of a stream. Slowly, words began to trickle into my consciousness, vivid imagery cascading like the leaves above. I scribbled furiously, pouring out my heart onto the pages, a cathartic release that felt like shedding an old skin.

In Jenna, I found a muse and a confidante, a reminder that ambition does not have to be a lonely path. She shared her own struggles with love, recounting a whirlwind romance that had flared brightly before extinguishing, leaving behind the ashes of heartbreak. Yet, there was no bitterness in her voice; instead, it was a celebration of the lessons learned and the strength gained. "Love is a beautiful mess," she laughed, her eyes sparkling with mischief. "It's worth every scar."

Her resilience inspired me to confront my fears, to embrace the uncertainty of pursuing my dreams while nurturing the love I cherished with Aiden. I started to draft stories that explored the very essence of this duality, weaving my characters through labyrinthine paths of passion and ambition. Each word felt like a step closer to reconciling the two parts of my life that had seemed so at odds.

Our days blended into a rhythm of creativity and camaraderie, our laughter echoing through the trees as we forged our narratives. But as the retreat began to wind down, I felt a pang of sadness. The looming departure threatened to shatter the fragile cocoon we had woven together, and I wondered how I would carry this newfound inspiration back to Brighton Shores. The thought of returning to the life I had paused for these precious days felt both exhilarating and daunting.

One evening, as we stood on the porch, the stars twinkling like diamonds in the velvet sky, Jenna turned to me, her expression serious. "Promise me you won't forget this feeling," she said, her voice low and earnest. "Don't let the world dim your spark." I nodded, feeling the weight of her words settle deep within me, a vow I intended to honor. We clasped hands, the connection between us electric, a reminder that I was not alone on this journey. With Jenna by my side, I felt ready to face whatever awaited me back home.

The final days of the retreat slipped away like grains of sand through my fingers, each moment laced with an electric urgency. The cabin pulsed with the energy of our collective creativity, a sanctuary transformed by the stories that danced through the air. Jenna and I spent our mornings tangled in our thoughts, scribbling fervently in our notebooks, and our afternoons wandering the trails, the rustle of leaves and the whisper of the wind offering us inspiration. The world outside seemed to fade, a distant memory of obligations and responsibilities that no longer felt as weighty in the face of our shared ambition.

With each passing conversation, Jenna peeled back the layers of my self-doubt, revealing the vibrant, ambitious soul that lay beneath. It was as if she had a map to my heart and dreams, guiding me toward paths I had long been too afraid to tread. One afternoon, we set out for a hike, the sun high in the sky, illuminating the forest like a golden tapestry. The air was alive with the scent of damp earth and blooming wildflowers, a sensory feast that felt both grounding and exhilarating.

"Sometimes, it's not about the destination," she remarked, her breath misting in the crisp air. "It's about the steps we take along the way." I glanced at her, admiring her confidence and the way she effortlessly navigated both the trail and the labyrinth of her thoughts. She had a way of making even the most mundane moments feel like epiphanies, her enthusiasm infectious. I found myself laughing more than I had in ages, my heart lightening with each shared story and silly quip.

At the summit, the view spread before us like a painter's canvas—mountains dipped in hues of blue and green, a shimmering lake reflecting the sky like a mirror. I felt a rush of exhilaration wash over me as I stood at the precipice, the world unfurling beneath my feet. It was a metaphor, I realized, for the leap I needed to take in my own life. "What if I just dive in?" I mused aloud, the thought spilling from my lips before I could second-guess it.

Jenna turned to me, her eyes gleaming with encouragement. "That's the spirit! Leap into the unknown. It's where the magic happens." Her words hung in the air, shimmering like the sunlight dancing on the water below. I closed my eyes, envisioning the stories I wanted to write, the characters I longed to breathe life into. This place, this moment, felt pivotal—a turning point where fear began to fade into the background.

As dusk fell, the world shifted from vibrant golds to deep indigos, the stars emerging like forgotten dreams. We settled on the porch once more, cups of steaming tea warming our hands against the chill of the evening. It felt like we were cocooned in our little bubble of creativity and understanding, the chaos of the outside world held at bay by the soothing rhythm of our hearts.

"Tell me about Aiden," Jenna prompted, her expression softening, genuine curiosity dancing in her eyes. I hesitated for a moment, the name lingering in the air between us. Aiden had been my anchor, my constant through the turbulent waters of my journey. I recounted the story of our whirlwind romance—the way he made me laugh until my sides hurt, the quiet moments spent watching the tide roll in, and the way his touch felt like home.

"Sounds like he's your grounding force," Jenna observed, tilting her head thoughtfully. "But don't forget to soar, too." Her gaze bore into me, a reminder that love could be a catalyst rather than a chain. I contemplated her words, realizing that I had often approached my relationship with Aiden as a delicate balancing act, afraid that pursuing my dreams might push him away.

But with every shared laugh, every flicker of understanding that blossomed between Jenna and me, I felt that the pieces of my life were aligning. "What if I write about us?" I mused, excitement bubbling to the surface. "Not just about me but the intricate dance between love and ambition. The way they intertwine, push and pull at each other." The idea took root, blossoming in my mind as I spoke, the story weaving itself into the fabric of my reality.

Jenna beamed, her enthusiasm palpable. "Yes! Write the kind of love that inspires and challenges. Love that doesn't apologize for its ambition." Her encouragement swirled around me, an empowering tide that pushed me closer to my truth. I envisioned my characters navigating the complexities of their relationships, mirroring the struggles I faced, the love I cherished, and the ambition I was only beginning to embrace.

The night deepened, a velvet cloak wrapping around us as we shared our fears and aspirations, our hopes spilling out like starlight. I felt a surge of gratitude, an acknowledgment of how much this retreat had transformed me. It was a beautiful mess, this friendship forged in the fires of creativity and honesty. In Jenna, I found not just a kindred spirit but a fierce ally in this journey toward self-discovery.

When the retreat finally came to a close, I felt a bittersweet ache settle in my chest, a tug of war between the anticipation of returning to Brighton Shores and the sadness of leaving this cocoon behind. On the last night, as we gathered around a crackling fire, the flames licking the air with a soft warmth, I looked around at the faces illuminated by flickering light—each one a reflection of dreams, struggles, and triumphs.

Jenna reached for my hand, squeezing it tightly, as if to solidify the bond we had forged. "Remember this moment. It's the beginning of something beautiful," she said softly, her voice thick with emotion. I nodded, my heart swelling with gratitude for the lessons learned and the friendships formed. The flicker of the fire mirrored the spark ignited within me, a flame that would continue to burn brightly as I returned home.

As I packed my belongings the following morning, the weight of my experiences felt like a mantle I was ready to wear. I held onto the promise of new beginnings and the belief that my love with Aiden would not hinder my dreams but would lift them higher, intertwining them into a narrative rich with passion and possibility. The road ahead may be uncertain, but with Jenna's words echoing in my mind and a heart full of ambition, I felt ready to embrace every twist and turn that awaited me in the vibrant tapestry of my life.

As the retreat faded into the distance, the morning sun spilled golden light across the landscape, illuminating the winding road that led me back to Brighton Shores. The gentle hum of the car engine was a soothing balm to my soul, the rhythmic cadence allowing my thoughts to wander freely. I could still feel the warmth of Jenna's laughter echoing in my heart, a comforting melody interwoven with the vibrant memories we had crafted. Each laugh, every shared dream, now accompanied me like an invisible companion, urging me to take the lessons learned and apply them to my life.

The shoreline was my first destination. As I stepped onto the familiar sand, the salty breeze kissed my cheeks, the ocean's roar wrapping around me like a beloved old sweater. I had missed this place, its ebb and flow mirroring the complexities of my own emotions. I took a moment to breathe, inhaling the sea air infused with a hint of nostalgia, a reminder of the countless days spent here with Aiden, lost in our little world. Yet, I felt a renewed sense of purpose alongside the warmth of familiarity.

I had promised myself to embrace both my love for Aiden and my passion for writing, and I was determined to keep that promise. I settled onto our favorite spot, a weathered log that overlooked the waves crashing rhythmically against the shore. I pulled out my notebook, its pages whispering tales of potential. The words poured forth like a tide, drawing from the well of experiences I had gathered during the retreat.

My pen moved with fervor as I crafted scenes that interlaced love and ambition. I wrote of characters that were reflections of myself and Jenna, each navigating the tumultuous waters of their dreams while holding tightly to the hands of those they adored. The sun dipped lower in the sky, casting hues of orange and pink that danced upon the water's surface. It was a perfect backdrop for my newfound inspiration, and I felt the fire within me rekindle, each stroke of the pen breathing life into the story I was destined to tell.

Days turned into weeks, each one a delicate dance of creativity and connection. Aiden and I fell back into our rhythm, but this time it felt different—more profound, layered with the understanding that our individual ambitions could coexist without one overshadowing the other. I often found him perched on the couch with a book in hand, the pages fluttering in the breeze from the open window, while I curled up beside him, typing furiously on my laptop. The sound of the keys clicking was a symphony, each note a declaration of my commitment to both him and my craft.

One evening, as we prepared dinner together, the scent of garlic and rosemary wafting through the air, I felt a surge of affection wash over me. Aiden was slicing vegetables, the muscles in his arms flexing with each precise cut, and I couldn't help but admire the way he moved with such effortless grace. "What's on your mind?" he asked, glancing at me over his shoulder, a playful smile dancing on his lips.

"I was just thinking about how much has changed since I came back from the retreat," I confessed, my voice light yet sincere. "I feel like I've finally found a way to balance my dreams and our love."

He put down the knife, turning fully to face me, his expression softening. "I'm proud of you. You've always had this light in you; I just wanted to make sure you didn't dim it for me." His words struck a chord, resonating with the promise I had made to myself. I stepped closer, wrapping my arms around him, my heart swelling with gratitude.

The kitchen was alive with warmth and laughter, a sanctuary where our love flourished amid the chaos of life. We cooked together, our movements synchronized like a well-rehearsed dance, and with each shared meal, the bond between us deepened, fortified by our willingness to embrace vulnerability. The evenings turned into opportunities for discussion, where we explored our dreams and fears, our aspirations colliding like the waves outside, bringing both chaos and clarity.

As I dove deeper into my writing, I began to explore the nuanced layers of relationships, how they could lift us up while simultaneously challenging us. I infused my characters with the essence of my experiences with Aiden and Jenna—complex, multifaceted individuals striving for connection amid the noise of the world. The characters were no longer just figments of my imagination; they became vessels for my emotions, embodying the duality of love and ambition, each page an exploration of that delicate balance.

The local coffee shop became my second home, a haven where creativity thrived. The smell of freshly brewed coffee mingled with the chatter of patrons, creating an ambiance that ignited my inspiration. I often found myself tucked in a corner, lost in the world I was creating, the clattering of cups and the soft hum of conversation fading into the background. I embraced the energy around me, absorbing it like a sponge, allowing it to seep into my writing, shaping it into something rich and relatable.

During one of those bustling afternoons, I caught sight of Jenna sitting at a nearby table, her presence immediately sparking joy within me. She looked as vibrant as ever, her fingers dancing over the keyboard, mirroring my own frenetic energy. I waved her over, and as she settled into the chair across from me, her eyes sparkled with mischief. "I knew I'd find you here," she declared, her tone teasing. "This place must be a writer's sanctuary."

"It really is," I agreed, a smile stretching across my face. "It's become my escape. I've been working on something new, and I feel like it's finally coming together."

"Tell me everything!" Jenna leaned forward, her enthusiasm palpable, igniting a fire within me as I began to share my progress, weaving in the complexities of my characters' journeys. She listened intently, her encouragement a steady pulse of motivation, and I felt a renewed sense of excitement ignite within me.

As we discussed our stories, I could feel the boundary between us dissolve, our friendship becoming an integral part of my creative process. Jenna had a knack for asking the right questions, challenging me to dig deeper, to explore the corners of my mind that were often left unexamined.

"Have you considered how your characters would handle failure?" she asked, her brow furrowing in thought. "It's often in those moments that we discover who we truly are." Her words struck me, igniting a spark of inspiration. I began to see how the setbacks and struggles could shape my narrative, how the essence of love could be tested, only to emerge stronger and more resilient.

As autumn painted the world in warm shades of amber and crimson, I found myself standing at a crossroads—an invitation to share my work with a wider audience had arrived, a local literary festival beckoning authors and dreamers alike. I felt both exhilarated and terrified at the prospect of reading my work aloud, baring my soul in front of strangers. But with Jenna's unwavering support and Aiden's love enveloping me, I knew this was my moment to embrace both my dreams and my heart.

The day of the festival arrived, a brisk breeze brushing against my cheeks as I stepped onto the stage. The sun was setting, casting a warm glow over the crowd, their expectant faces shimmering like stars. I took a deep breath, my heart racing with the pulse of a thousand emotions. With Aiden's reassuring smile and Jenna's fierce gaze anchoring me, I opened my notebook, feeling the words flow through me like a tide, ready to embrace whatever came next.

Chapter 15: A Letter from the Past

The sun dipped low on the horizon, casting a warm golden glow over the quaint town of Maplewood, a small slice of Americana that felt perpetually suspended in time. The air was crisp, carrying the scent of dried leaves and the faintest hint of woodsmoke from chimneys that had begun their seasonal work. I sat at my cluttered dining table, the wooden surface smoothed by years of meals shared and laughter echoing off the walls, while outside, children shrieked with delight, their voices mingling with the gentle rustle of the wind. The sky bled hues of orange and purple, a vibrant canvas that drew me in, yet my heart felt heavy, anchored by thoughts that refused to lift.

A soft thud interrupted my reverie, pulling me from the embrace of the fading sunlight. The postman had dropped off the day's mail, a daily ritual I usually embraced with glee. Today, however, my fingers hesitated as they brushed against the envelopes. Among the usual advertisements and bills, one stood out—a crisp, white envelope that bore my name in unmistakable handwriting. Aiden's handwriting. It was a style both familiar and foreign, each letter imbued with his essence, a delicate balance of strength and fragility. My breath caught in my throat as I held the envelope, my pulse quickening.

With a trembling hand, I slid my finger beneath the flap and opened it, the faint scent of his cologne wafting up to meet me, transporting me back to the long summer evenings we spent together, wrapped in the warmth of each other's presence. The letter unfolded like a tender promise, the words etched in ink flowing across the page, a river of emotion pouring from his heart to mine.

As I began to read, I was immediately struck by the rawness of his vulnerability. Aiden spoke of his struggles with a haunting clarity, describing the heavy shroud of guilt that enveloped him like a storm cloud refusing to part. Each line was laced with pain, his honesty both a comfort and a gut-wrenching ache that twisted my insides. He wrote of sleepless nights spent wrestling with memories that danced like phantoms in the shadows of his mind, taunting him with regrets he couldn't shake off. I could almost hear the echo of his voice, tinged with sorrow, as I read the words that bled from his soul.

"I feel like I'm trapped in a maze with no way out," he had penned, the anguish in his phrasing seeping through the paper. "The guilt weighs on me like a thousand bricks, and I'm afraid it will crush me before I find a way to escape."

With each sentence, I felt my heart constrict, a painful reminder of the man I loved and the battle he fought in silence. The memories of our time together flooded back, a bittersweet symphony of laughter, warmth, and the lingering shadows that had crept into our lives. I remembered the evenings spent beneath a blanket of stars, where dreams had danced on the tips of our tongues, and the world had felt so vast, yet so intimately ours. The contrast to his current turmoil was jarring, a cruel twist of fate that left me feeling helplessly adrift.

He continued, revealing a desire to shield me from his struggles, a sentiment that tugged at the very fibers of my being. "I don't want to drag you into my darkness," he wrote, "but I need you to know I'm not the man you fell in love with anymore. I'm still searching for him." Those words shattered something deep within me, a fragile hope that had flourished in the wake of our connection. I ached to reach out, to wrap him in my arms and shield him from his self-imposed exile, but the final lines of the letter struck me like a thunderbolt. Aiden requested space, a pause in our shared existence, as if he believed that distance might lighten the load he bore.

My heart raced, a tumultuous storm brewing within me. Could I really grant him the distance he sought? Love, I had always believed, was a tether that could weather any storm, but as I read those final words, I felt the weight of the decision settle heavily on my shoulders. Sometimes, love meant letting go. The realization unfurled like a dark cloud across my mind, casting shadows over my heart.

The laughter of children outside faded into the background, replaced by the relentless thrum of my thoughts. I pictured Aiden alone, wrestling with his demons, wishing fervently that I could reach into the letter and pull him back to me. The warmth of the day slipped away, leaving behind the chill of uncertainty, and I was left grappling with the knowledge that sometimes, the most loving act is to allow someone the space they desperately need, even when it feels like a betrayal of the love you share.

The sun finally dipped below the horizon, the vibrant colors fading into twilight, mirroring the shift in my own heart. I folded the letter carefully, as though it contained the very essence of Aiden himself. I would honor his request, even as it felt like a dagger to my heart. I would let him breathe, step back from the precipice of our connection, and hope that one day, he would find his way back to me, whole and unburdened.

The day slipped into night, and as the stars blinked into existence above me, I realized that this journey was not solely his to navigate. I too was on a path, and though it twisted and turned with uncertainty, it was mine to embrace. I would lean into the darkness that enveloped him from afar, trusting that love—true love—could weather even the most painful of separations. I would wait, grounded in the belief that one day, when the storm had passed, our paths would converge once more under the vast expanse of a hopeful sky.

The letter lingered in my mind, an echo of his anguish that refused to fade. I tucked it away in the drawer of the dining table, a secret tucked under the mundane chaos of unopened bills and stray receipts. Yet, its presence weighed heavier than anything else in that drawer, a tangible reminder of Aiden's struggle and my own internal conflict. As dusk deepened into night, the air grew cooler, and the comforting hum of my home shifted into a somber silence, amplifying the swirling thoughts in my head.

I wandered through the dimly lit rooms, each step accompanied by the creaking of the wooden floorboards beneath my feet. The walls were adorned with snapshots of our time together—sun-kissed days at the lake, laughter spilling out from behind the camera lens, our smiles captured in frames that now felt like distant memories. I paused by a picture of us at the county fair, the air thick with the smell of popcorn and cotton candy. Aiden had insisted on winning me a giant stuffed bear, his competitive spirit evident as he hurled rings with wild abandon. The thrill of that day, the exhilaration of being so blissfully present, was now a stark contrast to the sorrow that seemed to seep through every letter he penned.

In the solitude of my living room, I curled up on the faded couch, the fabric soft beneath me. My fingers absentmindedly traced the frayed seams, a habitual comfort in moments like this. I could still hear the echoes of our conversations, the playful teasing, and the way his laughter had filled the room, warming every corner. But now, the silence felt like a chasm between us, an unbridgeable divide brought on by his decision to retreat into himself.

The world outside was dark, the sky a tapestry of stars twinkling like distant candles. I turned my gaze to the window, where the soft glow of street lamps cast pools of light on the pavement. A flicker of movement caught my eye—Daisy, my neighbor's golden retriever, bounding across the yard in pursuit of her own tail, blissfully unaware of the weight of the world. In her joyful chaos, I found a momentary solace, a reminder that life continued to unfold, even in the face of heartache. Yet I longed for the warmth of Aiden's presence, the way he made the world feel less daunting and more vibrant.

With a deep breath, I leaned back, letting the couch cradle my weary body. A part of me wanted to bury myself in distractions—turn on the television, immerse myself in the latest bestseller, anything to escape the swirling emotions—but another part of me craved to sit with this feeling, to allow the ache of love and loss to flow through me like an unbidden tide. I reached for a blanket, wrapping it tightly around myself, cocooned in the fabric that felt like a hug, albeit a flimsy substitute for Aiden's warmth.

As the minutes stretched into hours, the quiet was interrupted by a soft knock at my door. My heart leapt. In this moment of solitude, the unexpected sound felt charged, as if the universe had conspired to pull me from my reverie. I rose cautiously, my heart racing as I approached the door. Maybe it was Aiden. Maybe he had reconsidered, his vulnerability giving way to a desire for connection. My breath quickened at the thought, and I hesitated, fingers hovering over the doorknob.

I opened the door to find Lily, my closest friend, standing on the doorstep, her expression a mixture of concern and determination. Her wild curls framed her face like a halo, and she wore a vibrant sweater that seemed to pulsate with energy, a stark contrast to the gloom that had settled over me. She pushed past me without waiting for an invitation, her presence filling the space with an undeniable warmth.

"Hey! I brought cookies," she declared, holding up a tin adorned with colorful stickers. The aroma wafted into the room, sweet and inviting, a brief respite from the weight of the world. "I figured you might need a pick-me-up."

I couldn't help but smile, the simple act of friendship stirring something deep within me. "You always know when to show up," I replied, leading her to the kitchen, where we settled at the small table cluttered with remnants of my day.

As she unwrapped the tin, revealing an assortment of chocolate chip and oatmeal raisin cookies, she shot me a knowing look. "You've been avoiding my calls. You okay?"

The question hung in the air, both gentle and probing. I took a moment to gather my thoughts, to piece together the kaleidoscope of emotions swirling within me. "I got a letter from Aiden," I finally admitted, the words slipping out with a mixture of relief and trepidation.

Lily's brow furrowed slightly as she reached for a cookie, breaking it in half, the chocolate still soft and gooey. "And?"

I shared the essence of his letter, carefully choosing my words, revealing the depth of his struggles and the request for space. As I spoke, I could see the concern etched on her face, a reflection of the worries that had taken residence in my own heart. "He's in a dark place, and I don't know how to help him. I feel so... powerless," I confessed, the weight of it crashing down on me anew.

Lily set down her half-eaten cookie, her gaze intense and unwavering. "You can't save him, you know. You can't be the solution to his problems. Sometimes the best thing you can do is to just be there when he's ready. It sounds like he's trying to navigate this on his own."

Her words resonated with me, a reminder that love isn't always about fixing; sometimes, it's about allowing space for healing. The realization felt like a balm, soothing the ache that had settled into my chest. As we shared cookies and laughter, I felt a flicker of hope rekindling within me, a warmth that whispered that perhaps love could withstand the distance, and that sometimes, letting go was an act of love in itself.

As the night deepened, we talked about everything and nothing, our laughter intertwining with the shadows. In that moment, surrounded by the familiarity of friendship, I found a small sanctuary amidst the chaos of my heart. Though Aiden's struggles loomed large in my mind, I realized that I didn't have to bear the weight alone. I could lean on those I loved, trusting that we would all find our way through the darkness together.

The lingering aroma of freshly baked cookies filled my home, weaving a comforting spell around the raw edges of my heart. With each bite, the warmth of sugar and chocolate danced on my tongue, momentarily distracting me from the tumult of emotions. As Lily and I sat across from each other, the kitchen light flickering gently overhead, I felt the heaviness in my chest start to ease, if only for a moment.

We laughed about the ridiculous antics of the neighborhood cats—how Mr. Whiskers had taken it upon himself to patrol the block as though he owned it, strutting with the confidence of a lion surveying his kingdom. I leaned into the playful banter, grateful for the reprieve from my swirling thoughts. Yet, even amidst our laughter, my mind kept returning to Aiden, the silent pull of his struggles beckoning me back to the letter tucked away in the drawer, a shadow that lingered at the edges of our conversation.

"Okay, but seriously," Lily said, suddenly earnest, setting her half-eaten cookie down with a delicate precision. "What are you going to do about Aiden? He needs you, and you need to be honest with yourself about what you want."

Her words held a weight I couldn't dismiss, nudging me to confront the truth that had been lingering just beneath the surface. The longing for Aiden was still palpable, a sweet ache that tugged at my heart. I had spent so many nights dreaming of his embrace, picturing his smile and the way his laughter felt like sunlight breaking through a storm. Yet now, I was faced with the reality that the very connection I craved was shrouded in shadows he couldn't escape.

"I don't know what he needs," I admitted, my voice barely above a whisper. "He wants space, and I don't want to crowd him. But that doesn't mean I don't want to be there for him."

"Then don't crowd him," she replied, her tone supportive yet firm. "Let him take the lead. But make sure he knows you're still here, ready to catch him when he falls. It's a fine balance, but you can do it."

Lily's perspective was like a compass guiding me back to solid ground. I could feel the shift within me, a soft stirring of determination nestled alongside the uncertainty. It was true; love didn't mean clinging desperately. Sometimes, it meant letting go, creating the space for someone to find their way back to themselves. Aiden had always been the anchor in my stormy seas; now, perhaps it was my turn to be the lighthouse, guiding him home without imposing my light too forcefully.

As the evening wore on, our conversation drifted to lighter topics—our mutual disdain for the latest reality TV show and our love for the vibrant farmers' market on Saturdays. The chatter flowed easily, filling the room with an air of familiarity that felt almost sacred. It reminded me of the times when Aiden and I would share dreams under the starlit sky, crafting plans for the future. Now, those dreams felt tangled, hidden beneath layers of unspoken words and unexpressed feelings.

Eventually, we settled into a comfortable silence, and I found myself gazing out the window again, watching as the shadows lengthened across the yard. The night was a tranquil canvas, painted with the soft glow of streetlights and the occasional flicker of a firefly, a reminder that beauty could still thrive amidst darkness. I felt a deep longing to reach out to Aiden, to bridge the distance with words of encouragement, yet I was also aware of the wisdom in restraint.

Just as I was lost in thought, my phone buzzed on the table, a sharp interruption that jolted me back to the present. I reached for it, my heart racing with anticipation. It was a message from Aiden. The breath I held caught in my throat as I opened it, my fingers trembling slightly.

Hey, I've been thinking about you. I hope you're okay. Can we talk?

The simple words struck a chord deep within me, an electric jolt of possibility. My heart swelled with a mix of hope and anxiety. I glanced at Lily, who had been watching me intently, her expression a mix of excitement and caution.

"Is it him?" she asked, eyes sparkling with curiosity.

"Yes," I breathed, the reality of his message sinking in. "He wants to talk."

"Then talk to him! No hesitation. Just go for it!" she urged, her enthusiasm infectious.

I knew she was right. This was the moment I had been waiting for, the chance to reconnect with him, to let him know that I was here, ready to embrace whatever came next. I nodded, steeling myself for the conversation ahead, and grabbed my phone, my fingers hovering over the keyboard as I considered my response.

I'd love that. When?

As I hit send, a nervous flutter danced in my stomach. The seconds felt like an eternity, each one stretching into the next. When my phone chimed back, I nearly jumped.

How about now?

I shot a quick glance at Lily, who smiled encouragingly. I took a deep breath, reminding myself of her words. This was my chance to show Aiden that love meant supporting him through his struggles, not shying away from them.

Okay. Call me.

I hit the call button, and my heart raced as the phone rang. The sound echoed in the quiet of my home, a rhythm that matched my pounding pulse. Each ring felt like a lifetime, but when his voice finally came through the line, it was like a balm to my spirit.

"Hey," he said, his tone tentative but warm, laced with an intimacy that felt both comforting and foreign.

"Aiden," I breathed, a mixture of relief and longing washing over me. "I'm here. I got your message."

There was a brief pause, and I could almost picture him on the other end, his brow furrowed in thought, perhaps running a hand through his hair, a familiar gesture that made my heart flutter. "I've been doing a lot of thinking. About us. About everything."

"I've been thinking too," I replied, my voice steadying with each word. "I want you to know I'm here for you, no matter what. I understand you need space, but I'm not going anywhere."

"Thank you," he said, his voice thick with emotion. "It's just... I feel so lost. And I don't want to drag you down with me. You deserve so much more than the chaos I'm dealing with."

"Aiden, you're not a burden. You're everything to me," I reassured him, feeling the sincerity seep into every syllable. "I want to share the good and the bad. That's what love is, right? It's being there for each other, even when it's hard."

A silence stretched between us, pregnant with unspoken truths. Then he sighed, a deep, soul-wrenching sound that seemed to resonate through the line. "I've been scared, you know? Scared that I'll push you away if I let you see the worst of me."

"But hiding doesn't protect us," I urged gently. "We can't pretend everything is okay when it isn't. You don't have to be perfect, Aiden. I don't need you to be."

"Maybe it's time to stop pretending, then," he finally said, the vulnerability in his voice a soft echo of the storm within me. "Can we take this slow? I want to figure things out, but I don't want to lose you in the process."

The warmth in my chest blossomed, a fragile flower emerging from the cracks of uncertainty. "I can do that. I'm here, ready to help you find your way back."

As we continued to talk, the shadows that had loomed over us began to recede, inch by inch. With each exchange, I could feel the connection between us reigniting, a spark that promised hope even amidst the turmoil. We shared stories, laughter, and tentative plans for the future, slowly weaving our way back to each other.

That night, as I finally hung up, the weight on my heart had lessened, replaced by a flicker of hope that illuminated the darkness. Aiden was still on his journey, but now, I knew I would walk beside him, each step an act of love and understanding. No longer would I shy away from the complexities of our lives; together, we would navigate the shadows and, in time, find the light again.

Chapter 16: Waves of Change

The scent of salt and pine hung heavily in the air as I stepped onto the familiar boardwalk of Brighton Shores, the wooden planks creaking softly underfoot like a nostalgic greeting. Sunlight danced on the surface of the waves, a bright, glittering blanket that made me squint and shield my eyes. The ocean had always been my refuge, a vast, shimmering expanse that mirrored the chaos of my thoughts. Now, as I stood there, I felt its gentle lapping against the shore echoing the tumult of emotions I could no longer contain.

Brighton Shores was a symphony of summer—children laughed and chased one another, their tiny feet kicking up the sand, while couples strolled hand in hand, whispering sweet nothings into the warm breeze. The smell of hot dogs sizzling from a nearby food cart mixed with the sugary scent of cotton candy, creating a carnival atmosphere that should have felt inviting. Yet, with every familiar face I passed, I felt the weight of the unsaid pressing down on me, as if each smile masked a thousand questions that hung uncomfortably in the air.

The sun was beginning its descent, casting long shadows across the boardwalk, and as I walked toward the pier, I could hear the distant laughter of my friends. They were gathered around a small table at our favorite beachside café, their jovial chatter like a balm to my frayed nerves. I missed them fiercely, their presence a comforting thread that tethered me to the joy of simpler times. As I approached, their eyes lit up, and for a brief moment, I felt like I had slipped back into the warmth of summer, but the joy was short-lived.

"Lila!" Mia shouted, her arms flinging open as if to embrace me in a giant hug that could erase all my worries. I stepped forward, and she pulled me into her infectious energy, the world around us blurring for a moment. The warmth of her body felt like sunshine breaking through the clouds, even as the storm within me brewed.

As I settled into a chair, the laughter felt like a fragile glass bubble, ready to pop at the slightest pressure. My friends talked animatedly about their summer escapades—concerts under the stars, spontaneous road trips, and nights spent stargazing on the beach. I tried to join in, to let their joy wash over me, but my mind kept wandering back to Aiden. Where was he? Why was he so distant? The chasm between us yawned wider, filled with silence that neither of us dared to cross.

"Have you talked to Aiden?" Mia's question sliced through my thoughts, her eyes narrowing with concern. The table fell silent, and I felt the weight of their gazes like a spotlight on my confusion.

"No, not really. It's... complicated," I replied, forcing a smile that felt brittle and thin. My heart raced at the thought of him, the way his smile could light up a room but had recently turned into a shadow of uncertainty. I could sense the storm brewing within him, as if the waves were crashing against his heart, eroding the connection we had once shared.

Mia bit her lip, glancing around at the others. "You know he's been a little off since you left, right? Maybe he's waiting for you to make the first move."

I felt the heat rush to my cheeks. Could it be that simple? I had always prided myself on being brave, but confronting Aiden felt like standing at the edge of a cliff, unsure if the leap would lead to flight or a free fall into despair. "I don't want to push him," I murmured, pushing a lock of hair behind my ear.

"Just be honest with him," Mia urged gently, her voice soothing like the sound of waves against the shore. "You guys have always been so good together. Don't let misunderstandings tear you apart."

The words hung in the air like a promise, yet they felt weighty, heavy with expectations. As the sun dipped below the horizon, painting the sky in hues of pink and orange, I couldn't shake the feeling that the tide was turning. Change was afoot, but I was unsure if it would wash over me like a gentle tide or crash down in a turbulent wave.

Later, as I strolled back towards the beach, the sand warm beneath my feet, I found solace in the rhythmic crashing of the waves. Each swell and recede felt like a heartbeat, a reminder that life continued, even when I felt frozen in place. I paused to take in the view—the ocean stretched infinitely before me, a canvas painted with the remnants of twilight. The darkening sky was speckled with stars, twinkling like diamonds, each one a beacon of hope in the vast darkness.

I wrapped my arms around myself, feeling a shiver of apprehension run through me. Would Aiden be able to see me beyond the confusion of this moment? Would he understand that I had come back, not just to reclaim my childhood but to reclaim us? The world felt vast and daunting, but there was a quiet determination rising within me.

Tomorrow would bring a new day, a fresh opportunity to breach the gap that had formed between us. I would find Aiden, confront the shadows that loomed over our friendship, and dare to tread the uncertain waters of our relationship. With each step back to my childhood home, I felt a flicker of resolve growing stronger, a silent promise to myself that I would fight for what mattered most.

As I settled into bed that night, the sounds of the ocean lulling me into a fragile peace, I realized that change was inevitable, but it was in the waves of change that I might find my footing again. All I needed was to summon the courage to ride the currents, to let them guide me back to the shores of my heart, where Aiden waited, lost but not beyond reach.

Morning light spilled through the sheer curtains of my room, casting delicate patterns on the floor like the lacework of a forgotten memory. I awoke with the taste of salt lingering on my lips, remnants of the ocean breeze that had snuck through the window, bringing with it the promise of another day. My heart fluttered with a mix of excitement and trepidation; today would be different, or at least, I intended for it to be. A quiet determination buzzed beneath my skin, pushing me out of bed and into the rhythm of a new routine.

After a quick shower, I slipped into a simple sundress—soft cotton that clung gently to my curves, the fabric a familiar embrace. I stepped outside, the sun warming my shoulders and the sounds of the town stirring to life around me. The boardwalk was alive with the scent of fresh pastries wafting from the bakery down the street, where I could almost see the golden-brown croissants resting beneath a glass display case, inviting and indulgent. I couldn't resist; I needed to fuel my courage before facing Aiden.

With each step toward the café, the cool morning air wrapped around me like a comforting shawl, and I took a moment to soak in the scenery. Children were already at play, their laughter bubbling over like the waves, and I could hear the distant call of seagulls circling above. Brighton Shores was alive in a way that felt both invigorating and achingly familiar, like a beloved song that reminded me of summers long past.

I pushed open the café door, and a bell jingled cheerfully above my head. The aroma of brewing coffee enveloped me, rich and inviting, mingling with the sweet scent of cinnamon rolls that danced temptingly in the air. I ordered a coffee and a croissant, taking my time to savor the moment, watching the patrons engage in their morning rituals. A young couple sat at the corner table, sharing a plate of pastries, their hands brushing against each other with a tenderness that tugged at my heart.

Once I had my breakfast, I found a seat outside on the patio, the sun warming my skin as I took a bite of the buttery croissant. The flaky layers melted in my mouth, a delightful reminder of why I had always loved this place. My gaze drifted toward the ocean, its waves crashing rhythmically against the shore. They seemed to whisper secrets, urging me to take the plunge, to speak the words I had been holding back for too long.

After finishing my breakfast, I made my way back to the beach. My heart raced as I walked along the shoreline, each step drawing me closer to the moment I'd been dreading and yearning for all at once. I had always found solace in the ocean, the vastness of its blue mirroring the expanse of my own thoughts. Yet today, it felt like a battlefield, a storm brewing beneath the surface of my resolve.

I spotted Aiden near the old wooden lifeguard stand, his silhouette framed against the sunlit horizon. He stood with his back to me, staring out at the water, his shoulders tense and rigid. My breath hitched in my throat. He looked so lost, as if the waves were pulling him under, and I knew I couldn't let that happen. Gathering my courage, I approached slowly, each step a silent plea for him to turn around, to acknowledge my presence.

"Aiden," I called softly, my voice barely rising above the sound of the crashing waves. He turned slightly, his profile caught in the golden light, and for a heartbeat, I could see the flicker of surprise in his eyes.

"Lila," he replied, his voice hoarse as if he hadn't spoken in ages. There was a distance in his gaze that made my heart ache. I stepped closer, the sand shifting beneath my feet, as if even the earth was uncertain about this moment.

"I've missed you," I confessed, the words tumbling out before I could stop them. They felt both liberating and terrifying. "I thought maybe we could talk? Just the two of us."

He hesitated, glancing back at the ocean, and I felt the weight of the silence stretching between us. I took another step forward, my resolve hardening. "I know things have been... different. But we can figure this out together, can't we?"

Aiden sighed, running a hand through his hair, the sun catching the strands and turning them a golden hue. "I don't know, Lila. I've been thinking a lot since you left, and I just—everything feels so... complicated now." His words were like a tide pulling away from the shore, leaving me standing on uncertain ground.

"I understand," I said gently, forcing myself to meet his gaze. "But we can't let complications drown us. I came back because I want to be here, with you. I want to face whatever this is together."

He finally turned to me, his eyes a stormy gray, and for a moment, it felt like the world around us faded away, leaving just the two of us and the whispering waves. "I don't want to hurt you," he admitted, his voice barely above a whisper. "I just... I've been struggling."

The vulnerability in his words broke something open within me, a tender realization that beneath his façade of strength, Aiden was just as lost as I was. "I'm here," I said, my heart racing, desperate to bridge the gap that had formed between us. "We can navigate this together, just like we always have. Let's not let fear drive us apart."

He stepped closer, and the space between us felt electrified, charged with unspoken words and lingering glances. "You have no idea how much I've missed this," he murmured, glancing at the ocean once more before locking his gaze on mine. "Missed us."

The tide surged around us, waves crashing against the shore, as if the ocean itself was cheering us on, urging us to take the leap. In that moment, I felt the tension begin to dissipate, replaced by something lighter, a tentative hope glimmering beneath the surface.

"Then let's not waste any more time," I whispered, stepping closer until our shoulders brushed. "Let's just be honest with each other. We owe it to ourselves, don't we?"

Aiden's gaze softened, and for the first time in what felt like forever, a smile tugged at the corners of his lips. "Yeah, we really do."

As the sun dipped lower in the sky, painting the world in shades of amber and gold, I felt a wave of relief wash over me. The currents were shifting, and together, we would ride them, hand in hand, ready to face whatever storms lay ahead. The warmth of his presence beside me felt like home, and for the first time since my return, I dared to believe that we could find our way back to the shore.

The warmth of the sun continued to bathe us in golden light as Aiden and I stood side by side, a fragile truce settling between us like the mist that rose from the ocean at dawn. We lingered in the gentle swell of the waves, the salty air wrapping around us, carrying with it the echoes of our shared laughter from days gone by. It felt surreal, standing there together again, as if time had taken a breath and held it, waiting for us to exhale our fears and uncertainties into the open air.

"I've missed talking to you," I said, the words surfacing like a buoy bobbing on the waves, desperate to keep afloat amidst the turbulence of emotions. "You always had this way of making everything feel lighter."

He turned to me, his expression softening. "And you always knew how to see the best in things. I forgot how much I needed that." His honesty was a balm, soothing the raw edges of my heart. We were teetering on the brink of something beautiful, and I was determined to leap, hand in hand, into the unknown.

"Let's go for a walk," I suggested, nodding toward the path that wound its way along the beach. The sand felt warm beneath our feet as we ventured further from the lifeguard stand, the sound of the ocean filling the spaces between our words. Each step was tentative yet exhilarating, as if we were learning to dance to a rhythm that had once been second nature.

As we walked, I stole glances at him, memorizing the way his hair tousled in the wind, how his shoulders relaxed just a bit with each wave that crashed against the shore. Aiden had always been my safe harbor, and though the storm had thrown us off course, I could sense the tide turning. "What have you been up to since I left?" I asked, curious to bridge the gap of silence that had enveloped us for so long.

He took a deep breath, as if summoning the right words from the depths of his heart. "Honestly? I've been trying to figure things out. School felt different without you. Everything felt different."

"Different good or different bad?" I pressed gently, eager to unravel the layers of his emotions, like peeling back the skin of a sun-ripened peach to reveal the sweet flesh within.

"Mostly bad," he admitted, his gaze drifting to the horizon, where the sun was a molten orb beginning its descent. "I missed our late-night talks, the way we used to brainstorm ideas. Everything was too quiet without you."

I felt a warmth bloom in my chest, the acknowledgment of our shared history igniting a spark of hope. "We can get back to that, you know. It doesn't have to be like this. We can rebuild what we had, one conversation at a time."

He nodded, his expression thoughtful. "I want that. I just didn't know if you'd want the same."

The moment hung between us, heavy with unspoken words and the promise of what could be. I stopped walking, turning to face him fully, the sunlight framing his face in a halo of warmth. "You mean everything to me, Aiden. Just because I left doesn't mean I stopped caring."

His eyes locked onto mine, the depth of feeling swirling within them spoke volumes, and for the first time, I saw the flicker of hope mirrored in his gaze. The distance that had once felt insurmountable began to shrink, and I could almost hear the waves whispering encouragement, urging us forward.

As we resumed our stroll, I began to notice the little things—the way the gulls called out to each other in the distance, the laughter of children playing in the sand, the sweet, sticky scent of melting ice cream from a nearby vendor. Each detail seemed amplified in the light of our newfound connection. "Let's stop by the old arcade," I suggested, feeling a rush of excitement. "Remember how we used to challenge each other at air hockey?"

Aiden laughed, a sound that filled my heart with warmth. "How could I forget? You were relentless."

We made our way to the arcade, and as we entered, the cacophony of bleeps and bloops greeted us like an old friend. The walls were lined with colorful machines, each one a portal to a different world. We quickly gravitated toward the air hockey table, our competitive spirits igniting like flames in a summer breeze.

"Prepare to lose," I teased, picking up the paddle and positioning myself, ready to defend my title.

"Not a chance," he shot back, his eyes glinting with mischief. The game began, and soon we were lost in the rhythm of the competition, laughter spilling from our lips like the coins that clinked into the machines around us.

With every goal scored, the tension between us melted away, replaced by the electric thrill of nostalgia. I reveled in the joy of our playful banter, the way our chemistry surged with each rally. It was as if time had folded in on itself, allowing us a momentary escape from the complexities of our lives.

After a few rounds, we took a break, panting and grinning like children. "Okay, you win this time," Aiden conceded, his eyes sparkling. "But just wait until the next round."

"Deal," I replied, unable to suppress my smile. As we wandered the arcade, I spotted a photo booth in the corner, its flickering lights calling to me like a siren's song. "Let's take a picture," I suggested, my heart fluttering at the thought. "For old times' sake."

He looked hesitant for a moment but then nodded, the corners of his mouth twitching in anticipation. We squeezed into the cramped booth, laughter bubbling up as we tried to find our places. The camera clicked, capturing our silly faces and carefree spirits, the moment freezing in time like a cherished memory.

As the final picture printed out, I held it in my hands, the glossy surface gleaming under the arcade lights. "This is perfect," I said, my heart swelling with a sense of hope. "Just look at us, ready to take on the world."

Aiden took the photo from me, examining it with a soft smile. "I want to keep this," he said quietly, tucking it into his pocket as if it were a secret treasure.

As we stepped back into the sunlight, the warmth enveloped us, and I felt a renewed sense of purpose. Aiden and I were walking hand in hand, not just through the streets of Brighton Shores but into a new chapter, one where we would navigate the complexities of our hearts together.

The ocean continued to roar beside us, the waves rhythmically crashing against the shore, reminding me of the journey ahead—one that would require courage, vulnerability, and trust. But I no longer felt afraid. We were anchored in a friendship that had weathered storms before, and I believed it could withstand whatever came next.

With each step along the beach, the horizon stretched before us like an open invitation, and I knew that this time, we would face it together, ready to embrace the waves of change that lay ahead. Together, we would find our way back to the shore, hand in hand, united by the tides of love and friendship.

Chapter 17: The Reunion

The summer air hung heavy with the scent of cotton candy and sizzling corn dogs, an intoxicating blend that wrapped itself around the heart of our small town like a well-worn quilt. The annual Summer Festival had arrived, a riot of color and sound that transformed our sleepy streets into a kaleidoscope of joy. Strings of twinkling lights crisscrossed overhead, casting a warm, golden hue on the faces of friends and neighbors, all gathered to celebrate the season. The sky, painted with shades of pink and orange, felt like a canvas waiting for the first brushstroke of nightfall, a prelude to the adventures yet to unfold.

As I stepped into the festival, my heart raced not just with excitement, but with an undercurrent of anxiety that twisted my stomach into knots. This was the place where Aiden and I had first discovered the kind of chemistry that felt almost tangible, as if the universe had conspired to align our paths amid the chaos of carnival games and laughter. Yet now, standing at the edge of the festivities, I found myself caught in a whirlwind of doubts. Would inviting him lead us back to the intimacy we once shared, or would it push him further into the shadows of our fractured history?

The festival surged around me, vibrant with life, yet I felt oddly detached, as if I were watching a favorite film from behind the glass of a window. I could hear the distant music, a lively banjo tune mingled with the shouts of children competing for prizes at the ring toss. The air buzzed with anticipation, yet my heart pounded for another reason entirely. Aiden's presence, so familiar and yet so elusive, filled the corners of my mind. It was a magnetism I couldn't ignore, a call to the heart that felt as irresistible as the sweet summer breeze.

Finally, the pull of the festival proved too strong to resist, and I surrendered to the excitement, weaving through the crowds. I paused near a booth where an elderly woman with a smile as warm as freshly baked pie was selling hand-painted pottery, each piece a testament to her years of craftsmanship. I admired a small bowl, its vibrant hues reflecting the sunset, but my heart wasn't truly in it. My thoughts lingered on Aiden, wondering if he was somewhere beneath the bright colors and laughter, lost in his own thoughts or perhaps mingling with memories of us.

As if summoned by my thoughts, I spotted him under a canopy of twinkling lights. Aiden stood there, a silhouette framed against the backdrop of shimmering stars, looking both lost and beautiful, his dark hair tousled by the gentle evening breeze. My breath caught in my throat as our eyes met, and in that moment, the chaos around us faded into a dull roar, leaving only the two of us suspended in time. The familiar warmth flooded my heart, a beacon calling me home, and I felt a rush of emotions I had tried so hard to bury.

I hesitated, caught in the crossfire of longing and fear. What if he turned away? What if the space between us had grown too vast to bridge? But the quiet intensity in his gaze pulled me forward, urging me to take the leap. With each step, I could feel the ground beneath me shift, as if the festival itself held its breath in anticipation. I stepped into his orbit, the world around us morphing into a blur as we closed the distance.

"Aiden," I said, the sound of his name slipping from my lips like a secret. There was something profound about the way it hung in the air, heavy with meaning and possibilities. He smiled, a tentative gesture that both warmed and broke my heart. It was a smile that seemed to acknowledge our shared history, the unspoken words lingering between us, like fireflies caught in a jar, flickering with memories of laughter and unguarded moments.

"Hey," he replied, his voice a low melody that wrapped around me like a favorite song. The tension that had built between us dissolved slightly, replaced by an electricity that felt familiar yet exhilarating. We stood there, both a little shy and a little bold, allowing the world around us to melt away, leaving only the two of us standing under the celestial canopy of lights.

"Want to get away from the crowd?" he asked, his eyes sparkling with a hint of mischief, the same glimmer that had once made my heart race. I nodded, and together we slipped away, leaving the laughter and music behind, seeking solace in the quieter corners of the fair. The noise faded into the background, but the anticipation crackled in the air like the first spark of a firework.

We wandered through a series of paths lined with food stalls and game booths, our feet finding a rhythm that felt both new and familiar. The air was thick with unspoken words, but beneath the surface, a spark ignited once more. It was as if the universe had spun the wheel of fate, bringing us back to this moment where everything felt possible again. I could almost taste the sweetness of what might be—a reunion not just of bodies, but of souls.

"Remember that time we got lost looking for the haunted house?" Aiden asked suddenly, breaking the silence, his laughter bubbling up like effervescent soda. The memory rushed back, vivid and alive. We had spent the better part of an hour wandering through the festival, our fingers intertwined, only to find the haunted house was just a flimsy facade decorated with cobwebs and a plastic skeleton.

"Of course, I do. You were so convinced it was just around the corner, and I kept insisting we should ask someone for directions," I replied, a smile stretching across my face.

He grinned, the kind of smile that sent my heart into a flutter. "And yet we still ended up having the best time that night, just being... us."

It was a simple statement, yet it hung between us like a fragile thread, binding us together in a tapestry of nostalgia and yearning. I realized then how much I had missed the lightness of our connection, the way our laughter felt like music playing in perfect harmony. Here, amid the festival's chaos, we were crafting our own little bubble, a sanctuary where time stood still.

The quiet corners of the festival welcomed us like a well-worn book, pages turned, but the story still fresh in our minds. We found ourselves wandering down a narrow path, lit only by the soft glow of lanterns strung haphazardly overhead. The bustle of the main event faded into a gentle hum, leaving only the rustling of leaves and the distant laughter that seemed like echoes of a time when everything was uncomplicated.

Aiden and I fell into a comfortable rhythm, our shoulders brushing occasionally, sending delightful shivers racing down my spine. The anticipation between us was palpable, hanging in the air like the sweet scent of funnel cakes that wafted through the trees. With every step, I could feel the weight of our shared memories pressing against the fabric of my heart, a patchwork of joy, longing, and the bittersweet taste of what could have been.

"Do you remember that old oak tree over there?" Aiden asked, gesturing toward a gnarled giant that stood sentinel at the edge of the fairgrounds. Its branches stretched wide, offering shade and secrets to those who dared to listen.

I chuckled, recalling the countless afternoons we spent beneath its sprawling limbs, weaving stories about the people who passed by, giving names to strangers based on the laughter and whispers we overheard. "How could I forget? It was our fortress against the world. And the leaves were our ceiling. I think we even named it something ridiculous."

"Right! We called it Sir Oakington," he laughed, his voice light and airy, a reminder of the boyish charm that had drawn me to him in the first place. "We believed it had magical powers, like it could grant wishes if you hugged it tight enough."

I grinned, a warmth spreading through my chest. "And you always hugged it like it was your long-lost friend. I think you even convinced me to try it once."

"Of course! And you made a wish to find the best slice of pizza in town," he replied, feigning seriousness. "I think we still need to follow up on that one."

We fell into easy banter, the kind that wrapped around us like a cozy blanket, reminding me of the nights spent sprawled on the grass, sharing dreams and secrets under a blanket of stars. The laughter bubbled between us, a language only we understood, each chuckle bridging the distance that had grown between us in recent months. It felt so incredibly right, like slipping into a favorite sweater after a long, cold winter.

As we approached the tree, the dim light cast intricate shadows on the ground, creating a mosaic of shapes that danced in rhythm with the rustling leaves. Aiden took a seat at the base, leaning back against the sturdy trunk, his gaze fixed on the twinkling lights that twirled above us. I followed suit, tucking my legs beneath me, the familiar ground feeling like a reassuring embrace.

"Have you ever really thought about wishes?" Aiden mused, his tone shifting to something deeper. "Like what you would ask for if you knew it would come true?"

The question lingered in the air, and for a moment, the levity of our earlier conversation gave way to something heavier. I glanced sideways at him, catching the flicker of vulnerability in his eyes. A weight settled between us, a reminder of the complex tapestry of our lives, woven with the threads of hopes, fears, and dreams deferred.

"I think I'd wish for simplicity," I said, surprising myself with the admission. "Just a day where everything felt uncomplicated, where decisions didn't carry the weight of what-ifs or regrets."

He turned to me, his gaze earnest. "I feel that. Sometimes, it's overwhelming, all the expectations and uncertainties. I think we forget how to just... be."

In that moment, we were two souls adrift in the vast ocean of our lives, seeking refuge in the familiarity of one another. I reached out, letting my fingers brush against his, a gesture so small yet charged with meaning. The connection felt electric, and I could sense the shift in the air, a collective breath held in anticipation.

"Do you ever think about what could have been?" Aiden's voice broke the silence, laced with a hint of longing that pulled at my heart.

All the memories swirled around us, a dizzying dance of laughter, arguments, shared dreams, and whispered secrets. The warmth of his presence anchored me, reminding me of everything we had built, even amidst the fractures. "Every day," I confessed, my voice barely above a whisper. "I think about the times we laughed until we cried, and the way you always knew how to make me smile, even on my worst days."

He leaned closer, the space between us narrowing to a whisper. "I miss that. I miss us. But I also know that things can't just go back to the way they were. We've changed."

"Maybe we can create something new," I suggested, my heart racing at the audacity of the idea. "A different kind of us that embraces all the changes, all the messiness of life."

He looked at me, his eyes sparkling with something unnameable, a mix of hope and apprehension. "I'd like that," he replied softly, the sincerity in his tone wrapping around me like a warm embrace.

Our fingers entwined, an innocent gesture that felt like a promise, a bridge over the chasm that had grown between us. In that moment, the music of the festival faded further into the background, leaving us cocooned in our own world, where only we existed.

A gentle breeze rustled the leaves above, and I could hear the distant laughter of children playing games, the cheerful chatter of friends reconnecting. The night felt alive, electric with possibilities. I could almost see the stars twinkling brighter, as if encouraging our fragile hopes to bloom.

Aiden squeezed my hand, a silent affirmation that we were both willing to explore this newfound connection. "Let's start with small steps," he suggested, his voice steady and reassuring. "We can figure it out as we go along. No pressure."

I nodded, feeling a wave of relief wash over me. The unspoken weight of expectation lifted, replaced by the thrill of discovery. "Just us, one day at a time?"

"Exactly," he smiled, a lightness returning to his eyes that made my heart soar.

As we sat beneath Sir Oakington, the world around us continued to spin, vibrant and full of life. Yet here, in this quiet sanctuary, we began to weave a new narrative, one that held the promise of laughter, adventure, and the kind of love that could withstand the test of time. The festival lights shimmered above us, a celebration not just of summer, but of rebirth, of rekindled hope and the joy of being utterly, beautifully alive.

The silence under the old oak enveloped us, a welcome cocoon that shielded our fragile moments from the chaos beyond. I could still hear faint echoes of laughter drifting from the carnival games and the cheerful chatter of festival-goers who seemed blissfully unaware of the seismic shift occurring just a few paces away. Aiden's fingers intertwined with mine felt like a lifeline, solid and reassuring, grounding me in a reality where we were no longer simply two people tangled in memories but rather architects of a future yet to be written.

"What do you think we should do first?" Aiden asked, his voice breaking the spell of quiet contemplation. "We could relive our old traditions or invent new ones."

The flicker of excitement in his eyes made my heart flutter. I imagined us wandering through the vibrant maze of stalls and games, tasting every morsel of the festival, collecting memories like precious gems to be tucked away for safekeeping. "How about we find that pizza place I wished for?" I suggested, a teasing smile playing on my lips, hoping to evoke a sense of nostalgia.

"Ah, Sir Oakington's legacy lives on!" Aiden chuckled, his laughter a balm that soothed the last remnants of tension in my heart. "Let's make it our mission. But first, we must pay homage to the funnel cakes."

With a mock-serious nod, I rose to my feet, brushing off bits of grass that clung to my jeans. "A sacred duty indeed. Lead the way, brave knight!" I declared, gesturing dramatically as I stepped back onto the path that wound through the festival grounds.

Aiden laughed again, his joy spilling over into the cool night air. He took the lead, guiding me through the familiar sights of the festival—the rowdy games of chance, where boisterous children clutched oversized stuffed animals, their eyes sparkling with the thrill of victory. The stalls were lined with colorful banners, each one beckoning us with promises of sweet delights and playful distractions.

"Look!" Aiden exclaimed, pointing at a booth where a juggler tossed colorful balls into the air with expert precision. "We have to see this!"

I followed him, enchanted by his enthusiasm. The juggler's performance was a vibrant chaos of colors and movements, and as we watched, I could feel the tension of the past few months melting away, replaced by the sweet warmth of companionship. The crowd erupted in applause when the juggler added a flaming baton to the mix, his deft hands working magic that held us all captive.

"Can you imagine if we tried to juggle?" I laughed, picturing us attempting and failing spectacularly. "We'd probably set something on fire."

"Probably ourselves," he grinned, his eyes sparkling with mischief. "But we'd have a great story to tell afterward."

The laughter continued to bubble between us, a connection reforging itself in the fires of shared joy. Once the performance ended, we drifted toward the booth that promised the best funnel cakes. The air was thick with the aroma of fried dough, sugar, and cinnamon, each scent weaving into the fabric of the festival atmosphere like a delicious spell.

As we placed our order, Aiden leaned close, a playful glint in his eyes. "You know, we could go for a record-breaking funnel cake. What do you think? The biggest one they have?"

"Oh, absolutely! If we're going to embrace our inner gluttons, we might as well do it in style." I laughed, our shared exuberance lighting a fire in my chest that chased away any lingering doubts.

When our order was ready, we each took a plate piled high with the sweet creation, the powdered sugar dusting the top like a light snowfall. Aiden dug in first, his eyes lighting up with delight. "This is everything I remembered and more!"

I took a bite, the sweetness exploding in my mouth, and I couldn't help but grin. "You're right! This is definitely the best in town."

As we indulged in our treats, I noticed a nearby group of friends engaged in a spirited game of cornhole, their cheers and playful banter a joyful backdrop to our intimate moment. I watched Aiden, his expression a mix of contentment and nostalgia as he took in the scene. "It's moments like this that remind me how much I've missed... this. Us," he said quietly, his gaze suddenly serious.

The sincerity in his voice sent a ripple of warmth through me. "I've missed this, too. The laughter, the spontaneity. It feels like we're reclaiming a part of ourselves we lost along the way."

He nodded, his expression softening as we stood side by side, sharing the moment in quiet understanding. "So, what do you want to do next?" he asked, his voice full of promise.

"Let's explore! I want to find that pizza place and see if it's as magical as we remembered," I replied, excitement bubbling within me.

With our plates now empty and our spirits soaring, we ventured deeper into the festival, the vibrant lights guiding our way. Each step brought us closer to rediscovering the parts of ourselves that had felt dormant for far too long.

As we navigated through the throngs of people, I couldn't shake the feeling that this night was more than just a reunion; it was a rebirth, an opportunity to redefine our relationship in the face of everything that had come before. I watched Aiden closely as he pointed out various booths and attractions, his enthusiasm infectious, pulling me into the flow of the festival's rhythm.

We passed a group of dancers, their twirling skirts a whirlwind of color, and I couldn't resist the urge to join them. "Let's dance!" I shouted, pulling him toward the makeshift dance floor.

Aiden laughed, caught off guard but undeniably excited. "You're on!"

We stepped into the circle, our movements awkward at first, but soon we found our groove, laughter spilling from our lips as we swayed and twirled, losing ourselves in the music. It didn't matter that we were surrounded by a crowd; in that moment, it was just us, two souls dancing under the stars, tethered together by the threads of shared history and newfound hope.

When the music finally slowed, we collapsed onto a nearby bench, breathless and exhilarated. "I think we might have just made a scene," Aiden joked, wiping sweat from his forehead.

"I wouldn't have it any other way," I replied, my heart racing not just from the dance but from the thrill of being with him, the spark between us igniting like fireworks in the sky.

"Okay, pizza next," he said, determination in his voice as he led the way.

We soon found ourselves at the small food truck nestled at the far corner of the festival, its neon sign flickering cheerfully. The aroma of fresh-baked dough and bubbling cheese wafted toward us, promising a taste of heaven. We placed our order, and while we waited, I couldn't help but steal glances at Aiden.

"Can you believe we're here, like this?" he mused, a hint of disbelief coloring his words. "It feels surreal."

"Surreal, yes. But it also feels right," I replied, my heart swelling with a sense of belonging. "We're not just reconnecting; we're writing a new story."

With pizza in hand, we meandered back toward the oak tree, settling beneath its sprawling branches once more. The first bite was heavenly, and we savored the gooey cheese and tangy sauce, laughter punctuating our meal as we swapped playful jabs and childhood stories.

As the festival continued to pulse with life around us, I realized that this was more than a simple reunion. It was a celebration of everything that brought us here, of every moment that had led to this new beginning. Each slice of pizza shared under the comforting shadows of Sir Oakington felt like a promise—a promise to embrace whatever came next, to explore the complexities of our hearts, and to cherish the vibrant tapestry we were weaving together.

With every bite, every laugh, and every shared glance, the past faded gently into the background, leaving space for the future—a future that sparkled like the stars above us, filled with the bright possibilities of love, friendship, and the beauty of rediscovery.

Chapter 18: Facing Fears

The sun dipped below the horizon, painting the Kansas sky in hues of violet and orange, the perfect backdrop for a reunion I'd longed for yet dreaded. I found myself in a cozy diner on the outskirts of Wichita, its neon sign flickering softly, casting a warm glow on the cracked vinyl booths. The scent of fresh coffee and frying bacon danced in the air, filling the space with an inviting familiarity. This place was our sanctuary, the scene of countless late-night conversations that had shaped the contours of our relationship. Now, it felt more like a battleground, one where I wasn't entirely sure which side I was on.

Aiden arrived with the quiet confidence that always unsettled me. His hair was tousled, hinting at a carefree charm, yet I could see the shadows of uncertainty etched across his face. As he slid into the booth opposite me, our eyes met, and for a brief moment, the world outside faded—the clattering of dishes, the murmurs of late-night patrons, all fell into a gentle hush. His presence was intoxicating, reminding me of everything I had missed: the way he smiled as if he were holding a secret, or how his laughter echoed like a familiar song. But tonight, that melody felt marred, a dissonance threading through our tentative reconnection.

We talked for hours, words tumbling over one another like waves crashing against a rocky shore. Aiden shared stories from the past few years, the ups and downs that sculpted him into a man I scarcely recognized. He spoke of heartbreak and healing, recounting his attempts to rebuild after my absence. I listened, my heart swelling and aching simultaneously, each revelation peeling back layers of nostalgia and regret. It was beautiful yet fragile, like a glass ornament left out in the cold, vulnerable to the slightest jolt.

Between sips of coffee that turned lukewarm, laughter punctuated the heaviness of the conversation. It bubbled up, a welcome distraction from the deeper emotions swirling beneath the surface. He told a story about his disastrous attempt at baking—a blackened cake that resembled a volcanic eruption more than a dessert—and we both erupted in laughter. In that moment, time slipped away, and the years that separated us felt like an illusion, a mirage in the vast desert of memory. I wanted to clutch onto that joy, to etch it into my heart so that I could always revisit it when the shadows crept back in.

But the shadows did come, creeping around the edges of our rekindled bond like a storm gathering in the distance. Just as I began to feel anchored in the present, the door swung open with a sharp jingle, and in walked Sarah. Her entrance felt like a thunderclap, shattering the fragile calm that enveloped our reunion. She glided in, her presence magnetic and unsettling, dressed in a fitted black dress that hugged her figure with an ease I found infuriating. I had always been aware of the lingering echoes of Aiden's past, but seeing her here, in this moment, sent a chill racing down my spine.

Aiden's smile faltered, the warmth that had enveloped us evaporating into a thick, suffocating fog. Sarah made her way to our booth, her eyes sparkling with a mix of determination and uncertainty. "I hope I'm not interrupting," she said, her voice laced with an artificial sweetness that felt anything but genuine. I wanted to roll my eyes but instead found myself frozen, caught in a whirlwind of emotions that threatened to consume me.

"Actually, we were just—" Aiden began, but she cut him off, her voice sharp, like a blade drawing blood.

"I just want to clear the air, Aiden. It's important." Her gaze shifted to me, assessing, dissecting. I could feel her eyes crawling over my skin, and I fought the urge to squirm under her scrutiny. It was a glance that told me everything I didn't want to know about her—a glimpse of the woman who had once held Aiden's heart.

"Sarah, now isn't the time," Aiden said, his tone clipped, but I could hear the guilt lacing his words, the remnants of old wounds that refused to heal. It was evident this confrontation was more than just a casual drop-in; it was an eruption of unresolved tension, bubbling beneath the surface for far too long.

"I think it's exactly the right time," she replied, crossing her arms as if bracing herself for impact. "You can't just pretend like I don't exist."

Aiden's jaw tightened, and I felt the weight of the moment bearing down on us. The laughter, the warmth—everything we had built in those fleeting hours dissipated like smoke in the air. My heart raced as insecurities took root, weaving a tapestry of doubt that threatened to smother the rekindled connection. Would I always be the girl standing in the shadow of his past? Would I ever be enough?

The booth felt smaller now, the air heavy with unspoken words and unresolved feelings. My fingers traced the rim of my coffee cup, seeking solace in the ceramic as the storm raged on. It was clear that the night had transformed into something much more complicated than I had anticipated. The question hung in the air: would I choose to confront my fears, to stand beside Aiden and fight for what we had reignited, or would I allow the weight of Sarah's presence to push me back into the shadows from which I had just begun to emerge?

With each heartbeat, the decision loomed larger, the ground shifting beneath me, as I grappled with the undeniable truth that this was just the beginning.

Sarah's presence warped the atmosphere around us, turning the diner's familiar warmth into a battleground where words would be weapons. Her gaze pierced through the awkward silence, and I felt the corners of my heart begin to harden. Aiden shifted in his seat, visibly wrestling with the tension, the old familiarity of the moment weighed down by the unresolved past hovering just out of reach. I wanted to reach for him, to pull him back into the safety of our laughter, but the distance between us felt insurmountable now.

"Look, I don't want to cause any trouble," Sarah began, her voice sugary yet tainted with bitterness, "but I think we owe it to ourselves to be honest. We had something real." Her eyes flared with a mixture of defiance and regret, as if she were challenging not just Aiden but also me, daring us to fight back against the nostalgia that seemed to cling to her every word.

Aiden's fingers drummed against the tabletop, a nervous rhythm that seemed to echo the chaos swirling within him. I could almost see the wheels turning in his mind, contemplating whether to shield me from the emotional debris or to face it head-on. "We've all moved on, Sarah," he said, his voice firm yet edged with an underlying vulnerability. "You know that."

But her laughter was sharp, cutting through the tension. "Moving on isn't always so simple, is it? Especially when you've left so much unresolved." Her eyes flitted between us, a predator sizing up her prey, and I could feel my heart racing, not in excitement but in a panic that was starting to bubble over.

There was a time when I might have melted under her scrutiny, when the mere mention of her name would have sent me spiraling into a sea of insecurity. But sitting here, amidst the remnants of what had once been a sanctuary, I felt a flicker of resolve ignite within me. I was tired of being the one cast in shadow, tired of allowing someone else's past to dictate my present.

"Maybe it's time we all learned to let go," I said, my voice steady as I attempted to weave courage into the fraying fabric of the moment. I could see Aiden's eyes widen, a spark of surprise mingling with pride, yet I pressed on, feeling emboldened. "It's easy to dwell on what once was, but that doesn't help anyone. We can't change the past, but we can choose how we move forward."

Sarah's smile faltered, the mask slipping just enough for me to catch a glimpse of uncertainty. "You're right, but it's not that simple. Emotions aren't that easy to untangle." Her voice softened, an unexpected vulnerability creeping in, but I could feel the tension still thickening the air.

Aiden's gaze darted to me, his expression an intricate mix of gratitude and alarm. He looked like a man caught between two worlds, each pulling at him in different directions. I wanted to comfort him, to tell him that I understood the struggle, that I too was grappling with shadows of my own. The truth was, I didn't want to be just another chapter in his story. I wanted to be the whole damn book.

"Maybe we need to start untangling," I said, my tone gentle but firm. "All of us. It's clear we've all been affected by what happened. But sitting here and hashing it out isn't going to change anything. If anything, it just brings up old wounds."

For a brief moment, I thought I saw a flicker of understanding in Sarah's eyes, a recognition that perhaps we were all more alike than we cared to admit. But then it was gone, replaced by a defensive posture, her arms crossing over her chest as if bracing against an unseen storm.

"I just thought we could talk, you know?" she said, her voice dropping a notch. "I never meant to hurt anyone." The words dripped with sincerity, yet I felt the air crackle with tension, the unwelcome remnants of the past threatening to engulf us again.

Aiden sighed, his shoulders sagging as if the weight of the world had settled upon them. "Talking is good, but sometimes it's not enough. We need to let the past stay where it belongs. I don't want to revisit old wounds anymore." The firmness in his tone drew me in, reinforcing the bond we had started to rebuild.

"Fine," Sarah said, her voice tightening. "If that's how you feel, I'll respect that." But I could hear the underlying edge, the flickering embers of unresolved feelings threatening to ignite.

The conversation lingered in the air, heavy and fraught with unspoken truths, and I knew that we were all standing on a precipice. The din of the diner around us faded into the background, as if the world had paused to listen, to witness this dance of emotions. My heart pounded with the realization that this moment was pivotal, not just for us but for what lay ahead.

"Maybe we can all just take a breath," I suggested, the words tumbling out as I glanced between them, a fragile peace hanging in the balance. "Maybe we all need to let go of the past, step back, and figure out who we are now."

Sarah studied me, a flicker of recognition crossing her features, and I could almost see the wheels turning in her mind. The tension was palpable, like the moment before a storm breaks, and I held my breath, hoping desperately that the clouds would clear.

"I guess you're right," she conceded slowly, her voice a mix of resignation and acceptance. "We can't keep reliving old mistakes. Maybe it's time we all moved on." The sincerity in her voice was almost shocking, and I felt the air shift ever so slightly, as if a layer of heaviness had been lifted, if only for a moment.

As the conversation drifted towards safer shores, I couldn't help but glance at Aiden, who watched Sarah with an intensity that made my heart flutter. There was a world of emotions flickering across his face—relief, apprehension, and maybe a hint of hope. In that instant, I realized that we were all just trying to find our way, to navigate the jagged edges of our history, and perhaps, if we were brave enough, carve a new path together.

The clinking of dishes and soft chatter of late-night diners swirled around us, and I felt a warmth spread through me, a sense of belonging amidst the chaos. It was a feeling I had craved, a reminder that perhaps love could be rekindled even in the most uncertain of times. Aiden's eyes met mine, and I smiled, a silent promise flickering between us. Whatever storms lay ahead, we would face them together, hand in hand, unearthing the beauty that awaited on the other side of fear.

The air hung heavy with a fragile truce, each breath a tentative dance between old wounds and new beginnings. Sarah's concession shifted the atmosphere, softening the sharp edges of our confrontation, though the weight of the moment remained palpable. She glanced down at the booth, her fingers tracing the edge of the table as if searching for something solid to hold onto. I could see her vulnerability beneath the bravado, and the realization hit me: we were all just trying to navigate this twisted maze of emotions, seeking closure amid the chaos of our intertwined histories.

"Let's just be real for a second," I said, taking a deep breath. My heart raced, but I pushed through the unease. "We all have baggage, don't we? Some heavier than others. But it doesn't mean we have to drag it around forever."

Sarah's head snapped up, and for a heartbeat, surprise flickered in her eyes. Aiden's gaze was a mixture of admiration and something akin to pride, and it filled me with warmth. Maybe standing here, navigating the tumultuous waters of our past, could forge a stronger bond. The diner, once a cozy enclave filled with the aroma of freshly brewed coffee and the chatter of late-night patrons, now felt like the stage of a play where we were all just actors striving for resolution.

"Fine," Sarah said again, her tone lighter this time, almost playful. "But if we're being real, I should probably apologize for how things ended between us, Aiden. It wasn't fair to you or to... whoever this is." She gestured vaguely toward me, and I felt a slight sting in my chest, but I swallowed it down.

"Aiden's not a pawn in anyone's game," I replied, the words tumbling out before I could second-guess myself. "He's here, now, and that's what matters. We're trying to figure things out."

Aiden's expression shifted, a flicker of surprise mixed with gratitude. He turned to me, his eyes bright with unspoken appreciation, and I could see the walls he had built around himself beginning to crumble. I felt a strange warmth coursing through me, as if this moment had opened a door, allowing vulnerability to seep in like sunlight through a dusty window.

As we continued to unravel the threads of our conversation, the world outside the diner faded into insignificance. It was just the three of us, caught in a storm of emotions—nostalgia, regret, and a flicker of hope threading its way through the darkness. The neon lights cast a warm glow around us, creating a cocoon of intimacy where the air was charged with possibility.

"Maybe we should all take a moment to share what we really want," Aiden suggested, his voice steady and calm. "Not just for ourselves, but for each other."

I nodded, heart pounding as the weight of his words sunk in. This was a chance—a real chance to lay everything bare and start fresh, even if the path ahead seemed daunting. I took a deep breath, the scent of coffee mingling with something sweeter in the air. "I want to be happy," I confessed, my voice barely above a whisper. "I want to explore what we have, Aiden. I want us to be real."

Sarah's expression shifted again, surprise giving way to something softer. "I want that too," she admitted, a hint of vulnerability threading through her words. "I want to let go of the past. I don't want to be the person who keeps hanging onto what's gone. It's exhausting."

It was as if the act of verbalizing our desires had lifted a weight off all of our shoulders, the burden of silence replaced with a newfound sense of clarity. The three of us were still tangled in each other's histories, but the promise of a brighter future began to shine through the clouds.

Aiden looked between us, his eyes reflecting the flickering neon lights. "Then let's make a pact," he proposed, leaning forward with a spark of determination. "Let's promise to be honest, to support each other through whatever comes next. We can't change what's happened, but we can create something new."

The diner hummed with life around us, and I felt a rush of excitement course through me. "I'm in," I said, the words spilling from my lips before I could think. Sarah nodded, a small smile breaking across her face as she offered her hand in agreement.

As our hands met in the center of the table, the connection felt electric. A simple gesture transformed into a vow—a promise that we would navigate the treacherous waters of our intertwined lives together. The world outside continued its chaotic dance, but within this little corner of Kansas, we had created our own sanctuary, a safe space where vulnerability was met with understanding.

Time slipped away as we shared stories and laughter, the evening stretching on, creating a tapestry of new memories. The warmth of connection wrapped around us, and I felt hope blooming in the space where insecurity had once thrived. The ghosts of our pasts didn't disappear, but they lost their power, transforming from menacing shadows into lessons that shaped who we had become.

As the clock ticked towards midnight, I caught Aiden's eye, a smile creeping across my lips. He looked like a man renewed, the burdens of yesterday lifting as he embraced the possibility of tomorrow. There was something magical about this moment—the way we were weaving our stories together, forging a bond that felt stronger than the sum of its parts.

"I can't believe we're here," Aiden said, his voice low, reverberating with sincerity. "It feels like the universe conspired to bring us back together."

I grinned, a warmth flooding my chest. "Or maybe it just knows how much we need each other."

With every word exchanged, every laugh shared, I felt the tapestry of our lives begin to shift, the threads intertwining into something beautiful and unbreakable. Outside, the world continued to swirl, but within the walls of this diner, we were carving out a piece of magic, a sanctuary built on hope and the promise of what could be.

As the night deepened, laughter echoed through the diner, weaving through the fabric of our shared past, wrapping around us like a warm embrace. It was a reminder that even amidst the tumult, joy could bloom in the most unexpected places.

I leaned back in my seat, feeling the comfort of the moment wash over me. This was just the beginning of something remarkable, a journey fueled by honesty and the courage to face fears together. The road ahead might be uncertain, but for the first time in a long while, I felt ready to embrace whatever came next, hand in hand with Aiden and Sarah, my heart open to the adventures that awaited us.

Chapter 19: The Tempest

The sun had just begun its descent, casting long shadows across the cracked pavement of our small Midwestern town. As I stood on the porch of the weather-beaten clapboard house, the air buzzed with the electricity of an impending storm. It mirrored the tempest brewing within me, a chaotic swirl of emotions that left my heart racing and my palms clammy. Aiden was inside, and I could hear the muffled voices, punctuated by the sharp edge of Sarah's laughter, a sound that once thrilled me but now grated on my nerves like nails on a chalkboard.

I leaned against the splintered wood of the railing, a sanctuary from the swirl of confusion and dread. The scent of damp earth filled the air, mingling with the sweet aroma of honeysuckle that crept along the fence, stubbornly thriving despite the impending chaos. The vibrant colors of the flowers stood in stark contrast to the darkening sky, a reminder that beauty could exist even in turbulent times. It was a lesson I needed to remember, especially now.

Aiden's laughter floated through the open window, warm and inviting, and for a moment, it lulled my anxious heart. But then came Sarah's voice, tinged with a teasing lilt that made my skin crawl. I knew their friendship ran deep; they had weathered storms of their own, but this time felt different. This time, it felt personal. As the clouds gathered ominously overhead, a tight knot of dread twisted in my stomach. I took a deep breath, trying to anchor myself in the familiar sounds of home, but the joy that once filled this space was morphing into a tension I could almost taste.

The front door creaked open, and Aiden stepped out, his sandy hair tousled by the wind, a hint of confusion flitting across his handsome face. He had an easy charm, a magnetism that drew people in, but that same quality now made me feel like a fish caught in a net.

"Hey," he said, offering a tentative smile that didn't quite reach his eyes.

"Hey," I replied, forcing my voice to remain steady, even as my heart hammered against my ribcage like a caged bird desperate to escape.

"Everything okay?" He was searching my face for answers, his brow furrowing in concern. I wanted to reassure him, to tell him everything was fine, but the truth hung heavily between us like the storm clouds overhead, thick and oppressive.

"Just... the weather," I said, glancing up at the swirling mass of gray. "Looks like it's about to pour." It was a flimsy excuse, but it was all I could muster. The truth was, I felt the storm brewing not just in the sky but within our fragile relationship, and I wasn't sure if I was ready to confront it.

Aiden stepped closer, the warmth of his presence washing over me like a summer breeze. "Do you want to go for a walk? It might help clear your head." There was genuine concern in his eyes, and for a fleeting moment, I thought about saying yes. But Sarah's laughter echoed in my ears, a reminder of the storm we were about to face.

Just as I opened my mouth to respond, the door swung wide, and Sarah appeared, her eyes sparkling with mischief. "What are you two whispering about?" she asked, the words draped in playful sarcasm. She was radiant, her confidence shining like a beacon, but that very brilliance felt like a dagger aimed at my heart.

"A walk," Aiden said, and there was a slight edge to his voice, a hint of defensiveness that made my chest tighten. I could see the shadows flicker in his eyes, the uncertainty that danced there, mirroring my own.

"Count me in!" Sarah exclaimed, as if her presence were essential to the outing. I watched her glide down the steps, an effortless grace that seemed to defy the storm brewing above us. In that moment, I felt like an unwelcome guest in my own life, trapped in a play I hadn't auditioned for.

"No, it's okay," I interjected, my voice wavering slightly. "I think I'll just stay here." The words tasted bitter on my tongue, a mix of defiance and resignation. I wanted to scream, to shake Aiden awake, to make him see what was happening, but instead, I stood there, rooted in place.

"Come on, it'll be fun!" Sarah coaxed, her smile disarming. But I saw the glint of competition in her eyes, a spark that ignited a flame of fear in my chest. I felt the ground shifting beneath me, the world tilting as I struggled to find my footing.

"I really don't feel like it," I said, my voice firmer this time, determination seeping through the cracks of my uncertainty. "You guys go ahead."

The air grew thick with tension, a palpable force that surged between us. Aiden shifted his weight, caught between loyalty and confusion. "Are you sure?" he asked, his voice low, almost tentative.

"Yes," I replied, the single syllable resonating with a strength I didn't know I possessed.

With a reluctant nod, he turned back toward Sarah, his face a mask of conflict. "Alright, let's go," he said, the words tinged with hesitation. I watched them walk away, a lump forming in my throat as the storm clouds rolled in, blotting out the sun.

As the first drops of rain began to fall, I felt the weight of my decision crashing down around me. I had chosen solitude over confrontation, but at what cost? The distant rumble of thunder echoed in the distance, a warning of the chaos yet to come, and I couldn't shake the feeling that the storm wasn't just outside; it was brewing inside me, too, a tempest I had yet to fully comprehend.

The rain started to pour, and I could hear it pounding against the roof, a cacophony of chaos that matched the turmoil within. I stood on the porch, drenched by the downpour of emotions and uncertainty, watching as Aiden and Sarah faded into the horizon, two figures swallowed by the storm.

Each drop of rain felt like a reminder of the fight I hadn't been brave enough to initiate, a constant chorus urging me to find my voice amidst the tempest, to reclaim the love I feared I was losing.

The rain transformed the world around me, washing the colors from the landscape into muted grays and greens. It fell in heavy sheets, drumming against the roof like a thousand tiny drummers marching to an unrelenting beat. I stood still on the porch, my heart thudding along in rhythm, lost in a tempest of my own making. The wind whipped around me, tugging at my clothes, almost as if it were trying to pull me back into the whirlwind I had just chosen to flee.

I wrapped my arms around myself, a feeble attempt to ward off the chill that penetrated not just my skin but my very core. My gaze drifted down the street, where Aiden and Sarah's silhouettes blurred under the relentless downpour. Each step they took felt like a step away from the love we had cultivated, the easy laughter and late-night talks that had once seemed unbreakable. Instead, a creeping vine of doubt began to twist around my heart, choking out the bright blossoms of affection I had for Aiden.

In the distance, thunder rumbled, a low growl of nature warning of the tempest brewing just as my own emotions churned violently within me. I turned back toward the house, stepping inside to escape the torrent that mirrored my turmoil. The warm interior felt like a sanctuary, yet it was tainted by the shadows of what was happening outside. I glanced at the photo of Aiden and me on the wall—a snapshot of a moment frozen in time, carefree and blissful, before the world had conspired to unravel everything.

A shuddering breath escaped my lips as I dropped onto the couch, the worn fabric familiar and yet foreign, a reminder of both comfort and conflict. I could still feel Aiden's lingering warmth on the cushion beside me, the way he sank into the space we shared, his laughter mingling with my own. That laughter now seemed distant, an echo fading into the background, replaced by Sarah's shrill mirth that seemed to taunt me even in its absence.

I pulled a throw blanket around my shoulders, the fabric a poor substitute for the embrace I craved. The storm outside intensified, rain hammering against the windows like tiny fists demanding entry. I felt every drop as a punctuation mark in the growing silence of my heart, each one reminding me of words left unsaid, battles left unfought. My mind spiraled into a labyrinth of insecurities, each corner revealing something new and unsettling: was I not enough? Had I ever truly been enough?

My thoughts spiraled further into the dark corners of my heart until a sharp rap on the door startled me from my reverie. It was as if the universe was pulling me back from the brink, urging me to confront the chaos instead of cowering beneath its weight. I hesitated, uncertainty coiling around my chest like a vice, but I pushed through it, rising from my cocoon of blankets.

I opened the door just as another bolt of lightning illuminated the street, casting long, ominous shadows that danced across the wet pavement. Aiden stood there, drenched and wide-eyed, his sandy hair plastered to his forehead and his clothes clinging to his frame as if they were trying to absorb the very essence of the storm.

"What happened to you?" I asked, the words tumbling out before I could stop them. I was surprised to find that I cared deeply about the state of his well-being, even amidst my own turmoil.

"I couldn't leave things like that," he replied, his voice steady yet tinged with urgency. "I had to come back."

The storm swirled around us, a living entity, yet in that moment, I felt suspended in time, a fragile bubble that could burst at any moment. I could see the turmoil in his eyes, a reflection of the turmoil I felt inside.

"I'm not sure I can do this right now," I admitted, my voice trembling. "Not with her in the picture."

Aiden stepped closer, the warmth radiating off him even through the chill of the rain. "She's just a friend," he insisted, but the words hung in the air, unconvincing and thin. "You know that, right?"

"Do I?" I challenged, the vulnerability in my voice cracking like thunder. "You laugh with her, you joke with her—she knows you in a way I don't."

"Because you won't let me in," he countered, and the hurt in his gaze sent a jolt through me. "You're pushing me away, and I don't know how to reach you when you do that."

For a moment, the storm roared louder, drowning out our words as if nature herself was trying to intervene in our fragile conversation. I felt the anger rise within me, a flame igniting in the depths of my frustration. "Maybe I'm trying to protect myself," I snapped, the truth spilling out, raw and unfiltered.

His expression softened, the storm clouds of his own emotions clearing just enough for me to see the concern beneath. "I get that. But running away will only make it worse. We need to talk."

"Talk?" I scoffed, bitterness lacing my tone. "About what? How I'm not the girl you thought I was? How every time I see you with her, it feels like a dagger to my heart?"

The wind howled outside, and for a moment, I thought I could hear it echoing my own inner chaos. But beneath my anger was a flicker of vulnerability, a part of me that longed for connection even as I built walls to protect myself.

Aiden took a deep breath, grounding himself as if searching for the right words. "Yes, we need to talk about all of it. But we also need to remember what brought us here, what we mean to each other. I don't want to lose you over something that can be resolved."

His plea cut through the tempest swirling in my mind. "It's not just about you and me," I replied, my voice barely above a whisper.

"It's about trust. It's about feeling safe. And right now, I don't feel safe."

Aiden stepped into the house, shaking off the rain like a dog fresh from a swim, leaving a trail of droplets in his wake. "Then let's create a safe space," he urged, a determination etched into his features. "Together."

As the storm outside raged, I found a sliver of hope in his words. Maybe this tempest could be navigated, not just for ourselves but for the love we both desperately craved. The air between us shifted, charged with possibilities. It was time to confront the storm head-on, to let the thunder roll and the rain fall, and to fight for the understanding and forgiveness that danced just out of reach.

With the storm raging on, I took a step toward Aiden, my heart pounding with a mix of fear and resolve, ready to face whatever came next.

The atmosphere in the house shifted as Aiden stepped closer, creating a cocoon of warmth that felt like a lifeline in the chaos. I watched the rain cascade down the windows, the droplets racing each other, competing for the ground like the emotions flooding my heart. A sense of urgency hung in the air, making every second stretch like taffy, the sweet taste of resolution just out of reach.

"I don't want to fight anymore," I finally admitted, the admission slipping from my lips like a confession in the dim light of the living room. "But I can't keep pretending that everything is okay when it feels like the ground is shifting beneath my feet."

Aiden's eyes softened, the storm clouds reflecting not just the rain outside but the turmoil in my heart. "Then let's talk about it," he urged, his voice steady, as if he were anchoring both of us in the midst of this swirling sea of doubt and fear. "I'm not going anywhere, okay? We'll face it together."

His reassurance wrapped around me like a warm blanket, yet I felt the weight of my insecurities pressing down. "You don't understand," I said, a tremor in my voice. "Sarah... she has this way of making you forget everything else. It's like she casts a shadow over us, and I'm terrified of fading into it."

He shook his head, the moisture in his hair glistening like spun gold under the dim light. "You won't fade. You're the light, remember?"

The sincerity in his gaze pierced through my doubts, and for a moment, I allowed myself to believe it. But as thunder rumbled in the distance, a reminder of the storm outside, I struggled against the instinct to shield myself. "But what if I'm not enough?"

"Enough for what?" he challenged gently, stepping even closer, his presence radiating comfort. "For me? You're everything to me. I chose you, and I will choose you again, every single day. I'm not going to let you convince yourself that you're anything less than that."

As his words washed over me, I felt the tight grip of fear begin to loosen, replaced by the flicker of hope igniting in my chest. "You have no idea how hard this is for me," I confessed, the words flowing like the rain outside, raw and unrestrained. "I've fought my whole life to prove that I belong, that I'm worthy of love. And now, just when I thought I had found it, I feel it slipping away."

Aiden's expression shifted, his brows knitting together with a mixture of concern and understanding. "Tell me what you need, and I'll do everything in my power to give it to you. I want to understand."

Taking a deep breath, I met his gaze, willing the honesty I had kept bottled up for so long to spill out. "I need you to see me—not just as a girlfriend or an option, but as someone who deserves to be prioritized. I need to know that when the storm hits, you won't be swayed by the wind."

The sincerity in his eyes deepened, and in that moment, I felt a flicker of recognition. We were navigating uncharted waters, each wave threatening to toss us off course, but perhaps this was the moment we would find our footing. "I promise," he said, the weight of his words hanging in the air like a fragile promise waiting to be kept. "I will fight for you, for us."

As if the heavens were conspiring with our words, the rain outside began to ease, a gentle drizzle that draped the world in a shimmering cloak. I felt the tension in my shoulders start to melt away, a sense of calm washing over me as I let Aiden's sincerity anchor me.

"Let's just breathe," he suggested, taking a step back but still holding my gaze. "We don't need to solve everything right now. We can take it one moment at a time."

I nodded, appreciating his willingness to be patient. "One moment at a time," I echoed, letting the phrase settle like a soothing balm over my racing heart.

We sat together on the couch, the distance between us evaporating as we sank into the cushions, the sound of rain now a gentle background melody to our quiet resolve. The air was thick with unspoken feelings, and yet there was a newfound clarity in the space we shared.

The minutes passed in comfortable silence, broken only by the occasional rumble of thunder and the distant patter of rain. I studied Aiden's profile, the way his brow furrowed in thought, the way his lips occasionally twitched as if he were fighting back a smile. I found solace in his presence, the way he seemed to make everything feel possible, even amidst the turmoil of the world outside.

"Do you remember the first time we met?" I asked, breaking the silence, my voice lightening the heavy atmosphere.

His lips curved into a smile, eyes sparkling with the memory. "Of course. You were running late, as usual, and you tripped over your own feet right in front of me."

I laughed softly, the sound breaking through the tension like sunlight piercing the clouds. "And you caught me, saving me from an embarrassing faceplant."

"Only to fall for you in the process," he teased, a hint of mischief dancing in his gaze.

"Flattery won't get you out of trouble," I shot back, but my heart swelled at his playful tone.

"Maybe not, but it's a start," he quipped, his grin infectious.

As we traded light-hearted banter, I felt the weight of the world lift, replaced by the warmth of connection that had always been the bedrock of our relationship. The playful exchanges became a thread that wove us back together, an intricate tapestry of memories binding our hearts with laughter and love.

But beneath the surface, the reality of Sarah still lingered like a shadow at the edges of our newfound joy. "What about her?" I asked, my tone growing serious once more. "We can't pretend she doesn't exist."

Aiden's expression sobered, and he took a deep breath, the lightness of our earlier conversation fading into the background. "I understand your concerns. I care about her as a friend, but you're my priority. I need you to know that."

His honesty left no room for doubt. "So, what do we do?" I asked, my voice trembling with uncertainty.

"We keep talking," he replied simply. "We address the elephant in the room and make sure it doesn't grow any bigger."

I nodded, feeling a sense of purpose rising within me. The storm outside had begun to fade, its ferocity dulled to a gentle hum, mirroring the shift in our conversation. Perhaps we could weather this storm together, addressing our fears and insecurities head-on.

As the rain drizzled gently against the window, I turned to face Aiden fully, courage bubbling up within me. "Then let's start right now. I want us to be stronger than this—together."

He smiled, that warm, genuine smile that had melted my heart from the very beginning. "Together," he echoed, and in that moment, the shadows of doubt and fear began to dissipate, revealing a path forward bathed in the golden light of possibility.

Outside, the clouds parted just enough for the sun to break through, sending a cascade of light flooding into the room. It felt like a promise, a reminder that even after the fiercest storm, there would always be a chance for renewal.

Chapter 20: A Heart Divided

The festival was alive with colors that seemed to pulse like a heartbeat, vibrant shades of orange, red, and gold swirling together in a dizzying display against the fading light of dusk. Lanterns dangled from trees, casting a soft glow that flickered like fireflies in the warm evening air, but all I could see was the distance that had formed between Aiden and me. He moved through the crowd, a striking figure caught in a tangle of emotions, his eyes darting like caged birds, searching for something beyond my reach.

The laughter of my friends bubbled around me, an intoxicating melody that should have filled me with joy, yet each giggle and cheer pierced through my heart like shards of glass. They twirled in their sundresses, carefree and gleeful, oblivious to the storm brewing just a few feet away. I tried to laugh along, forcing a smile that felt as brittle as the fallen leaves crunching beneath my feet. I was caught in the crossfire of emotions, my heart tugging in two opposing directions. On one side, Aiden, radiating confusion and hurt; on the other, my friends, who sought to lift my spirits, not knowing that their joy only amplified my pain.

The air was thick with the scent of caramel apples, cotton candy, and the smokiness of grilled corn, each fragrance weaving a tapestry of nostalgia that tugged at my heartstrings. I inhaled deeply, hoping to fill my lungs with sweetness, but all I tasted was the bitter tang of uncertainty. I glanced over at Aiden, who stood at the edge of the crowd, his silhouette outlined against the colorful chaos, looking as though he were contemplating a leap into the abyss. The ache in my chest deepened as I imagined what went unsaid between us—a chasm too wide to bridge, filled with misunderstandings and the unshed tears of our shared history.

The evening light grew dimmer, and the shadows of the festival stretched long, casting our hopes into obscurity. I felt a pulse of courage as I watched Aiden's brow furrow, as if he were wrestling with a decision that could change everything. With each heartbeat, I felt an urge to bridge the divide, to scream across the cacophony of laughter and music, to remind him that we were stronger than this rift. But what could I say? The words tangled in my throat, and I feared they would only fall flat, like the abandoned fireworks scattered across the sky.

Suddenly, laughter erupted nearby, pulling my gaze toward a booth where children lined up for face painting. The sight was both whimsical and jarring, the children transformed into vibrant butterflies and fierce tigers, their faces illuminated with the sheer joy of childhood. A pang of longing surged within me, and I remembered a time when everything felt simpler, when Aiden and I could bask in our shared dreams without the weight of expectations or past disappointments. I ached for that innocence, for a moment when we could paint our lives together, undeterred by external judgments or the ghosts of failed relationships.

With each passing moment, I felt myself drifting, the laughter of my friends echoing in the background like a fading memory. I wandered toward the face painting booth, entranced by the vibrant colors splattered across canvases of skin. My fingers itched with the desire to create, to add a splash of brightness to the monochrome reality that seemed to close in on me. I could almost feel the soft bristles of the brush against my cheek, a soothing balm against the turmoil within. I leaned closer, allowing myself to be enveloped in the allure of creativity, if only for a fleeting moment.

Then, just as the artist turned to me, my phone buzzed in my pocket, a stark reminder of the reality I had hoped to escape. It was a message from Aiden. My heart raced as I read the words, simple yet laden with weight: Can we talk? A wave of warmth surged through me, igniting a spark of hope. I glanced back toward him, and for the first time that evening, our eyes met. The world around us faded, and in that moment, I saw it—an echo of the connection we had once shared, flickering like the dying light of the lanterns above us.

My feet moved instinctively, the crowd blurring into an abstract swirl as I made my way toward him, each step a hesitant plea for understanding. As I approached, the festival's music faded into a muffled thrum, leaving only the sound of my heartbeat—a relentless drum echoing in my ears. He stood there, uncertainty etched on his face, yet behind it lay a glimmer of resolve, as though he had finally decided to confront the tempest swirling between us.

"Hey," I said, my voice soft yet steady, as if I were breaking a fragile silence. He shifted slightly, hands shoved deep into his pockets, a posture that betrayed the tension simmering beneath his calm exterior. I wanted to reach out, to bridge the gap with my touch, but the fear of rejection held me back, leaving me hovering in the space between hope and despair.

"Hey," he replied, his voice low and almost lost amidst the vibrant chaos of the festival. There was a vulnerability in his gaze that cracked the walls I had built around my heart, allowing a flood of emotion to seep through. "I... I've been thinking."

I held my breath, bracing myself for what was to come. In that moment, beneath the canopy of stars and the lingering scent of festival treats, our hearts hovered on the brink of revelation, suspended in a delicate balance between past pain and the potential for healing.

The air hummed around us, charged with the energy of a thousand conversations, yet in that moment, it felt like we were suspended in our own universe, a bubble against the chaos that raged just beyond our shared silence. Aiden's gaze held mine, and the flickering lantern light danced in his eyes, illuminating the unspoken words that hung between us like a delicate thread. It was as if every person around us had faded away, leaving only the two of us bound by an invisible force, an aching need to unravel the complexities that had tangled our hearts.

"Can we just... start over?" he asked, his voice barely above a whisper, yet it sliced through the din like a knife. The sincerity in his tone drew me closer, and for a fleeting moment, hope fluttered within my chest. It was a simple request, yet it bore the weight of everything we had endured—the heartaches, the misunderstandings, the love that felt simultaneously fragile and fierce.

I nodded slowly, the gesture heavy with the enormity of our shared past. "Yeah. I think I'd like that." My heart raced as I spoke the words, as if by voicing my desire for a fresh start, I was also daring to believe that we could be more than the shadows of our former selves.

He shifted, his posture relaxing just a fraction, a subtle indication that perhaps he was ready to peel back the layers of hurt and confusion that had enveloped us for far too long. "I just... I don't want to lose you," he admitted, his vulnerability raw and disarming. "Things got so tangled up after... everything with Sarah, and I don't know how to make it right."

The mention of her name sent a ripple through me, a flash of bitterness that was hard to swallow. Yet I recognized that she was not the true villain of our story; we had both played our parts in the drama that had unfolded. I took a deep breath, the scents of popcorn and fried dough wrapping around us like a warm embrace, grounding me in this moment. "You won't lose me," I promised, each word a balm against the unease that had festered between us. "But we have to talk about it. All of it."

As if on cue, the faint sound of fireworks burst overhead, showering the night with splashes of light and color. It felt like the universe was conspiring to ignite the very spark we had been missing. Aiden's eyes widened, reflecting the brilliance above, and for a brief moment, I could see the flicker of joy I had longed to witness again.

"Let's find somewhere quieter," he suggested, nodding toward a cluster of trees at the festival's edge, their shadows long and inviting. Without hesitating, I took his hand, the warmth of his touch anchoring me amid the swirling uncertainties. We navigated through the crowd, brushing past couples and families, the vibrant atmosphere buzzing with life, while our connection pulsed with a newfound intensity.

Once we settled under the canopy of trees, the festival sounds faded into the background, replaced by the rustling leaves and the distant laughter that felt like a world away. I could feel the coolness of the earth beneath us, grounding and real, as we leaned against the sturdy trunk of a tree, the bark rough against my back. Aiden turned to me, his face illuminated by the glow of the nearby lanterns, and I could see the hesitance etched in his features.

"Do you remember when we first met?" he asked, his voice softening. The question hung in the air, and I couldn't help but smile at the memory.

"Of course," I replied, my heart warming at the thought of that serendipitous moment in the crowded bookstore, surrounded by the scent of aged pages and the promise of stories yet to be told. "You were reading that ridiculous self-help book, and I was convinced you were trying to find the meaning of life between the pages of someone else's words."

Aiden chuckled, the sound rich and warm, and the tension in the air eased just a bit. "I was trying to impress you, actually. I thought if I read enough self-help books, I could finally figure out how to be the person you deserved."

The revelation caught me off guard, and I laughed softly, my heart fluttering. "You didn't need to read any books. You had me at the first smile."

He leaned in slightly, the air between us charged with the warmth of our shared memories. "And you stole my heart with your sarcasm," he replied, eyes twinkling. "I just didn't realize how fragile it all was until it shattered. I didn't protect you like I should have."

His honesty settled around us, a tangible weight that felt both daunting and liberating. I took a deep breath, the night air filling my lungs with clarity, and looked into his eyes, searching for the sincerity I had longed for. "Aiden, we've both made mistakes. I let my insecurities get the better of me, and I let them cloud my judgment. But I don't want to dwell on the past. I want to move forward."

His gaze softened, the lines of worry beginning to fade as he absorbed my words. "Together?"

"Together." I smiled, my heart swelling with the promise of what lay ahead. The sound of laughter and distant music floated toward us, a reminder of the vibrant world we had momentarily stepped away from. Aiden reached out, brushing a strand of hair behind my ear, his touch lingering like a whisper.

"I've missed this," he said, his voice low, almost reverent. "I've missed you."

The sincerity in his eyes pulled at my heart, reigniting a flicker of hope that had felt dim for far too long. In that moment, the festival around us blurred, and all that remained was the warmth of our connection, ignited once more. The memories of laughter and joy cascaded through my mind, fueling a quiet resolve within me.

"Let's make a pact," I proposed, the words tumbling out before I could second-guess myself. "No more hiding. No more letting outside influences pull us apart. We tackle things together, no matter how hard."

Aiden nodded, his expression serious yet hopeful, as though my words had taken root within him, awakening a dormant determination. "I promise. I want to face everything with you. You're the best part of my life, and I won't take that for granted again."

The sincerity in his voice sent warmth flooding through me, and I felt an almost magnetic pull toward him. In that quiet clearing, beneath the protective embrace of the trees, I realized that our hearts could still beat in unison, that we could navigate the tangled paths ahead, hand in hand. The world outside was still bright and chaotic, but together, we could find a way to carve out our own space, vibrant and alive. As the last remnants of daylight slipped away, the stars began to twinkle overhead, the universe twinkling as if celebrating the rekindling of a love that was far from over.

With the promise of rekindled connection hanging between us, I felt an unfamiliar weight lift from my shoulders, as if the festival's lanterns were burning brighter just for us. Aiden leaned closer, the warmth of his presence offering a comfort I had longed for. It was in that moment of vulnerability, standing under the ancient trees that whispered secrets of countless souls, that I realized we were navigating not just the immediate turmoil, but the legacy of our intertwined lives.

"We've built so much together," I began, my voice steady but tinged with uncertainty. "Friendships, dreams... memories. It's hard to imagine tossing that away because of one misstep." I studied his face, searching for traces of that easygoing boy I had first met, the one who had shared laughter over coffee and debated the merits of literature on rainy afternoons. That boy was still there, buried beneath layers of worry and confusion, and I yearned to unearth him.

"Life isn't like those novels we love," Aiden replied, his brow furrowing, each word measured as if he were choosing his steps carefully through an emotional minefield. "You can't just turn the page and hope everything will magically fix itself." There was a fire in his voice, but it was dampened by the hesitance that shadowed his eyes.

"No, but you can start writing a new chapter," I countered, emboldened by my own words. "We can create a narrative where we learn from our mistakes instead of being defined by them."

A faint smile crept onto his lips, one that felt like a fragile bloom in a winter landscape. "You always did have a way with words." He shifted slightly, the distance that once felt insurmountable narrowing just a touch. "Okay, let's say we do this. Where do we begin?"

The question hung in the air, heavy yet promising. "We start by being honest. I need to tell you how I really feel about everything—about Sarah, about us. And I want you to be honest too. No more pretending everything is fine when it isn't."

As I spoke, the music from the festival seemed to swell around us, wrapping our confessions in a cocoon of sound and spirit. I could hear the thumping of drums echoing like a heartbeat, the laughter of children mingling with the sizzle of food stalls, painting a vivid tapestry of life that felt both exhilarating and suffocating.

"I don't think you truly understand how hard this has been for me," Aiden began, the vulnerability in his tone demanding my full attention. "When Sarah confronted me, it stirred up everything I had buried. The insecurities I thought I had worked through came rushing back. I felt like I was losing the best part of myself—losing you."

His admission resonated within me, each word resonating like a note in a long-forgotten song. "I felt the same way," I confessed, my heart racing as the admission spilled out. "I thought I had lost you, and that fear was suffocating."

As the words left my lips, the dam I had built around my emotions began to crack. Memories surged to the surface—those countless evenings spent beneath the stars, sharing secrets and dreams, our laughter echoing into the void. I had missed that connection fiercely, the lightness that came from knowing we could share our darkest thoughts without fear of judgment.

"So, what now?" Aiden asked, his eyes searching mine, the vulnerability etched across his features. "How do we move forward?"

In the dim light, illuminated by flickering lanterns, I felt a swell of determination. "We take it one step at a time. We build our trust back, even if it means stumbling along the way. I want to understand your fears, Aiden. I want you to understand mine. No more hiding."

He nodded, and in that shared understanding, I saw the potential for healing, a pathway carved through the uncertainty. "Okay," he said softly, his voice almost a whisper as if afraid to disturb the fragile peace we were constructing. "Let's do it. But I need to know—are you sure you can trust me again? After everything?"

The question hit me like a sudden gust of wind, stirring my thoughts and fears, but the flicker of hope ignited a sense of clarity within me. "I want to trust you," I replied, my voice steady, the weight of my heart resting on those words. "But trust is built, not given. It takes time, and I'm willing to invest that time if you are."

As the festival continued to unfold around us, I felt a sense of solidarity bloom. I could see couples and friends embracing, laughter echoing through the night, each interaction a reminder of the vibrancy of life. I wanted that for us—to not just exist but to thrive amid the chaos, to dance together through the ups and downs that life inevitably threw our way.

Aiden's gaze softened, and in that moment, the shadows of doubt began to dissipate. "Then let's start now. Let's promise to be there for each other, no matter how messy things get."

I held his gaze, feeling the gravity of his words settle within me. "I promise." My voice rang clear, each syllable a vow echoing in the cool night air.

Just as we sealed our unspoken pact, the first firework erupted overhead, bursting into a brilliant cascade of colors that lit up the night sky. The explosion of light was a celebration of possibility, a reminder that even amid darkness, beauty could emerge. I glanced up, captivated by the display, and when I turned back to Aiden, I could see the reflection of the fireworks mirrored in his eyes, igniting a spark that transcended the chaos surrounding us.

The moment felt electric, and I wanted to grasp it, to hold it tightly against the uncertainties that lay ahead. As we stood beneath the canopy of stars, a myriad of emotions swirled between us—hope, fear, love, and a growing desire to nurture what we had almost lost. I felt an overwhelming surge of gratitude for the journey that had brought us to this point, for the trials that had tested us, and for the lessons we had yet to learn.

With the festival lights shimmering around us, I leaned in closer, brushing my lips against his, tasting the sweetness of renewal. In that kiss, I felt the tentative threads of trust weaving together once more, a tapestry of resilience and love that promised to weather any storm. As the last of the fireworks faded into the night, the world around us pulsed with life, echoing the rhythm of our hearts as we stepped forward into a future uncharted, yet bright with the promise of togetherness.

Chapter 21: A Journey of Healing

The salty breeze swept through my hair, a wild dance that played with each strand as I perched on a weathered rock, the sun dipping low into the horizon, setting the Pacific ablaze in hues of orange and pink. Big Sur was an artist's canvas, every moment a brushstroke of nature's raw beauty. The waves crashed below, their rhythmic symphony both exhilarating and calming. I could almost hear the secrets whispered by the tides, tales of resilience that echoed through the ages. Here, I felt a tether to something greater, something timeless that helped put my own fragmented thoughts into perspective.

As I took in the vast expanse of the ocean, I could taste the brine on my lips, mingling with the bittersweet tang of memories that flickered in the back of my mind. I had come here to escape, to find solace, but more than that, I sought clarity. The kind of clarity that felt almost like a warm embrace, wrapping around me like the comforting layers of a well-worn quilt. Each wave crashing against the rocks felt like nature's way of reminding me of the power of perseverance, and for the first time in a long time, I felt a flicker of hope igniting within me.

Sitting there, my notebook balanced precariously on my knees, I began to write. My pen flew across the page, the ink spilling out my heart in a flurry of emotions, each word a drop of the ocean, deep and profound. I wrote about Aiden—the way his laughter sparkled like sunlight on the water's surface, the warmth of his hand enveloping mine, the look in his eyes when he spoke of dreams that reached far beyond the horizon. The memories came flooding back: our shared moments of joy, the mundane transformed into magic just by his presence. But with the sweetness came the tang of sorrow, memories woven together like threads in a tapestry, each one intricately linked to the next.

I recalled the darkness that had threatened to engulf me, the shadows that danced at the edges of my mind. Life had thrown more than a few storms my way, and I was still learning how to navigate through them. But in this moment, with the sun setting and the world bathed in twilight, I felt a burgeoning strength. I wasn't simply a victim of my past; I was a warrior, learning to fight for my happiness, for Aiden, for us.

As the sky shifted from vibrant colors to a soft indigo, the first stars began to peek through the veil of night. They twinkled like tiny promises, reminding me that even in darkness, there was light. Each star told a story, just like the scars etched on my heart. I traced the edge of my notebook with my fingertips, the paper warm from being cradled against my body. I realized that writing was my lifeline—a way to untangle the emotions that threatened to choke me, a way to breathe life into my hopes.

In the distance, a couple strolled along the shore, hand in hand, their laughter mingling with the sound of the ocean. Their joy felt infectious, a sweet reminder of love in all its forms. I watched as they paused to take in the breathtaking view, their silhouettes framed against the fading light. My heart ached for that kind of uncomplicated happiness, but I also felt a warmth spread through me, a realization that my own happiness was not out of reach. I had Aiden, and our love, while imperfect, was beautiful in its complexity.

The cool sand beneath my feet felt grounding as I wandered closer to the water's edge. Each step left a fleeting mark, an imprint that would be washed away with the next wave, just like the worries that had once consumed me. The ocean's pull was magnetic, and as I stood there, I closed my eyes, letting the breeze wrap around me like an embrace, whispering promises of healing and renewal.

In that moment of solitude, I felt an overwhelming urge to scream, to release the pent-up energy coursing through me. But instead, I breathed deeply, inhaling the salty air, the scent of wild sage and sun-warmed earth, exhaling the remnants of my pain. Healing wasn't a linear journey; it was a winding road full of curves and bumps, a path where I would stumble but always rise again. I resolved to embrace each part of my story, the good and the bad, like pieces of a mosaic that created a larger picture.

And then, as if the universe had conspired to remind me of my resolve, my phone buzzed in my pocket. I hesitated before pulling it out, a sudden rush of anxiety flooding over me. What if it was news I wasn't ready for? What if it was Aiden, reaching out with words that could shatter this fragile moment of peace I had carved for myself? But I knew I had to face whatever lay on the screen. The display lit up with a message, his name shining like a beacon in the darkness, and my heart soared at the thought of him.

With a mix of hope and trepidation, I opened the message, and a smile crept across my face. It was simple—a photo of him grinning, a dorky expression plastered across his face as he held up a sign that read, "Missing you like crazy."

At that moment, I knew I would fight for our love, not just for the memories but for the future we could still create together. The ocean roared in the background, and I stood taller, my spirit buoyed by the vastness of the world around me. I was not just a collection of past hurts; I was a story in progress, ready to embrace every twist and turn that awaited me.

The sun dipped lower in the sky, its golden rays casting a warm glow over the jagged cliffs of Big Sur. The ocean's surface shimmered like a sea of diamonds, each wave reflecting the light with a glimmer of hope. I could hear the distant calls of seabirds, their cries weaving through the salty air, mixing with the rhythmic pulse of the tide. This was my sanctuary, a place where the weight of the world felt just a little lighter, and I could breathe without feeling constricted by the past.

With my notebook cradled in my lap, I took a moment to relish the tranquility enveloping me. The cliffs loomed like ancient guardians, steadfast against the relentless crash of the surf below. Each rock formation told a story, layered and complex, much like my own life. I let my fingers trace the contours of the pages, the smoothness grounding me in this moment. The last few days had been a whirlwind, but here, time felt fluid—an ebb and flow rather than a march towards an uncertain future.

I was determined to unpack the tangled threads of my emotions. Words flowed from my pen, each stroke of ink a cathartic release. The power of writing had always been my refuge, a space where I could unleash the whirlwind inside me. I scrawled about Aiden and how the very thought of him made my heart race like a child chasing the tide as it receded. I delved into the complexities of our relationship, the laughter we shared like ripples on the surface of the water, and the conflicts that sometimes crashed over us like rogue waves, threatening to pull us under.

But as I wrote, I began to unearth something deeper—an understanding that love is not merely an emotion; it's an art form that requires nurturing. It demands vulnerability, a willingness to expose the raw edges of our hearts. I paused, letting my pen hover over the page as I absorbed this revelation. Aiden had shown me that love is also about the brave act of standing together against the tempest.

The sun continued its descent, painting the horizon in shades of lavender and soft pink, as if the universe was holding its breath in anticipation of twilight. I took a deep breath, allowing the fresh ocean air to fill my lungs, pushing aside the remnants of doubt that lingered. With renewed purpose, I resolved to reach out to Aiden, to share my thoughts, my fears, and the love that continued to swell within me like the rising tide.

My phone buzzed again, a gentle vibration against my thigh. I glanced down, heart racing as I saw his name light up the screen. "What's the ocean like?" he asked, his playful tone nearly tangible, a warmth that radiated from my device. I grinned, feeling a rush of affection for him. I began typing, each word infused with the excitement of connecting with him, a reminder of why I had come to Big Sur in the first place.

"It's breathtaking," I typed back, fingers moving eagerly across the keyboard. "Like nature's way of saying, 'You are small, but you are mighty.' I feel like the waves are telling me to embrace the chaos."

He replied quickly, a response that made my heart flutter. "You are mighty. Just remember that. I'm here, cheering you on from afar. I can't wait to see you."

The simplicity of his words wrapped around me like a warm blanket on a chilly night. I smiled, a genuine one that felt foreign yet familiar, as if my heart was stretching into a new shape, one that could accommodate both joy and vulnerability. I didn't want to merely survive the trials of our relationship; I wanted to thrive, to flourish amid the uncertainty.

As the sun finally dipped below the horizon, a canvas of stars began to emerge, twinkling like the countless possibilities that lay ahead. I closed my notebook and stood, feeling the cool earth beneath my feet as I made my way closer to the water. The waves lapped at my ankles, the chill sending a shiver up my spine. It was exhilarating, a reminder that even the most unpredictable elements could be beautiful.

Standing there, enveloped in the soothing sounds of the ocean, I could feel the threads of my past slowly loosening their grip. I had spent too long holding onto fears that didn't serve me, and it was time to let go. Each wave that rolled in was a gentle nudge, urging me to release the weight I carried. I closed my eyes, letting the salty mist kiss my cheeks, and breathed deeply, inhaling the promise of renewal.

Suddenly, the air shifted, and I opened my eyes to see a flicker of light dancing on the water. It was a boat, its lanterns glowing softly against the darkening sky, cutting through the night like a beacon. The sight pulled at something deep within me—an adventure waiting to unfold, a reminder that life is often a journey rather than a destination.

As the boat sailed gracefully, I thought about the journey Aiden and I had embarked upon. There would be rough waters ahead, of that I was certain, but I was ready to navigate them together. I envisioned the two of us on this very beach, sharing dreams and fears, standing shoulder to shoulder against the crashing waves. I wanted to dive deeper, to explore the depths of our relationship, to unveil every hidden corner of our hearts.

My phone buzzed again, breaking me from my reverie. "Are you there?" Aiden's message brought me back to the moment, the warmth of his presence wrapping around me even from miles away.

"Yes," I replied, my fingers flying across the screen. "And I feel so alive. Like I'm ready to fight for us, for everything we can be."

The reply came almost instantly. "You've always been a fighter. Just promise me you won't forget that."

I stood there, the ocean swirling at my feet, the stars twinkling above, feeling more connected to Aiden than I had in ages. This journey was mine to shape, and with him by my side, I was ready to embrace the chaos, ready to weather the storms, ready to celebrate the beautiful moments that would undoubtedly come our way. In the heart of Big Sur, under the watchful gaze of the moon, I began to understand that love, much like the ocean, was vast, unpredictable, and utterly transformative.

The moon hung low in the night sky, a brilliant orb casting silver light across the undulating waves, illuminating the world in a soft glow. The air felt electric with possibility, every breath I took filled with the scent of salt and the promise of renewal. I wandered along the shore, each step a conversation with the sand, which crumbled beneath my weight like the fragile whispers of my past. I could feel the cool water licking at my ankles, a gentle reminder that change was constant, ebbing and flowing like the tides.

As I moved farther down the beach, I found a secluded spot away from the occasional couple sharing their moments under the stars. Here, the sound of the waves crashing against the rocks seemed to synchronize with my heartbeat, a rhythmic reminder that I was alive and capable of feeling again. Sitting on the cool, damp sand, I pulled my knees to my chest, watching the luminescent surf and allowing the tranquility of the night to wash over me.

I thought of Aiden, his laughter echoing in my mind, a melody that lightened even the darkest corners of my heart. I recalled the little things—the way his hair caught the sun, turning golden; the slight crinkle around his eyes when he smiled; the way he made even the simplest moments feel extraordinary. In a world that often felt heavy with expectation and disappointment, he was my buoy, a lighthouse guiding me through the fog of uncertainty.

But I was also painfully aware of the weight I carried, the shadows that lingered at the edges of my mind like stubborn fog refusing to dissipate. Would I always be at war with my own memories? I closed my eyes, letting the sounds of the ocean wrap around me like a comforting blanket. I needed to acknowledge these fears, to confront them rather than bury them beneath the soft sand.

In that quiet moment, I made a decision. It was time to be honest—not just with myself but with Aiden. No more hiding behind walls built from doubt and insecurity. I would share my vulnerabilities with him, expose the scars I had collected like shells on the shore, and invite him to understand the depths of my heart.

A soft breeze rustled through the palm trees lining the beach, carrying with it the faint scent of jasmine and hints of wood smoke from distant campfires. I opened my eyes to see the stars twinkling like diamonds scattered across a velvet canvas, each one a reminder of the love I had to offer. The universe felt alive with stories waiting to unfold, and I was ready to contribute my own.

Pulling out my notebook once more, I began to write, the words flowing effortlessly as I poured my heart onto the pages. "Aiden," I wrote, "I've been holding back. There are pieces of me that I want to share, parts of my soul that I need you to see." The ink flowed freely, as if the very act of writing was a conduit for all the things I had buried deep within.

I wrote about my fears—of failure, of losing him, of being unable to be the person he believed I could be. I documented the moments of joy we had shared, the way we'd laughed until our sides hurt and the comfortable silences that had wrapped around us like a warm embrace. I wanted him to know that every time I hesitated to open up, it was because I was terrified of being unworthy of the love he so freely gave.

The moonlight shimmered on the pages, illuminating my confessions. It felt liberating, cathartic even, as I poured every ounce of myself into the words. This wasn't just a letter; it was an unveiling, a promise to let him in, to invite him to witness the beautiful mess I had become.

As I finished writing, a sense of calm settled over me, the weight on my shoulders lifting, if only slightly. I stood and stretched, letting the cool breeze caress my skin, feeling more like myself than I had in weeks. It was time to head back, to seek out Aiden and let him read my heart laid bare.

The walk back felt shorter, each step filled with newfound purpose. My phone buzzed again, and I glanced down to find a new message. "Are you still there? The stars are out, and they're incredible tonight," Aiden wrote. My heart fluttered at the thought of him, missing me as I missed him.

"I'm on my way back. The ocean is beautiful, but it's missing something—someone," I typed back, my heart racing as I hit send. The response came swiftly, a burst of warmth that wrapped around me like the waves lapping at the shore.

"Come home, then. I can't wait to see you."

His words ignited a fire within me. Home wasn't just a place; it was wherever we were together. With a sense of determination, I quickened my pace, feeling the pull of love guiding me back.

When I reached our cabin, nestled among the trees, I found him standing on the porch, silhouetted against the soft glow of the lights within. The sight of him sent butterflies racing through my stomach, a giddy sensation that made me feel alive. I climbed the steps, the wood creaking beneath my weight, and as I drew closer, I could see the concern etched on his face.

"Hey," I said softly, my voice barely above a whisper.

"Hey," he replied, his expression softening as he stepped forward, enveloping me in his arms. I melted against him, the familiar scent of sandalwood and warmth grounding me. "I was worried. I know how much this place means to you, and I didn't want you to feel alone out there."

"I wasn't alone," I confessed, pulling back slightly to look into his eyes. "I was writing."

Aiden raised an eyebrow, intrigued. "Writing? You're full of surprises. What were you writing about?"

With a deep breath, I retrieved my notebook from my bag, my fingers trembling with both excitement and apprehension. "I wrote about us—about everything. I need you to understand me, to see the pieces of myself I've been too afraid to share."

He took the notebook gently, his fingers brushing against mine, sending a spark of connection coursing through me. I watched as he opened it, his brows furrowing slightly as he began to read my words.

With each sentence, I could see the emotions flickering across his face—curiosity, concern, and, finally, understanding.

When he reached the end, he closed the book softly, and I felt my heart pounding in my chest. "You're incredible," he said, his voice thick with emotion. "You have no idea how much courage it takes to lay yourself bare like this. I'm honored that you chose to share this with me."

His words wrapped around me like a warm embrace, igniting a flicker of hope. I reached for his hand, intertwining our fingers, feeling a sense of unity that had been absent for far too long. "I'm ready to fight for us, Aiden. I want us to navigate this journey together, to embrace everything that comes our way."

He stepped closer, his breath warm against my skin. "Then let's do it. Together."

In that moment, under the blanket of stars and the watchful gaze of the moon, we stood side by side, ready to embrace the unpredictability of love and life. With the ocean crashing in the distance and the warmth of each other's presence, we knew we were not just writing our story; we were crafting a masterpiece, one filled with hope, healing, and a love that would withstand the tests of time.

Chapter 22: The Call of the Sea

The sun hung low over Brighton Shores, draping the beach in a golden glow that danced across the waves. It was a day that begged for the salty embrace of the ocean, the kind of day where the sand seemed to sparkle with a life of its own, whispering secrets from beneath my toes. I had invited Aiden to join me, the hope for rekindling something precious shimmering in the air like sunlight on water. The moment he arrived, I felt a flutter in my chest, a familiar excitement mingled with the nagging weight of what lingered between us.

We strolled along the shoreline, the gentle tide lapping at our feet as if the ocean itself wanted to cradle us in its arms. Aiden's hand brushed against mine, and for a heartbeat, the world around us faded into the background. I studied him, the way the late afternoon light caught the edges of his jaw, giving him an ethereal glow that I remembered so vividly. His smile, though tinged with shadows, still held that same warmth that could melt the iciest of hearts. Each step we took left an imprint in the wet sand, a temporary mark that echoed our shared past—fleeting yet beautiful, like the waves that washed over them.

"Do you remember the last time we were here?" I asked, my voice barely rising above the rhythmic crash of the surf.

Aiden chuckled softly, the sound like music to my ears. "How could I forget? You insisted on trying to surf, and I ended up rescuing you from the waves more than once."

I laughed, picturing myself floundering like a fish out of water, the salty brine stinging my eyes as I desperately paddled back to shore. "You were my lifeguard and my greatest fan, all rolled into one."

He looked down, a wistful smile creeping onto his lips. "And you were the bravest person I knew, throwing yourself into the waves without a second thought."

As we walked, the sun dipped lower, casting long shadows that stretched toward the horizon like fingers yearning to touch the edge of night. The beach was alive with the sounds of seagulls squawking overhead and children's laughter dancing through the air, filling me with a sense of nostalgia and longing. This place was a treasure trove of memories—each grain of sand a reminder of who we once were. Yet the weight of our past loomed large, an uninvited guest lurking at the edges of our reunion. I could sense it, the specter of Sarah, always present, reminding us of what we had lost.

"I miss this," I admitted, trying to grasp the ephemeral nature of our moments together. "I miss us."

Aiden's gaze drifted out to the ocean, where the horizon met the sky in a blur of oranges and pinks. "I do too, more than you can imagine," he replied, his voice heavy with unspoken words. "But things are different now."

The truth of his statement hung in the air like a storm cloud, a dark reminder of the chaos that had invaded our lives. I wanted to push past it, to step into the sunlight of our shared laughter and the warmth of the beach, but Sarah's name still clung to the edges of our conversation like seaweed tangled in my toes. It was a name that had become synonymous with heartache, the ghost of a love that had carved deep lines into our story. I wanted to reach for him, to erase the distance that had grown like barnacles on a shipwreck, but I feared that doing so might invite the tumultuous waves of our reality crashing back in.

"Let's forget about everything for today," I suggested, trying to summon a sense of lightness, hoping to banish the shadows that threatened to engulf us. "Just you and me, like the old days. Let's build a sandcastle."

He turned to me, surprise flickering in his eyes, and then a slow grin broke through. "A sandcastle? I haven't done that since I was a kid."

"Exactly!" I exclaimed, feeling a rush of enthusiasm. "We can pretend the world doesn't exist. Just for a little while."

With that, I dashed toward a patch of untouched sand, scooping up handfuls as I began to mold a fortress fit for royalty. Aiden joined me, his laughter infectious as he recounted tales of our childhood mischief, the memories becoming a bridge between us. We piled sand high, sculpting towers and moats, pouring our hopes into each grain as we shaped the castle of our dreams.

The sun continued its descent, painting the sky in brilliant hues, and the golden hour felt like a soft embrace. We lost ourselves in the rhythm of creation, our hands working in tandem, our laughter mingling with the whispers of the sea. I could almost forget the weight of Sarah's shadow—almost.

As the last rays of sunlight kissed the horizon, casting a fiery glow over our creation, I sat back on my heels and admired our handiwork. The sandcastle stood tall, a testament to our shared spirit, resilient despite the inevitable waves that would eventually come to reclaim it.

"This is our kingdom," I declared with a playful flourish, and Aiden chuckled, shaking his head.

"More like a temporary fortress, but I'll take it."

His eyes sparkled, and for a moment, I could see the boy I had fallen in love with long ago, unburdened and free. The ghost of Sarah faded, if only for an instant, and I grasped that flicker of hope, the possibility that perhaps we could rebuild, stronger this time.

But as the tide lapped at our feet, inching closer to our creation, I felt the tightening in my chest again—the reality that our fortress, like our love, was at the mercy of forces beyond our control. Would it stand against the waves? Would we?

The waves were relentless, each one crashing against the shore with an enthusiasm that seemed to mock the precariousness of our creation. I watched as the tide licked closer to our sandcastle, a stark reminder of the transience of everything we were building. Aiden remained beside me, his gaze fixed on the water, a furrow of concentration on his brow that made him look both handsome and pensive. It was as if he were calculating the odds of our fortress surviving the impending wave—a bet I wasn't sure we could win.

"Are you ready for the inevitable?" he asked, his tone light yet edged with seriousness.

I shrugged, a playful grin creeping onto my face. "It's just a sandcastle, right? It's meant to be washed away." I picked up a seashell, smooth and glistening, and placed it on the parapet like a precious jewel. "But until it goes, let's pretend it's the strongest structure on the beach."

Aiden chuckled, his eyes flicking to mine, sparkling with a warmth that melted the chill of uncertainty. "Okay, your highness," he said, taking on a mock-serious tone. "We shall defend this castle with all our might!"

And just like that, we settled into a rhythm, a playful banter that filled the air around us with laughter. I could feel the years of distance between us beginning to close, the space where resentment and confusion had taken root slowly giving way to nostalgia and hope. The sun slipped lower, casting the beach in hues of orange and purple, wrapping us in a cloak of warmth that felt both safe and ephemeral.

As the tide crept closer, I found myself distracted by the music of the evening—the soft strumming of a guitar wafting through the air from a nearby bonfire gathering, mingling with the sound of laughter from friends reuniting over s'mores and stories. The smell of toasting marshmallows drifted to us, tempting and warm, like the comfort of shared moments past. I could almost taste the sweetness, a blend of childhood memories and fleeting summer nights.

"Do you want to join them?" Aiden asked, nodding toward the bonfire. "It looks fun."

I hesitated, my eyes lingering on our half-built fortress. The castle felt like a manifestation of us, an effort to reclaim something lost, something tangible we could mold together. "I don't want to leave our castle unguarded," I replied playfully, though I felt a pang of longing for the camaraderie of laughter and warmth.

He laughed softly, the sound like waves rolling in. "I think it's about to fall, regardless of whether we're here or not."

Before I could respond, a wave surged forward, crashing against the castle with a fierce determination, water splashing around us. Our structure buckled, and I gasped, watching as a section of our painstaking work crumbled into the sea. Aiden's laughter rang out, and I couldn't help but join him, the sound mingling with the ocean's roar.

"Defended valiantly, my queen," he proclaimed dramatically, bowing as if he were a knight in shining armor.

I couldn't hold back my grin. "Let's go, then! We can either drown our sorrows in s'mores or build a better castle."

"Onward!" Aiden shouted, grabbing my hand and pulling me toward the bonfire, our laughter echoing across the sand like a melody meant just for us.

The closer we got, the more the scent of charred marshmallows and smoky wood enveloped us, the sounds of joy washing over me like a wave. We joined a small group, and my heart swelled at the sight of familiar faces, friends who had once been constants in my life. They welcomed us warmly, offering toasted marshmallows as though it were an offering to the gods of friendship.

"About time you two showed up!" Jenna exclaimed, her cheeks rosy from the fire's warmth. "We thought you were lost at sea!"

"More like drowning in sand," Aiden joked, pulling me closer to the circle.

As the flames crackled, I felt a cocoon of safety envelop us, the camaraderie wrapping around me like a warm blanket. We settled onto the sand, laughter bouncing between us, stories flowing freely. I watched Aiden interact with our friends, the ease of his laughter blending with theirs, and for a moment, it felt like we were a family once more.

As the night deepened, the stars emerged, sparkling overhead like diamonds scattered across a dark velvet canvas. I glanced at Aiden, who was lost in conversation, his face lit by the firelight. I marveled at the way the flames danced in his eyes, igniting something inside me that had been dormant for far too long. The ache in my heart softened, the looming shadows of doubt temporarily banished.

"Hey," he said, catching my gaze, his voice lowered amidst the merriment. "Want to take a walk?"

I nodded, intrigued by the flicker of something deeper behind his eyes, the way he had looked at me earlier—the warmth and the pain intertwined. We stood and walked away from the crowd, the soft sand shifting beneath our feet. The rhythmic sound of the waves crashing against the shore accompanied us, a soothing lullaby against the backdrop of the night.

We wandered farther down the beach, the bonfire's glow diminishing behind us, replaced by the silvery shimmer of moonlight on the water. The world around us faded until it was just the two of us, standing under the vastness of the universe, where the only sound was the gentle rush of the tide.

"Aiden," I began, the words hanging between us, almost tangible, thick with emotion. "Do you think we can ever—"

"Forget?" he finished for me, the question heavy with understanding. "No. But we can move forward."

His honesty startled me. I wanted to scream, to cry out against the injustice of our past, but instead, I simply nodded, feeling the truth of his words settle deep within me. "I miss what we had," I admitted, my voice barely a whisper.

"I miss it too," he said softly, stepping closer. The air was electric, charged with memories and the promise of what could be. "But maybe it's not about going back. Maybe it's about finding something new together."

As he spoke, the weight of uncertainty that had clung to me began to lift, replaced by a tentative hope. I looked out at the waves, the moonlight glistening on the surface, and for the first time in a long time, I felt the stirrings of possibility.

The tide swelled and receded, relentless in its rhythm, a reminder that life was always in motion. I could hear laughter from the bonfire drifting down the beach, but here, in the quiet, we found something sacred—a moment suspended in time, where the past and future collided, and I realized I was ready to embrace whatever came next.

The night unfurled like a velvet tapestry, each star a shimmering reminder of the countless dreams we had once whispered to each other under the vast sky. Aiden and I stood on the beach, caught in the delicate web of possibilities, each wave a soft heartbeat echoing the turmoil of our past. As the moon cast its silvery glow over the ocean, illuminating our faces, I realized how fragile our moment felt, like glass poised on the edge of a table, ready to shatter at the slightest nudge.

"Do you ever think about the future?" Aiden asked suddenly, his voice low and contemplative.

The question hung in the air, heavy with implications. I gazed out at the dark expanse of water, the way it ebbed and flowed, an eternal cycle. "Sometimes," I replied, my mind racing to the endless what-ifs that had plagued my thoughts since our paths had diverged.

"But it's hard to see it clearly when the past keeps crashing in like the tide."

He stepped closer, the warmth radiating from him drawing me in like a moth to a flame. "The past shapes us," he said, his tone earnest. "But it doesn't have to define us."

With those words, he reached for my hand, fingers intertwining with mine in a way that felt both familiar and foreign. The simple act of holding hands sent a jolt through me, a warmth blooming from our touch, awakening dormant feelings I had almost buried. I searched his eyes for clarity, for reassurance that this wasn't merely an illusion—a fleeting moment before the storm of reality broke upon us once more.

"I want to believe that," I murmured, my voice barely audible above the surf. "But it's hard when Sarah's name is an anchor pulling us back."

A flicker of pain crossed his face, a reminder that her shadow loomed larger than either of us wanted to admit. "I know," he said softly. "But I also know that what we had—what we still have—deserves a chance to grow."

We stood there, the world around us dissolving into a blur of salty air and starry skies, and for the first time in a long time, I felt the weight of my doubts begin to lift. Aiden's presence was like a lighthouse cutting through the fog of uncertainty, guiding me back toward something I had long thought lost.

"Let's promise to try," I said, my heart racing at the prospect of what lay ahead. "No matter how scary it feels."

He nodded, his grip tightening around my hand. "Together," he affirmed, a quiet determination in his eyes that mirrored my own resolve.

With newfound courage, we walked along the beach, the moonlight illuminating the path ahead. We left the remnants of our sandcastle behind us, a monument to our shared past, and stepped into the vast unknown of the future. As we strolled, the rhythmic sounds of the ocean became a comforting melody, each wave washing away the remnants of our heartache, cleansing the air of unspoken fears.

We passed clusters of people gathered around bonfires, their laughter spilling over like sparks in the night. The aroma of sizzling hot dogs and toasted marshmallows wafted through the air, igniting our hunger. I pulled Aiden toward a small group where a guitar was being strummed, a lively rendition of a familiar tune filling the night with warmth and cheer.

"Look at those marshmallows!" I exclaimed, pointing to a young couple laughing as they attempted to roast theirs over the flames, only to end up with a charred mess.

"Not everyone can be as talented as we are," Aiden quipped, feigning seriousness as he gestured to our earlier sandcastle disaster.

I burst into laughter, the sound bright and genuine. "Clearly, we are the true artists of the beach."

He leaned closer, his breath warm against my ear. "We should add sand sculptors to our resumes."

As we settled into the circle, surrounded by friends and familiar faces, I felt a sense of belonging wash over me. The worries that had tangled in my mind like seaweed began to dissipate, replaced by the laughter and camaraderie that filled the air. We shared stories, sipped drinks, and exchanged smiles, the barriers that had once separated us slowly dissolving with each passing moment.

I watched as Aiden engaged with our friends, his laughter infectious as he recounted tales of our childhood escapades. The way he spoke animatedly, his eyes dancing with mirth, reminded me of the boy I had fallen for all those years ago. It was like witnessing a reunion of sorts—not just of our friendship, but of the spark that had ignited between us long ago.

"Hey, you two!" Jenna called out, her eyes sparkling as she nudged Aiden. "When are you going to perform your famous duet?"

I felt heat rise to my cheeks, the memory of our last karaoke performance—the terrible rendition of an iconic love song—sparking a flurry of embarrassment and laughter.

"Only if you promise to join us," Aiden challenged, a glimmer of mischief lighting up his expression.

Jenna raised her hands in mock surrender. "Alright, but only if you promise to spare us the details of your 'love' life afterward!"

The night wore on, laughter echoing through the darkness like fireflies, illuminating the memories we were weaving together. As the embers of the bonfire flickered and faded, I felt a profound shift within myself—a sense of acceptance, a dawning realization that perhaps it was possible to carve a new path while carrying the weight of our past.

Later, as the party began to wind down, Aiden and I wandered back toward the water's edge, our feet sinking into the cool sand, each step drawing us closer to the edge of the waves. The night air was thick with salt, invigorating and alive, stirring something deep within me that had lain dormant for far too long.

"What if we make a pact?" Aiden suggested, his voice soft yet unwavering. "To always come back to this place, no matter where life takes us. A reminder that we can always find our way back to each other."

The thought sent a thrill through me. I could already envision us returning, years from now, sharing stories with children or partners about the summers we had spent under the stars, the way the ocean had woven our lives together.

"I'd like that," I replied, my voice laced with sincerity. "To always have this place—this moment—no matter what happens."

With a gentle nod, he stepped closer, our hearts in sync, the weight of our past still present but no longer a burden. Instead, it became a foundation upon which we could build. As we stood there, gazing out at the vast expanse of ocean and sky, I realized the future, much like the waves, would ebb and flow—an unpredictable rhythm we could learn to dance to together.

And just like that, with the sound of the surf crashing in a soothing cadence, we took a step forward, ready to embrace the unknown, hand in hand, our hearts open to whatever adventures awaited us on the horizon.

Chapter 23: Tides of Emotion

The crisp autumn air carries a slight chill as I step out onto the bustling streets of New Orleans, the sun casting a golden hue over the wrought-iron balconies and the vibrant murals that decorate the alleys. Each breath is infused with the scent of gumbo simmering in nearby kitchens and the sweet tang of beignets dusted with powdered sugar, the kind that whispers secrets of the city into your ear. I wrap my scarf tighter, feeling the weight of the fabric against my skin, as if it could cocoon me from the frigid bite of uncertainty that looms over my heart.

As I stroll past Jackson Square, the lively chatter of tourists fills the air, blending harmoniously with the distant strum of a street performer's guitar. I allow myself a fleeting smile, absorbing the sounds and sights, yet the joy feels muted, overshadowed by the absence of Aiden. We once laughed here, sharing spontaneous moments that stitched us together in the fabric of this city. I miss the way he would pull me into the rhythm of the music, his laughter echoing against the historic buildings as we danced like nobody was watching. Now, the vibrant energy feels almost mocking, a reminder of what we had and what hangs in limbo.

I find my way to Café du Monde, the iconic green-and-white striped awning a beacon calling me home. The line snakes out the door, but I don't mind; I let myself sink into the collective anticipation, breathing in the rich aroma of coffee mingling with the sweetness of frying dough. Each step forward brings me closer to the counter where I can order my usual—an iced café au lait, a plate of warm beignets waiting to be devoured. As I stand there, I pull out my notebook, the familiar pages feeling like an old friend beneath my fingers. It's the sanctuary where I pour my thoughts, weaving stories that keep the essence of Aiden alive even in his absence.

With each line I write, I see fragments of our memories flickering like fireflies. I can't help but scribble about that rain-soaked evening when we found ourselves huddled under an umbrella, his shoulder brushing against mine as we shared our dreams and fears. The words flow as I explore the vast ocean of emotion within me, my pen dancing across the page, capturing not just the laughter, but the profound longing that gnaws at my insides like an uninvited guest. Yet, with every stroke, I realize I'm merely skimming the surface; the depths of my feelings are an uncharted territory that both excites and terrifies me.

Lost in this reverie, I suddenly sense a shift in the air. A familiar voice cuts through the ambient noise like a warm breeze breaking through the autumn chill. I look up, heart racing, and there he is—Aiden, framed against the backdrop of the café, his tousled hair glinting in the sunlight. Time seems to still as I drink in his presence, the way his lips curl into a hesitant smile that ignites a flicker of hope within me. My heart hammers against my ribcage, a mix of joy and apprehension swirling in my chest. What do I say? How do I bridge the chasm that has opened between us?

He takes a tentative step closer, his eyes searching mine as if he's trying to decipher a language only we understand. The air is thick with unspoken words, the kind that could either heal or shatter us further. I close my notebook, the pen slipping from my fingers as I rise, caught in a moment that feels both achingly familiar and utterly new. I want to reach out, to pull him into a hug that would melt away the distance, but the fear of rejection holds me back like a vice.

"Aiden," I manage, my voice a soft whisper, laced with uncertainty. He looks at me as if he's seen a ghost, or perhaps an angel, caught between disbelief and yearning. "I didn't expect to see you here."

"I—" he starts, faltering slightly, as though the weight of the world rests upon his shoulders. The vulnerability in his voice sends a shiver down my spine. "I came to find you. I miss this place... us."

His words hang in the air, filled with unbridled potential, like the first brush of twilight painting the sky in shades of lavender and gold. My heart swells at his admission, yet it's tinged with caution, the past hovering like a specter between us. I search his face for signs of the man I fell for, and there he is—somewhere beneath the layers of uncertainty and fear.

"I've been writing," I say, eager to bridge the gap, to share my world with him. "Trying to make sense of everything." I gesture to the notebook on the table, where pages flutter like wings in the breeze, eager to take flight.

He looks down, his brow furrowing as he flips through the pages, absorbing the essence of my thoughts, my struggles. "You've been busy," he murmurs, his voice thick with emotion. "I never wanted to push you away. I just... didn't know how to handle what we were becoming."

The honesty in his words seeps into the cracks of my heart, a soothing balm for the wounds we both carry. "We were both scared," I reply, the truth spilling out, raw and unfiltered. "But I want to understand. I want to know where we stand." The moment stretches, charged with possibility, and I take a step closer, emboldened by the flicker of hope that ignites between us.

The city hums around us, alive with stories waiting to be told, and in this moment, I realize that perhaps we are not as lost as I thought. Maybe, just maybe, the tides of emotion that have swept us apart can also bring us back together, carrying us toward a new horizon.

The sunlight drapes itself over the city like a comforting blanket, warm yet fleeting, a reminder that the days are growing shorter, mirroring the emotional distance I've felt since Aiden walked back into my life. The café buzzes with life, yet I can't help but feel as if we're enveloped in our own cocoon, a world separate from the laughter and chatter surrounding us. Our conversation picks up the pace, words tumbling out like hesitant dancers, some graceful and others tripping over the awkwardness that lingers.

"I'm really sorry," he says suddenly, his voice low, as if the weight of his apology demands that we keep our voices hushed. "For everything. For not reaching out sooner. I thought giving you space was what you needed, but I see now how much I misjudged things."

The sincerity in his eyes warms the chill that had settled in my heart. "Aiden, we both needed to figure things out," I assure him, but my words feel flimsy against the wall of hurt built between us. "We were caught in a storm of emotions, and I—"

"No," he interrupts gently, a soft determination in his gaze. "I want you to know that I'm here now, and I want to work through this. Together."

The sincerity in his words rekindles that flicker of hope within me, the kind that threatens to burn brightly if only we nurture it. My heart races with the possibility of rebuilding what we had, even if it means delving into the murky waters of our fears. The sunlight shifts as the breeze plays with the leaves, causing shadows to dance across our table, mimicking the uncertainty we're trying to navigate.

"Then let's talk," I propose, my voice steadying as I gather my thoughts. "What are you afraid of? I know I am."

He takes a deep breath, his expression contemplative as he gazes past me, into a distance only he can see. "I'm scared of losing you. The connection we had felt so real, but then everything spiraled. I thought maybe distance would make it easier, but it just made me realize how much I need you."

His admission hangs in the air, palpable and raw, drawing me closer to him. "I feel the same," I admit, my heart thundering. "Every day without you felt like a page left blank in a book I wanted to fill with our story. I've been writing, trying to piece together how I feel, but it's not the same without you."

Aiden's eyes soften as he leans in, the intimacy of the moment enveloping us like a warm embrace. "What have you written?"

I hesitate for a heartbeat, the vulnerability creeping in, but then I realize that this is exactly what we need. "It's a mess, really. Just scattered thoughts and bits of poetry about how the world feels incomplete when you're not around. Like a song missing its melody."

He smiles, the corners of his lips lifting in a way that ignites a spark within me. "I'd love to hear it."

I take a breath, my heart racing, and I begin to share fragments of my writing, the words tumbling out in a rhythm that feels both familiar and foreign. I recount moments from our past—the rain-soaked afternoons, our laughter echoing down the streets, the quiet moments when we simply existed together in the same space. Each recollection dances in the air, illuminating the connection we share.

With every word, I watch his expression shift, the laughter flickering in his eyes giving way to something deeper, more profound. He nods, absorbing my words like a sponge, and I can see that he's moved by the feelings I've poured onto the page. "You have a way of capturing emotions," he says, his voice thick with admiration. "It's like you breathe life into them."

"Thank you," I murmur, feeling the warmth spread through me. "But it's easier to write about emotions than to actually confront them."

"Maybe it's time we do both," Aiden suggests, the intensity in his gaze anchoring me. "We can't keep dancing around what we feel. If we want this to work, we need to lay everything out on the table."

His words resonate deeply within me, like the sweet notes of a jazz saxophone cutting through the air. It's time to stop avoiding the hard conversations that linger like shadows in the corners of our minds. "Okay," I reply, my voice steady, emboldened by his willingness to dive deeper. "What scares you the most?"

He pauses, his brow furrowing in thought, and then he leans back, crossing his arms as he weighs his response. "It's not just losing you," he finally admits. "It's the fear of never being enough. What if I can't be the person you need?"

His vulnerability takes my breath away, but it also ignites a fire within me. "Aiden, you're more than enough. You make me feel alive. It's not about being perfect; it's about being real."

His eyes search mine, and I can see the flicker of hope returning, slowly replacing the doubt. "I want that," he says softly. "I want to be real with you."

"Then let's be honest," I urge. "What do we want from each other?"

The question hangs between us, heavy with possibility, and as he opens his mouth to respond, I feel the world around us fade, the café and the city dissolving into a blur. It's just us, caught in this moment, our hearts beating in synchrony, our souls intertwining like vines reaching for sunlight.

"I want to explore this with you," he says finally, his voice steady. "I want to know your dreams, your fears, everything that makes you, you. I want to be a part of your life again."

A flood of warmth washes over me, and in that instant, I know we are ready to navigate the turbulent waters ahead, hand in hand. There's a long road before us, filled with uncertainties and challenges, but with Aiden by my side, I can finally see the possibility of something beautiful emerging from the chaos.

The world outside continues to whirl around us, but inside, a quiet calm envelops our hearts, a reassurance that whatever lies ahead, we are willing to face it together. As the sun begins to set, casting hues of amber and rose across the sky, I realize that this moment is just the beginning of our next chapter, a chance to write a new story filled with hope and endless possibilities.

The air thickens with the promise of change as Aiden and I step outside the café, leaving behind the comforting embrace of familiarity. The sunset bathes the streets of New Orleans in a rich tapestry of oranges and purples, casting a warm glow that dances off the cobblestones. It feels as if the city is holding its breath, waiting for us to make our next move.

We walk side by side, our footsteps echoing against the historic buildings that line the street, each one holding secrets and stories of its own. The hum of a nearby jazz band drifts through the air, mingling with the laughter of tourists and the scent of creole spices wafting from a nearby restaurant. It's intoxicating, and yet, beneath the surface, there's a current of tension that neither of us can ignore.

"I've missed this," Aiden says, breaking the silence, his voice barely above a whisper, but it cuts through the noise around us. "The city, but more importantly, you."

I glance up at him, the sincerity in his eyes sending a shiver down my spine. "I've missed you too. Every part of you—the laughter, the debates over the best po' boy, even the quiet moments when we didn't need words."

He smiles softly, a look of relief washing over his features. "Can we reclaim some of that? I don't want to rush anything, but I also don't want to tiptoe around what's between us."

"Neither do I," I reply, feeling the weight of his words settle comfortably in the pit of my stomach. "Let's take it one day at a time, but with intention. I want to build something real, something strong."

As we walk, I can't help but notice the vibrant street art that colors the alleyways we pass. Each mural tells a story, splashes of paint capturing the essence of life in the city—joy, sorrow, love, loss. It's a perfect metaphor for our relationship, one I wish to explore further. "You know," I say, gesturing to a particularly striking mural of a woman's face, vibrant and expressive, "this reminds me of us. We have layers, and sometimes those layers are messy, but they're beautiful in their own way."

He stops to look at the mural, nodding thoughtfully. "I see what you mean. It's like we're all works in progress, aren't we? Trying to paint our own stories despite the chaos."

The conversation flows as effortlessly as the river that winds through the city, and I can feel the tension begin to dissipate, replaced by a sense of camaraderie. We find ourselves meandering toward the riverfront, where the Mississippi glistens under the fading light, its surface sparkling like diamonds scattered upon a deep blue velvet cloth. The sound of the water lapping against the shore acts as a soothing backdrop to our deepening connection.

Sitting on a bench overlooking the river, I can't help but feel a sense of peace wash over me. The gentle breeze carries with it the echoes of laughter from nearby riverboat cruises and the distant notes of a jazz trumpet, blending seamlessly into the atmosphere. "This place feels like home," I say, leaning back against the cool wood of the bench.

Aiden glances over, his eyes softening. "Home is a feeling more than a place, don't you think? It's the people we share it with."

"Exactly," I reply, feeling the truth of his words resonate within me. "I want us to create a home together, wherever that may be."

He turns to me, the earnestness in his gaze making my heart flutter. "Then let's start right here. We can explore together, find the nooks and crannies of this city that still hold secrets for us."

I nod, enthusiasm bubbling inside me. "What about visiting the French Market tomorrow? It's a treasure trove of everything New Orleans—art, food, culture. We can pick up fresh ingredients and cook together."

His smile is infectious, a beam of light breaking through the shadows that had lingered between us for far too long. "I'd love that. Cooking is an adventure in itself. And who knows what else we'll stumble upon?"

As the sun sinks lower, the sky transforms into a riot of colors, hues blending in a final dance of day. The warmth of Aiden's presence feels like an anchor, grounding me in a world that had once felt so uncertain. "Let's promise to be honest with each other," I suggest, the thought bubbling up from the depths of my heart. "If we want to make this work, we need to face our fears together."

He nods, the determination etched in his features. "Agreed. No more running. Let's be brave, for ourselves and for each other."

With that vow hanging in the air, I can almost hear the weight of unspoken words lifting, replaced by the promise of new beginnings.

The following day, the sun rises with a renewed energy, casting golden rays that filter through the palm trees lining the streets. The city awakens slowly, vibrant and alive, and as I make my way to the French Market, I can already feel the buzz of anticipation coursing through my veins. The market itself is a kaleidoscope of colors and sounds, with vendors calling out their wares, the scent of spices mingling with the sweetness of fresh fruits, and the laughter of families exploring together.

When I spot Aiden near a stall overflowing with fresh produce, my heart skips a beat. He's leaning over a basket of bright red tomatoes, the sunlight catching the warm tones of his hair. "These look perfect for a sauce," he says, looking up as I approach, a grin spreading across his face.

"They do! What about some basil? And maybe a little garlic?" I suggest, excitement bubbling in my chest.

The simple act of picking out ingredients feels like a dance, our movements fluid and synchronized, as if we've done this a thousand times before. As we wander through the market, our conversations flow like the river, filled with laughter and the gentle teasing that reminds me of the connection we're rebuilding. We sample local delicacies, our faces lighting up at the first taste of beignets dusted with powdered sugar, the soft pastries melting in our mouths like sweet memories.

At one stall, a vendor sells handmade jewelry, and I can't resist picking up a delicate silver bracelet adorned with tiny charms, each one representing a piece of New Orleans. "Look at this," I exclaim, holding it up for him to see. "It's like a charm for every moment we've shared."

Aiden takes it from me, examining the intricate details. "It's beautiful," he says, and I notice the way his fingers brush against mine, a spark igniting at the contact. "You should get it. It'll be a reminder of our adventures here."

I hesitate, suddenly aware of the emotions swirling around us like the colors of the market. "What if it's a reminder of everything we lost?"

"Then let it be a reminder of how far we've come," he replies, the conviction in his voice wrapping around me like a warm embrace.

After a moment of consideration, I nod, the decision solidifying in my mind. "You're right. Let's make new memories."

As we pay for the bracelet, I slip it onto my wrist, the weight of it feeling just right, like the beginning of a new chapter waiting to be explored. With bags filled with fresh ingredients in hand, we make our way back to my apartment, laughter and playful banter punctuating the air around us.

In the kitchen, the scent of garlic sizzling in olive oil envelops us, and as we chop and mix, our movements become a language of their own. The chopping sounds and the bubbling of sauce fill the space, blending harmoniously with our laughter. Cooking together becomes more than just a meal; it's a ritual of connection, the rhythm of our actions echoing the heartbeats that have grown stronger together.

"Just a pinch of salt," Aiden says, looking over his shoulder with a playful glint in his eye. "We want to season our dish with just enough flavor to make it memorable."

I chuckle, appreciating the metaphor he so effortlessly weaves into our cooking. "So, is this a reflection of us? Just the right amount of spice to keep things interesting?"

"Exactly," he responds, stirring the sauce with a flair that makes me smile. "And maybe a splash of unexpected sweetness."

As we set the table, the atmosphere shifts, the quiet intimacy between us enveloping the room. We share stories over dinner, laughter mingling with the rich aroma of our creation. I can see the flicker of hope in Aiden's eyes, mirroring the one blossoming in my heart, and in that moment, everything feels right.

With the sun setting outside, casting a warm glow through the windows, I realize that we are not merely cooking; we are crafting our own story, one filled with the kind of richness and depth that can only come from shared experiences. And as the evening unfolds, I can't shake the feeling that this is just the beginning of a beautiful tapestry, woven with threads of laughter, honesty, and love, ready to be embraced in all its imperfections.

Chapter 24: Revelations

The sun hung low in the sky, a molten orb that surrendered its light to the embracing arms of dusk. Hues of pink and orange danced across the canvas of the heavens, transforming the ordinary into the extraordinary. The waves, restless and rhythmic, lapped at the shore, each crest and trough a heartbeat in the symphony of nature that surrounded us. I stood at the water's edge, feeling the cool surf kiss my ankles, my heart pounding in time with the cadence of the tide. Tonight, the ocean felt alive, charged with an energy that mirrored the tumultuous storm brewing within me.

Aiden stood beside me, his silhouette stark against the fading light. He was a constant in my chaotic life, an anchor in the churning waters of my emotions. I turned to him, taking in the gentle curve of his jaw, the way his hair caught the evening breeze, tousling about in careless abandon. A deep breath filled my lungs as I summoned the courage to confront the thoughts that had haunted me since Sarah's arrival.

With the sound of the waves crashing behind us, I felt the weight of unspoken words pressing against my chest, begging for release. "I can't keep pretending everything is fine," I said, my voice barely above a whisper, the fear of breaking the fragile peace between us palpable in the salt-kissed air. "Since Sarah came into our lives, it's like I'm living in a shadow. I feel... inadequate."

His brow furrowed slightly, and I could see the wheels turning in his mind as he processed my confession. "You think she's better than you?" he asked, his tone earnest and searching, as if he were trying to unravel the layers of my insecurity.

"It's not about that," I replied, wrapping my arms around myself as though to shield my vulnerability from the cool breeze. "It's about how she fits in with everyone. She seems so effortless, so... perfect. Meanwhile, I feel like I'm just floundering."

Aiden turned to face me fully, the warmth of his gaze piercing through the cool evening air. "You're not floundering," he said, the conviction in his voice grounding me. "You've always been strong. You've been the one holding everything together while I've been lost in my own head."

His words hung in the air, a tangible truth that I hadn't fully grasped until that moment. The ocean behind us swelled and receded, mirroring the ebb and flow of my emotions. I had always been the one to put on a brave face, to act as the sturdy vessel for our little family, but now it felt as if the weight of the world was resting squarely on my shoulders, and I was afraid I would sink beneath it.

"I don't know how to navigate this," I admitted, the vulnerability flooding my voice, mixing with the salty sea breeze. "I want to be there for you, but with her around, I feel like I'm not enough. Like I can't compete with the memories you both share."

Aiden's expression softened, a flicker of understanding crossing his features. He stepped closer, the space between us shrinking until I could feel the warmth radiating from his body. "You don't have to compete with anyone, least of all Sarah. What we have is something different, something real."

His words wrapped around me like a comforting blanket, but the tension that had been building in my chest refused to dissipate. The fear that had taken root in my heart gnawed at me, urging me to lay bare not just my insecurities but the raw truth of my feelings for him.

"I care about you, Aiden," I said, each word a deliberate step deeper into the vulnerable territory I had been avoiding. "More than I thought was possible. But every time I see you two together, it feels like I'm watching a scene unfold that I'm not a part of, and it terrifies me."

Aiden sighed, running a hand through his hair as the wind tousled the strands. "You have to know that my feelings for you are stronger than any nostalgia I might have for the past. With you, everything feels alive again. You make me want to be better, to push past my demons."

A flicker of hope ignited within me, casting aside the shadows that had loomed so heavily. "But what about the guilt?" I pressed, the unease still lingering like a ghost. "You still have feelings for her."

He closed the distance between us, his presence a steadying force against the uncertainty swirling in my mind. "I do, but it's complicated. She's a chapter of my life, but you... you're my story. You're the one I want to share my future with."

His confession unfurled before me like the vibrant colors of the sunset above, each word a brushstroke adding depth to the canvas of our shared experiences. In that moment, I realized that the bond we had forged in the quiet spaces between laughter and tears was worth fighting for.

As the last rays of sun dipped below the horizon, a deeper understanding dawned between us. The world around us faded into shadows, but the light that flickered between our hearts illuminated the path forward. I could feel the warmth of his gaze holding mine, the pull of something deeper than mere attraction anchoring us in place.

And there, in the soft embrace of twilight, with the ocean whispering secrets of the past and future alike, I let go of the trepidation that had held me captive for too long. Instead, I embraced the possibility of trust, of love renewed amidst the swirling chaos of our lives. The air was electric, charged with the promise of what lay ahead, and I was ready to step into the unknown, hand in hand with the man who had captured my heart.

The soft whispers of the ocean became a soothing balm for my frayed nerves, the rhythmic lull of the waves merging with the quiet heartbeat of the moment we shared. I could still feel the warmth of Aiden's gaze enveloping me, a sanctuary amidst the chaos of my thoughts. The tension in my chest began to dissolve, replaced by an unguarded hope that perhaps the foundation of our relationship was solid enough to weather this storm. As I searched his eyes, the depths of his sincerity washed over me, urging me to embrace this fragile connection that had started to grow once more.

"Do you really mean it?" I asked, the vulnerability of my question tinged with a mixture of hope and trepidation. "You want to share your future with me?" The moon began its ascent, casting a silvery light over the beach, illuminating our entwined paths in this tangled narrative we were writing together.

Aiden nodded, the corners of his mouth lifting in that lopsided grin that had always made my heart race. "Every moment I spend with you feels like a glimpse into what could be. You're more than just a chapter in my life; you're the whole book. The one I want to write every day, filled with laughter, adventure, and yes, even the occasional conflict."

His admission swelled within me, a warmth spreading through my body as the cool evening breeze brushed against my skin. It was like a flicker of a flame reigniting, the embers of our connection glowing brighter amidst the ashes of doubt.

"But what about the guilt?" I asked again, my voice softer this time, still haunted by the shadows of uncertainty. "You can't just erase that."

"It's not about erasing it; it's about learning to live with it," he replied, his tone earnest, like he was sharing a secret he had uncovered. "Sarah was a part of my past, yes, but she's not my future. I can't ignore what we had, but it doesn't overshadow what we have now. That's what you need to understand."

I studied him, his earnestness cutting through the fog of my insecurities. The gentle waves rolled in rhythm with my racing heart, each crash a reminder of the strength I had within me. Maybe, just maybe, we could find a way to navigate this together. The sound of our shared laughter mingled with the ocean breeze, lightening the heavy air around us.

"Okay," I breathed, a tentative smile breaking across my face. "Let's figure this out together. I want to build something new with you, something we can both be proud of."

Aiden reached for my hand, our fingers intertwining in a gesture that felt both comforting and electrifying. The world around us faded, the beach transforming into our own private sanctuary, untouched by the outside world. I could feel the warmth of his skin against mine, a gentle reminder of the connection we were rebuilding, layer by layer.

As we began to walk along the shore, the sand soft and cool beneath our feet, the tide ebbed and flowed like the emotions swelling within me. Each step felt like a commitment to facing whatever lay ahead together. We shared stories, laughter drifting on the evening breeze as the moon hung like a sentinel overhead, casting its silver glow upon us. Aiden spoke of dreams, some ambitious and others whimsically mundane. He talked of travels to far-off lands, the kind where every sunset promised a new adventure, while I found myself sharing snippets of my childhood—days spent chasing fireflies in the backyard, laughing with friends under the summer sky, and the warmth of my mother's embrace.

In those moments, I saw the building blocks of our future taking shape, a mosaic pieced together with memories both new and old. The beach transformed into a canvas of possibilities, the darkening sky our backdrop as the stars began to flicker into existence above us.

"Do you ever think about what our life would look like in a year?" Aiden asked, pausing to let the waves rush around our feet. The question hung in the air like the lingering taste of salt on my lips, inviting exploration.

"Honestly? I never really let myself imagine it before," I admitted, my heart fluttering at the thought. "But now, it feels...

exhilarating to think about. I can picture us waking up in a little cottage by the sea, the sun streaming in through the windows. Maybe there'd be a garden filled with wildflowers, and we'd spend lazy afternoons just enjoying the simplicity of it all."

Aiden chuckled, a rich sound that made me smile even wider. "I can see you getting lost in that garden, talking to the flowers like they're your best friends."

"Hey, I would not talk to flowers," I protested, laughing. "They might not talk back, but they'd definitely listen."

"Exactly! You'd have an entire conversation about their day and what they're planning for tomorrow," he teased, his eyes sparkling in the moonlight.

The playful banter flowed easily between us, a delicious mixture of warmth and laughter that stitched the seams of our hearts back together. As the moonlight bathed us in its ethereal glow, I realized that these moments were building the foundation of a life that we could both cherish, a tapestry woven from laughter, trust, and the willingness to navigate the unknown together.

With every shared secret, every burst of laughter, I felt the walls I had built around my heart begin to crumble, exposing the raw, vibrant core of my feelings for Aiden. The stars above, twinkling like distant dreams, seemed to echo the silent promises we were forging in the soft sand beneath our feet. The worries that had once consumed me began to fade into the backdrop of our lives, replaced by an intoxicating hope that shimmered in the night air.

As we strolled along the beach, I felt a sense of belonging that I hadn't known in so long—a feeling that perhaps I was not merely a spectator in my own life but an integral part of this unfolding narrative. A story filled with laughter, adventures, and the occasional tangle of emotions that made the journey worthwhile. With Aiden by my side, I was ready to dive headfirst into whatever awaited us, to embrace the chaos and beauty of our intertwined destinies. The night stretched on, an endless expanse of possibility, and for the first time in what felt like ages, I felt truly alive.

The moon rose higher, spilling its silver light onto the shoreline, illuminating the grains of sand that sparkled like tiny jewels beneath our feet. With every step we took, the laughter and warmth we shared washed away the shadows of doubt that had lingered in the corners of my heart. The air was rich with the scent of salt and freedom, a heady mix that urged me to let go of the past and embrace the present.

As we meandered along the water's edge, the sound of the ocean became a gentle companion, whispering secrets that only we could understand. I glanced at Aiden, his profile highlighted against the moonlit backdrop, and I felt a surge of affection so powerful it almost took my breath away. There was a strength in his presence, a steadiness that anchored me in this moment, even as the tides of uncertainty ebbed and flowed around us.

"I used to think love was simple," I said, the words slipping from my lips as we walked. "You love someone, they love you back, and everything falls into place. But this... it's messy and complicated, like trying to fit a square peg into a round hole."

Aiden chuckled softly, the sound warm and inviting. "Love has a funny way of keeping us on our toes. Just when you think you've figured it out, it throws you a curveball. But I think the messiness is what makes it beautiful. It's in those tangled moments that we discover who we really are."

I nodded, the truth of his words resonating deep within me. There was something profound about our struggles, a shared experience that bonded us in ways I had never imagined. With each revelation, each flicker of vulnerability, we were weaving a tapestry rich with texture—one that celebrated not only our flaws but also our strengths.

The beach began to feel like a sacred space, a realm where only we existed, the world beyond fading into a blur. The stars above twinkled like tiny beacons of hope, and for the first time, I allowed myself to dream about a future—our future—unencumbered by fear or jealousy.

"Do you remember the first time we came here?" I asked, a smile breaking across my face as memories danced in my mind. "You were trying to impress me by skipping stones, and you ended up splashing half your drink all over yourself instead."

"Oh, please," he grinned, shaking his head. "That was all part of my master plan to make you laugh. And it worked, didn't it?"

"It did. But only because you looked so utterly ridiculous." I laughed, the sound ringing out into the stillness, a melody of shared history that anchored us to this very moment.

"Maybe I should make a habit of embarrassing myself to keep that laughter coming," Aiden said, his voice low and teasing. "A good laugh is priceless, especially when you have such a beautiful audience."

We continued to walk, the water brushing against our ankles, each wave lapping like a playful child tugging at our feet. The warmth of his hand in mine was a tangible reminder of how far we had come and the journey that still lay ahead. The path was not without its hurdles, but I felt a flicker of determination igniting within me. We were both capable of growing and changing, learning from the past instead of allowing it to define us.

"Do you think we can really make this work?" I asked, the weight of my question settling heavily in the air between us. "With everything that's happened, the past, the complications, the people in our lives... can we find a way to build something lasting?"

Aiden stopped walking and turned to face me, his expression earnest and unwavering. "I believe we can," he said, his voice steady. "It won't always be easy, and there will be days when we stumble.

But I know what I feel for you. It's not just a fleeting moment; it's something deeper. I'm committed to figuring this out with you, no matter what."

My heart swelled at his words, a rush of emotion coursing through me. In that moment, I understood that love was not simply about the idyllic moments or the fairy-tale endings; it was about the willingness to face the storms together, to forge a connection that could withstand the tests of time.

"Then let's promise to always communicate," I suggested, the idea forming as I spoke. "No matter how uncomfortable it may feel. I don't want us to end up like... well, like Sarah and you. I want us to be open, honest, and brave."

"Agreed," Aiden replied, his grip on my hand tightening slightly. "From now on, no more holding back. We tackle everything together, come what may."

As if to seal our promise, the wind picked up, sending a playful gust through the air, tugging at my hair like a mischievous child. I laughed, reveling in the moment, in the beauty of the connection we were fostering.

With the horizon darkening, we decided to settle on the sand, our bodies sinking into its warmth. The world felt infinite as we sat side by side, the waves serenading us with their ceaseless lullaby. In that intimate silence, our thoughts drifted, mingling with the sound of the ocean.

"Aiden," I said softly, breaking the stillness. "What are you most afraid of?"

He turned to me, surprise flickering across his face before giving way to contemplation. "I'm afraid of losing you. That somehow I'll mess this up and you'll walk away. I don't know how I would cope without you."

The sincerity in his voice wrapped around my heart like a warm embrace, and I felt a swell of compassion for him. "You won't lose me," I assured him, my gaze steady. "But we have to promise to be open, to address our fears instead of letting them fester."

He nodded, his eyes reflecting the shimmering light of the moon, a promise etched into the very fabric of the night.

As we sat in the quiet, the stars beginning to twinkle like distant echoes of dreams yet to be realized, I felt a shift within myself. The weight of my past began to lift, replaced by a buoyancy that surged with every shared glance and unspoken promise. The future was no longer a daunting abyss but a vast expanse filled with potential—a journey we were embarking on together, hand in hand.

We shared stories long into the night, the kind that deepened our bond and painted vivid pictures of the lives we envisioned. Laughter intermingled with dreams, creating a melody that echoed across the ocean, a promise to ourselves and each other that we were ready to embrace whatever came next.

In the end, it was more than just words exchanged on a moonlit beach. It was the birth of something beautiful, a tapestry woven from the threads of hope, love, and resilience. Together, we were ready to face the waves, not as two separate entities but as one, carving our own path through the vast, unpredictable ocean of life.

Chapter 25: A New Beginning

The sun hung low in the sky, casting a golden hue over the quiet town of Ocean Springs, Mississippi, where the salty breeze intertwined with the scent of magnolia blossoms. I stood barefoot in the cool sand, feeling the grains shift beneath my toes like the gentle pulse of the earth. This place, with its charming southern architecture and friendly locals, had been my refuge, a cradle of memories woven tightly with laughter and tears. Just days ago, the thought of facing my past felt like dragging an anchor through these waters, but now, with a heart stitched together by hope, I was ready to embrace what lay ahead.

As I watched the waves roll in, rhythmically kissing the shore, I spotted Amelia, my best friend since childhood, bounding toward me with an infectious grin plastered across her sun-kissed face. Her laughter, a melody that danced in the air, was a balm to my weary soul. We had shared countless sunsets, whispered secrets under the stars, and navigated the labyrinth of teenage angst together. Yet, life had taken us down different paths, diverging like the branches of the magnolia tree under which we'd spent countless afternoons.

"Hey! You're actually early for once," she teased, plopping down beside me, her vibrant sundress fluttering like a flag in the warm breeze. Her hair, a wild cascade of curls, framed her face as she tilted her head, her green eyes sparkling with mischief. "Thought I'd have to send a search party."

"Just wanted to soak in the peace before the chaos of the weekend," I replied, the corners of my mouth lifting involuntarily. It felt good to reconnect, to be in the presence of someone who had witnessed my ups and downs, someone who understood the weight I carried.

Amelia turned her gaze to the horizon, where the sun dipped lower, igniting the sky with splashes of pink and orange. "So, what's the plan? You can't keep dodging the town's gossip forever. They'll come for you like seagulls to a fry."

"Trust me, I know," I sighed, the weight of my recent choices heavy on my heart. "But I'm trying to take things slow. Rebuilding takes time."

"Rebuilding, huh? Like a relationship?" She nudged my shoulder playfully, her voice filled with a mix of curiosity and concern. I hesitated, the thoughts swirling in my mind like leaves caught in a gust of wind. I was still trying to piece together the fragments of my relationship with Jonah, the man who had once felt like home and yet had left me feeling more lost than ever.

"It's complicated," I admitted, staring out at the waves. "We've had our share of storms, but I believe we can weather this one, too."

"Good. You deserve happiness, you know?" Her voice softened, the teasing replaced with genuine warmth. "I've seen how much you both care, even when the world feels heavy. Just... don't forget to enjoy the little things. Life is too short for anything less."

A gentle silence enveloped us as we let the tranquility of the moment wash over us. The sound of the waves and the distant laughter of children playing on the beach created a soothing symphony that pulled at my heartstrings. Memories flooded my mind—Jonah and I, sprawled on this very beach, stealing kisses under the cloak of twilight, sharing our dreams as the stars flickered overhead like tiny fireflies. We had been two souls dancing to the same rhythm, yet somehow, life's dissonance had led us astray.

As the sun dipped below the horizon, painting the sky in the deep hues of dusk, Amelia stood and extended her hand to me, a mischievous grin returning. "Come on, let's grab some ice cream at that little shop down the street. I'm craving a scoop of that lavender honey flavor. Plus, you need to show your face to the locals. They miss you, you know?"

I chuckled, accepting her hand and allowing her to pull me up. "Alright, but you're treating! My budget's a little tight until I find my footing again."

"Deal!" she laughed, her carefree spirit lighting up the dimming day. We walked toward the town, the glow of the streetlamps casting warm circles of light that flickered like stars scattered across the pavement.

Ocean Springs buzzed with life—artists showcasing their works in vibrant galleries, families enjoying dinner at sidewalk cafes, and the rhythmic strumming of guitars echoing from the nearby park. It felt as if the town had been waiting for me to return, to rediscover its heart, and in that moment, a flicker of excitement ignited within me.

As we approached the quaint ice cream shop, its neon sign flickering with promise, I caught a glimpse of Jonah standing outside, a tall figure framed against the backdrop of the warm light. My heart raced, an involuntary reaction that betrayed the calm facade I tried to maintain. He looked different—older, perhaps, but the same kindness lingered in his blue eyes, the kind that had once melted my worries away.

"Is that...?" Amelia whispered, her voice barely a breath.

"Yeah," I replied, my pulse quickening. We stopped, uncertainty weaving itself into the air around us. It was as if the universe had conspired to place us in the same path again, the threads of our lives intertwining in a way that felt both terrifying and exhilarating.

The moment hung between us, a delicate balance of fear and hope, as I took a step forward, drawn to him as if by an invisible force. The noise of the town faded into a distant hum, and for a fleeting second, it felt like we were the only two souls in existence, suspended in a space where time had forgotten to move.

"Hey," Jonah said, his voice a familiar melody that tugged at my heartstrings. "I didn't expect to see you here." The warmth in his tone wrapped around me like a comforting embrace, igniting the embers of feelings I thought I had buried deep.

"Neither did I," I managed, my voice barely above a whisper. Here, standing before him, I felt the familiar tug of the past, the gentle reminder of laughter and love interlaced with the pain of what we had lost. But perhaps, just perhaps, this could be the beginning of something beautiful.

The warmth of Jonah's presence enveloped me like the comforting embrace of a familiar blanket, and I was caught between nostalgia and the uncertainty of the future. He looked at me with an expression that flickered between surprise and something deeper, a glance that seemed to linger on unspoken memories. It was surreal, standing here, just a breath away from the man who had once been the centerpiece of my world, yet felt like a ghost of my past.

"Are you, uh, here for the ice cream?" he asked, his hands shoved deep into the pockets of his jeans, as if he were grounding himself against the tide of emotions that surged between us. A fleeting smile played on his lips, the corners twitching upward as though he were wrestling with an internal struggle.

"Actually, I am," I replied, my heart doing an ungraceful tap dance against my ribcage. "Amelia's dragging me here for her lavender honey fix."

His laughter came like a refreshing wave, light and infectious. "Of course she is. That flavor is her guilty pleasure. I swear she's addicted to it." He gestured toward the entrance, the soft glow of the shop's lights casting a warm ambiance that felt inviting yet charged with tension.

"Do you want to join us?" Amelia interjected, her enthusiasm punctuating the air like the sound of a clanging bell. "I mean, it's not every day you run into old flames. We could turn this into an impromptu reunion."

The word "reunion" hung in the air like a delicate ornament, and I held my breath, waiting for Jonah's response. The sunlight dipped lower, and a few stars began to peek out from the velvet sky, twinkling with potential and promise.

"Sure," Jonah said finally, his voice steady, but I could sense a slight tremor beneath the surface. "Why not? I could use a scoop myself."

As we entered the shop, the sweet scent of waffle cones and freshly churned ice cream enveloped us, and I couldn't help but smile at the familiar sights. The walls were painted a cheerful mint green, adorned with quirky artwork that screamed small-town charm. My heart ached with the memories of countless visits here with Jonah, each scoop of ice cream a scoop of shared laughter, stolen kisses, and whispered dreams.

Amelia bounded to the counter, animatedly discussing flavors with the young girl scooping ice cream, while Jonah and I hung back, caught in the magnetic pull of our shared history. I could feel the warmth radiating from him, a soft glow that illuminated the corners of my heart.

"So, how have you been?" Jonah asked, breaking the silence that wrapped around us like a cozy shawl. His gaze was steady, yet his vulnerability was palpable.

"Busy," I replied, struggling to keep the mood light, as if the mere mention of my challenges could dissolve the tension between us. "Work has kept me on my toes, and I've been figuring out what comes next for me."

"Same here," he said, running a hand through his hair, a gesture that was achingly familiar. "It's been a wild ride. Sometimes I wonder if I'm just treading water, you know? Like I'm stuck in a loop, waiting for a sign."

A wave of empathy washed over me, and I realized that beneath the surface, we were both navigating the murky waters of uncertainty, a place we had once shared so intimately. "Maybe this is our sign," I offered, attempting to coax a flicker of hope into the conversation. "A chance to reconnect and figure things out together."

He paused, his expression shifting into something softer, more contemplative. "I'd like that," he finally admitted, his voice barely above a whisper, but it resonated within me, a quiet promise echoing through the air.

Amelia returned, her arms laden with colorful cups of ice cream. "Here we go! Lavender honey for me, vanilla bean for you, and..." she held up a scoop of chocolate fudge, looking at Jonah expectantly. "You can't go wrong with classic chocolate, right?"

"I'll take it," Jonah replied, a grin breaking free as he took the cup from her. The moment felt charged with possibility, and as we settled into a small table outside, laughter and chatter of passersby floated around us, painting a vibrant tapestry of life that felt both exhilarating and daunting.

With the sun now a distant memory, the night air settled around us, cradling the warmth of our conversation like a cherished secret. We took turns sharing stories—Amelia regaled us with tales from her job at the local bookstore, while Jonah shared his recent adventures in photography, showcasing the vibrant landscapes that lay just beyond the horizon of our town. Each shared laugh drew us closer, blurring the lines between past and present.

As I savored the sweet, floral notes of my lavender honey ice cream, I found myself glancing at Jonah, drinking in the way the streetlights danced in his eyes, the way his smile crinkled at the corners, each detail a reminder of everything I had once cherished. My heart swelled with a heady mixture of nostalgia and longing, and it struck me how easily we fell into our old rhythm, as if no time had passed at all.

"Remember that summer we spent at the lake?" Jonah asked, his voice a warm caress. "You were convinced you could teach me to kayak, and I nearly tipped us over a dozen times."

I chuckled, the memory unfurling like a flower in bloom. "You made it an adventure, that's for sure. I thought we were going to sink at one point!"

"Your scream still haunts me," he joked, laughter lighting up his features.

Amelia rolled her eyes, feigning exasperation. "You two should really write a memoir. The Adventures of the Clumsy Kayakers: A Tale of Love and Almost Drowning."

As the laughter ebbed, a comfortable silence settled among us, the kind that felt like a warm embrace, familiar yet charged with the potential for something new.

"Things have changed, haven't they?" Jonah said quietly, his tone shifting as he looked out toward the street, the passing cars casting shadows that danced in the light. "But I still believe in us, you know?"

Those words wrapped around my heart like a soft embrace. "I do too. We've both grown, and maybe we can learn to navigate this together."

His gaze met mine, and in that moment, the world around us faded into the background, leaving only the pulsing connection between us, a delicate thread woven with shared dreams and quiet hopes.

"I'd like to take things slow, figure it out, if you're willing," he said, vulnerability glistening in his blue eyes. "No pressure, just... one step at a time."

"Slow sounds perfect," I whispered, my heart racing with the knowledge that we were on the brink of something beautiful, something worth fighting for. The stars above seemed to shimmer in agreement, watching over us as we embarked on this new chapter, hand in hand, ready to embrace the uncertain future ahead.

The evening air was thick with the rich scent of blooming jasmine, and the stars shimmered like scattered diamonds above us as we lingered outside the ice cream shop. Jonah and I sat opposite each other, the small wooden table bearing witness to the unspoken words that danced between us. Amelia, finishing her lavender honey scoop with zeal, was oblivious to the moment's gravity. She recounted tales of our childhood mischief, her laughter a joyful balm that lightened the atmosphere.

With every shared story, I felt Jonah's presence pull me closer, not in the physical sense, but as if the very fabric of our connection was being rewoven with each memory we revisited. I watched him as he listened, his eyes bright with the playful light of youth, yet carrying a depth that spoke of experiences that had shaped him during our time apart. His fingers absentmindedly played with the edge of his cup, tracing patterns that mirrored the intricate paths of our own lives.

"Remember the Halloween when we dressed up as the dynamic duo?" he asked, a teasing grin playing on his lips.

"Oh, how could I forget?" I replied, the memory bursting forth like confetti in my mind. "You were the world's clumsiest superhero, complete with a cape that you nearly tripped over every five seconds. I thought for sure the villain would have a heart attack laughing at us."

His laughter rang out, rich and full, echoing through the night. "And you were the most convincing sidekick. I don't think I've ever seen someone manage to throw confetti and trip an entire street of kids while attempting to hand out candy."

Amelia chimed in, her eyes twinkling with mischief. "The Great Candy Catastrophe! I remember that! You two were the highlight of my night!"

We fell into a rhythm, words flowing freely, the barriers that had once felt insurmountable now crumbling into dust. With each shared laugh, I began to envision a future where the past didn't hold us hostage. Instead, it became the backdrop for a vibrant canvas of possibility.

As the night deepened, we decided to take a stroll along the beach. The moon hung low, a glowing orb casting a silvery path across the water, leading us toward a horizon filled with whispered promises and dreams yet to be written. The waves rolled gently to shore, their soft murmurs lapping at my feet, urging me forward, urging us all forward into the future.

Jonah walked beside me, a comfortable silence enveloping us, broken only by the sounds of nature weaving through the night air. I glanced sideways, stealing glances at him as he gazed out at the ocean. The moonlight danced across his features, highlighting the strength in his jawline, the softness in his eyes. It was easy to forget the pain of the past in moments like this, to lean into the magic of the present.

"Do you ever miss it?" he asked suddenly, his voice low, the weight of the question heavy between us.

"Miss what?" I replied, feigning ignorance as I drew a line in the sand with my toe, wanting to prolong this moment of suspended time.

"Us," he said, turning to meet my gaze, the vulnerability in his eyes a mirror to my own. "I know it's been a long time, but sometimes I think about the good times. The laughter, the plans... the dreams we shared."

The memories washed over me like the tide, each wave a reminder of the bond we had once shared. "I miss it too," I admitted softly, my heart racing at the admission. "But I also know that it's not just about what we had. We need to create something new, something that can stand on its own."

He nodded, understanding flaring in his gaze. "You're right. I think the best relationships evolve, like the seasons. They change, and sometimes they come back stronger."

As we continued to walk, our steps in sync, the conversation ebbed and flowed effortlessly, like the gentle rhythm of the ocean beside us. The beach stretched out in both directions, a canvas waiting for us to paint our story anew.

"I want to explore more with you," I said, a sudden spark igniting within me. "Remember those spontaneous beach picnics we used to have? Just a blanket, some snacks, and the sound of the waves?"

"Count me in," he replied, his eyes lighting up. "I'll bring the sandwiches if you bring the dessert. And we can set up a blanket right here, under the stars."

"Deal," I smiled, envisioning the carefree afternoons filled with laughter and stolen moments. "We can do late-night stargazing too. I've forgotten how beautiful the sky is without the city lights."

As the conversation flowed, I could sense the distance between us shrinking, our lives intertwining like the roots of a tree, reaching for sunlight and growth. Each day would be an opportunity to nurture our connection, to redefine what we had once lost and cultivate it into something richer.

Amelia, sensing the shift in our dynamic, joined us with her usual exuberance. "I vote we also schedule some game nights. I'm thinking board games and all the snacks. You two can relive your childhood competitiveness!"

"Oh, that could get dangerous," Jonah chuckled, shooting me a knowing glance. "I seem to remember a certain someone sulking when they lost at Monopoly."

I feigned indignation. "That was a strategic choice! You don't just give up the title of Monopoly Champion without a fight."

Jonah laughed, the sound vibrant against the night. "Alright, but fair warning: I've improved since then. I've been practicing my strategy on my cat."

Amelia shook her head, laughter bubbling up again. "Only you would take on a cat in a battle of wits."

With each shared joke and playful banter, we created an invisible thread that seemed to weave our hearts closer together. As the night stretched on, we made plans, each detail a promise to ourselves.

Eventually, we arrived at the pier, a sturdy wooden structure that jutted out over the water. The sound of the waves crashing below mixed with the distant laughter of families enjoying the cool night air. The sky above was a tapestry of stars, twinkling like a thousand little hopes. I leaned against the railing, gazing out at the endless expanse of water, feeling the cool breeze dance through my hair.

"Let's make a pact," Jonah said, his tone serious now as he leaned beside me. "No more running away. No more avoiding what we feel. We face everything together, no matter how hard it gets."

I turned to him, heart swelling with emotion. "I promise. We'll do this together. We'll take it slow and cherish every moment."

As we sealed our pact with a shared smile, the world around us faded, leaving only the two of us, our hearts entwined in a delicate dance of hope and renewal. With the weight of the past lifted and the future stretching out before us like an open road, I realized that love, with all its complexities, truly had the power to conquer all. And in this moment, with Jonah beside me, I believed in the magic of new beginnings.

Chapter 26: The Echoes of the Past

In the heart of a late summer afternoon, I stood at the kitchen counter, the sun spilling golden light through the window, illuminating motes of dust that danced in the air like tiny fairies caught in a moment of bliss. The scent of fresh basil mingled with the lingering aroma of roasted garlic from the night before, a comforting reminder of simple joys in a life that had become anything but simple. My fingers deftly tore into a ripe tomato, the juice spilling over my palm as I prepared a salad, while outside, the familiar sounds of children's laughter and cicadas filled the air, creating a soundtrack that felt both timeless and fleeting.

Aiden had promised to be home early that day, his presence a soothing balm for the tumult that had begun to brew in our relationship. We'd woven together a tapestry of moments—shared coffees at dawn, lazy afternoons on the porch, laughter echoing through our home as we bickered over the simplest of things. Yet, with the arrival of that letter, a dark cloud threatened to shadow our sun-soaked existence. The letter was an uninvited guest, one whose arrival I had sensed in the tightening of Aiden's jaw and the way his fingers brushed against the envelope, as if it were a live wire.

I set the knife down, my heart pounding with an urgency that felt foreign. My instincts, sharp as the edge of that knife, told me something pivotal was about to unfold. I watched him, his face a landscape of emotions that shifted like the weather, each crease of his brow and flicker of his eyes revealing a turmoil he had kept buried beneath layers of charm and resilience. I could feel the tension radiating off him, palpable and heavy, like humidity before a storm.

"What does it say?" I asked, my voice steadier than I felt.

He looked up, the sunlight catching in his dark hair, making it glint like polished wood. "It's from Sarah," he finally replied, his voice a low rumble, as if each word required a monumental effort to release. I hated the way my heart sank at the mere mention of her name, a name that echoed in the recesses of our shared history, resonating with memories neither of us could truly escape.

I wanted to rush to him, to pull the letter from his hands and tear it to shreds, to banish her from our lives as though that could somehow erase the remnants of their past. But I stayed rooted, a spectator to a drama unfolding with the slow, cruel precision of a train wreck. "You need to tell me what this means for us," I insisted, forcing my eyes to hold his.

He took a deep breath, the weight of the air thickening around us. "It's... complicated," he murmured, his gaze drifting back to the letter as if it held answers to questions he hadn't yet dared to ask himself. I could see the internal struggle etched across his features, the way his brow furrowed with a mixture of regret and longing, and I felt a surge of empathy, the kind that gnawed at my insides.

"Complicated how?" I pressed, unable to mask the frustration lacing my words. My heart raced, a wild thing trapped within my chest, desperate for clarity, for honesty. "She's part of your past, Aiden. You need to decide if you're going to let her affect our future."

The silence stretched between us, thickening with unspoken thoughts, as Aiden wrestled with the remnants of a history that was not his to ignore. I could almost see the gears turning in his mind, each click echoing with the unresolved feelings that lingered like shadows in our bright kitchen.

He finally met my gaze, determination flickering behind his eyes. "I want to be honest with you. I have feelings for her, but they're complicated. I thought I was over it, but... maybe I haven't been." His admission hit me like a punch to the gut. I felt raw, exposed, as if he had stripped away the comforting layers of our relationship and laid bare the truth beneath.

"Is that why you've been distant?" I asked, the sting of tears welling up as I searched his face for answers. "Because you're trying to sort out your feelings for her?"

He ran a hand through his hair, a gesture I had come to recognize as a sign of frustration. "I've been trying to figure out how to balance it all. You're everything to me, but Sarah... she was part of my life for so long. I don't want to hurt you." His voice dropped to a whisper, vulnerability spilling into the space between us like the fading sunlight.

I stepped closer, the air crackling with tension and the weight of unspoken words. "You can't keep her in your life and expect us to move forward. It doesn't work that way." My voice trembled, a mixture of anger and heartbreak curling like smoke in my throat. "You need to set boundaries. You need to close that chapter."

He nodded, determination rekindling in his gaze, a glimmer of hope that flickered like a candle in the dark. "You're right. I need to confront this, once and for all." The resolve in his voice sparked something within me, igniting a flicker of hope amidst the storm.

As he reached for my hand, I could feel the warmth of his skin, a reminder of everything we had built together. The kitchen, once a sanctuary filled with laughter and love, now felt like a battleground, but I clung to the possibility that we could emerge from this stronger. The road ahead was fraught with uncertainty, but in that moment, standing on the precipice of revelation, I chose to believe in us.

As Aiden's fingers brushed against mine, a flicker of warmth ignited in the air, battling the chill of uncertainty that had crept into our world. I could see the determination settling in his gaze, a resolve that held the potential to alter the trajectory of our relationship. Yet, just beneath the surface, doubt curled like smoke—fragile, yet persistent. A storm was brewing, one that had little to do with the clouds gathering on the horizon but rather with the tumult of emotions threatening to break apart the careful equilibrium we had forged.

We stood there, our fingers intertwined, a lifeline in the swirling chaos that threatened to consume us. The sunlight, now dipping low in the sky, painted everything in warm, honeyed hues, but I felt an icy knot in my stomach as Aiden continued to hold that letter, the embodiment of his past. The intensity of the moment magnified as I wrestled with my own thoughts, each pulse of my heart echoing with questions that had no easy answers. Would he truly be able to shut that door? Would he truly choose me?

"I need to go," he finally said, breaking the silence that had thickened around us. The urgency in his voice sent a shiver through me. "I need to talk to her. I can't keep pretending it doesn't matter. I owe it to both of us."

The words hung in the air like a bitter fruit, ripe for plucking but with the potential to rot from within. I felt the heat of anger rise within me, a tumultuous wave crashing against the shore of my patience. "You can't just waltz back into her life, Aiden. What if she tries to pull you back in? What if you end up getting swept away by whatever unresolved feelings you have?"

He took a step back, and the distance between us felt like an ocean. "I'm not doing this for her. I'm doing this for us." His words, meant to reassure, only fueled my anxiety. "I need to clarify things, to set the boundaries I should have set long ago."

The reality of his impending conversation with Sarah felt like a blade twisting in my gut. I wanted to scream, to shake him, to make him understand how fragile our connection felt at that moment. But I also recognized the wisdom in his approach. It was the only way to move forward, to clear the fog that had clouded our journey. My heart waged a silent war as I battled with the duality of my emotions—fear and hope, anger and love.

"Promise me you'll be careful," I said, my voice barely above a whisper, the tremor betraying the courage I was trying to muster. I squeezed his hand tighter, as if my grip could keep him from slipping away. "I can't lose you to the ghosts of your past."

He nodded, his expression softening as he tucked a loose strand of hair behind my ear, a tender gesture that ignited a flicker of warmth in the chill of uncertainty. "I promise," he said. "And when I come back, I want to talk about everything—about us. I want to know what you want, what you need."

The sincerity in his voice calmed the storm within me, if only slightly. "I need you to be all in," I replied, finding strength in my vulnerability. "No more half-measures, Aiden. I want us to be real, to be solid."

With one last squeeze of my hand, he released me, his footsteps echoing down the hallway as he made his way toward the front door. I watched him go, the door clicking shut behind him, severing the fragile thread of connection that had just begun to reestablish itself. The silence that enveloped me felt almost oppressive, pressing in like a heavy weight that threatened to crush my resolve.

I moved through the kitchen like a restless spirit, cleaning up the remnants of our meal—a forgotten basil leaf here, a misplaced knife there—each action a way to distract myself from the gnawing uncertainty. Outside, the evening began to settle, wrapping the world in twilight's gentle embrace. The streetlamps flickered on one by one, casting pools of golden light on the pavement, as if the universe was reminding me that darkness does not last forever.

As the minutes ticked by, my mind spiraled with scenarios, each darker than the last. I envisioned Aiden sitting across from Sarah, laughter bubbling between them, the tension of old feelings crackling in the air like static. What if she was everything I wasn't—someone he had once loved, someone he could easily slip back into a comfortable rhythm with? My stomach churned at the thought.

I grabbed my phone, a wave of impulse crashing over me as I considered reaching out to him. But no, I had to let him navigate this alone, just as I had to trust him. So instead, I turned my attention to the window, staring out at the darkening sky. The stars began to twinkle, tiny diamonds scattered across the velvet backdrop, and with each blink, I whispered a silent prayer for clarity—for Aiden to find his way back to me, with all the pieces intact.

An hour crawled by, heavy with anticipation, before my phone finally buzzed against the countertop. My heart leaped as I glanced at the screen, only to find a text from Aiden: I'm on my way home. We need to talk.

I took a deep breath, a mixture of relief and dread flooding through me. The evening had turned cool, and I grabbed a sweater, wrapping it around my shoulders as I made my way back to the kitchen. I flicked on the kettle, the comforting hiss of water filling the silence as I prepared tea, a ritual that had become our tradition—a balm for the inevitable conversations that lay ahead.

When the door opened, Aiden stepped inside, his face slightly flushed and his eyes filled with a mixture of determination and vulnerability. He crossed the threshold, the heaviness of what had just transpired evident in the way his shoulders sagged ever so slightly, like a weight had been lifted but had left behind an imprint.

"Hey," he said, his voice low, almost tentative, as he leaned against the doorframe, surveying the room as if seeking refuge in the familiar. "I did what I needed to do."

My heart raced at the uncertainty behind his words. "And?"

He stepped forward, closing the distance between us, his gaze searching mine as if trying to piece together the emotions swirling in the space between us. "I set the boundaries," he said slowly, choosing his words carefully. "I told her I couldn't be in her life the way she wanted me to be. It's not fair to either of us."

Relief washed over me, but it was tinged with something more complex—an echo of his pain, the struggles he had faced. "And what does that mean for us?" I asked, my voice steadier than my heart felt.

He took my hands in his, grounding me in that moment. "It means I'm ready to move forward with you. I want to build our life together, but I need you to know it won't always be easy. I'm still figuring things out."

The sincerity in his voice reached into the depths of my heart, and as I stared into his eyes, I saw the shadows begin to recede, replaced by a hopeful glimmer that ignited something within me. A smile crept onto my lips, tentative but genuine. "Then let's figure it out together."

In that moment, with the promise of tomorrow hanging in the air like the first light of dawn, I felt the walls around my heart begin to soften. Together, we would navigate the complexities of love and the echoes of our pasts, stepping forward into a future that shimmered with possibility.

The moments that followed felt like standing on the precipice of a vast, uncharted landscape, one where the air shimmered with the promise of hope and the threat of despair. Aiden's resolve hung in the atmosphere like a thread, delicate yet unyielding. I took a moment to soak in the familiarity of our kitchen, with its worn oak table and the eclectic mix of pottery that adorned the shelves—a testament to our shared lives. Each item held a story, a memory forged in laughter and love, and I clung to them like talismans, hoping they would anchor us in the tumult of unresolved emotions.

As we settled into the rhythm of the evening, the kettle whistled sharply, breaking the spell that had woven itself around us. I poured steaming tea into our favorite mismatched mugs, the comforting warmth radiating through the ceramic, wrapping us in a cocoon of intimacy. I could see Aiden's fingers tapping nervously against the side of his cup, a rhythm betraying the calm facade he tried to maintain.

"Tell me everything," I urged, leaning forward, the anticipation prickling along my spine like a live wire. His gaze dropped to the swirling steam rising from his mug, as if the answers he sought were hidden within the vapor.

"I told her that I needed space," he began, his voice steady yet layered with complexity. "That I couldn't be what she wanted, not anymore. It's like... she was stuck in a memory of who I used to be, and I'm not that person anymore. I've changed, and I need her to understand that."

His words spilled forth, tumbling over each other like a cascade of water, each one laced with the weight of his past. "But it felt like a betrayal," he continued, a shadow passing over his features. "I didn't want to hurt her, and yet, I could feel the ghosts of our history wrapping around me like a shroud. It's hard to explain—"

I interrupted gently, my voice softening, "You don't owe her anything, Aiden. You've built a life with me now." The honesty of my statement reverberated between us, resonating with the shared understanding of what we had fought to create. "You deserve to choose your path, and if that means letting go of the past, then do it. We deserve to move forward, free from that weight."

He nodded, and I saw a flicker of relief dance behind his eyes. "I know. It's just... complicated. I think she's still holding onto the hope that we could go back to what we were. But I don't want to go back. I want to go forward with you."

My heart surged at his declaration, a bright light cutting through the darkness that had settled around us. "Then let's build our future," I said, feeling the words solidify the bond we were trying to mend. "Let's fill our lives with things that are ours—memories that belong solely to us."

Aiden smiled, a genuine smile that crinkled the corners of his eyes and made my pulse quicken. It felt like the first breath of fresh air after being submerged in water for too long. I could sense the walls around his heart slowly crumbling, replaced by an openness I had longed for.

The minutes morphed into hours as we talked, unraveling the threads of our fears and desires, weaving them into a tapestry of understanding. We shared dreams of travel, of wandering through sun-soaked vineyards in Italy, of standing at the edge of the Grand Canyon, breathless at nature's majesty. With each word, I could feel the old wounds begin to heal, replaced by the warmth of new aspirations and possibilities.

"I want to make new traditions," Aiden declared suddenly, his voice brightening. "Let's start a weekend ritual—every Saturday, we'll do something different. A hike, a cooking class, anything! Just to keep the spark alive." His enthusiasm was infectious, pulling me along like a current.

"Okay, but I draw the line at goat yoga," I teased, my laughter spilling into the room, chasing away the shadows of uncertainty. He grinned, the warmth of it spreading through me, melting away the last remnants of doubt.

Just then, the gentle chime of my phone cut through the moment, and I glanced at the screen, my smile faltering slightly as I saw Sarah's name flash across it. The realization that she had not vanished from our lives, despite Aiden's promises, pulled at the corners of my mind. "It's her," I murmured, uncertainty threading its way into my voice.

"Don't answer it," Aiden said immediately, his expression tightening, a flicker of defensiveness igniting within him. "You don't need to engage with her."

"But it could be important," I countered, caught in the tug-of-war between my instinct to protect our fragile bond and the curiosity that flared within me.

"Or it could just be her trying to draw you into the mess we're trying to leave behind," he replied, his tone firmer this time, underscoring the seriousness of the situation.

I hesitated, the phone still vibrating softly in my palm, and then made a decision. I silenced the notification, placing the device face down on the table. "You're right. I don't need that distraction right now. I want to focus on us."

Aiden let out a breath he didn't realize he was holding, and the relief on his face was palpable. "Thank you," he said, reaching for my hand again, the warmth of his touch igniting a sense of security that wrapped around me like a cozy blanket.

Time slipped away as we reveled in our newfound understanding, but I could sense that the echo of Sarah's presence still lingered at the edges, a reminder that we weren't free just yet. When Aiden eventually stood to leave the kitchen, I felt a ripple of uncertainty flicker through me again, a hesitation that clung to the corners of my mind.

"Let's make a pact," I suggested, turning to face him, my heart pounding in my chest. "Whenever you feel the weight of the past creeping in, promise me you'll talk to me about it. No more holding things in."

He nodded, a serious glint in his eye. "And I promise to keep the lines of communication open. You're my priority now, and I want to make sure you feel that every day."

As the night deepened, we found ourselves wrapped in the quiet intimacy of shared space. With the kitchen lights dimmed, shadows danced on the walls, and the soft hum of the world outside faded into a soothing backdrop. We shared stories, laughter spilling between us like a cherished secret, each moment reinforcing the connection we had fought so hard to reclaim.

With the moon hanging low in the sky, its glow spilling through the window like liquid silver, I realized that the echoes of our past were not just burdens to bear, but also lessons to learn from. They had shaped us, molding the contours of our hearts and our relationship. We were standing at the threshold of a new beginning, one where love could thrive amidst the remnants of what had come before.

As the evening wound down, Aiden took my face in his hands, his touch tender and electric, drawing me closer. "No matter what happens, I choose you," he whispered, the sincerity in his voice settling over me like a warm embrace.

I leaned into him, surrendering to the moment. In that brief space of time, with the world falling away, I felt an unshakeable conviction rise within me. The journey ahead would be fraught with challenges and uncertainties, but it was one we would navigate together, forging our path through the echoes of our past into the vibrancy of our shared future.

Together, we stepped into the unknown, ready to embrace the intricacies of love and the beauty of forging a life entwined with both the shadows and the light. With our hearts laid bare, we were prepared to write our story anew—one filled with laughter, resilience, and a love that could weather any storm.

Chapter 27: A Night of Choices

The ballroom buzzed with an electric energy, the kind that ripples through your skin, igniting a thrill in your stomach. Crystal chandeliers sparkled overhead, casting prismatic reflections across the polished marble floor, where couples glided gracefully, their movements a symphony of elegance and rhythm. The air was thick with the mingling scents of jasmine and freshly polished wood, laced with a hint of excitement that felt almost tangible. My dress, a deep emerald green that flowed like water, hugged my figure in all the right places, yet it felt more like a costume than my true self, the layers of fabric almost oppressive beneath the weight of my thoughts.

As I adjusted the delicate bracelet Aiden had gifted me, I caught sight of him across the room. He stood tall, his posture commanding yet relaxed, the faintest hint of a smile gracing his lips as he conversed with a group of our friends. There was something magnetic about him, a warmth that radiated like the glow of the chandeliers, drawing people in and wrapping them in his charm. But tonight, that charm felt like a double-edged sword, glinting with promise yet hiding the potential for pain, especially when my mind drifted to Sarah.

I had spent the last week oscillating between excitement for the gala and a gnawing anxiety that clawed at my insides. Aiden's past with her loomed like a specter at the edge of my thoughts, ever-present and haunting. Despite the many conversations we had about their history, the unresolved feelings tethered to their shared memories seemed to shackle my heart. Would tonight be the night when those chains would finally be tested?

As we wove through the throngs of elegantly clad guests, my senses heightened with every step, the laughter and chatter rising like a crescendo. The band played a lively tune, the notes soaring through the air, wrapping around us in an embrace of joy. I clutched Aiden's arm a little tighter, needing his strength as I stole glances around the room. Each face seemed to blend into the next, a blur of color and fabric, but my gaze kept returning to the grand entrance, where the double doors stood as a portal to the past.

Just then, as if conjured by my worries, Sarah appeared. She swept into the ballroom, her presence instantly commanding attention like a sudden gust of wind shifting the tide of a calm sea. Dressed in a flowing silver gown that shimmered like moonlight on water, she looked every bit the goddess, her hair cascading down her shoulders in glossy waves. I could see the way people turned to watch her, their eyes wide with admiration, and in that moment, the room seemed to hold its breath, a collective pause in the face of her undeniable allure.

Aiden's reaction was immediate; his posture stiffened, and I felt the tension radiating from him like heat from a flame. He swallowed hard, and I could see the conflict flickering behind his eyes. My heart thudded painfully against my ribs as dread coiled in my stomach. There was an unspoken understanding between us; the weight of history was like a leaden shroud draped over the evening's merriment, and I knew I had to act.

"Let's step outside," I said, my voice barely above a whisper, but firm enough to convey my urgency. Aiden hesitated, glancing back at Sarah, but I could feel my resolve hardening, a protective instinct flaring to life. I wasn't going to let her shadow loom over us tonight. We slipped through the ornate double doors onto the terrace, the cool night air wrapping around us like a soothing balm, the stars above twinkling in silent witness to our struggle.

"Are you okay?" I asked, my voice low and gentle, but it felt like I was navigating a minefield. Aiden rubbed the back of his neck, his brow furrowing as he exhaled sharply, his breath misting in the cool air.

"It's just... seeing her again, it brings back so much," he confessed, his gaze drifting to the horizon where the city lights twinkled like distant constellations. "I thought I had moved on, but..."

I stepped closer, the gravity of his unspoken words anchoring me in place. "You don't have to explain anything to me," I said softly, yet I knew that wasn't entirely true. I wanted to understand. "But we can't let this define us, Aiden. Whatever happened between you two is the past. I want us to focus on what we have now."

He turned to me, his eyes reflecting the moonlight, a mixture of gratitude and fear swirling within them. "I don't want to hurt you, Sarah. I love what we have, but seeing her just brings back all those memories."

My heart swelled at his admission, a warmth blooming in my chest. "Then let's confront it. We need to talk about it, clear the air, whatever it takes. I refuse to let her shadow our relationship. We can't let the past hold us hostage."

Aiden's shoulders relaxed slightly, and I could see him wrestling with his thoughts. "You're right. I don't want you to feel threatened by her presence. It's not fair to you."

As we stood on that terrace, the distant sounds of laughter and music faded into the background, leaving only the two of us in our little bubble of vulnerability. I could feel the weight of the night pressing in, but there was also an unmistakable thrill in the air, the promise of a pivotal moment. Aiden's hand found mine, fingers intertwining in a gesture that felt both reassuring and electric. In that simple connection, I felt the strength of our bond, a reminder that love can be a sanctuary amid the storm of emotions swirling around us.

"Let's go back inside," I said finally, my voice steady. "Together." Aiden nodded, his expression resolute, and as we stepped back into the brightness of the ballroom, I held my breath, ready to face whatever came next.

As we stepped back into the ballroom, the energy enveloped us like a warm blanket, but I felt like I was walking into a storm. The laughter and music swirled around us, but it all seemed muted, like we were encased in glass, isolated from the joy that danced in the air. My heart raced, and I could feel Aiden's presence beside me, steady yet fraught with an undercurrent of tension.

The crowd swayed to the music, lost in the rhythm of their own lives, blissfully unaware of the emotional turmoil churning beneath my surface. I glanced at Aiden, his brow still slightly furrowed as he scanned the room, his mind undoubtedly caught between the past and the present. There was a magnetic pull between us, one that I felt would either tether us together or unravel the delicate threads of our relationship. I squeezed his hand, a silent reminder that we were in this together.

In that moment, I spotted Sarah again, standing near the punch bowl, laughing with a group of friends. She was a vision of confidence, her laughter ringing out like chimes in the breeze, and I couldn't help but feel a flicker of resentment. I hated the way she seemed so at ease, as if the past didn't weigh her down at all. Her laughter, bright and infectious, cut through my thoughts, sparking a flicker of anxiety that danced at the edges of my mind.

"What do you want to do?" Aiden asked, breaking my reverie. His voice was low, a gentle rumble that sent a shiver down my spine, yet I could hear the uncertainty woven into his words.

"Let's just enjoy the night," I suggested, forcing a smile that felt more like a mask than genuine cheer. "We came here to celebrate, didn't we? We can't let her ruin it for us."

He nodded slowly, yet the tightness in his jaw suggested that my words hadn't erased the conflict within him. As we moved further into the crowd, the music swelled, and couples twirled in dizzying patterns, their laughter weaving through the air like an elaborate tapestry. I leaned into Aiden, feeling the warmth radiate from him, his presence anchoring me in a world that felt increasingly surreal.

We made our way to the dance floor, where the rhythm of a slow song beckoned us. The soft lights dimmed slightly, casting a golden hue that transformed the space into a dreamscape. Aiden wrapped his arms around my waist, pulling me close. The world outside our embrace faded into oblivion, leaving just the two of us, lost in the moment. I rested my head against his chest, the steady thump of his heart syncing with the pulse of the music, and for a fleeting second, all the worries dissipated.

"See?" I whispered, tilting my head up to meet his gaze. "This is what matters."

He smiled, the warmth of it melting away the shadows in his eyes, but I could still see that the specter of Sarah lingered in the back of his mind. The song flowed like a river, and we danced as if nothing else existed. My worries momentarily faded, replaced by the sensation of his fingertips brushing against my back and the sweet intimacy of being wrapped in his embrace.

As the song drew to a close, the moment of peace was shattered when Sarah's laughter erupted nearby, drawing our attention like a moth to a flame. I felt Aiden stiffen, his gaze riveted on her as she stepped closer to us, radiant and effortlessly charismatic, with a mischievous glint in her eye that sparked a sense of dread within me.

"Hey there, lovebirds," she said, her tone light and teasing, though her eyes bore a seriousness that belied her playful facade. "I see you two are enjoying yourselves."

"Just celebrating," I replied, forcing a smile that felt more like a grimace. Aiden's hand tightened around mine, and I could feel his muscles tense, ready to shield me from whatever verbal sparring was about to unfold.

"Good to see you, Sarah," Aiden said, his voice steady but edged with caution. The air thickened, and I could feel the tension coiling around us like a serpent, ready to strike.

"Likewise," she replied, tilting her head slightly, her gaze flicking between us. "I didn't expect to run into you tonight. It's been a while."

"Yeah, a while," Aiden echoed, his voice clipped. The unspoken words hung between us, pregnant with the weight of memories and unresolved feelings. I felt the heat of embarrassment creeping up my neck; the last thing I wanted was to play the part of the jealous girlfriend.

"So, how's life treating you? Still running that little cafe?" she asked, her tone laced with a sweetness that felt disingenuous.

"Yes," I replied, forcing a confidence I didn't fully feel. "It's going really well, actually. I've been experimenting with new recipes."

"Oh, I remember how passionate you were about that," she said, her smile genuine but edged with an undertone of something sharper. "It's nice to see you pursuing your dreams."

The conversation felt like a dance of its own, steps carefully measured, each word chosen as if it could trigger an avalanche of emotions. Aiden shifted slightly beside me, and I could sense his discomfort, the internal battle raging just beneath the surface.

"I think it's great," Aiden interjected, his voice firm. "Sarah, I'm glad you're doing well." The sincerity in his tone took me by surprise, but it also made the tension sharper, like a taut wire ready to snap.

"Thanks," she replied, her eyes flicking back to me, a challenge lurking just beneath her polished exterior. "You know, Aiden and I had some great times together. It's nice to reminisce about the past, isn't it?"

The way she said "the past" sent a chill down my spine, and I tightened my grip on Aiden's hand. He met my gaze, and I could see the flicker of concern mirrored in his eyes. "That was a long time ago, Sarah. We're in different places now," he replied, his tone resolute.

The atmosphere shifted, electric with unspoken tension, as we stood there, three characters in a story fraught with history and emotion. I felt like I was in a precarious balancing act, my heart thumping wildly, adrenaline coursing through my veins.

Sarah's gaze lingered on Aiden for a heartbeat longer than necessary, her smile faltering slightly. "I hope you both enjoy the rest of the night," she said, her voice smooth yet edged with something I couldn't quite place.

As she walked away, I let out a breath I didn't realize I'd been holding, the rush of relief mingling with the remnants of uncertainty that still clung to the air. Aiden turned to me, and the worry etched across his features crumpled slightly, a flicker of vulnerability peeking through the cracks.

"That was intense," I murmured, trying to keep my voice light, but the tremor in it betrayed me.

"Yeah," he agreed, running a hand through his hair, his frustration palpable. "I didn't expect her to be here. I thought we could just enjoy the night without—"

"Without her coming in and stirring everything up," I finished for him, my heart racing as I took a step closer. "But we're here together, and that's what matters. I mean, she can't take that away from us, right?"

He nodded, but I could see the lingering doubt in his eyes. "I just don't want you to feel uncomfortable because of my past," he said softly.

I reached up to cup his face in my hands, forcing him to look at me, to see the certainty in my eyes. "You're not responsible for her feelings, Aiden. We're building something here, and I won't let the past overshadow what we have. I love you, and that's all that should matter."

His eyes softened, and the tension in his shoulders began to ease, melting away the barriers we had both been holding up. In that moment, it felt as if we were on the precipice of something transformative, a threshold that separated the weight of what had come before and the promise of what lay ahead. Together, we could face the shadows, navigating the complexities of love and trust with open hearts.

"Okay," he murmured, leaning down to press a gentle kiss to my forehead. "Let's make the most of tonight."

With a shared understanding, we stepped back into the warmth of the ballroom, ready to embrace the rest of the evening. As the music swelled once more, the vibrant world around us pulsed with life, and I held on to Aiden, my heart filled with hope and determination, prepared to dance our way through whatever awaited us.

The music swirled around us, an intoxicating blend of notes that seemed to caress my skin, wrapping us in a cocoon of sound as we rejoined the thrumming pulse of the gala. Aiden's presence was like an anchor, his warm hand clasped firmly around mine as we navigated the throngs of elegantly clad attendees. The kaleidoscope of colors spun before my eyes, the deep reds and blues of dresses swirling like petals caught in a gentle breeze. Laughter danced like fireflies among the shadows, yet beneath that vibrant facade, a current of uncertainty crackled, a reminder that the night was far from simple.

I spotted the bar—an ornate mahogany structure adorned with glimmering glassware and bottles that caught the light like jewels. "How about a drink?" I suggested, my voice a touch louder than necessary to be heard over the music. Aiden nodded, his eyes still flickering toward the entrance where Sarah had made her grand appearance moments ago. It felt as if the air had been sucked out of the room, replaced by a tension that threatened to snap like a taut string at any moment.

As we approached the bar, the bartender—a tall man with a neatly trimmed beard and an apron that looked more like a piece of fine art than a work uniform—greeted us with a smile that lit up his face. "What can I get for you two?"

"Two glasses of your finest red wine," I replied, my voice steady despite the chaotic thoughts swirling in my mind. Aiden leaned against the bar, and I could see the tension in his shoulders easing, if only slightly, as he watched me.

"Coming right up," the bartender said, pouring the rich crimson liquid into crystal glasses that glimmered like prisms. As he slid them toward us, I raised my glass, its cool surface reflecting the lights above.

"To us," I said, meeting Aiden's gaze, the unspoken promise hanging between us like a fragile thread.

"To us," he echoed, clinking his glass against mine, and for a moment, the warmth of connection chased away the shadows that loomed on the edges of my mind. We sipped, the velvety taste enveloping my tongue and sending a comforting warmth coursing through me. I savored the moment, allowing the richness of the wine to blend with the joy I felt being by his side.

As we stood there, I took in the grand hall—a spectacular space filled with towering columns draped in silken fabrics, and exquisite floral arrangements that seemed to bloom from the very air. The scent of roses mingled with the warmth of the evening, creating a fragrant backdrop to the unfolding drama. Couples swayed to the music, lost in each other's eyes, while laughter echoed like sweet chimes throughout the room. Yet, no matter how enchanting the scene, my thoughts were anchored to the specter of Sarah, lingering just out of reach.

Aiden's gaze drifted once more toward the entrance, and my heart sank as I followed his line of sight. Sarah stood there, radiant and poised, effortlessly commanding the attention of those around her. She was the star of her own show, her laughter ringing like silver bells, inviting and intoxicating. I could feel Aiden tense beside me, the weight of his past palpable, and a protective instinct flared within me.

"We can do this," I whispered, the words barely escaping my lips as I sought to reassure both him and myself. "We're stronger than this."

Just then, Sarah caught Aiden's gaze and offered a smile that shimmered with a hint of mischief. I could feel a knot forming in my stomach, the sense of impending conflict wrapping around me like a suffocating fog. "Come on," I said, determination igniting within me. "Let's show her that we're together, that we won't let her disrupt our night."

He looked at me, a mix of uncertainty and admiration flashing across his features, and then nodded. Together, we wove our way through the crowd, the music swelling as we approached her, the delicate clinking of glasses underscoring the moment.

"Sarah," Aiden said, his voice steady despite the slight tremor in his hands. "Glad to see you here."

"Of course! I wouldn't miss it for the world." Her eyes sparkled, but beneath the veneer of friendliness, I could sense the underlying tension. "You two look adorable together."

"Thanks," I said, trying to sound casual, though my heart raced. "How have you been?"

"Oh, you know," she said, her tone light, "just living life and keeping busy. This gala is lovely, isn't it?" Her eyes flicked to Aiden, a challenge in her gaze that made my skin prickle. "It's always nice to catch up with old friends."

"We've been enjoying it," I interjected, forcing a smile that felt like a fragile mask. "Especially the dancing."

"Ah, yes, the dancing." She glanced at Aiden, her gaze piercing through the atmosphere like a blade. "You always did have two left feet, didn't you, Aiden?"

His laughter was strained, yet he played along. "Some might say I've improved."

Sarah leaned closer, her voice dipping to a conspiratorial whisper. "I remember when you tripped over my dress at the last gala. It was quite the spectacle!"

The way she said it was both playful and pointed, and I felt my jaw clench involuntarily. Aiden chuckled, but I could see the discomfort simmering just below the surface. "Let's hope that doesn't happen again tonight," he replied, his tone light but laced with tension.

As the conversation meandered, I sensed Sarah's intent, a subtle attempt to reclaim her hold on Aiden's attention. Yet, I refused to let it phase me. A flicker of determination ignited within me as I exchanged glances with Aiden. In that brief moment, I felt the unwavering strength of our bond, a connection that transcended the whispers of the past.

"I think it's time for another dance," I said suddenly, pulling Aiden by the hand. "What do you think?"

"Sounds great," he agreed, relief washing over his features as he followed my lead. We stepped away from Sarah, her laughter trailing behind us like a distant echo, and I felt the tension in my shoulders ease slightly as we rejoined the swirling mass of couples on the dance floor.

The music shifted to a slow, romantic ballad, and I wrapped my arms around Aiden's neck, feeling the warmth radiating from his body. He held me close, our movements syncing effortlessly, and for a moment, I let myself get lost in the melody, the world around us fading into a beautiful blur. The weight of Sarah's presence lifted as I breathed in the familiar scent of Aiden's cologne, the richness of it anchoring me in this moment of bliss.

"You were amazing back there," I murmured, gazing up at him, the sincerity of my words weaving into the air between us. "I'm proud of you for handling it so well."

"Thanks," he replied, a softness in his voice that made my heart swell. "I just... I don't want to hurt you. You're everything to me."

"I know," I said, my voice steady. "And I won't let anyone, not even her, come between us. We're stronger than that."

He smiled down at me, the warmth in his gaze sending butterflies fluttering through my stomach. "You're right. Let's just focus on this moment, on us."

As we danced, I let the music carry me away, and the world around us transformed into a shimmering dream. The laughter and chatter of the crowd faded, leaving only the soft melody and the connection that crackled between us. I marveled at the way he moved, each step an unspoken promise, a reassurance that we were forging a path all our own, one that shimmered brightly against the backdrop of the past.

Yet, the moment was fleeting. The crowd surged, and the air crackled with excitement as a lively tune broke through the haze, drawing people into a whirl of frenetic energy. Aiden glanced toward the entrance again, and I felt a familiar twist of anxiety in my chest. But instead of letting it overwhelm me, I squeezed his hand, my resolve solidifying.

"Let's join them," I said, my eyes sparkling with mischief. "I refuse to let this night be dictated by anyone else."

He grinned, and I saw the glimmer of joy return to his eyes as we danced our way through the crowd, losing ourselves in the rhythm. The music enveloped us, each beat reverberating through my body as we laughed and twirled, our movements weaving a tapestry of connection that felt more potent than any words could express.

The vibrant world around us pulsed with life, the lights flickering like stars against the velvet backdrop of the night. As we danced, I allowed myself to forget the shadows that had threatened to steal our joy, to lose myself in the beauty of this moment. Aiden's laughter mingled with mine, rising above the cacophony, a sweet symphony that echoed through the air.

But just as the night seemed to reach its peak, I felt a gentle tap on my shoulder. Turning, I found myself face-to-face with Sarah once more, her expression a mask of cheerful curiosity. "Mind if I cut in?" she asked, her tone light but the underlying tension unmistakable.

I hesitated, caught off guard. Aiden looked at me, his expression a blend of surprise and uncertainty.

"Actually," I began, my heart racing, "I think we're good."

"Oh, come on," she said, her smile widening. "Just one dance? It'll be

Chapter 28: The Storm Within

The gala buzzed with life, a tapestry of laughter and the clinking of glasses woven together in a grand, opulent ballroom that echoed the richness of its surroundings. Crystal chandeliers cast a warm glow over the polished hardwood floors, while the scent of freshly arranged lilies and roses danced in the air, mingling with the fragrance of expensive cologne and perfume. Guests twirled in elegant gowns and tailored suits, their smiles bright, but beneath the surface, tensions simmered like a pot ready to boil over.

I stood on the fringes, a glass of sparkling water cradled in my hand, watching as the scene unfolded in front of me, the chaos of emotions a vibrant backdrop to my own internal turmoil. Aiden was across the room, a dashing figure with his dark hair falling just so over his forehead, his blue eyes sharp and attentive. He was engaging in polite conversation, but the tightness in his jaw hinted at an underlying frustration. I could sense the discontent swirling around him, a storm brewing just beneath the surface.

Then she entered. Sarah. The name itself felt like a jolt of electricity surging through the room, sparking curiosity and unease alike. She glided in with an air of confidence, her presence demanding attention, as if the very atmosphere had shifted to accommodate her. Dressed in a striking crimson dress that hugged her figure perfectly, she was the embodiment of seduction and chaos. I felt a pang of insecurity ripple through me, followed by an all-consuming wave of anger. I hadn't seen her in months, and yet here she was, like a specter rising from the past, uninvited and unashamed.

The moment our eyes locked, I felt the air thicken, a charged silence enveloping us, heavy with unspoken words and unresolved feelings. Her lips curled into a sly smile, as if she held all the secrets of the universe. I clenched my jaw, willing myself to remain calm, but the tremors of anxiety were impossible to ignore. I could see Aiden's focus shifting towards Sarah, his expression unreadable. I wanted to scream, to push through the crowd and shield him from her magnetic pull, but my feet felt glued to the floor, caught in an invisible web of dread.

"Isn't it lovely?" Sarah called out, her voice dripping with false sincerity as she approached us. "The gala, I mean. So many people here, yet it feels so... empty."

Her gaze flicked between Aiden and me, a predator assessing its prey. My heart raced, pounding in my chest like a war drum. The room faded away, and all I could hear was the steady thrum of my pulse, the rising tide of my fears swelling with each passing second.

Aiden, seemingly caught in the gravity of her presence, shifted his weight, but it was too late. "You shouldn't have come, Sarah," he said, his voice steady yet strained. There was an edge to his tone that made my breath catch. The crowd around us blurred into a murmur, their laughter fading like a distant echo as our world shrank down to just the three of us.

"Oh, come now, Aiden," she purred, stepping closer, her gaze unwavering. "You know I can't resist a good party. Besides, I missed you. We had such fun last time, didn't we?"

The words hung in the air, thick with implication, and I could feel my world crumbling around me. I glanced at Aiden, searching for reassurance, but the look in his eyes was clouded, uncertainty battling against affection. "We need to talk, Sarah. Not here, not now," he insisted, his voice low, but the tension in the air crackled like static.

The crowd continued to swirl around us, oblivious to the tempest brewing just outside their line of sight. I could feel the heat of anger rising within me, sharp and unyielding. It bubbled over as I stepped forward, breaking the invisible barrier. "You need to leave.

This is not your place anymore," I said, my voice a mixture of defiance and desperation.

She turned her gaze towards me, her eyebrows arching in mock surprise. "Oh, sweet little thing," she cooed, her tone dripping with condescension. "You really think you can dictate what I do?"

Before I could respond, Aiden's hand found mine, squeezing tightly, grounding me even as the storm of emotions threatened to overwhelm us. "We've moved on, Sarah," he said, the firmness in his voice resonating through the space between us. "You should too."

The room held its breath, and in that moment, I saw it—the flicker of vulnerability in his eyes, the rawness of our shared struggle. The words he whispered next felt like a lifeline, breaking through the cacophony of doubt swirling around us. "I love you, and this is where I want to be."

His admission hung in the air, a defiant proclamation against the chaos that threatened to tear us apart. A sharp breath escaped me, the weight of my fears crashing down like waves against a crumbling shore. But as tears prickled my eyes, threatening to spill over, I felt his warmth envelop me. Aiden pulled me close, our foreheads touching, and in that instant, the world around us faded, leaving just the two of us suspended in our own moment.

The crowd faded to a murmur, the bright lights dimmed, and I could only focus on his voice, low and steady. "We can face this together," he whispered, his breath warm against my skin, and I felt a spark of hope ignite within me. No matter how tumultuous the storm, I realized that as long as we stood side by side, we could weather anything.

In the charged silence that followed Aiden's whispered declaration, the world felt suspended, the din of the gala a distant echo. I could feel the warmth of his body radiating against mine, a sanctuary amidst the chaos swirling around us. My heartbeat, steady yet frantic, began to synchronize with the rhythm of the moment, each pulse reinforcing our connection, fortifying our resolve.

But Sarah wasn't done; she wouldn't let us off that easily. The confident smile she wore like armor faded, replaced by a calculating gaze that assessed every nuance of our fragile alliance. "Oh, darling," she began, her tone syrupy sweet but laced with an undercurrent of malice. "You really think you can just ignore me? You don't just walk away from the past. It has a way of clawing its way back, doesn't it?"

The words hit like a slap, slicing through the comforting cocoon Aiden had wrapped around us. I tightened my grip on his hand, searching for the courage to stand firm against her onslaught. "You're wrong," I said, my voice steadier than I felt. "We are moving forward. Together. And you're part of the past."

She scoffed, amusement dancing in her eyes. "How quaint. Do you really believe love can shield you from reality? From me?"

My heart raced as I glanced at Aiden, a spark of anger igniting in my chest. "Love isn't just a word, Sarah. It's a commitment, a promise to face challenges together. And right now, our challenge is you."

The crowd had begun to stir, glances darting our way, curiosity mingling with concern. I could feel the weight of their scrutiny, the way eyes followed our confrontation like a dramatic scene in a play. I wished I could fade into the background, become invisible, yet I stood my ground, buoyed by the strength emanating from Aiden beside me.

With a determined shift in posture, Aiden stepped forward, asserting his presence. "I won't let you disrupt our lives any longer," he said, his voice echoing with conviction. "You're a chapter we've closed."

The tension snapped like a taut string, and I felt a rush of adrenaline as Sarah's façade cracked. For the first time, her cool composure wavered, revealing a flicker of vulnerability beneath her bravado. "You think you can just erase me?" she hissed, her voice a dangerous whisper. "You think this is over?"

As she leaned closer, I could see the faint tremor in her hands, a flicker of desperation masked by her bravado. There was something deeply unsettling about the way she refused to back down, her eyes narrowing as if plotting her next move. I refused to let her intimidate me any longer.

"Enough," I said, my voice cutting through the noise of the room. The command echoed in the charged space, commanding silence and attention. "You are not the storm you think you are, Sarah. You can't tear us apart. Not now, not ever."

In that moment, something shifted. Aiden's grip on my hand tightened, a silent affirmation of our unity. I could feel the energy crackle between us, an electric charge that seemed to push back against her presence. We were a force to be reckoned with, a testament to love's resilience, even when faced with the ghosts of the past.

The air was thick with tension as I met Sarah's gaze, unflinching. It felt like a duel of wills, our resolve clashing against her defiance. In the crowd, murmurs rippled through the audience, but I was blissfully unaware of their fascination; all I could focus on was the whirlwind of emotions swirling in my chest, a potent mix of fear and determination.

Finally, after what felt like an eternity, Sarah's expression shifted. The defiance faded, replaced by an inscrutable mask of indifference. "You're cute," she said, almost dismissively. "But cuteness doesn't win battles. Just remember, the past has a way of creeping back when you least expect it."

With that, she turned on her heel, striding away with a flourish that suggested victory. But there was a moment, a fleeting glimpse, where I saw the cracks in her facade—the vulnerability masked by bravado, the insecurity cloaked in confidence. I felt a twinge of sympathy, yet it quickly dissipated as I turned to Aiden, my heart pounding in my chest.

He reached out, brushing a strand of hair behind my ear. "You were amazing," he said, admiration lacing his voice. "I don't know how you did that."

The moment was sweet, yet I could still feel the remnants of tension in the air, the remnants of Sarah's words echoing in the back of my mind. "I just couldn't let her win," I confessed, my breath shaky. "She's been lurking in the shadows for too long. It's time we take control of our story."

Aiden's smile softened, and I felt the warmth of his gaze steady me. "We will," he promised, his voice low and full of intent. "Together."

As the gala resumed its rhythmic pulse around us, laughter and music swelled, enveloping us in a cocoon of normalcy. Yet, beneath the surface, a current of anticipation lingered. We had faced a storm tonight, and while we stood together against the remnants of the past, I knew the journey wasn't over.

We stepped further into the throng, our hands interlocked like a lifeline, the world swirling around us in vibrant hues. I could see the faces of friends, acquaintances, and strangers flickering in and out of focus, but all that mattered was Aiden beside me. The night blossomed into life as we navigated the crowd, laughter mingling with the soft strains of music, weaving a spell that dulled the edges of our earlier confrontation.

With each step, the weight of uncertainty began to lift, replaced by a newfound clarity. Our love was a force, a beacon shining brightly against the backdrop of shadows. And as we danced beneath the dazzling chandeliers, I realized that every heartbeat, every whispered word of encouragement from Aiden, was a step forward—a step into the unknown, hand in hand, ready to face whatever storm awaited us.

The music swelled around us, a comforting backdrop that enveloped our moment of solidarity as if the universe itself was tuning in to our emotional frequency. We stepped deeper into the pulsating heart of the gala, the rhythm of our steps echoing in sync with the soft thump of the bass. Aiden's presence beside me felt like an anchor, grounding me against the tempest of feelings still swirling in my chest. Every glance and murmur from the crowd reminded me of our earlier confrontation with Sarah, yet the spark of defiance kindled a fire within me that I hadn't known I possessed.

As we glided across the dance floor, Aiden's hand found the small of my back, guiding me with a gentle pressure. The world around us shimmered, the golden chandeliers twinkling like stars against the darkening sky of the evening. With every turn, I could feel the tension slipping away, replaced by an exhilarating sense of freedom. The laughter of our friends bubbled up like effervescent champagne, lifting our spirits as the weight of that encounter began to feel more like a fleeting shadow than an impending storm.

"You have no idea how incredible you were," Aiden said, his breath warm against my ear as we swayed to the music. The band played a slow, romantic melody that wrapped around us, inviting intimacy even amid the crowd. "You stood your ground, and it was... inspiring."

A smirk tugged at my lips, a playful challenge lighting up my eyes. "You mean it was 'cute'?"

Aiden chuckled, his laughter a sweet sound that melded seamlessly with the surrounding music. "Cute doesn't quite capture it. It was fierce."

Fierce. The word hung between us, a banner under which we could rally our fears and hopes. I felt emboldened, the remnants of Sarah's presence fading like smoke, yet the reality of our situation loomed large. Her warning still echoed in the corners of my mind, lingering like a stubborn stain that refused to wash away.

"I know she's not going to just disappear," I confessed, my voice low and earnest. "She'll come back, won't she?"

Aiden's expression shifted, the easy smile replaced by a more serious demeanor. "We'll handle it. Together," he reassured me, but I could see the flicker of concern in his eyes.

We danced for what felt like hours, our bodies moving in perfect harmony, the world around us blurring into a mosaic of colors and sounds. The taste of uncertainty lingered on my tongue, but so did the sweetness of Aiden's touch, a tender reminder that our love was worth fighting for. The evening felt like a dream, and I wished to hold on to it forever, to keep the chaos at bay for just a little longer.

As the music shifted to a faster tempo, we released our hold on one another and stepped back, allowing the vibrant rhythm to take over. The dance floor transformed into a sea of movement, couples twirling and laughing, lost in their own moments. My heart swelled with gratitude, and I couldn't help but smile at the joy radiating from our friends.

"Let's grab a drink," Aiden suggested, and we maneuvered through the throng, weaving in and out of laughter and camaraderie. I could feel the weight of the world lifting with each passing moment, the shimmering promise of what could be ahead nudging me closer to hope.

At the bar, Aiden ordered us two flutes of sparkling wine, the bubbles shimmering like stars as they rose to the surface. We clinked our glasses together, a small ritual that felt monumental in the face of uncertainty. "To us," he said, his eyes locking onto mine with an intensity that made my heart flutter.

"To us," I echoed, the words sweet and meaningful on my tongue.

As we sipped our drinks, laughter erupted nearby, drawing our attention to a group of friends who had gathered to toast the evening. I recognized their faces—the shared experiences etched in their smiles, the stories in their laughter. For a moment, I allowed myself to bask in the warmth of belonging, the camaraderie of friends who had become our chosen family.

But even in this moment of joy, the shadow of Sarah lingered. I could feel her presence like a distant storm, hovering on the horizon. I stole a glance at Aiden, who was engaged in conversation with a mutual friend, his smile infectious. My heart swelled with love for him, a fierce and protective kind of love that made me realize just how much I was willing to fight for what we had built together.

When he turned back to me, I could see the light in his eyes—an unwavering assurance that filled me with strength. "What's on your mind?" he asked, tilting his head slightly, a knowing look playing at the corners of his mouth.

"Just thinking about how we're going to handle Sarah," I admitted, my voice barely above a whisper. "I don't want her to ruin this, to ruin us."

Aiden stepped closer, the warmth of his body providing comfort amid the cool night air wafting through the open terrace doors. "She won't. I promise you that. But we need a plan."

The determination in his voice sparked something within me. I straightened my back, feeling emboldened by our alliance. "You're right. We should strategize. Maybe we could talk to a few friends for support, let them know what's going on."

"Absolutely. We're not in this alone," Aiden agreed, and the conviction in his words washed over me like a wave of reassurance.

With renewed vigor, we rejoined our friends, laughter enveloping us like a cozy blanket. We shared stories and dreams, weaving a tapestry of memories that grounded us in the present. I felt the evening morph into something greater than a mere gala; it became a celebration of resilience and love, a testament to the bond Aiden and I had forged through the tumultuous waters of uncertainty.

But even as we danced and laughed, a part of me remained vigilant, ever aware of the storm brewing on the horizon. Sarah's voice echoed in my mind, her words a haunting reminder of the past's grip. Yet, standing beside Aiden, I knew that whatever came our way, we would face it together.

As the night deepened, the music shifted once more, and Aiden pulled me into a slow dance, our bodies moving in perfect sync as if the universe had conspired to bring us together. I rested my head against his shoulder, allowing the comfort of his presence to wash over me.

With each gentle sway, I felt a sense of hope rising within me, buoyed by the love we had built against the backdrop of chaos. The world around us faded, and in that moment, it was just us—a singular entity navigating the complexities of life together.

The gala might have been a stage for others, but for us, it was a sanctuary, a reminder that love could weather even the fiercest storms. And as I inhaled the scent of his cologne, a warm blend of cedar and citrus, I knew that whatever challenges lay ahead, we would face them hand in hand, ready to rewrite our story, one step at a time.

Chapter 29: Embracing the Journey

The morning air carries a crispness that tingles against my skin, an invigorating reminder that each new day is a canvas waiting for strokes of ambition and hues of laughter. As I sit cross-legged on the warm sand, the grains, fine and golden, sift through my fingers like time slipping away. I look out at the endless stretch of water before me, the ocean unfurling like a vibrant tapestry, each wave a whisper of the adventures that lie ahead. The horizon blushes with the promise of dawn, splashing soft pastels across the sky, a breathtaking prelude to the sun's ascent.

Aiden's presence beside me feels both grounding and electrifying. His fingers intertwine with mine, a simple gesture that radiates warmth and reassurance. The sun peeks above the horizon, casting a golden glow that dances upon the surface of the water, making it shimmer like a thousand diamonds. It feels like a secret shared between the two of us—a moment carved out of time where everything else fades into insignificance. The world feels enormous, yet in that moment, it's just us, suspended in our own bubble of quiet connection.

"I can't believe we did it," I say, my voice barely more than a whisper, carried away by the gentle breeze. The memory of the gala still tinges the air with excitement, a kaleidoscope of glittering gowns, laughter, and the clinking of glasses echoing in my mind. It was a night of new beginnings and tentative hopes, a celebration that felt like the first breath after a long dive underwater.

Aiden chuckles, a deep, rich sound that rolls over the waves, bringing warmth to the cool morning. "You were a force out there, you know. I don't think anyone expected you to steal the show quite like that."

I flush with the compliment, a mix of pride and disbelief. "Maybe I just stumbled into it. One moment I was waiting for the event to start, and the next, I was standing at the podium, pouring my heart out. It's surreal."

"Surreal is good," he replies, his gaze steady and unwavering. "You've always had a spark, and last night, it was like you lit a bonfire."

His words envelop me, infusing me with warmth and hope. It's no small feat to share one's dreams with an audience, especially when those dreams feel as fragile as the shells scattered along the shore. I glance down, tracing the delicate patterns in the sand, thoughts whirling around my aspirations. I've always wanted to be a writer, to capture the essence of life's fleeting moments, but that desire has sometimes felt overshadowed by self-doubt and fear of inadequacy.

"What if I'm just fooling myself?" I confess, the words tumbling out, laden with vulnerability. "What if this is just a fleeting moment of confidence, and I'll go back to being the same uncertain girl?"

Aiden squeezes my hand tighter, the strength of his grip anchoring me. "Then you'll keep trying. It's not about perfection, Ellie. It's about growth. You don't have to have everything figured out right now. This is your journey, not a race."

His unwavering faith in me is a balm to my soul, igniting a fire within that I thought had long since flickered out. I watch the waves crash against the shore, their relentless rhythm a metaphor for the challenges I face. Each wave ebbs and flows, and like them, I can find my own rhythm, my own voice in this vast expanse of existence.

"I want to write stories that matter," I say, my voice stronger now. "Stories that inspire and connect people. I want my words to resonate, to remind people they're not alone."

Aiden's eyes glimmer with pride, and he tilts his head, as if weighing the significance of my words. "Then you need to write, Ellie. You need to get out there and pour yourself onto the page. Don't wait for someone to validate your passion. You have to own it."

His conviction envelops me, wrapping around my heart like a warm embrace. It's in these moments of clarity that I realize how vital it is to have someone who believes in you—who sees the potential where you see uncertainty. I feel a swell of determination rising within me, pushing aside the doubt that had clung to my heart like seaweed on a rocky shore.

"I will," I promise, the words falling from my lips with newfound certainty. "I'll take the plunge. I'll start writing again, no matter how messy it gets."

Aiden grins, and the sunlight catches in his hair, illuminating his features like a celestial being. "That's the spirit. And I'll be here, cheering you on, every step of the way."

As the sun climbs higher, the sky transforms into a brilliant canvas of blue, dotted with fluffy clouds that seem to drift lazily, unhurried by time. The world awakens around us, the distant laughter of children mingling with the sound of seagulls soaring overhead. It's a reminder that life continues, each day a new opportunity to embrace our dreams.

I lean back on my palms, feeling the warmth of the sun seep into my skin, the grains of sand cradling me in their embrace. A sense of clarity washes over me, a feeling that maybe, just maybe, I am capable of more than I've ever dared to imagine.

The waves beckon me to let go of the past, to ride the tides of uncertainty with open arms. With Aiden by my side, I feel fortified against whatever storms may come. Our love feels like a lighthouse, guiding me through the fog, assuring me that no matter how turbulent the journey, I am never alone.

Together, we are ready to embrace this journey—every rise and fall, every triumph and setback—because in the end, it is not just about the destination but the memories we create along the way.

As the sun rises higher in the sky, spilling its light over the beach like molten gold, the symphony of the ocean takes on a new melody, blending with the gentle rustling of palm fronds and the laughter of children playing in the distance. The air is thick with the scent of salt and sun, a heady mixture that makes my heart race with possibilities. Each wave crashes against the shore with a rhythmic persistence, a reminder that life, much like the ocean, is ever-changing and beautifully chaotic.

Aiden leans back, propping himself on his elbows, and I can't help but steal glances at him. The sunlight dances across his face, illuminating the angles of his jaw and the playful curl of his hair. In these moments, he seems almost ethereal, a figure carved from sunlight and shadow. The way he watches the horizon, as if searching for answers among the waves, brings a smile to my lips. I wonder if he's contemplating the same things I am—how far we've come, the uncharted territories we're eager to explore together.

"Remember when we first met?" I ask, a nostalgic grin spreading across my face. "You were convinced I was a tourist, lost and looking for directions."

His laughter bubbles up like the tide, filling the air with warmth. "You did look a bit out of place in that oversized sun hat and those ridiculously bright sunglasses. I almost offered to take you to the nearest gift shop."

I chuckle, picturing that moment—the awkward, sunburned me, standing on the bustling boardwalk, overwhelmed by the cacophony of music, chatter, and the scent of fried dough wafting through the air. "It's funny how things work out. I was just trying to find my way, both literally and figuratively."

Aiden shifts to face me, his expression softening. "Sometimes the best paths are the ones we stumble upon. You showed up on that beach as a lost tourist, but you found more than just directions. You found me."

My heart swells at the sincerity in his words. The serendipity of our meeting feels like a small miracle, a twist of fate that led me to him. It's in those moments of vulnerability that I realize how deeply intertwined our lives have become, how much we have supported each other through the whirlwinds of uncertainty.

As the sun climbs higher, a flock of seagulls swoops down, their cries punctuating the serene atmosphere. I watch as they dive and soar, unfettered by the worries that seem to cling to me like an old sweater. Aiden's presence serves as a gentle reminder that I can learn to glide, too, that I can embrace the winds of change without fear.

"Do you ever think about what the future holds for us?" I ask, tracing the outline of a small seashell with my finger. The shell is fragile yet resilient, a fitting metaphor for the way I want to approach my own dreams. "I mean, beyond the beach and this moment."

His brow furrows slightly as he considers my question. "Of course. I think about it all the time. But the future is like the ocean; it's vast and unpredictable. What matters is that we're together to navigate whatever comes our way."

The simplicity of his response brings a wave of calm over me. He's right; the future may be uncertain, but the steadfastness of our partnership feels like an anchor, steadying me against the storms that threaten to blow us off course. Together, we can face the unknown with courage and laughter, our hearts woven together in a tapestry of shared dreams and whispered hopes.

"Let's make a pact," I propose, my eyes sparkling with mischief. "Let's promise to chase our dreams, no matter how outlandish they may seem."

Aiden's eyes light up with intrigue. "What do you have in mind?"

"Let's set tangible goals," I say, leaning forward. "I want to write a book—something that captures the essence of life and love, maybe even our story in a way. And you... you need to work on that photography project you keep putting off."

He tilts his head, a playful smirk dancing on his lips. "You mean the one where I capture the beauty of our favorite places? I've been meaning to start that, but every time I pick up the camera, I freeze up."

"Then let's do it together!" I exclaim, excitement bubbling within me. "We can inspire each other, keep each other accountable. Picture it—a beachside writing retreat where you capture moments and I craft stories inspired by your photographs."

Aiden laughs, the sound bright and infectious. "That sounds incredible. A creative collaboration with the two of us at the helm—how could we fail?"

The thought of merging our passions fills me with anticipation, a vivid picture forming in my mind of us wandering through picturesque landscapes, losing ourselves in our respective crafts. I can envision long afternoons sprawled on the sand, words flowing as freely as the tide, and Aiden capturing it all through his lens, each click a testament to our journey together.

"Let's make it a weekend ritual," I suggest. "Every month, we find a new spot, whether it's here, the mountains, or even a cozy café downtown. We can explore new places while chasing our dreams."

His eyes twinkle with enthusiasm, mirroring my excitement. "I love it. And we'll document our adventures along the way. Who knows what stories we'll create or what beauty we'll uncover?"

As the waves roll in, I feel a surge of motivation coursing through me. This is more than just a promise to each other; it's a commitment to our growth as individuals and as a couple. I can already see the seeds of inspiration blossoming, the thrill of exploration igniting a fire within me.

I lean back, allowing the warmth of the sun to envelop me like a comforting blanket, and I close my eyes, breathing in the scent of the ocean. This moment, this feeling, is what I want to capture in my writing—the raw, unfiltered joy of being alive, of dreaming, and of loving fiercely.

Aiden nudges me gently, breaking my reverie. "What are you thinking about now?"

"Just how grateful I am," I reply, opening my eyes to meet his gaze. "Grateful for you, for this moment, and for all the possibilities ahead."

With a smile that could light up the darkest of days, Aiden leans closer, his forehead resting against mine. "Me too. We're just getting started, Ellie. The best is yet to come."

In that moment, the world fades away, and all that exists is the connection between us, the unshakeable bond forged through dreams and desires. We sit together, intertwined in our aspirations, ready to face whatever waves may come, anchored by love and buoyed by hope.

The sun continues its ascent, painting the sky with splashes of orange and soft lavender, an artist working feverishly to create a masterpiece. I close my eyes, allowing the warm rays to seep into my skin, a comforting embrace that melts away the remnants of doubt lingering in my heart. With Aiden by my side, each breath feels lighter, infused with the exhilaration of new beginnings.

As I peel my gaze away from the horizon, I can't help but admire the serene beauty surrounding us. The beach, once a mere backdrop to my worries, transforms into a vibrant sanctuary filled with possibility. Sand dunes rise like gentle hills, dotted with tufts of sea grass swaying lazily in the breeze, while the rhythmic crashing of waves feels like a heartbeat, steady and reassuring.

"Let's make a list," I suggest, my mind buzzing with ideas. "Not just of our dreams, but of all the places we want to explore, the experiences we want to have."

Aiden raises an eyebrow, his curiosity piqued. "A bucket list? I'm intrigued. What's at the top of yours?"

"Definitely Paris," I reply without hesitation. "The romance, the cafés, the writers' nooks. I want to wander the streets with a notebook in hand, soaking in inspiration from every corner."

His smile is infectious, lighting up his face. "Paris sounds perfect, but let's add a little spice. How about a photography tour through the streets, capturing the magic of the city while you write?"

"Now you're speaking my language," I say, the thought igniting a fire within me. "We could blend our passions and create something beautiful."

We fall into a delightful rhythm, brainstorming the places we'd love to visit, our excitement swirling in the air like a delicate dance. Italy slips onto the list next, its rich history and mouthwatering cuisine calling to us like sirens. I can almost taste the fresh pasta and gelato as I imagine us sitting in a sunlit piazza, writing our stories amid the chatter of locals and the strumming of guitar strings in the background.

As we jot down more destinations—New Orleans for its vibrant music scene, the Scottish Highlands for their breathtaking landscapes—I begin to feel a sense of adventure surging within me. It's not just about the places; it's about the memories we'll create together, the laughter and love woven into every experience.

"Let's not forget about home," Aiden suggests, glancing at the familiar shoreline that has become our haven. "There are hidden gems right here that we haven't explored. Local spots where we can find inspiration just as easily."

I nod, realizing that sometimes the most profound experiences can be found right outside our door. "I want to discover those quirky little coffee shops, the ones tucked away in alleys, where we can sit for hours, sipping lattes and brainstorming our next adventures."

Aiden's eyes sparkle with mischief. "We could even host a writing workshop on the beach! Invite some friends, make it a weekend retreat where we all share our stories and passions."

"Now that's a dream worth pursuing," I say, feeling the excitement bubble up again. "Imagine the bonfires at night, sharing our work under the stars, laughter mingling with the sound of the waves."

With each new idea, the world expands around us, transforming the future from a nebulous uncertainty into a vibrant landscape of possibility. I can feel the weight of my insecurities lifting, replaced by a thrilling anticipation for what lies ahead.

As the sun hangs high in the sky, its warmth enveloping us like a tender embrace, I take a moment to reflect. This journey is not just about the destinations we'll explore; it's about the way we choose to live our lives—boldly, fearlessly, and with unyielding love for one another.

"Here's to us," I raise an imaginary glass, laughter bubbling forth. "To the adventures we'll embark on and the stories we'll write."

Aiden clinks his invisible glass with mine, a twinkle of mischief in his eyes. "And to the detours that will inevitably take us off the beaten path."

"Those are the best ones," I agree. "Like when we ended up at that little beachside diner, feasting on greasy burgers after getting lost on our last road trip."

"Or when we found that art festival and you tried to paint, creating a masterpiece that resembled a squashed tomato," he retorts, laughter spilling from his lips.

I can't help but giggle at the memory, the joy of those moments intertwining with the excitement for what lies ahead. With each shared memory, our bond deepens, stitching us together in a tapestry of love, laughter, and adventure.

In the days that follow, we embark on our quest to explore both near and far. Aiden and I find ourselves wandering through charming little towns, discovering hidden bookshops that smell of aged paper and nostalgia, as well as quaint coffee shops buzzing with the energy of creatives like us. Each encounter enriches our journey, igniting the flames of inspiration that had once flickered dimly.

One rainy afternoon, we huddle in a cozy café, sipping steaming cups of chai, surrounded by the soft murmur of conversations and the comforting aroma of freshly baked pastries. I take out my notebook, the pages still crisp and new, and begin to jot down thoughts, snippets of dialogue, and bursts of inspiration that have been bubbling beneath the surface.

Aiden, with his camera in hand, captures candid moments of our adventure, his laughter echoing through the small space as I act out ridiculous scenarios in my quest for inspiration. Each photograph tells a story, a moment frozen in time, and I can't help but admire the way he sees the world—the beauty in the mundane, the magic in the everyday.

"Look at this one!" he exclaims, showing me a picture of an elderly couple sharing a plate of pastries, their eyes twinkling with joy. "It's like they're living a fairytale right here in this café."

"That's the beauty of life," I reply, my heart swelling with warmth. "Every ordinary moment has the potential to become extraordinary."

As the weeks unfold, our adventures blend into a vibrant tapestry of experiences, each thread woven with love and laughter. We find inspiration in places we never expected—in the conversations with strangers, the quiet moments of solitude, and even in the chaos of a bustling farmers' market, where we dance between stalls, our arms full of fresh produce and laughter.

With every sunset we watch together, I feel more grounded, more confident in my writing. The words begin to flow, and with Aiden's encouragement, I pour my heart into stories that reflect not only my experiences but also the beauty of our journey. He becomes not just my partner but my muse, pushing me to take risks, to dive into the depths of my creativity.

It is in the quiet moments, late at night when the world is still, that we often find ourselves wrapped in each other's arms, sharing our dreams and fears. Aiden speaks of his aspirations to showcase his photography in galleries, while I unveil the stories that are blossoming within me, eager to break free from the confines of my mind.

"I want to create something that resonates," I tell him one night, the stars twinkling above us like tiny diamonds scattered across velvet. "Something that reminds people of the beauty in everyday life."

He nods, his expression earnest. "And I want my photos to evoke emotions, to capture moments that people might overlook. Together, we can create a world where our stories and images intertwine."

In those shared dreams, I see a future bright with promise—a future where we not only embrace our passions but also lift each other up as we chase them. The journey stretches before us like an open road, filled with possibilities that beckon with whispers of adventure.

As the sun sets once more, casting a golden hue over the horizon, I realize that life, much like the waves, will always have its ebbs and flows. But with Aiden by my side, I am ready to ride those waves, to embrace the journey ahead, knowing that together we can navigate the vast ocean of uncertainty, hand in hand, heart to heart, forever chasing the light.

Milton Keynes UK
Ingram Content Group UK Ltd.
UKHW040257181024
449757UK00001B/98